Abby

Cass Kellie

1 REVELATIONS

Spring – March - 2015

"You are my sunshine, my only sunshine. You make me happy when skies are grey, you'll never know dear how much I love you. Please don't take... my... sunshine... away..."

Abby jolted upright, her heart pounding against her ribcage as if trying to escape. The remnants of her nightmare clung to her like a second skin, the images seared into her mind. She gulped in air, trying to steady her breathing, but the panic had already taken hold. It was the same dream that had haunted her for months, a jumble of facilize and voices that she couldn't quite place. Beside her, Drake stirred, his handsome features etched with concern in the dim light of their bedroom.

"Another one?" he asked softly, his voice thick with sleep.

Abby nodded, not trusting herself to speak. She noticed the perspiration cooling on her skin, with the sheets entwined around her legs. Drake sat up and wrapped his arms around her, pulling her close. "It's okay," he murmured, stroking her hair. "You're safe."

Her phone was on the nightstand. She paused, knowing her mother would still be awake, reading mystery novels. Yet, she hesitated, reflecting on their growing distance.

"You should call her," Drake said, reading her mind as he always did. "Your mom would want to know."

Abby withdrew her hand. "It's late. And anyway, she'll worry."

"Isn't that what moms are supposed to do?"

The kitchen was quiet the next morning as Abby moved through her routine, the coffee maker gurgling in the background. Drake stood at the stove, making his signature weekend omelets, the ones that had first won her heart during their law school days.

"So, are you still planning to stop by your mom's place today?" he asked, sliding a perfectly folded omelet onto her plate.

Abby poked at her breakfast with her fork. "I should. Mom's been calling all week about having lunch."

"But?"

"I don't know. Things have been... off lately. Every time I see her, it's like she's about to say something important, but then she doesn't." Abby took a bite of omelet, savoring the familiar comfort of cheese and herbs. "Maybe I'm projecting because of these dreams."

Drake leaned against the counter, his expression thoughtful. "You've been having them more frequently. Maybe talking to your mom would help? She always seems to know what's going on with you, sometimes before you do."

"That's what worries me," Abby muttered.

The law firm was quieter than usual for a Friday morning, most of her colleagues had already headed out for long weekend lunches. Abby sat at her desk, staring at the family law case file on her screen without really seeing it. The details kept blurring together – custody arrangements, visitation rights, the complex web of relationships that defined a family.

A photo on her desk caught her eye: herself at eight years old, grinning widely despite her missing front teeth, her mother's arms wrapped protectively around her at some long-forgotten birthday party. The memory stirred something else, a fragment of conversation she'd overheard years ago between her parents: "We have to tell her someday..."

Tell her what?

The thought nagged at her through the afternoon, through case reviews and client calls, until she finally gave up pretending to work and grabbed her keys.

The drive from downtown took her past familiar landmarks that marked the progression of her life like chapters in a book. The Marcus Cinema theatre in Kronenwetter, where she'd had her first date stood more vibrant than she remembered, its marquee a digital display instead of plastic letters showing the movie times, progression. She thought. Heading into Mosinee, at the intersection of W. Main Street and Twelfth Street, the crossing guard who'd helped her navigate elementary school had been replaced by impersonal traffic lights, progress marching on without sentiment.

She passed the ice cream parlor where she'd celebrated every report card. Its faded awning still sporting the same red and white stripes

As she navigated the tree-lined avenues of her childhood neighborhood, melting ice remained scattered across her windshield like fragments of memory. Robertson's house still had the tire swing where she'd spent countless summer afternoons. Mrs. Smith still tended her prize-winning roses, though her back stooped more than it used to. Each house contained a story, a part of her history that seemed temporary, like books she'd have to return someday.

The late afternoon sun filtered through the maple trees, casting dappled shadows on her steering wheel as she made the final turn onto Cedar Lane. Her mother's house appeared ahead, looking exactly as it always had – the cream-colored walls, the carefully tended garden, the wind chimes tinkling softly in the afternoon breeze. Abby sat in her car for a long moment, gathering her courage. Through the living room window, she observed her mother adjusting the arrangement of throw pillows on the couch.

The doorbell chimed, and Liz Davis's face lit up at the sight of her daughter. "Abby! I wasn't expecting you until dinner time." She hugged Abby with a mix of familiarity and desperation.

"I left work early," Abby said, following her mother into the house. The living room exuded the aroma of cinnamon and coffee, a consistent remedy employed by her mother for every crisis since Abby's earliest memories.

"Is everything alright?" Liz asked, observing her daughter's face attentively. "You look tired, sweetheart."

"I haven't been sleeping well," Abby admitted, sinking into the overstuffed armchair that had been her favorite reading spot growing up. "These dreams..."

"Dreams?" Liz's hand trembled slightly as she poured coffee into delicate china cups – the good ones, usually reserved for holidays and serious conversations.

"It's probably nothing. Just... there's this lullaby, and faces I can't quite see..." Abby watched her mother's face carefully. "Mom? What aren't you telling me?"

Liz set down the coffee pot with deliberate care. She seemed to age ten years in the space of a heartbeat, her shoulders sagging under an invisible weight. "I've rehearsed this conversation a thousand times," she said quietly. "And I still don't know how to begin."

"Begin what?"

"When you were born..." Liz's voice cracked. She took a deep breath, steadying herself. "When you came into our lives, it was the happiest day of my existence. Your father and I... we'd tried for so long to have a baby. The doctors said it wasn't possible. And then there you were, this perfect little miracle."

Understanding dawned slowly, like ice spreading across a pond. "What are you saying?"

"We adopted you, Abby. You were three days old." Tears spilled down Liz's cheeks. "Your birth mother... she was very young, in a difficult situation. She wanted you to have the best life possible."

The world tilted sideways. Abby gripped the arms of the chair, her knuckles white. "Twenty-five years," she said, her voice barely a whisper. "You've had twenty-five years to tell me this."

"We were going to tell you when you were older, but then you were so happy, so secure. I was afraid..." Liz reached for her daughter's hand. "I was afraid you'd feel different about us, about your place in the family."

Abby pulled away, standing so abruptly that coffee sloshed over the rim of her untouched cup. The room felt too small, too filled with memories that suddenly seemed like elaborate props in a play she hadn't known she was performing in. Abby gripped the arms of the chair, her knuckles white. The date—March 20th, 2015—would forever be etched in her memory as the day her world tilted sideways.

"I need... I can't..." She grabbed her keys, barely registering her mother's pleading voice as she fled to her car.

The sun was setting by the time Abby's car pulled into the parking lot of Rising Sun Dojo. The familiar scent of wood and canvas wrapping pads greeted her as she pushed through the doors. The main training area was empty this late, the evening classes long finished.

Abby moved to the center of the mat, her bare feet silent on the padded surface. She began to move through the forms, each punch and kick a meditation in motion. Every technique eased the knots in her shoulders and steadied her breathing.

A lullaby echoed in her memory, no longer a dream but perhaps a real voice from her past. Who had sung it? The woman who gave birth to her? The same woman who had chosen to give her away?

The last rays of sunlight filtered through the high windows, casting long shadows across the training floor. Abby completed her final kata and stood still, centering herself. The truth lay behind her like a door suddenly discovered in a familiar wall and ahead stretched a path into unknown territory.

She pulled out her phone and dialed Drake's number.

"Hey," she said when he answered. "I need to tell you something. And then... then I need your help finding someone."

The setting sun painted the dojo in shades of gold and shadow, and somewhere in the distance, a wind chime sang a fragmented lullaby to the evening breeze.

2 FRACTURES

My fingers trace the edges of the family photo on my desk, searching for signs I should have seen years ago. The smiling eight-year-old girl with missing front teeth stares back at me, ignorant and happy in Mom's embrace. Mom. The word tastes different now, like something familiar gone sour.

The family law case file glows on my computer screen, mocking me with its talk of custody arrangements and parental rights. Two hours ago, I was an astute attorney capable of navigating these emotional complexities with professional detachment. Now every word feels personal, every case notes a possible echo of my own story.

My phone buzzes. Another missed call from Mom. That makes five since I fled her house yesterday, since the moment she shattered everything, I thought I knew about myself with nine simple words: "We adopted you when you were three days old."

The office around me blurs as the memory crashes back. The familiar scent of Mom's cinnamon coffee. The delicate China cups she only uses for serious conversations. The way her hands trembled as she set down the coffee pot. I should have known then, should have braced myself for the impact.

But how do you brace yourself for learning your entire life is built on carefully constructed lies?

I shut down my computer, gathering my things with mechanical precision. The familiar routine feels wrong, like muscle memory that no longer fits. Sandra from Corporate waves as I pass her office. Does she see it? Can everyone tell that I'm not who I thought I was?

The drive home is a blur of spring colors and fragmented thoughts. Every red light becomes a moment to spiral into questions. Who is my birth mother? Why did she give me up? What else don't I know about myself?

Drake's car was already on our driveway when I pulled up. Of course he came home early. He's been watching me unraveling since the nightmares started, since before I knew why I was coming apart.

"Hey," he says as I walk in, his voice gentle. He's at the kitchen island, chopping vegetables with the precise attention he usually reserves for contract negotiations. The familiar domestic scene makes my throat tight. "Your mom called me."

"She's not—" The words stick, and I can't finish the sentence. Because she is my mom, isn't she? Twenty-five years of love and care and shared history don't disappear with one revelation. Do they?

"Come here," Drake says, setting down the knife. His arms open, offering the comfort I've been craving and dreading in equal measure. I step into his embrace, breathing in the familiar scent of his cologne mixed with fresh basil from his cooking.

"I don't know who I am anymore," I whisper into his shirt.

"You're Abby Thompson," he says firmly. "The most brilliant attorney at Morrison Wright. & Wellington. The woman who kicks my ass at chess and stress-bakes banana bread at midnight. The person I love more than anything."

But am I? The name Thompson feels borrowed now, a costume I've been wearing without knowing it. "I keep thinking about my birth mother," I admit. "Was she young? Scared? Did she sing to me in those three days before..." My voice cracks. The lullaby from my dreams echoes in my mind, tantalizingly familiar yet out of reach.

"We can find out," Drake says carefully. "If you want to. There are agencies and resources."

"I don't know what I want." The words come out sharper than intended. "Sorry I... every time I think about it, about her, I feel like I'm betraying Mom. The mom who raised me," I clarify, hating how I now must specify, have to categorize and label the relationships I once took for granted.

Drake's hands rub soothing circles on my back. "You're allowed to have complicated feelings about this. You're allowed to be angry and hurt and curious all at once."

My phone buzzes again. Mom's contact photo lights up the screen — a snapshot from last Christmas, both of us wearing matching reindeer sweaters and genuine smiles. The sight sends a fresh wave of pain through my chest.

"I should talk to her," I say, not moving to answer.

"Only when you're ready."

But will I ever be ready? The thought of facing her again, of sitting in that familiar living room where every photo and trinket now feels like evidence of a carefully maintained fiction... My chest tightens, the edges of panic creeping in.

"I need to move," I say abruptly, pulling away from Drake's embrace. "I need... I can't think straight right now."

He understands immediately. "Go. I'll have dinner ready when you get back."

Twenty minutes later, I'm at Rising Sun Dojo, the familiar scent of wood and canvas wrapping pads grounding me in the present. The evening classes are done, leaving the training area empty and peaceful. My bare feet find their positions on the mat automatically as I begin the first kata.

Each movement is meditation, a chance to exist purely in my body without the chaos of my thoughts. Punch. Block. Kick. The forms I've practiced thousands of times become a language of their own, telling a story of balance and control when everything else feels like it's spinning apart.

A memory surfaces: Mom bringing me to my first karate class at twelve, worried it was too violent but supporting my interest anyway. Was that real? Were any of the sacrifices and compromises she made for me genuine, or were they attempts to compensate for the original lie?

The last rays of sunlight paint shadows across the training floor as I complete the final kata. My breathing has steadied, but the questions remain, circling like birds of prey.

I pull out my phone and pull up Mom's contact. My finger hovers over the call button as I consider Drake's words: You're allowed to have complicated feelings about this.

Maybe that's the first truth I need to accept – that love and anger, betrayal and gratitude, can exist in the same heart at the same time. That the woman who kept this secret for twenty-five years is the same woman who held me through every heartbreak, who celebrated every victory, who shaped the person I've become.

I press the call button before I can change my mind. It rings once, twice—

"Abby?" Mom's voice is rough, like she's been crying.

"Hi." I swallow hard. "I think... I think we need to talk. Really talk. About everything."

The silence stretches between us, heavy with twenty-five years of unspoken truths. Finally, she says, "Yes. Yes, we do."

The setting sun casts long shadows across the dojo floor, and somewhere in the distance, a wind chime sings a fragmented lullaby to the evening breeze. I close my eyes, letting the sound wash over me. One conversation won't fix everything, won't answer all my questions or heal all my hurt. But it's a start.

And maybe that's all anyone can ask for – the courage to take the first step into an uncertain truth.

3 THE FIRST STEP

April 2015 - Three Weeks Later

Abby checked her watch for the third time in five minutes, the leather chairs in Dr. Chen's waiting room doing little to ease her anxiety. Behind the closed door, her mother was delving into memories that had been buried for decades. What truths would emerge? And was Abby ready to hear them? The room was tastefully decorated, but she felt uneasy. On the plush couch in Dr. Chen's office, she fidgeted with her shirt hem, waiting for the intake session to start. Seeking help had taken courage, and now the reality of it all was sinking in.

"Abigail Thompson?" a soft voice called, and Abby looked up to see a woman standing in the doorway. She was older, perhaps in her mid-50s, with warm, intelligent eyes and a gentle smile. "I'm Dr. Emily Chen. Please, come in."

Dr. Chen, a warm and compassionate woman in her mid-50s, sat across from Abby, a notepad balanced on her lap. She offered a reassuring smile, sensing Abby's unease. "Abby, I want you to know that this is a safe space," she began, her voice gentle and soothing. "Whatever you share here is confidential, and my goal is to help you navigate the challenges you're facing."

Abby followed Dr. Chen into her office, taking a seat on the comfortable couch opposite the therapist's armchair. She fidgeted with the hem of her blouse, suddenly unsure of where to begin.

Abby nodded, taking a deep breath to calm her nerves. She knew that opening up about her past and her current struggles wouldn't be easy, but she also knew it was a necessary step in her healing journey.

As the intake session progressed, Dr. Chen gently guided Abby through a series of questions, gathering information about her background, family history, and the specific issues that had brought her to therapy. Abby found herself slowly opening up, sharing details about her recurring nightmares, panic attacks, and the recent revelation of her adoption.

Dr. Chen listened attentively, jotting down notes and offering empathetic nods and words of encouragement. She helped Abby identify patterns and connections in her experiences, providing insights that Abby had never considered before.

Dr. Chen seemed to sense her hesitation. "Why don't we start with what brought you here today, Abby?" she prompted, her voice gentle and encouraging.

Abby took a deep breath, trying to steady the tremor in her hands. "I've been having panic attacks," she began, her voice barely above a whisper. "And nightmares. They've been getting worse lately, and I don't know how to make them stop."

Dr. Chen nodded, her expression compassionate. "Can you tell me more about these panic attacks and nightmares? When did they start?"

Abby hesitated, the memories flooding back in a rush. "I've had them for as long as I can remember," she admitted. "But they've been more frequent lately. The nightmares are always the same - I'm trapped in a burning building, and I can't breathe. I wake up screaming, and it takes me hours to calm down."

Dr. Chen made a note on her pad, her brow furrowed in

concentration. "And what about your life outside of these episodes, Abby? Can you tell me a bit about yourself?"

Abby began to talk, the words spilling out of her in a torrent. She told Dr. Chen about her job as a corporate attorney, the long hours and high-pressure cases. She spoke of her husband, Drake, and the love and support he provided. And finally, she revealed the bombshell her mother had dropped just days before - the truth of her adoption.

"I feel like my entire life has been a lie," Abby confessed, her voice breaking. "I don't know who I am anymore. I don't know if I can trust anything or anyone."

Dr. Chen leaned forward, her expression compassionate. "Abby, what you're feeling is completely normal given the circumstances. The revelation of your adoption has undoubtedly shaken your sense of identity and trust. And the panic attacks and nightmares you've been experiencing are likely tied to unresolved trauma from your past."

Abby experienced a sense of relief following the therapist's remarks. It was comforting to know that her feelings were valid, that she wasn't losing her mind.

"In our sessions, we'll work together to explore the roots of your anxiety and trauma," Dr. Chen continued. "We'll develop coping strategies to help you manage your symptoms and work towards healing. It won't be an easy journey, but I promise you, Abby, you don't have to face it alone."

Abby nodded, feeling a glimmer of hope amidst the chaos of her emotions. She understood that the road ahead would be challenging, but she recognized a potential path forward for the first time in a while.

As the session drew to a close, Abby thanked Dr. Chen, a tentative smile on her face. She stepped out of the office, feeling lighter than she had in years. The first step had been taken, and though the journey ahead was uncertain, Abby knew that she had the strength to face whatever lay ahead.

Dr. Chen leaned back in her chair, studying Abby with a thoughtful expression. "Abby, before we wrap up today's session, I'd like to discuss the frequency of our meetings," she said, her tone gentle but professional. "Given the complexity of the issues we've discussed, I recommend that we meet weekly, at least initially. This will allow us to establish a solid foundation and make consistent progress in your healing journey."

Abby nodded, feeling a sense of relief at the prospect of regular support. "I think weekly sessions would be good," she agreed, her voice steadier than it had been at the start of the session.

Dr. Chen smiled, making a note on her pad. "Excellent. We'll schedule your next appointment before you leave today." She paused, considering her next words carefully. "I also wanted to mention that, as we progress in our work together, we may explore the option of hypnotherapy."

Abby's eyebrows rose in surprise. "Hypnotherapy?" she repeated, a hint of uncertainty in her voice.

"Yes," Dr. Chen confirmed, her expression reassuring. "Hypnotherapy can be a powerful tool in accessing and processing deep-seated emotions and memories. It's not something we need to decide on today, but I wanted you to be aware of the possibility. We'll only move forward with it if and when we both feel it's appropriate for your treatment."

Abby experienced a moment of curiosity combined with a sense of apprehension. The idea of delving into her subconscious mind was both intriguing and daunting. "I'll keep that in mind," she said, her voice thoughtful. "Thank you, Dr. Chen."

As the session concluded, Abby shook Dr. Chen's hand, feeling a newfound sense of hope and determination. She scheduled her next appointment with the receptionist and stepped out into the bright sunshine, taking a deep breath of the crisp autumn air.

On the drive home, Abby reflected on the revelations of the past few weeks. The truth of her adoption, the fractured trust with her mother, and the unresolved trauma that had haunted her for so long. It was a significant amount of information to consider, but Abby recognized a clear way ahead.

She thought of Dr. Chen's words, the promise of healing and self-discovery. The journey ahead would be challenging, but Abby knew that she had the strength to face it. With Drake's support and the guidance of her therapist, she experienced a sense of hope for the future.

As she pulled into the driveway of her home, Abby felt a sense of determination settle over her. She would unravel the mysteries of her past, confront the demons that had plagued her for so long, and emerge stronger and more whole than ever before.

With a deep breath and a smile, Abby stepped out of the car and into the warmth of her home, ready to embrace the journey ahead.

4 DRAKE

Later that evening, as Abby sat on the couch with her husband, Drake, she found herself opening up about her experience with Dr. Chen. Drake listened intently, his arm draped comfortingly around Abby's shoulders.

"I'm so proud of you, Abby," he said, his voice filled with warmth and understanding.

"I can only imagine the immense courage it took to finally open up and share the weight of your struggles with someone else. The darkness you've been battling must have been suffocating, but you took that brave step forward and faced it head on."

Abby leaned into Drake's embrace, feeling a surge of gratitude for his unwavering support. "It was hard," she admitted, her voice barely above a whisper. "But I know it's something I need to do. I can't keep carrying this weight alone."

"I promise to stand by you, when the road ahead looks perilous. Having Dr. Chen guide you through these shadows is a blessing I deeply appreciate."

Drake nodded, pressing a gentle kiss to Abby's temple. "You're not alone, Abby. I'll never leave your side, no matter how treacherous the journey may seem. And I'm grateful that you have someone like Dr. Chen to steer you through this dark and daunting path."

Abby experienced a surge of emotion, tears forming at the corners of her eyes. She acknowledged that the forthcoming journey would be difficult, but with Drake's companionship and Dr. Chen's guidance, she perceived a sense of optimism for the first time in an extended period.

"Thank you, Drake," she whispered, snuggling closer to him. "I don't know what I'd do without you."

Drake smiled, his love for Abby shining in his eyes. "You'll never have to find out, Abby. I'm here, now and always."

As they sat there, wrapped in each other's arms, Abby felt a sense of peace settle over her. The journey to healing and self-discovery was just beginning, but with the love and support of her husband and the guidance of Dr. Chen, she knew she had the strength to face whatever lay ahead.

.

5 LAWYER TROUBLES

Abby had settled into her office chair, ready to dive into the complex details of the multi-million-dollar lawsuit she was handling, when her phone buzzed with an incoming call. She glanced at the screen and saw her mother's name flashing insistently.

With a sigh, Abby picked up the phone, knowing that her mother's timing was less than ideal. "Hi, Mom," she greeted, trying to keep the weariness from her voice.

"Abby, sweetheart, I wanted to check in and see how your first therapy session went," her mother's warm voice came through the receiver. "I know how important this is to you, and I've been thinking about you all day."

Abby recognized a twinge of guilt for not calling her mother sooner, but the demands of her job had been unrelenting. "It went well, Mom," she replied, cradling the phone between her ear and shoulder as she shuffled through a stack of legal documents. "Chen seems like a good fit, and I feel like I'm taking a step in the right direction."

Her mother's relief was palpable, even through the phone line. "That's wonderful, Abby. I'm so proud of you for taking this step. I know it couldn't have been easy."

Abby smiled, appreciating her mother's support. "Thanks, Mom. It means a lot to have your encouragement."

Then, a knock sounded at Abby's office door, and her assistant poked her head in, mouthing the words "conference call in five minutes." Abby nodded, holding up a finger to indicate she needed a moment.

"Listen, Mom, I hate to cut this short, but I'm in the middle of a huge lawsuit, and I have a conference call starting in a few minutes," Abby said apologetically. "Can I call you back later tonight?"

Her mother's understanding tone came through the receiver. "Of course, sweetheart. I know how important your work is. Remember to take care of yourself, too. Don't let the stress of the job overshadow your own well-being."

Abby felt a surge of love and gratitude for her mother's unwavering support. "I won't, Mom. I promise. Thanks for checking in on me."

"Anytime, Abby. I love you."

"I love you too, Mom. Talk to you soon."

As Abby ended the call, she took a deep breath, trying to refocus her mind on the task at hand. The multi-million-dollar lawsuit loomed large, demanding her full attention and legal expertise.

She glanced at the framed photo on her desk, a candid shot of her and Drake on their wedding day, smiling and laughing with carefree abandon. The image served as a reminder of the love and support she had in her life, during the chaos and stress of her job.

With renewed determination, Abby straightened her shoulders and gathered her notes for the conference call. She knew that balancing her personal journey of healing with the demands of her career would be a challenge, but she also knew that she had the strength and resilience to handle whatever came her way.

As she walked into the conference call, Abby silently thanked her mother for the reminder to prioritize her own well-being. She knew that the road ahead would be difficult, but with the love and support of her family and the guidance of Dr. Chen, she was more equipped than ever to face the challenges head-on.

Abby strode into the conference room, her high heels clicking against the polished marble floor. The room was a symphony of power and prestige, with its sleek mahogany table, plush leather chairs, and floor-to-ceiling windows that offered a stunning view of the city skyline. It was a space designed to impress, and Abby knew that every detail mattered when dealing with high-profile clients.

- She took her seat at the head of the table, her posture impeccable and her expression one of cool confidence. Around her, a team of junior associates and paralegals bustled, arranging stacks of legal documents and preparing to take meticulous notes.

The client, a prominent business tycoon embroiled in a contentious legal battle, sat across from Abby, his brow furrowed with concern. He leaned forward, his voice low and urgent. "Ms. Thompson, I cannot stress enough how important this case is to me and my company. The stakes are incredibly high, and I need to know that you and your firm are fully committed to securing a favorable outcome."

Abby met the client's gaze unflinchingly, her voice smooth and assured. "Mr. Thompsen, I can assure you that my team and I are dedicating all of our resources and expertise to this case. We understand the gravity of the situation, and we will leave no stone unturned in our pursuit of a successful resolution."

The client nodded, his shoulders relaxing slightly. "I appreciate your confidence, Ms. Thompson. But I must warn you, the opposition is ruthless. They will stop at nothing to destroy my reputation and my company."

Abby's eyes flashed with determination. "We are well aware of their tactics, Mr. Thompsen. But I can promise you this - we will fight fire with fire. My team and I are the best in the business, and we will not be intimidated by their attempts to derail this case."

As Abby spoke, her mind raced with the countless details and strategies she had meticulously planned. Late nights spent pouring over legal precedents, intense strategy sessions with her team, and the constant pressure to stay one step ahead of the opposition - it all coalesced in this moment, in this room where the fate of her client's empire hung in the balance.

The meeting stretched on for hours, with Abby leading her team through a complex web of legal maneuvering and calculated risks. She fielded questions with precision, countered arguments with razor-sharp intellect, and exuded an aura of unflappable control.

But beneath the surface, Abby could feel the weight of the pressure bearing down on her. The expectations of her client, the reputation of her firm, and the knowledge that one misstep could spell disaster - it all combined to create a suffocating sense of responsibility.

As the meeting finally ended, the client shook Abby's hand, his grip firm and his eyes filled with tentative hope. "I'm counting on you, Ms. Johnson. My company's future is in your hands."

Abby nodded, her smile polished and reassuring. "I won't let you down, Mr. Thompsen. You have my word."

As the client and her team filed out of the conference room, Abby allowed herself a moment to exhale, her shoulders sagging slightly under the weight of the momentous task ahead. She knew that the coming weeks would be a grueling marathon of legal strategy and high-stakes negotiations, with little room for error.

But as she gathered her notes and prepared to dive back into the fray, Abby felt a flicker of gratitude for the support system she had in her life. Her husband's unwavering love, her mother's constant encouragement, and the promise of healing through her sessions with Dr. Chen - these were the things that would sustain her through the challenges ahead.

With a deep breath and a steely resolve, Abby stepped out of the conference room and into the corridors of power, ready to face whatever obstacles lay in her path. She was Abigail Thompson, a legal powerhouse and force to be reckoned with, and she would not be deterred from her mission to secure justice for her client, no matter the cost. ...As she walked into the conference call, Abby silently thanked her mother for the reminder to prioritize her own well-being.

6 SESSION 2

Abby arrived for her second session with Dr. Chen, feeling a mix of anticipation and nervousness. As she settled onto the familiar couch, she noticed that Dr. Chen seemed a bit distracted, shifting uncomfortably in her seat.

"Abby, it's good to see you again," Dr. Chen greeted her, a tight smile on her face. "How have you been since our last session?"

Abby began to recount the events of the past week, delving into the emotional ups and downs she had experienced. As she spoke, she couldn't help but notice that Dr. Chen's discomfort seemed to be increasing.

Suddenly, mid-sentence, Dr. Chen let out a resounding belch that echoed through the room. Abby's eyes widened in surprise, her words trailing off as she stared at the therapist in shock.

Dr. Chen's face turned a deep shade of red as she quickly covered her mouth with her hand. "Oh, my goodness, I am so sorry," she apologized, her voice muffled behind her fingers. "Please excuse me, I don't know what came over me."

Abby blinked, unsure of how to respond. "Are you alright, Dr. Chen?" she asked hesitantly, concerned mingling with the absurdity of the situation.

Dr. Chen waved her hand dismissively, taking a deep breath. "I'm fine, Abby, thank you. Let's proceed with our session, shall we?"

Abby nodded, trying to refocus on the topic at hand. However, as she began to speak again, a pungent odor wafted through the room. Abby's nose wrinkled involuntarily as she glanced at Dr. Chen, who was shifting in her seat, a pained expression on her face.

"I apologize, Abby," Dr. Chen said, her voice strained. "It seems I'm experiencing some rather uncomfortable gas pains today."

Abby tried to suppress a laugh, the absurdity of the situation overwhelming her. Here she was, in the middle of a therapy session, and her esteemed therapist was battling a case of flatulence.

Dr. Chen, to her credit, tried to maintain a professional demeanor. She straightened her posture and cleared her throat, determined to continue the session. "Now, Abby, let's discuss the coping strategies we talked about last week. Have you had a chance to practice any of them?"

Abby opened her mouth to respond, but before she could utter a word, another loud, prolonged burst of gas escaped from Dr. Chen. The therapist's eyes widened in mortification as she clutched her stomach, a look of pure horror on her face.

Unable to contain herself any longer, Abby burst into a fit of laughter. Tears streamed down her face as she gasped for air, the tension of the past few weeks melting away in the face of the ridiculous situation.

To her surprise, Dr. Chen joined in the laughter, her own giggles mixing with Abby's as they both succumbed to the hilarity of the moment. The office filled with the sound of their shared mirth; the seriousness of the therapy session temporarily forgotten.

As their laughter subsided, Dr. Chen wiped tears from her eyes, a sheepish grin on her face. "Well, Abby," she said, her voice still tinged with amusement, "I think it's safe to say that this session has taken an unexpected turn."

Abby grinned, feeling a newfound sense of connection with her therapist. "I guess therapists have off days too," she remarked, her eyes sparkling with mirth.

Dr. Chen chuckled, nodding in agreement. "Indeed, we do. But perhaps this is a good reminder that we're all human, with our own quirks and imperfections."

As the session resumed, the atmosphere in the room had shifted. The laughter had broken down barriers, creating a sense of camaraderie between therapist and client. And though the serious work of therapy still lay ahead, Abby felt a renewed sense of hope and determination.

Sometimes, amid life's challenges, a little laughter could be the best medicine of all.

As the session continued, Abby found herself increasingly distracted by a peculiar and pungent odor that seemed to be permeating the room. At first, she tried to ignore it, focusing on Dr. Chen's words as she discussed the importance of self-care and mindfulness. However, with each passing moment, the smell grew more intense, invading her nostrils and making her stomach churn.

Abby shifted uncomfortably on the couch, her nose wrinkling in disgust as she discreetly tried to wave the odor away with her hand. She glanced around the room, trying to pinpoint the source of the stench, but nothing seemed out of place. The bookshelves were neatly organized, the potted plants were vibrant and well-maintained, and the windows were closed, sealing out any external influences.

Unable to bear it any longer, Abby interrupted Dr. Chen mid-sentence. "I'm sorry, but do you smell that?" she asked, her voice strained as she tried to breathe through her mouth to avoid inhaling the noxious fumes.

Dr. Chen paused, her brow furrowing as she took a deep breath. She tilted her head, sniffing the air with a puzzled expression. "I don't smell anything unusual, Abby," she replied, her voice calm and reassuring. "Can you describe what you're sensing?"

Abby's face contorted in revulsion as she struggled to find the words. "It's like a mix of rotten eggs, spoiled milk, and something that died in the walls," she said, her stomach churning at the mere thought. "It's absolutely horrid."

Dr. Chen leaned forward, taking another sniff. "I honestly don't detect anything out of the ordinary," she said, her tone apologetic. "Perhaps it's a sensitivity you have that I don't share. Let's try to proceed with our session, and if it becomes too overwhelming, we can take a break."

Abby nodded, trying to push the smell to the back of her mind. She took a deep breath, immediately regretting it as the stench filled her lungs, causing her to gag. In a desperate attempt to block out the odor, Abby grabbed the hem of her shirt and pulled it up over her nose, creating a makeshift mask.

Dr. Chen watched with a mix of concern and amusement as Abby sat there, her shirt covering half her face, her eyes watering from the intensity of the smell. "Abby, are you sure you're alright?" she asked, struggling to suppress a smile at the absurdity of the situation.

Abby nodded, her voice muffled behind the fabric of her shirt. "I'm fine," she mumbled, her words barely audible. "Please, let's keep going."

Dr. Chen shrugged, picking up where she left off. As she spoke, Abby found herself becoming more and more distracted by the stench. It seemed to be growing stronger by the minute, seeping into every corner of the room and clinging to her clothes and hair.

Abby's eyes darted around the office, desperately searching for the source of the smell. She eyed the potted plants suspiciously, wondering if some strange fungus had taken root in the soil. She glanced at the bookshelves, half-expecting to see a decomposing rodent tucked between the volumes.

As Dr. Chen droned on about the benefits of journaling and self-reflection, Abby felt her patience wearing thin. The combination of the overpowering odor and the therapist's seeming oblivious to it was pushing her to the brink of frustration.

As Abby was about to rip her shirt off and demand a full-scale investigation into the source of the stench, Dr. Chen suddenly paused. Her eyes widened as she sniffed the air, a look of realization dawning on her face.

"Oh my," she said, her voice tinged with embarrassment. "I think I might have figured out the culprit behind that smell."

Abby lowered her shirt, her eyes narrowing in suspicion. "What is it?" she demanded, her voice edged with irritation.

Dr. Chen reached beneath her chair and pulled out a small, plastic container. She held it up, a sheepish grin on her face. "I forgot that I had packed a tuna fish sandwich for lunch today," she admitted, her cheeks flushing pink. "It must have been sitting there, fermenting in the heat of the office."

Abby stared at the container, her jaw dropping in disbelief. The source of the horrendous odor, the thing that had been tormenting her for the past half hour, was nothing more than a forgotten lunch.

Dr. Chen quickly disposed of the offending sandwich, opening the windows to air out the room. As the fresh breeze wafted in, carrying away the lingering stench, Abby couldn't help but burst into laughter.

"I can't believe it," she gasped, tears of mirth streaming down her face. "All this time, I thought there was some terrible, hidden source of the smell, and it was just your lunch!"

Dr. Chen joined in the laughter, shaking her head at her own forgetfulness. "I guess this goes to show that sometimes, the things that bother us the most can have the simplest explanations," she said, her eyes twinkling with amusement.

As the laughter dissipated and the session recommenced, Abby experienced a renewed sense of ease. The absurdity of the situation had somehow managed to break through the heaviness of her emotions, reminding her that even in the midst of life's challenges, there was always room for a little humor.

As the session progressed, Dr. Chen's discomfort became increasingly apparent. She shifted in her seat, her face contorting in a grimace as she tried to maintain her professional composure. Abby, still grappling with the lingering odor of the forgotten tuna fish sandwich, watched with growing concern as her therapist seemed to be battling an internal struggle.

Dr. Chen took a deep breath, her voice strained as she spoke. "Abby, I apologize, but I think we may need to end our session a bit early today," she said, her words punctuated by a barely suppressed groan. "I'm not feeling very well at the moment."

Abby's eyebrows furrowed in worry, her own discomfort momentarily forgotten. "Is everything alright, Dr. Chen?" she asked, leaning forward on the couch. "Is there anything I can do to help?"

Dr. Chen shook her head, a tight smile on her face. "No, no, it's quite alright," she assured Abby, even as her body betrayed her words. "I need a moment to..." Her voice trailed off as a sudden, intense pressure built up within her.

Abby watched, her eyes widening in a mix of shock and morbid fascination, as Dr. Chen clenched her jaw and tensed her muscles. The therapist's face turned a deep shade of red as she fought against the inevitable, trying desperately to maintain her dignity in front of her client.

Despite her best efforts, a muffled, high-pitched squeak escaped from Dr. Chen's tightly pursed lips. The sound hung in the air for a moment, followed by a deafening silence. Abby's mouth fell open, her mind struggling to process what had happened.

Dr. Chen's eyes squeezed shut, mortification etched across her features. She took a shaky breath, her voice barely above a whisper as she spoke. "Please excuse me, Abby. I seem to be experiencing some rather... uncomfortable gastrointestinal distress."

Abby, in a valiant attempt to preserve her therapist's dignity, quickly pulled her shirt back up over her nose, creating a makeshift barrier against the impending onslaught. She nodded, her voice muffled behind the fabric. "Of course, Dr. Chen. I completely understand."

As if on cue, a series of muffled, yet unmistakable sounds began to emanate from Dr. Chen's direction. The therapist's face contorted in a mix of relief and embarrassment as she tried to pass gas as quietly as possible, her efforts failing miserably in the confines of the small office.

Abby, her nose now firmly covered by her shirt, tried to focus on anything but the audible evidence of her therapist's digestive distress. She studied the patterns on the ceiling, mentally recited the alphabet backwards, and attempted to recall the lyrics to her favorite childhood song, all in a desperate bid to distract herself from the awkward reality of the situation.

Dr. Chen, meanwhile, continued to battle her rebellious bowels, each muffled toot and squeak adding to the growing tension in the room. The air grew thick with the unmistakable scent of flatulence, mingling with the lingering aroma of the tuna fish sandwich to create a truly unholy olfactory experience.

After what felt like an eternity, Dr. Chen finally exhaled, her shoulders sagging in relief. She took a deep breath, her face still flushed with embarrassment. "I am so terribly sorry, Abby," she apologized, her voice tinged with mortification. "This is highly unprofessional, and I assure you, it won't happen again."

Abby, her nose still safely hidden behind her shirt, nodded in understanding. "It's okay, Dr. Chen," she mumbled, her words slightly muffled. "These things happen to everyone."

Dr. Chen smiled weakly, grateful for her client's compassion. "Thank you, Abby. I think it's best if we end our session here for today. I promise, next week, we'll have a proper, uninterrupted session."

Abby stood up, carefully lowering her shirt as she made her way to the door. She paused, turning back to face her therapist with a sympathetic smile. "Take care of yourself, Dr. Chen. And maybe consider packing a different lunch next time."

Dr. Chen chuckled, the tension in the room finally dissipating. "Noted, Abby. I'll stick to salads from now on."

As Abby left the office, she couldn't help but feel a newfound sense of camaraderie with her therapist. After all, they had just survived one of the most awkward and humorous therapy sessions imaginable. And in a strange way, the shared experience had brought them closer together, reminding them both importance of laughter, compassion, and the ability to find humor in even the most uncomfortable situations.

And as she left Dr. Chen's office that day, Abby couldn't help but smile, knowing that the memory of the Great Tuna Fish Sandwich Debacle would forever be etched in her mind as a reminder that sometimes, laughter truly was the best medicine.

7 LAUGHTER AND LEVITY

Three days after the strategy meeting, Abby stood frozen in Dr. Chen's waiting room, her heart pounding against her ribcage...

Abby sat across from her best friend, Lila, in their favorite cozy booth at the local wine bar. The soft lighting and gentle hum of conversation created a warm, inviting atmosphere, and Abby felt herself slowly unwinding from the stresses of her day.

Lila leaned forward, her eyes sparkling with curiosity as she swirled her glass of pinot noir. "So, spill the beans, Abby. How was your second therapy session with Dr. Chen? I'm dying to know all the juicy details."

Abby couldn't help but chuckle, the memories of the session flooding back in vivid detail. She took a sip of her own wine, savoring the rich, velvety flavor before setting the glass down and grinning at her friend.

"Well, let's just say it was an experience I won't soon forget," Abby began, her voice laced with amusement. "Picture this - Dr. Chen and I are deep in conversation, discussing my childhood memories and emotional triggers, when suddenly, the room is filled with the most pungent odor imaginable."

Lila's eyes widened, her mouth forming a perfect "O" of surprise. "No way! What happened?"

Abby laughed, the sound ringing out through the bar. "Turns out, Dr. Chen had forgotten about a tuna fish sandwich she had packed for lunch. It had been sitting in her office all day, fermenting in the heat.

The smell was absolutely horrendous!"

Lila burst into laughter, her hand flying to her mouth to stifle the sound. "Oh my god, Abby! That's hilarious! I can't believe your therapist forgot about a tuna sandwich in her office. Talk about unprofessional!"

Abby nodded, her own laughter mingling with Lila's. "But wait, it gets better. Just as we're trying to recover from the tuna incident, Dr. Chen starts experiencing some serious gastrointestinal distress. I'm talking full-on gas attacks, Lila. The woman was tooting like a brass band!"

Lila nearly choked on her wine, her eyes watering with mirth. "Stop it, Abby! I can't handle this. Your therapy sessions sound more like a comedy sketch than a deep dive into your psyche."

Abby grinned, taking another sip of her wine. "I know, right? I mean, there I was, pouring my heart out about my childhood traumas, and all I could focus on was the fact that my therapist was letting out silent-but-deadlies every five minutes."

The two friends dissolved into fits of laughter, drawing curious glances from the other patrons in the bar. They clinked their glasses together, toasting to the absurdity of life and the unexpected moments of levity that could be found in the midst of emotional turmoil.

As their laughter subsided, Lila reached across the table, her hand resting comfortingly on Abby's arm. "In all seriousness, though, Abby, I'm really proud of you for going to therapy and facing your demons. I know it's not easy, but you're one of the strongest people I know. And if a few gassy moments with your therapist can bring a smile to your face, then I say embrace the humor where you can find it."

Abby felt a surge of warmth and gratitude for her friend's unwavering support. "Thanks, Lila. You're right. Sometimes laughter is the best medicine, even in the most unexpected places."

The two friends spent the rest of the evening sipping wine,

swapping stories, and finding joy in the simple pleasure of each other's company. As Abby returned home that evening, she experienced a sense of relief, confident that irrespective of the forthcoming challenges, the support and camaraderie of her friends would sustain her.

Abby leaned back in her seat, a contemplative look on her face as she considered Lila's question. The memory of her second therapy session, with all its gassy interruptions and tuna-scented distractions, was still fresh in her mind.

Lila tilted her head, her expression a mix of curiosity and concern. "I mean, I know I was joking around earlier, but seriously, Abby, are you going to go back to Dr. Chen after that whole side-splitting scene? I can't imagine trying to have a serious conversation with someone who's constantly battling their own bodily functions."

Abby took a deep breath, her fingers absently tracing the stem of her wine glass. "You know, Lila, I've been asking myself that same question. Part of me wonders if I should find a new therapist, someone who doesn't come with a built-in laugh track."

Lila nodded, her eyes filled with understanding. "I can totally see why you'd be hesitant. It's hard to open up and be vulnerable when you're constantly waiting for the next gassy interruption."

Abby chuckled softly, a wry smile tugging at the corners of her mouth. "Exactly. I mean, how am I supposed to delve into the depths of my psyche when all I can think about is the fact that my therapist's intestines are staging a rebellion?"

The two friends shared a knowing look, the absurdity of the situation hanging in the air between them. Abby sighed, her brow furrowing as she grappled with the decision.

"But then again," she continued, her voice growing more thoughtful, "there was something kind of refreshing about the whole thing. I mean, yes, it was awkward and uncomfortable and downright hilarious at times, but it also reminded me that therapists are human.

They have their own quirks and bodily functions, just like the rest of us."

Lila considered Abby's words, her head nodding slowly in agreement. "I can see that. It's like, if your therapist can own up to her gassy moments and still maintain a sense of professionalism, then maybe it's okay for you to be vulnerable and imperfect, too."

Abby felt a surge of warmth and affection for her friend's insight. "Exactly. And honestly, Lila, I don't know if I'm ready to start over with a new therapist. Dr. Chen may have her quirks, but she also has a way of making me feel heard and validated. I don't want to lose that because of a few awkward bodily functions."

Lila reached across the table, her hand resting comfortingly on Abby's arm. "Then I say go for it, Abby. Stick with Dr. Chen and see where this journey takes you. And if nothing else, you'll have some pretty hilarious stories to share over wine with your amazing best friend."

Abby grinned, raising her glass in a toast. "To therapy, tuna sandwiches, and the unbreakable bond of friendship."

Lila clinked her glass against Abby's, a mischievous sparkle in her eye. "And to the hope that Dr. Chen invests in some heavy-duty air freshener before your next session."

The two friends dissolved into laughter once more, the decision made and the path forward clear. Abby knew that therapy wouldn't be easy, and there would undoubtedly be more awkward and uncomfortable moments ahead. But with the support of her best friend and the determination to face her demons head-on, she was ready to embrace the journey, gas and all.

8 FINDING YOUR INNER PEACE

The next day, the sun had barely begun to peek over the horizon when Abby stepped into the quiet, unassuming building that housed her karate dojo. The familiar scent of polished wood and worn mats filled her nostrils, instantly putting her at ease. This was her sanctuary, the place where she could shed the weight of her worries and focus solely on the strength and discipline of her craft.

Abby made her way to the changing room, her footsteps echoing softly in the empty space. She donned her crisp, black gi, the fabric a comforting second skin. With each tug of her belt, She transitioned, setting aside the stress and uncertainty of her everyday life and assuming the role of sensei.

As she entered the main training area, Abby took a moment to center herself, her eyes closed and her breathing steady. She moved through a series of stretches, her muscles warming and her mind clearing with each fluid motion. The outside world faded away, replaced by a singular focus on the present moment.

The first students began to trickle in, their faces a mix of excitement and determination. Abby greeted each one with a bow and a warm smile, her confidence and poise evident in every interaction. She watched as they lined up, their stances strong and their eyes fixed forward, ready to begin the day's lesson.

"Today," Abby began, her voice ringing out clear and strong, "we focus on the power of stability. In karate, as in life, a strong foundation is key. Without a stable base, we are easily knocked off balance, prone to falling and losing our way."

She moved to the front of the class, her movements fluid and precise as she demonstrated a series of stances. The students watched, their eyes eager and their muscles tensed, ready to follow her lead. Abby guided them through each position, her instructions firm but encouraging.

As the class progressed, Abby found herself drawing parallels between the principles of karate and the challenges she faced in her own life. Just as a strong stance could withstand the force of an opponent's blow, a solid foundation of self-awareness and emotional resilience could weather the storms of personal upheaval.

Abby's thoughts drifted to her latest real estate development project, a towering skyscraper set to reshape the city's skyline. She had thrown herself into the planning and negotiations, pouring over blueprints and contracts late into the night. It was a massive undertaking, one that required a level of focus and determination that mirrored her approach to karate.

In the dojo, Abby watched as her students sparred, their movements quick and decisive. They tumbled and rolled, their falls controlled and their recoveries swift. Each time they hit the mat, they sprang back up, their eyes blazing with renewed determination. It was a testament to the resilience of the human spirit, the ability to face challenges head-on and emerge stronger for the struggle.

As the class wound to a close, Abby led her students through a final series of stretches, their bodies loose and their minds calm. She looked out at the sea of faces, each one a reflection of the progress and growth she had witnessed over the course of the lesson.

"Remember," she said, her voice soft but firm, "true strength comes from within. It is the ability to face our fears, to confront our demons, and to rise above the challenges that life throws our way. Whether in the dojo or in the boardroom, we must always strive for stability, for a foundation that can weather any storm."

The students bowed, their faces glowing with a sense of accomplishment and inner peace. As they filed out of the dojo, Abby sensed a surge of pride and gratitude for the opportunity to guide and inspire others on their own journeys of self-discovery.

She knew that her own path was far from over, that there would be many more obstacles and setbacks to come. But here, in the sanctuary of the dojo, surrounded by the strength and resilience of her students, Abby now had a renewed sense of purpose and determination.

With a final, centering breath, she stepped out into the bright, bustling world beyond the dojo's walls, ready to face whatever challenges lay ahead. She was Abigail Thompson, black belt and real estate powerhouse, and she would not be deterred from her quest for stability, both in her personal life and in the towering skyscrapers that would soon shape the city's horizon.

9 ABBY'S SEARCH FOR HER BIOLOGICAL MOTHER

Abby sat in her plush office, staring at the computer screen, her brow furrowed in concentration. As a successful lawyer, she knew the ins and outs of the legal system, but despite weeks of scouring online databases, reaching out to adoption agencies, and hiring researchers to comb through public records, she kept hitting dead ends. It was as if her mother had vanished into thin air.

Frustrated and desperate, Abby decided to take a different approach. She reached out to her network of contacts in the legal world, asking for recommendations for the best private investigators. That's how she found Sam Hawkins.

Sam was a former FBI agent who had made a name for himself working on high-profile cases. His keen eye for detail and relentless determination had earned him a reputation as one of the best in the business. After leaving the Bureau, he had started his own private investigation firm, taking on cases that others deemed impossible. But his success came at a price - his obsession with work had cost him his marriage and strained his relationship with his teenage daughter. He poured himself into his cases, using work as a way to avoid the painful realities of his personal life.

When Abby first contacted him, Sam was immediately intrigued by her story. He could hear the desperation in her voice, the longing for answers that had consumed her for so long. As he sat across from her in his sparse office, listening to her story, he felt a familiar pull - the need to uncover the truth, no matter where it led. Something about this case felt different. Maybe it was the raw emotion in Abby's voice, or maybe it was how it reminded him of his own daughter, whom he barely saw anymore. Whatever the reason, he knew he had to help her.

"I don't know much," Abby explained, her hands clasped tightly in her lap. "Her name was Amanda, and she was from a small town near here. She was only fifteen when she had me." Her voice cracked slightly. "I just... I need to know where I came from."

Sam nodded, studying the adoption papers spread across his desk. "I'll find her," he promised, his voice gentle but firm. "No matter what it takes."

For weeks, Sam immersed himself in the search. He followed leads that went nowhere, dug through dusty archives, and called in favors from old contacts. Each dead end only made him more determined. He recognized the same determination in Abby's eyes whenever she called to check on his progress.

Then, finally, a breakthrough. The pieces started falling into place, but what they revealed made Sam's blood run cold. He stared at his computer screen, double-checking the information, hoping he was wrong. But the facts were undeniable.

The morning he had to break the news to Abby felt heavy with dread. She sat across from him, hope shining in her eyes, as he carefully laid out what he'd found.

"Your birth mother's name is Amanda Cole, formerly known as Amanda Johnson - she legally changed her last name while in prison," he began, his voice steady despite the weight of what he had to say. "She's been in Taycheedah Correctional Institution for the past twenty-five years." He paused, watching Abby's face carefully. "She was convicted of attempted murder and first-degree murder."

Abby felt her world crumbling around her. She collapsed into Drake's arms, who had insisted on coming with her for support. "How could she..." Her voice trailed off, unable to complete the thought.

Sam leaned forward, his expression grave. "There's more, Abby.

The victims... one of them was John Elder, attempted murder. The other..." He hesitated, his eyes moving to Drake. "The other was Michael Maddox Johnson. Drake's father."

The silence that followed was deafening. Drake's arms tightened around Abby, but she could feel him trembling. The universe, it seemed, had a cruel sense of irony.

"I need to see her," Abby whispered, her voice barely audible. "I need to understand."

Sam nodded, understanding the compulsion to face hard truths head-on. "I'll make the arrangements. But Abby..." He caught her eye. "Are you sure you're ready for what you might learn?"

The morning sun cast long shadows across Abby Thompson's kitchen as she gripped her coffee mug, trying to still the trembling in her hands. Papers were scattered across the table - adoption records, prison documents, old newspaper clippings - each one a piece of a puzzle she wasn't sure she wanted to complete.

"Maybe we should wait," Drake said softly, his own coffee untouched. He stood by the counter, car keys clutched in his hand so tightly his knuckles had gone white. "It's too soon after everything with Liz. And with what Sam found out..." His voice cracked on the last words.

Abby's heart ached watching him struggle. The revelation about her birth mother's identity had hit Drake harder than either of them could have imagined. Amanda - the woman who had given birth to her - was also the woman who had taken Drake's father from him. The universe, it seemed, had a cruel sense of irony.

"I need to know," Abby whispered, echoing the words she'd said in Dr. Chen's office yesterday. Her therapist had cautioned her about moving too quickly, about the risks of piling trauma upon fresh trauma. But she had also understood Abby's desperate need for answers. "The not knowing is worse than any truth could be."

Drake crossed the kitchen, pulling her into his arms. "Then let me come with you," he pleaded, his voice rough with emotion. "You shouldn't have to face her alone."

Abby pressed her face against his chest, breathing in his familiar scent. "You know you can't," she said gently. "Not yet. Not until..." She couldn't finish the sentence. How could she explain that she needed to protect him from seeing his father's murderer? That she needed to understand who Amanda was before she could ask Drake to face her?

The unspoken truth hung between them: every step Abby took toward her birth mother was a step into the darkest chapter of Drake's life. Every answer she sought was tied to his deepest wound. Their love had always felt predestined - now they knew it had been built on an intersection of tragedy neither could have imagined.

Abby nodded, tears welling up in her eyes. "I just need to know, Drake. I need to understand who I am and where I came from."

Abby felt her world crumbling around her. She collapsed into Drake's arms, sobbing uncontrollably. "How could she do something like that? What does that make me?"

Drake held her tightly, stroking her hair. "It doesn't make you anything, Abby. Her actions don't define you."

Abby stared at the blank piece of paper before her, pen poised in her hand. How could she begin to write to the woman who gave her life, but also took the lives of others?

Drake sat beside her, his presence a steady comfort. "Speak from your heart, Abby. Tell her how you feel."

"With a shaky breath, Abby began to write, her fingers trembling so badly she could barely hold the pen. The words swam before her eyes as Sam's phone call echoed in her mind - 'She's in prison, but she wants to meet you.' Twenty-five years of wondering, and now this.

'Dear Amanda,' she wrote, then stopped, her stomach clenching. What do you call a mother you've never met? The woman whose face had haunted her nightmares, always just out of reach? Liz—Mom—had only told her about the adoption a few weeks ago, and now...

'I don't know where to start,' she continued, a tear splashing onto the paper, blurring the ink. 'I've spent my entire life wondering about you, dreaming of the day I would finally meet you. But now, knowing what I know... I'm scared. I'm confused. The mother I imagined and the reality of who you are—they're such different people. And I don't know if I'm ready for what comes next.

Tears splashed onto the paper as Abby poured out her heart, her emotions raw and unbridled. "I need to understand, Amanda. I need to know what led you to that place, to those actions. I need to know if the love you once felt for me was real."

Sam Hawkins was a former FBI agent who had made a name for himself working on high-profile cases. He had a keen eye for detail and a relentless determination that had earned him a reputation as one of the best in the business. After leaving the Bureau, Sam had started his own private investigation firm, taking on cases that others deemed impossible.

But Sam's success came at a price. His obsession with his work had cost him his marriage and strained his relationship with his teenage daughter. He poured himself into his cases, using work as a way to avoid the painful realities of his personal life.

When Abby first contacted him, Sam was intrigued by her story. He could hear the desperation in her voice, the longing for answers that had consumed her for so long. He knew that this case would be a challenge, but he was determined to help Abby find the truth, no matter where it led.

ICE AWAKENS

The envelope landed on Amanda's metal bunk with a soft thud during afternoon count. Another piece of junk mail, she thought, probably some religious group trying to save her soul. She'd seen enough of those over the last twenty-three years to wallpaper her 6x8 cell twice over. But this one was different – handwritten, personal. As she read the first line, her coffee-stained fingers began to tremble.

"Dear Amanda, I believe I'm your daughter..."

"What kind of sick fucking joke is this?" She crumpled the letter in her fist, the cheap prison-issued paper crinkling like dead leaves. The familiar taste of bile rose in her throat – the same taste she got every morning when the guards rattled their keys at 4 AM, every afternoon when her cellmate's girlfriend visited and they played happy families in the visitation room, every night when the screams from C-block reminded her where she was.

Twenty-five years. Twenty-five years of the same routine: wake up to the sound of metal on metal, stand for count, eat whatever slop they served in the mess hall, work in the laundry breathing in bleach fumes until her head spun, stand for count again, an hour in the yard if she was lucky, more counting, more slop, more screaming, more counting. The days bled into weeks, those bled into years until time became meaningless. The only marker of its passing was the growing collection of scars – some from fights, some self-inflicted during those dark nights when the walls closed in too tight.

"A daughter? Bullshit." She spat the words at the concrete wall, her voice rough from years of chain-smoking whatever cigarettes she could trade for. The last thing she needed was some con artist trying to play on her emotions. She'd seen enough inmates fall for that scam – long-lost relatives suddenly appearing when they thought there might be money or favors to gain. But something about this letter nagged at her, picked at that locked door in the back of her mind where she kept all the memories she couldn't face.

"Listen here, you little bitch," she began writing, her pen pressing so hard it nearly tore through the paper. "I don't know what kind of scam you're trying to pull, but I've been in here long enough to spot a con from a mile away. You want to play pretend? Let me tell you what it's really like to be connected to someone like me. Let me tell you about waking up every fucking day knowing you'll die in a cage. Let me tell you about watching your own mother's funeral through a grainy video feed because they wouldn't let you attend. Let me tell you about the nights I've spent listening to my cellmate cry for her kids while I try to remember if I ever held you – IF you exist."

She paused, her hands shaking so badly now she could barely hold the pen. That last thought had slipped out unbidden, unwanted. There were things she didn't let herself think about, memories that stayed buried beneath layers of anger and denial. The spring of '90 was one of them. The hospital. The pain. The blood. No. NO. She wouldn't go there.

Instead, she channeled her confusion into rage, the one emotion that had never failed her in this place. "You want a mother? Go back to whoever raised you. I'm not your fucking fairy godmother. I'm not your salvation. I'm not your anything. And if you ever write to me again, I'll show you exactly why I ended up in here in the first place."

The look that Abby gave Drake was filled with determination and fear. "I don't know if I can do this," she said quietly, her voice trembling. "Amanda is so angry, she thinks we're trying to trick her into believing she has a child." The truth was, Amanda didn't know she had a child. It was a repressed memory, a painful reminder of the years of abuse she suffered as a young girl. But now, faced with the possibility of having a daughter, Amanda couldn't help but entertain the idea. Maybe having a child could give her some sense of purpose and help her escape from this prison she had been living in for so long. As she wrote in her letter to Drake, "it may have been the only good thing I did during that dark time in my life." But deep down, Amanda couldn't shake the guilt and regret that consumed every day since then, knowing she could never be the kind of mother her child deserved.

Abby read the letter over and over, her tears blurring the ink. She knew what she had to do.

The morning sun cast long shadows across Abby Thompson's kitchen as she gripped her coffee mug, trying to still the trembling in her hands. Two weeks. It had only been two weeks since her mother Liz had shattered her world with seven simple words: "We adopted you when you were three days old." Now here she was, about to meet her birth mother - in prison, of all places.

"Maybe we should wait," Drake said softly, his own coffee untouched. He stood by the counter, car keys clutched in his hand so tightly his knuckles had gone white. "It's too soon after everything with Liz. And with what Sam found out..." His voice cracked on the last words.

Abby's heart ached watching him struggle. The revelation about her birth mother's identity had hit Drake harder than either of them could have imagined. Amanda - the woman who had given birth to Abby - was also the woman who had murdered Drake's father. The universe, it seemed, had a cruel sense of irony.

"I need to know," Abby whispered, echoing the words she'd said in Dr. Chen's office yesterday. Her therapist had cautioned her about moving too quickly, about the risks of piling trauma upon fresh trauma. But she had also understood Abby's desperate need for answers. "The not knowing is worse than any truth could be."

Drake crossed the kitchen, pulling her into his arms. "Then let me come with you," he pleaded, his voice rough with emotion. "You shouldn't have to face her alone."

Abby pressed her face onto his chest, breathing in his familiar scent. "You know you can't," she said gently. "Not yet. Not until..." She couldn't finish the sentence. How could she explain that she needed to protect him from seeing his father's murderer? That she needed to understand who Amanda was before she could ask Drake to face her?

A knock at the door interrupted them. Lila stood on their porch, her expression a mixture of determination and concern. She had been Abby's rock through everything - through the initial shock of learning about her adoption, through the sleepless nights of questioning everything she thought she knew about herself, and now through this latest devastating revelation.

"Ready?" Lila asked simply, holding up a manila envelope containing all the documentation they might need - adoption papers, birth records, everything that proved Abby's connection to Amanda.

Four hours earlier, in a six-by-nine-foot cell at Taycheedah Correctional Institution, Amanda jolted awake to the familiar sound of keys rattling against metal bars. The pre-dawn darkness pressed against her small window, not yet touched by the approaching sunrise. 4 AM count – same as every other day for the past twenty-five years.

"Count time, ladies!" Officer Martinez's voice echoed through the cellblock, followed by the rhythmic sound of doors being unlocked and relocked. Amanda could identify most guards by their footsteps now – Martinez had a slight drag to his left foot, probably from the knee injury he'd mentioned last summer.

The cellblock came alive with the sounds of women preparing for count: toilet flushes, whispered conversations, the rustle of cheap prison blankets. In the cell next door, someone was crying again – probably the new girl, still adjusting to the reality of a twenty-year sentence.

Amanda sat up on her thin mattress, muscle memory taking over as she swung her legs over the side and planted her feet firmly on the cold concrete floor. Her few possessions were arranged with military precision: three books from the prison library stacked by size on the small metal shelf, state-issued toiletries lined up in perfect rows, photos she never looked at tucked away in an envelope beneath her mattress.

"Cole!" Officer Martinez's flashlight beam cut through the darkness, illuminating Amanda's face. She kept her expression neutral, her posture rigid - half-asleep, ICE never showed weakness.

"Present," she responded, her voice carrying the practiced flatness that had become her trademark. The beam moved on, leaving her in darkness once more.

From the bottom bunk, Rosa stirred. "You were talking in your sleep again, ICE," she murmured, her voice still heavy with drowsiness. "Something about sunshine?"

Amanda's shoulders tensed. Rosa Garcia had been her cellmate for three years now, serving time for embezzlement. She was one of the few inmates who wasn't intimidated by ICE's reputation – perhaps because she'd arrived after Amanda's most notorious prison yard fights, when the name ICE still carried fresh terror.

"Mind your business, Garcia," Amanda snapped, but there was less bite in her tone than usual. The dream fragments were still too close to the surface: a hospital room bathed in afternoon sunlight, the weight of something small and warm in her arms, a melody she couldn't quite...

No. She slammed that door shut, as she had for the past twenty-five years. ICE didn't have a past. ICE didn't have regrets. ICE didn't have a...

"Suit yourself," Rosa shrugged, swinging her feet off her bunk. At fifty-two, she moved with the careful precision of someone who knew exactly how much her aging body could handle. "But you might want to work on your game face before your visitor shows up. You're slipping, mama."

Amanda's hand moved unconsciously to her abdomen, an ancient muscle memory she didn't recognize. "What do you mean, slipping?"

Rosa's dark eyes, lined with twenty years of wisdom earned in women's correctional facilities across three states, studied Amanda carefully. "Three years I've been in this cell with you. Never seen you check the visitor board. Never seen you get mail that wasn't legal notices. Never seen you flinch at count. But this week?" She shook her head. "Something's got ICE starting to melt."

The morning bell cut off Amanda's retort. 5:30 AM – time to prepare for breakfast. The cellblock erupted into its usual choreography: one hundred and twenty women negotiating four sinks and three toilets, all under the watchful eyes of guards who'd rather be anywhere else.

Amanda moved through her morning routine with mechanical precision, but Rosa's words had shaken something loose. In the scratched metal mirror above the sink, her reflection seemed less certain than usual. The gray in her hair was more pronounced, the lines around her mouth deeper. When had ICE started showing her age?

A flash of memory: staring into a different mirror, twenty-five years ago. A terrified fifteen-year-old girl with a swollen belly, singing softly to her unborn child. "You are my sunshine, my only sunshine..."

The toothbrush snapped in Amanda's grip. "Shit," she muttered, watching a drop of blood well up where the broken plastic had cut her palm.

"Here," Rosa said quietly, holding out a spare toothbrush. Their fingers brushed during the exchange – the most physical contact Amanda had allowed in years. "You know, ICE, whatever's coming at ten o'clock... maybe it's time to let some of those wall's thaw."

Amanda's reflection stared back at her, hollow-eyed and uncertain. The visitor's notification had disrupted her carefully ordered world: "Cole, Amanda. Visitor approved for Thursday, 10 AM. Legal visit." But something about it felt different from regular legal visits. Something about it felt like doors long frozen shut were beginning to crack.

The breakfast line moved with its usual sluggish efficiency. Amanda took her place, hyper-aware of how other inmates gave her space – a habit born from years of witnessing what happened to those who got too close to ICE. The morning's offerings were the same as every Thursday: lumpy oatmeal, dry toast, coffee that tasted like warm dishwater.

But today, even the familiar routine felt off-kilter. As she mechanically spooned oatmeal into her mouth, more memories tried to surface: the taste of hospital food, a kind nurse showing her how to hold a bottle, a tiny hand gripping her finger before they took...

"Eating alone again, ICE?" Rosa's voice cut through the memory. She set her tray down opposite Amanda – something she'd never done before. "You know, my grandmother used to say that memories are like water. The harder you try to hold them back, the more ways they find to leak through."

Amanda's spoon clattered against her tray. "Your grandmother sounds like a fool."

"Maybe," Rosa agreed mildly. "But she raised seven kids by herself after my grandfather died, including one that wasn't hers by blood. Said that love doesn't care about biology." She stood, gathering her tray. "Just think about something before your visitor arrives."

Back in their cell, Amanda found herself doing something she hadn't done in over twenty years — she cared about her appearance. She ran the cheap prison comb through her hair multiple times, trying to tame the gray strands into submission. She smoothed her state-issued blues, noticing how the fabric hung looser than it used to.

"Use my lipstick," Rosa offered, holding out a pale pink contraband tube. When Amanda hesitated, Rosa added softly, "Even ICE is allowed to look human sometimes."

The color on her lips felt foreign, vulnerable. In the mirror, she looked less like ICE and more like... Amanda. The name itself felt strange, like clothes that no longer fit. When was the last time anyone had called her anything but ICE or Inmate Cole?

Another memory surfaced: a nurse's gentle voice. "Do you want to name her before..." Amanda had shaken her head, knowing that name meant attachment, and attachment meant pain.

"Ten minutes to visitor check-in," Officer Martinez called down the block. Amanda's hands began to shake.

"Breathe, mama," Rosa said quietly. "Whatever's coming through that door... maybe it's time to let it in."

But as Amanda walked toward the visitor's area, each step echoing on the concrete floor, she felt ICE's familiar frost creeping back over her heart. ICE didn't have visitors. ICE didn't have feelings. And ICE certainly didn't have a...

The guard at processing looked up from her paperwork. "Cole, your visitor's here. Legal counsel, first time visit." She peered at Amanda curiously. "You're wearing lipstick."

Amanda straightened her spine, letting ICE's cold mask settle into place. Whatever waited in that visitor's room, she would face it as she had faced everything else in the past twenty years – with walls of ice too thick to breach.

But deep in the recesses of her mind, in places ICE pretended didn't exist, a lullaby continued to play: "You are my sunshine, my only sunshine..."

Four Hours Earlier

The drive to Taycheedah Correctional Institution was mostly silent. Abby's knuckles were white on the steering wheel as she navigated through the city's north side. The morning sun caught the institution's distinctive red roofs as they crested the final hill, making the sprawling complex look deceptively peaceful against the winter landscape.

A knot formed in her throat at the sight of the American and state flags snapping in the wind above the entrance plaza. The modern octagonal gatehouse with its wall of windows seemed to watch their approach, a stark contrast to the older brick buildings beyond. She followed Lila's quiet directions to the visitor parking lot, trying not to stare at the razor wire that traced the perimeter like metallic ivy.

"You can still change your mind," Lila said softly as they pulled into a spot facing the entrance building, its tan brick and large windows attempting a warmth that couldn't quite mask its true purpose.

Abby shook her head, taking in the manicured lawns and neat walkways that somehow made everything feel more surreal. "No," she said, her voice steadier than she felt. "I need to know."

"Remember what Dr. Chen said," Lila spoke up as they approached the prison. "You're not defined by her actions or her choices. You're still you - still the same Abby who kicks ass in court and stress-bakes at midnight and has the biggest heart of anyone I know."

Abby managed a weak smile, grateful for her friend's presence. Dr. Chen had been right to suggest having someone there for support. The imposing brick structure of the correctional center loomed ahead, its razor wire glinting in the morning sun like cruel jewelry. She had driven past this building countless times during her years practicing law in, never imagining that somewhere behind those walls was the woman who had given her life - and taken Drake's father's.

The intake process felt surreal. Abby, used to entering courthouses with a simple flash of her bar card, found herself removing her wedding ring, her watch, emptying her pockets. Each item placed in the small locker felt like shedding a piece of her carefully constructed life.

"Arms out," the guard instructed, running the metal detector wand over her body. Her eyes flickered between the ID and Abby's face, lingering a moment too long on the surname. "Johnson? No - Thompson, sorry about that. Any relation to Michael Maddox Johnson?"

Abby felt Lila's steadying hand on her arm, grateful for the anchor as the guard's stumble over names stirred memories she'd rather keep buried. "He was my father-in-law," she managed, her voice steady despite the churning in her stomach. Let the guard assume what she wanted about the different surnames. Some stories weren't meant for metal detector small talk.

55

The guard's face softened with recognition. "That was a tough case. ICE showed no remorse at sentencing." She paused, studying Abby's face. "You sure you want to do this?"

Abby nodded, unable to form words. The walk through the series of security doors felt like a descent into another world. Each buzzing lock, each heavy metal door clanging shut behind them, marked another boundary crossed. The sound of distant voices, muffled announcements over crackling speakers, and the constant hum of industrial fluorescent lights created a disorienting symphony.

The visiting room assaulted her senses. The sharp smell of industrial cleaners barely masked years of institutional living. Children's drawings decorated one wall in a failed attempt at warmth, their bright colors jarring contrast to the grey-green paint and reinforced windows. A vending machine hummed in the corner; its offerings arranged in neat rows like empty promises.

And then there she was. Amanda entered with the practiced movement of someone who had walked through institutional doors for decades. Her prison blues hung loose on her frame, but she carried herself with a predator's grace. Her eyes, grey as winter ice, swept the room with calculated precision before landing on Abby.

Something flickered in their depths – confusion, recognition, fear? – before being swallowed by cold calculation. The distance to the visiting station felt endless. Abby's heels clicked against the linoleum, each step echoing with finality.

And then, there she was. Amanda, her birth mother, sitting behind the glass, her eyes filled with a lifetime of pain and regret. Abby picked up the phone, her hand shaking. "Amanda?"

"So you're the one claiming to be my daughter." Amanda's voice came through with mechanical flatness on the intercom, stripped of emotion by the aging system. Her eyes scanned Abby's face with the precision of someone looking for tells in a poker game. "Funny, I don't remember having a kid."

The words hit Abby like a physical blow. First Liz's decades of lies, and now this - her birth mother denying her very existence. She felt Lila's steady presence beside her as she forced herself to speak.

"I have the adoption papers," she managed, her lawyer's instincts kicking in despite her trembling hands. "From the Wausau Hospital, 1990. You were fifteen—"

The words hit Amanda like a physical blow, shattering the ice that had protected her mind for twenty-five years. Suddenly, she wasn't in the prison visiting room anymore. The fluorescent lights transformed into afternoon sunshine streaming through hospital windows. The hard plastic phone receiver became cold metal bed rails under her white-knuckled grip.

Amanda was back in the Wausau Hospital, 1990. The pain was overwhelming, ripping through her teenage body in waves that left her gasping. The starched sheets scratched against her skin; every sensation too sharp, too real. She could smell the antiseptic, hear the steady beep of monitors, feel the sweat plastering her dark hair to her forehead.

"Breathe through it, Amanda," the nurse was saying, her kind face swimming in and out of focus. "You're doing so well. Your baby's almost here."

Baby. The word echoed in her mind like a gunshot. She hadn't allowed herself to think of it as a baby during the months she'd hidden her growing belly under baggy sweaters, during the long nights she'd lain awake feeling it move inside her. A baby meant it was real. A baby meant she'd have to face what had happened to her, what he had done...

Another contraction seized her. She heard herself scream, the sound raw and primal. Fifteen years old, alone in a delivery room because her parents couldn't even look at her after they'd found out. Fifteen years old and about to become a mother when she was still a child herself.

"I see the head!" the doctor announced. "One more big push, Amanda."

She bore down, tears streaming down her face. The pressure built to an impossible crescendo, and then... release. A tiny wail pierced the air, high and indignant. Despite herself, Amanda's eyes snapped to the source of the sound.

They were holding up a small, wrinkled thing, pink and perfect and angry at the world. "It's a girl," the nurse said softly. "A beautiful baby girl."

Before Amanda could process what was happening, they placed the baby on her chest. She felt the warm weight of her, smelled that indescribable newborn scent. Tiny fingers flexed against her skin. And something inside Amanda's chest cracked open, letting in love so fierce it terrified her.

"You are my sunshine," she found herself singing, her voice cracking. Her mother used to sing it to her, before everything went wrong. "My only sunshine..."

The baby's cries quieted. She turned her head, unfocused eyes blinking up at Amanda. So, trusting. So, innocent. So unaware of the darkness in the world, of the violence that had created her.

"Would you like to name her?" the nurse asked gently. "Before the adoption paperwork is processed?"

Reality crashed back like a bucket of ice water. Amanda turned her face away. "No," she whispered. "No name. Just... just take her. Please."

She felt them lift the baby's weight from her chest. The tiny cry started up again, growing fainter as they carried her away. Amanda curled onto her side, pulling her knees to her chest, making herself as small as possible. She felt the ice beginning to form around her heart, protecting her from the pain that threatened to tear her apart.

By the time she left the hospital three days later, the ice had spread. It covered her completely, turning her into someone new. Someone hard. Someone who would never be hurt again. ICE was born in that hospital room, in the absence of a baby's warmth.

The memory released Amanda with the same violence with which it had gripped her. She was back in the prison visiting room, staring through the glass at a young woman with her eyes, her jaw, her determination. A woman who had shattered twenty-five years of carefully maintained frost with five simple words: "Wausau Hospital , 1990. You were fifteen—"

"Shut up!" Amanda's fingers whitened around the receiver, tendons standing out like cords. She could feel the ice cracking, memories seeping through like water in spring. Too much. It was too much. "You don't know anything about—"

But she couldn't finish the sentence. Because for the first time in twenty-five years, she remembered everything. The hospital. The baby. The lullaby. And the terrible, wonderful love she'd felt for those brief moments before the ice took over.

"Shut up." Amanda's fingers whitened around the receiver, tendons standing out like cords. Something flickered behind her eyes — fear, maybe, or rage. A bead of sweat traced down her temple despite the room's chill. "You don't know anything about—" She stopped abruptly, her face contorting as if fighting against a memory trying to surface.

Behind them, a child squealed with delight at seeing their mother. Amanda flinched at the sound, her hardened facade cracking for just a moment. Her free hand moved unconsciously to her abdomen, an ancient muscle memory she seemed unaware of.

"Listen here," Amanda finally said, leaning forward until her breath fogged the glass. Her voice had taken on a honeyed tone that didn't match her eyes. "Maybe you are who you say you are. Maybe you're not. Either way, I can see you're a woman of means. Professional clothes, wedding ring that's worth more than my first three cars combined..."

"I married Michael Maddox Johnson's son," Abby interrupted, her voice steadier than she felt. "Drake Johnson. The boy who was twelve when you killed his father."

Amanda's mask cracked completely. She recoiled as if struck, the receiver clattering against the glass. A string of emotions flashed across her face — recognition, horror, calculation, and something deeper, more primal. "No," she whispered. "No, no, no..."

"I need to understand," Abby pressed, watching her birth mother unravel. "Not only for me. For Drake. For the family you destroyed when you became ICE."

Amanda's hands began to shake violently. "You married..." She couldn't finish the sentence. Her eyes darted around the room like a trapped animal's, decades of carefully buried memories threatening to surface. "This isn't... you can't be..."

"Your victims had names, Amanda. They had families. One of them became mine."

The predatory smile that had played on Amanda's lips earlier was gone, replaced by raw panic. This wasn't how her usual manipulations went. The neat lines she'd drawn between her past and present were blurring, reality becoming too messy, too interconnected to control.

"Get out," Amanda hissed, her ICE persona frantically trying to reassert itself. "You think you can come here, wearing his name, claiming to be... GET OUT!"

The outburst drew the attention of nearby guards. As one approached their station, Amanda leaned close to the glass, her voice dropping to a desperate whisper. "You don't know what you're doing, girl. Some doors shouldn't be opened. Some truths..." She glanced around furtively. "Drake Johnson's father wasn't merely another victim. There's more... there's so much more..."

Amanda approached the guard. "Hey, you! I don't know what just happened, but I think that girl has the wrong person. I don't know her."

The guard chuckled. "Mama, you said that to every pretty girl who came in here for a visit. It's part of your act, trying to hook up with some rich sap on the outside."

Amanda's heart raced. "No, I swear, officer! I don't know her!"

The guard rolled his eyes and turned away, leaving Amanda alone with her thoughts and the haunting realization that she might have just turned away a real connection.

The words tumbled out, a torrent of grief, guilt, and anguish. Amanda spoke of her troubled past, the abuse she suffered, the drugs that consumed her. She spoke of the night that changed everything, the night she lost herself completely.

Abby listened, her heart breaking with each revelation. But as Amanda spoke, something shifted within her. She saw beyond the crimes, beyond the pain, to the broken woman before her. A woman who, despite everything, had loved her enough to let her go.

"I forgive you, Amanda," Abby whispered, her voice choked with emotion. "I forgive you, and I want to know you. Not the person you were, but the person you are now."

Amanda wept, her tears a release of years of pent-up shame and longing. "Thank you, Abby. Thank you for giving me a chance."

As Abby left the prison that day, hand in hand with Drake, she felt a sense of peace wash over her. She had found her truth, her history, and a glimmer of hope for a future with the mother she had always longed for.

Amanda sitting in her cell, thinking to herself. Who was that bitch! I never had a kid. What the fuck!

Truth be told, Amanda was a notorious con artist who had claimed motherhood over 50 times before. The system was so messed up that it never caught on to her little game. Abby, however, was unaware of all this.

Abby would come to regret the day she ever considered forgiving Amanda...

Abby felt her world crumbling around her. She collapsed into Drake's arms, sobbing uncontrollably. "How could she do something like that? What does that make me?"

Drake held her tightly, stroking her hair. "It doesn't make you anything, Abby. Her actions don't define you."

"But she's my mother, Drake. Her blood runs through my veins," Abby whispered, her voice barely audible through her tears. "What if I'm just like her? What if this... this deception is hereditary?"

Drake gently tilted her chin up, forcing her to meet his gaze. His eyes were fierce with conviction. "Listen to me. You are nothing like her. You've spent your whole life searching for truth while she's built hers on lies. The fact that you're even worried about becoming like her proves how different you already are."

Abby's breathing steadied slightly as she leaned into his solid presence. The weight of Amanda's betrayal still pressed heavily on her shoulders, but Drake's unwavering faith provided a small island of stability in the chaos.

"I just feel so stupid," she confessed. "I wanted to believe her so badly that I ignored all the warning signs. I practically handed her my trust on a silver platter."

"We see what we want to see sometimes," Drake said softly. "You wanted a mother. There's nothing wrong with that."

As the last light of day faded from the window, they sat together in the growing darkness, the truth of Amanda's deception settling around them like dust after an explosion. Abby knew the path forward would be difficult, but with Drake beside her, she would find a way to rebuild from the ruins of her shattered hopes.

10 THAWING WALLS

The drive back from Taycheedah Correctional Institution felt endless. Lila kept her eyes on the road, hyperaware of every subtle shift in Abby's breathing from the passenger seat. Her friend's hands trembled as she clutched the manila envelope containing the adoption papers – papers that now felt like matches that had ignited an explosion.

The morning sun pierced through the windshield with painful brightness, a stark contrast to the institutional fluorescent lighting they'd left behind. Each mile seemed to carry them further from ICE's calculating stare, but the weight of Amanda's final whispered warning hung in the car like smoke.

"Do you want to talk about it?" Lila finally asked, her voice barely above a whisper. The question felt inadequate against the magnitude of what they'd witnessed.

Abby's laugh was hollow, almost hysterical. "Talk about what? About how my birth mother denied my existence until I mentioned Drake's name? Or about how completely she fell apart after that?" She pressed her forehead against the cool glass of the window, her breath fogging the surface. "God, Lila, what have I done? What am I going to tell Drake?"

Lila thought back to Amanda's transformation in that visiting room – how the infamous ICE's practiced control had shattered at the mention of Michael Maddox Johnson. That wasn't the reaction of a simple murderer having her crime recalled. That was something deeper, more visceral.

When they pulled into Abby's driveway, Drake was already waiting on the porch. He wore the same clothes from breakfast, as if he hadn't moved since they left. One look at Abby's face told him everything he needed to know. He crossed the distance in long strides, pulling her into his arms before she could collapse.

"I'm so sorry," Abby whispered into his chest, her tears finally breaking free. "I shouldn't have gone. I shouldn't have opened this door. Now everything's worse and Amanda knows about us and—"

"Shh," Drake soothed, though Lila could see the tension in his jaw, the way his own hands shook slightly as he held his wife. "Let's get you inside. Mom's here."

Liz Davis sat at the kitchen table, her normally perfectly styled hair disheveled as if she'd been running her hands through it all morning. Her eyes carried the weight of twenty-five years of secrets. The sight of her adoptive mother – the woman who had raised her, loved her, lied to her – sent fresh pain through Abby's chest.

"I had to come," Liz said, half-rising from her chair. "When Drake called and said you were meeting her, I..." She trailed off, uncertainty written across her face. These past two weeks had transformed their relationship into something fragile, full of landmines neither knew how to navigate.

Lila moved to the counter, starting the familiar ritual of making tea – something she'd done countless times during late-night study sessions in law school, during Abby's wedding planning, during the shocking aftermath of learning about her adoption. The routine helped ground her as she processed what she'd witnessed in that visiting room.

"She knew who Drake's father was," Abby finally said, her voice barely above a whisper. "The moment I mentioned Michael Maddox Johnson, it was like... like a mask cracked. She completely lost control." She looked up at Drake, tears streaming down her face. "What if this isn't some cosmic coincidence? What if there's more to why she killed your father?"

Drake knelt beside her chair, taking her hands in his. "Hey, look at me. Whatever Amanda did, whatever secrets she's keeping – that's on her. Not you. You're my wife, the love of my life. Nothing she says or does changes that."

"But she's my mother," Abby choked out. "My blood. What if I'm somehow part of—"

"Stop right there," Liz cut in, her voice sharp with maternal protectiveness. "Biology isn't destiny, Abby. I may have lied about being your birth mother, and I will spend the rest of my life trying to make that right. But I raised you. I know your heart. You are nothing like her."

Lila set the mugs of tea on the table, remembering how Amanda's facade had crumbled. "She said something else at the end," she reminded gently. "Something about Drake's father not being 'just another victim.' Maybe that's where we need to focus."

Through the window, they could see their neighbor's children playing in the spring sunshine, their laughter carrying across the yard – a reminder that somewhere, normal life continued. But in this kitchen, four people who loved Abby held their breath, knowing that whatever came next would change all of their lives forever.

Meanwhile, in her cell at Taycheedah Correctional Institution, Amanda paced like a caged animal, the ice in her veins beginning to crack. Rosa watched from her bunk, concern etching deeper lines around her eyes.

"Twenty-five years," Amanda whispered, more to herself than her cellmate. "Twenty-five years I kept those secrets buried. Let them think I was a cold-blooded killer. And now my daughter – the baby I gave up, the one pure thing I ever created – has married into the very family I destroyed to keep those secrets."

"You okay, mama?" Rosa asked softly, using the nickname that usually earned her a sharp rebuke.

Amanda stopped pacing, staring out the small window at the same spring sunshine that fell on her daughter's kitchen across town. "No," she whispered, pressing her hand against the cold glass. "I'm not okay. And soon... soon no one else will be either."

The truth was clawing its way to the surface, and this time, not even ICE could stop it.

11 ICE IS BACK

Later that night, curled up on her couch with Drake's arms around her, Abby felt the full weight of the day crash over her. "I don't know who I am anymore," she whispered into his chest. "Two weeks ago, I thought I was Liz Davis's daughter. Now I'm the daughter of a murderer, married to her victim's son. How do we begin to process this?"

Drake held her tighter, his own tears falling into her hair. "We process it together," he whispered fiercely. "And tomorrow, we talk about it with Dr. Chen. One step at a time, like she says."

Meanwhile, in her cell, Amanda paced like a caged animal. The girl's face kept morphing into Michael's in her mind – the same determined set of the jaw, the same unflinching gaze. And now her daughter – if she really was her daughter – had married his son? The universe had a sick sense of humor.

A slow, calculating smile spread across Amanda's face as new possibilities began to form. This complicated things, but complications meant leverage. Maybe she couldn't remember if the girl was really her daughter, but the Johnson connection... that she could use. After all, that's what ICE did best – turn chaos into opportunity.

But as she finally lay on her bunk, staring at the ceiling, different memories began to surface – memories of Michael Maddox Johnson's last words, of secrets she'd killed to keep buried, of a teenage girl's desperate choices. Secrets that, if they came to light, could destroy not just Abby and Drake's marriage, but the very foundation of everything they thought they knew about their connected past.

The question was, would Abby see through her birth mother's lies before it was too late? Or would the tragic truth about Michael Maddox Johnson's murder surface first, shattering both families all over again?

12 BREAKING THE ICE

Three days after the prison visit, Abby found herself back in Dr. Chen's office, still getting used to the leather armchair that didn't quite feel like hers yet. The gentle patter of spring rain against the windows filled the silence as she struggled to articulate the chaos of the past few days to this woman she barely knew.

Dr. Chen sat quietly, her patience evident but not yet familiar. Only their second real session together, after that rushed initial consultation two weeks ago when everything with Liz had first exploded. It felt strange, laying bare such intimate family wounds to someone who was still essentially a stranger.

"When Amanda first denied knowing me," Abby finally began, her voice uncertain, "it felt like being abandoned all over again. But then..." She stopped, glancing at Dr. Chen, trying to gauge if this new therapist could handle the weight of what came next.

Dr. Chen leaned forward slightly, her expression open. "Take your time, Abby. I know we're still getting to know each other, but this is a safe space to process what happened."

Something in her tone gave Abby the courage to continue. "When I mentioned Drake's father, something broke in her. I've watched hundreds of witnesses crack on the stand – that's what I do, I'm a lawyer – but this was different." Her hands twisted in her lap. "This wasn't just guilt or fear. It was like watching someone's whole world implode."

"That must have been intense to witness," Dr. Chen observed, her tone carefully neutral but engaged. "Especially given your connection to both Amanda and Drake's father."

"That's just it." Abby stood, drawn to the window by restless energy. "Everything I've learned about Amanda – or ICE, as they call her – suggests someone who maintains absolute control. The guards, the other inmates, even her reputation... she's spent decades building these walls. But one mention of Michael Maddox Johnson and those walls just..." She pressed her hand against the cool glass. "They shattered."

Dr. Chen waited a moment before asking, "What do you think that tells you about her?"

Abby turned back, appreciating how Dr. Chen didn't rush to fill the silence with premature interpretations. "That maybe the woman who killed Drake's father isn't the whole story. That maybe there's more to why she became ICE." She took a shaky breath. "That maybe she's as scared of the truth as I am."

"I hear you wanting to understand," Dr. Chen said carefully. "And that's natural. But since we're beginning our work together, I want to make sure you have support as you navigate this." She paused, making sure she had Abby's full attention. "Whatever Amanda's reasons were, whatever secrets she's keeping... your well-being has to come first."

"I know," Abby said softly. "But I can't just walk away. Not now. Not when I might finally understand why she gave me up, why she..." She swallowed hard. "Why she killed Drake's father."

"Then perhaps we can talk about how to approach this safely." Dr. Chen's voice held a balance of support and caution that Abby found steadying. "What might it look like to explore these questions while protecting yourself emotionally?"

Abby sank back into the chair, considering. "Letters, maybe? Through my lawyer, so there's some distance? And I'd tell Drake everything – no secrets between us, even if it's hard."

"That sounds like a thoughtful approach," Dr. Chen nodded. "What other support systems do you have in place?"

"My friend Lila," Abby said immediately. "She was there at the prison. She'll tell me if I'm moving too fast. And..." She managed a weak smile. "I'd like to keep coming here, keep processing everything with you. If that's okay."

"Of course." Dr. Chen returned the smile. "I know we're just beginning to build trust, but I'm here to support you through this journey. Think of exploring this relationship with Amanda like approaching a frozen lake. You need to test each step, have safety lines in place, and be ready to pull back if the ice starts to crack."

As their session wound down, Dr. Chen scheduled their next appointment for three weeks out – the earliest she had available. Abby felt a flicker of anxiety at the gap but reminded herself that she had other support systems in place.

Leaving the office, Abby pulled out her phone and called Drake. "Hey," she said when he answered. "Remember how you said we'd face everything together? I think... I think I need to write Amanda a letter. But I want us to write it together. Can we talk about it over dinner?"

Across town, Amanda sat in her cell, staring at the wall. Rosa's words from that morning echoed in her mind: "Even ICE has to thaw sometime, mama." She thought about her daughter's face – so much like her own at that age, before everything went wrong. Before Michael Maddox Johnson. Before the secrets that had turned her to ice.

Maybe it was time. Maybe after twenty-five years of frozen silence, some truths needed to come to light. Even if those truths changed everything.

She reached for a piece of paper and began to write.

That evening, Abby sat cross-legged on their living room floor, surrounded by crumpled drafts of letters. Drake appeared from the kitchen carrying two mugs of chamomile tea, the kind they always drank when cases kept them up late. He settled beside her, close enough that their shoulders touched.

"What if we're making a huge mistake?" Abby whispered, staring at the blank paper before them. "What if reaching out just makes everything worse?"

Drake set their mugs on the coffee table and took her hand, his thumb tracing familiar patterns across her palm. "Then we face it together," he said softly. "Like we always do."

Abby turned to study his face – the face she'd fallen in love with in law school, long before either of them knew how their pasts were entangled. "How can you be so calm about this? About me wanting to understand the woman who..." She couldn't finish the sentence.

"Who killed my father?" Drake completed gently. He was quiet for a moment, gathering his thoughts. "You know, I've spent twenty-five years trying to understand why. Mom never talked about it. The trial transcripts only told part of the story. Maybe..." He squeezed her hand. "Maybe this is a chance for both of us to find some answers."

Abby leaned into him, drawing strength from his steady presence. "Dr. Chen suggested writing through my lawyer, keeping some professional distance. But that feels... wrong somehow. Cold."

"Then we write from the heart," Drake said. "But carefully. Like you always tell your clients – be honest, but measured." He reached for a fresh sheet of paper. "Want me to start?"

Abby nodded, watching as Drake's familiar handwriting began to fill the page:

"Dear Amanda,

This letter comes from both of us – Abby and Drake. We know our first meeting was overwhelming, for all of us. We also know there are truths that need to be spoken, stories that need to be heard. We're writing because we believe in second chances, in the possibility of understanding even the hardest things.

We're not asking for immediate answers or explanations. We're simply opening a door, if you're willing to walk through it with us..."

"Too much?" Drake asked, glancing at Abby.

She shook her head, tears pricking at her eyes. "No, it's perfect. It's... human." She took the pen from him, adding her own words:

"I know seeing me brought up painful memories. I saw it in your eyes when I told you who I married. But maybe that's not just cosmic cruelty. Maybe it's an opportunity – for truth, for healing, for understanding why our lives intersected the way they did.

We're not naive. We know this won't be easy. But we're willing to listen, to try to understand. Not just about why you gave me up, but about everything that happened after. About who you were before you became ICE. About my father..."

Abby's hand trembled on the last words. Drake steadied her wrist, helping her finish the sentence.

"About what really happened with Michael Maddox Johnson."

They spent the next hour crafting each careful paragraph, finding words to bridge twenty-five years of silence and pain. When they finally signed their names at the bottom, the letter felt like both a peace offering and a leap of faith.

"I'll have my office send it tomorrow," Abby said, sealing the envelope. "Through official channels, so she knows it's really from us."

Drake pulled her close, pressing a kiss to her temple. "Whatever happens next," he murmured, "remember what Dr. Chen said about safety lines. You have me. You have Lila. You have your mom – both your moms. You don't have to carry this alone."

Abby nodded against his chest, listening to his heartbeat. "I keep thinking about what you said at our wedding," she whispered. "About how love isn't just the easy parts – it's choosing each other through the hard stuff too."

"And I choose you," Drake said firmly. "Through whatever this brings up, whatever truths we uncover. The past doesn't get to define us."

Later that night, as they lay in bed, Abby thought about Amanda in her cell, and about the walls of ice she'd built to survive. Maybe those walls were finally starting to thaw. The question was: what would they find when the ice melted completely?

But for now, wrapped in Drake's arms, Abby let herself believe that sometimes the hardest paths could lead to healing – if you were brave enough to walk them together.

13 HIDDEN FRACTURES

Abby's heels clicked against the polished marble of Thompsen Industries' executive floor, the sound sharp as breaking ice. Her mind was still half-focused on the letter she and Drake had sent to Amanda three days ago, but she forced herself to center on the case files clutched against her chest. This merger dispute could make or break her career at Caldwell Ross & Wellington – she couldn't afford distractions.

Richard Thompsen's corner office commanded a view of Wausau's skyline, but today the blinds were drawn. He stood at his desk, moving papers with jerky, anxious movements that immediately set off warning bells in Abby's courtroom-honed instincts.

"The opposition's called for an emergency hearing," she said, settling into her usual chair. "They claim to have new evidence that could affect the merger timeline." She watched Thompsen's face carefully, noting how he wouldn't quite meet her eyes. "Want to tell me what they might have found?"

"Nothing substantial." Thompsen's voice was steady, but his

fingers drummed against his desk — a tell she'd noticed during prep sessions. "Just Smith & Klein trying to delay the inevitable."

Abby set her briefcase aside, leaning forward. Five years of cross-examining witnesses had taught her to trust her gut. "Mr. Thompsen, I need you to be straight with me. Is there anything, anything at all, that could blindside us in that courtroom?"

He finally looked at her then, and something in his expression made her throat tighten. It reminded her of how Liz had looked that night two weeks ago, right before shattering her world with the truth about her adoption.

"You're an excellent attorney, Ms. Thompson," Thompsen said softly. "One of the best I've worked with. Your ability to see connections, to understand the human element behind corporate facades..." He trailed off, running a hand through his silver hair. "That's what makes this so difficult."

The familiar surge of adrenaline — the one that had carried her through countless courtroom victories — kicked in. "Make what difficult?"

But Thompson had already shuttered whatever moment of vulnerability he'd shown. "Nothing. Just pre-trial nerves. Now, about the shareholder meeting minutes..."

Later, preparing in her office until the city lights blurred outside her window, Abby couldn't shake the feeling that she was missing something crucial. She spread the case files across her desk, searching for patterns, connections, anything that might explain Thompsen's behavior.

Her phone buzzed – a text from Drake: "Any word from Amanda yet?"

The question made her chest tight. "Nothing," she typed back. "Focus on prep for tomorrow's hearing. Love you."

She returned to the files, but now her mind kept overlaying them with another set of documents – the adoption papers, the prison records, the transcripts from Amanda's trial. All those papers that had revealed one truth while hiding others.

The next morning dawned grey and cold, spring sunshine losing its battle with heavy clouds. Abby stood before the bathroom mirror, adjusting her suit jacket – armor for the battle ahead. Drake appeared behind her, wrapping his arms around her waist.

"You've got this," he murmured against her hair. "Whatever happens in that courtroom today, you've got this."

She leaned back against him, allowing herself one moment of vulnerability before the day's performance began. "Something feels off about this case. Thompson's hiding something, I can feel it. But I can't put my finger on what."

"Trust your instincts," Drake said. "They've never steered you wrong before."

But as Abby strode into the courtroom two hours later, her instincts were screaming. Thompsen sat too stiffly beside her, his usual corporate confidence replaced by something that looked almost like fear. The opposition's lead counsel, Jessica Chen, wore the slight smile Abby had learned to dread – the smile that said she was about to flip the board.

"Your Honor," Chen began, "we've recently obtained documentation that calls into question not only the validity of this merger but the very foundation of Thompsen Industries' financial history." She approached the bench with a manila envelope that made Thompsen go rigid beside Abby. "Specifically, a series of transactions from twenty-five years ago, involving a financial consultant named Amanda Johnson."

The name hit Abby like a physical blow. Johnson– her birth mother's former name, before she became Amanda Cole, before she became ICE.

"These documents," Chen continued, "show a pattern of fraudulent activities that Mr. Thompsen and Ms. Johnson engaged in together, activities that laid the groundwork for Thompsen Industries' current market position. Activities that ended abruptly when Ms. Johnson was arrested for the murder of Michael Maddox Johnson."

The courtroom tilted sideways. Abby heard herself object, heard the judge overrule her, but it was all happening at a distance. She turned to Thompsen, whose face had gone ashen.

"You knew," she whispered, ice spreading through her veins. "All this time, you knew who I was. Who she was."

"Abby," he started, reaching for her arm, "I can explain—"

But the ice had already claimed her, just as it had claimed Amanda twenty-five years ago. She rose, her voice steady despite the chaos in her mind. "Your Honor, in light of this new evidence and what appears to be a significant conflict of interest, I move for an immediate recess to confer with my client and firm leadership."

As she walked from the courtroom, Abby felt the weight of history repeating itself. Another trusted figure, another web of lies, another truth that would change everything. The question was: how many more secrets were still waiting to be uncovered? And how many more relationships would shatter when they finally came to light?

In her office, her phone buzzed again. A message from the prison: "Your letter received. Visiting hours Thursday at 10. – Amanda."

The ice in Abby's veins cracked, letting in something that felt dangerously like hope. Or maybe it was just the peculiar clarity that comes with having nothing left to lose.

14 SURFACE CRACKS

The day before Abby's second visit, Amanda paced her cell like a caged tiger, her mind racing with possibilities. Rosa watched from her bunk, dark eyes tracking each turn.

"You're plotting something, mama," Rosa said quietly. "I can smell it on you like prison soap."

Amanda's lips curved into the smile that had earned her the nickname ICE – beautiful and deadly cold. "My daughter married Michael Maddox Johnson's son," she said, tasting the words like bitter medicine. "Tell me that's not divine intervention."

"Or maybe it's karma coming to collect," Rosa muttered. "Twenty-five years of secrets don't stay buried forever."

Amanda paused at the window, watching clouds gather over the exercise yard. She thought about the letter Abby and Drake had sent – so earnest, so hopeful, so perfectly vulnerable. And now with that

Thompsen Industries connection surfacing... the timing couldn't be better if she'd orchestrated it herself.

"You know what the worst part of being ICE is, Rosa?" Amanda asked, not turning around. "Everyone expects you to be cold. Heartless. They never see the calculation behind it." She pressed her hand against the glass. "My daughter's a lawyer. She'll be looking for lies, for manipulation. So instead, I'll give her just enough truth to make her doubt everything else she thinks she knows."

Rosa sat up, concern etching deeper lines around her eyes. "These aren't just games anymore, Amanda. This is your daughter. Your flesh and blood."

"My daughter," Amanda whispered, "is my second chance. And this time..." Her smile sharpened. "This time I won't lose everything."

She spent the rest of the day preparing – not just her words, but her posture, her expressions, the precise tremor she'd allow in her voice when speaking of Michael Maddox Johnson. ICE hadn't survived twenty-five years in prison by accident. Every reaction was choreographed, every emotion carefully rationed.

But as night fell and the cell block quieted, Amanda found herself humming that old lullaby again: "You are my sunshine..." The melody caught her off guard, cracking something in her chest that felt dangerously real.

"Damn it," she whispered, pressing her palms against her eyes. She couldn't afford real feelings. Not now. Not when she was so close to...

To what? Freedom? Revenge? Or something else entirely, something that felt too much like hope?

"I think I should come with you," Drake said the next morning, watching Abby apply her makeup with too-careful precision. "After that Thompsen Industries bombshell... maybe it's time we faced her together."

Abby's hands stilled on her mascara wand. "Are you sure? The last time anyone mentioned your father's name to her..."

"That's exactly why." Drake moved behind her, meeting her eyes in the mirror. "All these secrets about my father's murder... they're not just your burden to carry anymore. They're ours."

Lila's voice cut in from the doorway: "Which is exactly why you shouldn't go yet." She held up a hand before either could protest. "Think about it. Amanda's already showing cracks in her ICE persona. Throwing Drake into the mix now might make her shut down completely. Let me go with Abby again – I can watch for the things you both might miss because you're too close to it."

Abby turned to Drake, seeing the war between protection and pain play across his face. "Lila's right," she said softly. "I need to understand who Amanda was before she killed your father. And I need you to help me process whatever I learn, with a clear head."

The drive to the prison felt different this time. Lila drove while Abby reviewed her mental notes – not just about Amanda's tells from their first meeting, but about Thompson's revelations. Twenty-five years ago, Amanda Winters had helped build the company that now employed her daughter. The coincidence felt too neat, too calculated.

"Remember," Lila said as they parked, "you're not just Abby the daughter today. You're also Abby the lawyer. Use those courtroom instincts."

Amanda was already seated in the visiting room when they arrived, her posture softer than last time, her smile almost warm. But something about it raised the hair on Abby's neck – it was the same smile she'd seen defendants use right before lying on the stand.

"I wasn't sure you'd come back," Amanda said, her voice carefully modulated. "After how our last meeting ended..."

"A lot has happened since then," Abby replied, watching her birth mother's face. "Including some interesting revelations about Thompsen Industries."

The flicker in Amanda's eyes was so quick Abby almost missed it. Calculation? Fear? Or something else entirely?

"The past has a way of surfacing," Amanda said softly. "Sometimes all at once, like spring ice breaking up on a river." She leaned forward, dropping her voice. "But Abby... there are things about Michael Maddox Johnson – about your husband's father – that even the

86

court records don't show. Things that could change everything you think you know about what happened that night."

Lila's hand found Abby's knee under the table, steadying her. Grounding her.

"Then help me understand," Abby said, keeping her voice level despite her pounding heart. "Help me understand why my mother became ICE. Why the woman who sang lullabies to her unborn child became someone capable of murder."

Amanda's face crumpled in a display of emotion that would have been Oscar-worthy if Abby hadn't spent years reading witnesses. But underneath the performance, something real flickered – a shadow of genuine pain that suggested even ICE's most practiced lies held seeds of truth.

"Some stories," Amanda whispered, "can only be told in pieces. Some truths are too sharp to handle all at once." She reached across the table, her fingers stopping just short of Abby's. "But if you're willing to listen... if you're willing to understand... I'll tell you everything. Starting with why I really gave you up. And why, twenty-two years later, I had no choice but to kill Drake's father."

Behind them, a guard called time. As they stood to leave, Amanda caught Abby's wrist – the touch electric, dangerous. "Next time," she said, "come alone. Please. There are things... things I can only tell my daughter."

Walking out, Lila's arm steady around her shoulders, Abby felt the weight of manipulation and truth tangled so tightly she couldn't separate them. But one thing was clear – Amanda was playing a game within a game. The question was: were her revelations about Michael Maddox Johnson's murder just another con, or was ICE finally starting to thaw?

In her cell that night, Amanda added another mark to her mental tally. Each calculated revelation, each perfectly timed emotion, brought her closer to her goal. But that damn lullaby kept playing in her head, and the ice around her heart felt thinner than it had in twenty-five years.

Rosa watched her from the shadows. "You're playing with fire, mama," she warned. "Lie to the daughter too many times, you might lose her forever."

Amanda closed her eyes, remembering the weight of a newborn in her arms. "You can't lose what you never really had," she whispered. But for the first time in decades, she wasn't sure if she was lying to Rosa or to herself.

15 THAWING DECEPTIONS

The newspaper clipping trembled in Amanda's hands as she sat on her narrow bunk in the Taycheedah Correctional Institution. Through the institutional windows, she could see the manicured lawn outside, a deceptively peaceful view that belied the careful surveillance of every movement within these brick walls. Thompsen Industries. The words burned into her vision like acid, melting through twenty-five years of carefully constructed plans. Behind her, Rosa's familiar presence waited, watchful as always, both women acutely aware of the guard station positioned at the end of their unit.

The afternoon count had just finished, the institutional routine as predictable as the seasons. Outside their window, visitors' cars filled the small parking lot, each one subject to the strict regulations that governed every aspect of life at TCI. Amanda knew the rules by heart now - no more than twelve approved visitors on her list, every interaction monitored, every movement observed. But rules had always been her favorite kind of challenge.

"Your past is catching up, mama," Rosa said softly. "Question is, are you gonna run from it or use it?"

Amanda's laugh held no humor, just the sharp edge of calculated satisfaction. "Thompson was always the weak link. Too soft, too prone to guilt." She smoothed the article against her knee, mind already three moves ahead on the chessboard she'd spent decades arranging. "His exposure doesn't change the game – it just moves up our timeline. And with Abby's position at Caldwell & Ross, her access to corporate documentation..." She paused, savoring the perfection of it. "Well, let's just say having a corporate attorney for a daughter has its advantages."

"We?" Rosa's eyebrow arched. "Or just you?"

Before Amanda could answer, the cell block erupted with the familiar chaos of shift change. Through the bars, she watched the guards swap positions, their movements as predictable as the tides. Everything in prison ran on routine – even freedom, if you knew how to orchestrate it.

"Did you know?" Rosa asked after the noise died down. "About your daughter working for Thompson?"

"Know?" Amanda's smile was pure ICE. "I made sure of it. Why do you think I waited until now to make contact?" But even as the words left her mouth, something shifted beneath her practiced persona. The look in Abby's eyes during their last visit – that mixture of hope and wariness, of desperate longing and professional suspicion – had cracked something inside her that refused to refreeze.

She stood abruptly, pacing the confined space of their cell. "Get word to Martinez and Prescott. We need to accelerate the timeline. With

Thompsen's connection exposed—"

"You're scrambling," Rosa cut in, her voice carrying the weight of fifteen years shared in eight-by-ten concrete boxes. Her fingers absently traced the faded tattoo on her wrist - a reminder of her own daughter, lost to the system years ago. "The ICE I know doesn't scramble. She calculates. She waits. What's really got you rattled? The plan being exposed, or the fact that your daughter might actually be melting that frozen heart of yours?"

Amanda caught the familiar shadow crossing Rosa's face. They'd never discussed the parallels between them - Rosa's own lost child, the choices that had led them both here. It was an unspoken understanding that made Rosa's counsel more valuable than any other inmate's. She knew the true cost of using family as currency in the prison economy.

Amanda's steps faltered. The lullaby that had been haunting her nights rose unbidden: "You are my sunshine..." She pressed her palms against her eyes, trying to block out the memory of singing to her swollen belly in a different cell, in a different time. "This changes nothing. Abby is still the key. Now she'll just be more... motivated to help once she learns the full truth about Thompson's involvement in her father-in-law's death."

"The truth?" Rosa's laugh was bitter as prison coffee. "Or your version of it?"

"There are layers to truth, Rosa. You know that better than most." Amanda moved to the window, watching clouds gather over the exercise yard. "Thompson's guilt is real enough. His fingerprints are all over what happened that night, even if he never pulled the trigger. Once Abby sees the documentation..."

"The documentation you made sure would surface right when you needed it?" Rosa shook her head. "You're playing a dangerous game, mama. Using your own daughter as both lock pick and leverage..."

"She's a corporate attorney," Amanda snapped, a note of pride slipping through her calculated facade. "She understands power dynamics, leverage points, strategic timing. The long game is in her blood, whether she knows it or not." But even as she spoke, her fingers traced patterns on the glass, drawing the shape of a baby's face she'd only held once. "Besides, everything I told her about Michael Maddox Johnson was true. He deserved what he got. The fact that his death served multiple purposes doesn't make him any less guilty."

The afternoon sun caught the silver in her hair, reminding her of how much time had passed. Twenty-five years of waiting, watching, planning. Twenty-five years of building ICE into a legend that could survive anything. Except, perhaps, the warmth of her daughter's desperate need for connection.

"Gather the others," she told Rosa, her voice steady despite the turbulence beneath. "Tonight, after lights out. If Thompsen's talking, we need to be ready. Everything we've built, everything we've waited for... it all hinges on what happens in the next few weeks."

Rosa settled onto her regulation bunk, carefully arranged

according to TCI's strict protocols. Her fingers found the worn photograph she kept hidden beneath her state-issued blanket – Marina at sixteen, dark eyes defiant beneath graduation cap tassels, before everything fell apart. The photo was one of the few personal items allowed in their cell, a precious reminder of the world beyond the red-brown buildings and institutional fences of North 10th Street. "My girl was like your Abby once. Honor student. Debate team captain. Full ride to Northwestern." She met Amanda's eyes. "Then she found out what her mama really did for a living."

Amanda paused in her pacing, catching the raw edge in Rosa's voice. She'd heard pieces of the story over their years together – how Rosa's precision with locks had funded Marina's private school tuition, how each perfect heist had paid for SAT prep and college applications. A mother's love expressed through perfect crimes.

"Marina was supposed to be my redemption," Rosa continued, her accent thickening with memory. "Everything I did, every house I entered, every safe I cracked – it was all for her future. But when she learned the truth..." She traced the tattoo again, the stylized M intertwined with prison bars. "She spent three years trying to numb the shame. Heroin. Street life. By the time I got arrested, she was already lost to me."

"But she's clean now," Amanda said, the words somewhere between question and statement.

Rosa's smile held decades of regret. "Eight months sober. Working at a women's shelter in Chicago. My friends on the outside says she's studying for her counseling certification." Pride and pain mingled in her voice. "She's helping girls who remind her of herself. Daughters who lost their way because their mothers made all the wrong choices for all the right reasons." "Just remember," she said, pausing at the cell door, "some of us have more to lose than just freedom. My connection on the outside... she's been watching my daughter. Says she's clean now, trying to make something of herself." Her dark eyes met Amanda's. "If this plan goes sideways, if your corporate attorney daughter starts asking the wrong questions..."

"Your girl stays protected," Amanda assured her, recognizing the rare crack in Rosa's usually impenetrable facade. "That was part of our deal from the beginning. Besides, having your daughter's fresh start as leverage keeps everyone's priorities aligned."

The words came automatically, wrapped in ICE's familiar calculation, but something in Rosa's knowing look made Amanda wonder if she was still the only one playing both sides of the maternal bond.

The night deepened around them, prison sounds fading into the familiar rhythm of lockdown. Rosa watched the methodical patrol of guards through their unit's window, her years of experience as a professional thief automatically noting the timing of each round, the rotation of staff, the subtle patterns within TCI's rigid routine. The facility's layout on North 10th Street was both blessing and curse - a converted medical building that lacked the towering walls and razor wire of maximum security, but made up for it with sophisticated surveillance and the watchful eyes of a well-trained staff.

"Your corporate attorney daughter," Rosa mused, her voice

pitched low enough that only Amanda could hear it, "she'll have to navigate more than just visiting hours to help with your plans. Every visit is monitored here - no contact visits if they suspect anything, and they're quick with those suspensions." She traced the outline of her daughter's photo, remembering the last time she'd seen Marina in the visiting room, the strict rules about embracing only at the beginning and end of visits, the way every movement was observed and logged.

"I learned that the hard way when Marina was sixteen," Rosa continued, her accent thickening with memory. "Back when I was working the Gold Coast circuit, before this place. I had a perfect setup - high-rise condos, lakefront mansions, private galleries. Fond du Lac's elite never knew what hit them." Her lips curved in a bitter smile. "I paid for Marina's private school tuition with Tiffany diamonds and Cartier watches. Every perfect heist was another semester at Divine Savior Holy Angels, another step toward the future I never had."

Amanda paused in her pacing, the familiar sound of the 3 PM shift change echoing through the corridors. "But something went wrong."

"Everything went wrong." Rosa's eyes tracked the movement of guards outside their door - three minutes until the next patrol, like clockwork. "Marina found my stash of newspaper clippings about the Ghost's latest heists. Smart girl - she'd already figured out the connection between my 'business trips' and the break-ins at her classmates' homes. The shame in her eyes..." Rosa shook her head. "That's when the heroin started. Three years on the streets while I kept working, telling myself one more job would fix everything."

Through their window, they could see new visitors being processed at the entrance, going through the meticulous search procedures required by TCI. No more than four visitors at a time, no contact visits for anyone under suspicion, every interaction recorded and analyzed.

"Now look at us," Rosa said, gesturing at their shared space in the converted medical facility. "You plotting to use your attorney daughter's access, me getting updates about my girl's recovery through carefully monitored phone calls. Eight months clean at that women's shelter in Chicago. She's helping girls who remind her of herself - daughters who lost their way because their mothers made all the wrong choices for all the right reasons."

Amanda watched a young woman being turned away at the entrance for inappropriate attire - the facility's strict dress code was just one of countless barriers between them and the outside world. "You never told me how they caught you."

Rosa's laugh was soft and bitter as institutional coffee. "Would you believe it was something as simple as a traffic stop? Twenty years of perfect crimes, international fences, millions in stolen merchandise - and Fond du Lac PD got me because of a broken taillight three blocks from my last job. They found Marina's college acceptance letters in my glove compartment, right next to my lock picks and security system blueprints."

The conversation paused as Officer Martinez made her scheduled round, her keys jingling with institutional authority. Both women knew the importance of appearing compliant, unremarkable. In

TCI, survival meant understanding not just the written rules, but the invisible ones - the complex dance of power and perception that governed every interaction.

"You know what's really going to trip you up?" Rosa asked after Martinez passed, her voice carrying decades of hard-won wisdom. "It's not going to be the visiting room cameras or the staff surveillance. It's going to be the moment your daughter looks at you the way Marina looked at me - like she's seeing past the mask for the first time, understanding exactly what kind of mother she really has."

Amanda's posture stiffened, but Rosa pressed on, her words carrying the weight of shared experience. "You think you can control it all - the visits, the timing, the perfect play of emotion. But in this place?" She gestured at their surroundings, at the institutional routine that governed their every moment. "In this place, even ICE can melt. Especially when it comes to daughters."

The institutional schedule at TCI ticked by with military precision: 5 AM wake-up call, 5:30 breakfast lineup, 6:15 work assignments. Amanda watched the familiar dance of inmates and officers through her window, each movement a reminder of the routines that both confined and protected them. The morning sun cast long shadows across the facility's parking lot, where early visitors were already lining up for processing.

"Frost would have loved this setup," Amanda murmured, more to herself than to Rosa. "All these perfectly timed rotations, the predictable patterns. Remember how he used to say timing was everything?"

Rosa's head snapped up at the mention of their former partner. "Careful, mama. Those aren't waters you want to stir up, especially not with your attorney daughter starting to dig."

Amanda's smile held a hint of her ICE persona. "Frost is ancient history. Twenty-five years in the ground, or so everyone believes." She paused, watching a guard escort a line of inmates to their work assignments. "Though sometimes I wonder if Thompsen knows different. The way he looked at Abby in that courtroom..."

The morning routine continued around them: medication distribution at 7 AM, cell inspection at 7:30, programming blocks starting at 8. Every movement monitored, every interaction logged in the facility's meticulous records. Through their window, they could see the visiting room entrance being prepared for the day - metal detectors calibrated, search procedures reviewed, the careful choreography of security measures that made TCI's maximum-security status more illusion than reality.

"You never did tell me the whole story about Frost," Rosa said carefully, arranging her bunk to regulation standards before the morning inspection. "Just whispers about that last job - the one that went wrong right before Michael Maddox Johnson turned up dead."

"Some stories are better left buried," Amanda replied, but her eyes tracked the movement of Officer Chen with unusual intensity. "Like the real reason Thompsen Industries grew so fast in those early years, or why certain security systems in Fond du Lac's financial district had convenient blind spots."

The conversation paused as the morning medication cart rolled through, the nurse's cheerful greeting a stark contrast to the undercurrent of tension. Both women were acutely aware of the surveillance cameras positioned at each corridor junction, the careful monitoring of every conversation.

"Your daughter's going to find those breadcrumbs eventually," Rosa warned as they joined the line for morning head count. "Between her firm's connection to Thompson and her husband's link to Johnson... Frost's shadow is longer than you think."

The visiting room was visible from their position, its setup deceptively casual - small tables arranged for maximum observation, every sight line carefully calculated. Amanda had memorized every detail: the three security cameras with overlapping coverage, the positions of the guard stations, the exact distance between tables that prevented private conversations.

"You know what makes TCI so perfect?" Amanda asked, pitching her voice low as they moved through the breakfast line. "Everyone sees the minimal security, the community corrections model. They don't notice the sophisticated surveillance systems, the behavioral monitoring, the way every interaction is analyzed. Just like they never noticed how Frost's legitimate security business made the perfect cover for testing Fond du Lac's most advanced alarm systems."

Rosa accepted her breakfast tray, noting how the newest guard, Matthews, was positioned to observe the entire dining area. "Until it all went wrong. Just like your plan could go wrong if Abby starts connecting those dots. Thompsen, Johnson, Frost - there's a pattern there for anyone smart enough to see it."

"Frost always said the best security was invisible," Amanda mused, her eyes distant. "Like this place - no walls, no razor wire, just layers of observation and control. The perfect trap is the one you don't see until it's too late."

They ate in silence, each woman lost in thought as the morning routine continued around them. Through the dining area windows, they could see visitors beginning to arrive, each one subject to TCIs rigorous screening process: ID checks, dress code enforcement, metal detector scans, personal property restrictions.

"Your girl's smart," Rosa said finally, watching a young attorney being escorted to the professional visiting area - the same route Abby would take. "She's got her father's instincts for investigation, from what I hear. If she starts pulling at the Frost thread..."

"Then she'll learn what every good investigator eventually discovers," Amanda replied, her voice carrying the chill that had earned her nickname. "Some secrets stay buried because the truth is too dangerous to touch. Even for a corporate attorney with her resources."

The morning sun climbed higher over Fond du Lac's skyline, casting sharp shadows across TCI's grounds. Somewhere in the city, Abby was probably preparing for another day at Caldwell, Ross & Wellington unaware of the intricate web of past connections that linked her mother's crimes to her present position. And somewhere, in files sealed by time and fear, the truth about Frost's disappearance waited like a landmine for the unwary.

Rosa watched her cellmate's face, reading the calculations behind every expression. "You're playing a dangerous game, mama. Using your daughter to engineer your freedom is one thing, but if she stumbles onto Frost's connection to Thompsen Industries..."

"Then maybe it's time certain truths came to light," Amanda said softly, her words nearly lost in the institutional background noise. "After all, every good con needs a convincing backstory. And Frost... well, she always did have perfect timing."

"You know what's funny?" Rosa said into the darkness. "All those years of perfect crimes, and it was my daughter's tears that finally broke me. Made me sloppy. Made me take risks I shouldn't have." She looked at Amanda, seeing echoes of her own struggles in ICE's careful facade. "Love makes us vulnerable, mama. Even when we think we're using it as a weapon."

Amanda's posture stiffened, but Rosa pressed on. "You think you're playing Abby, using her attorney status and her need for connection. But she's playing you too, whether she knows it or not. Those walls you built? That ice you wrapped around your heart? It's already cracking. I see it every time you say her name."

"This is different," Amanda insisted, but her voice lacked its usual steel. "Abby's involvement is calculated. Controlled. Every move, every emotion – it's all part of the plan."

Rosa's laugh held all the warmth of a prison yard in winter. That's what I told myself too. That I could control everything, calculate every risk. But daughters... they have a way of breaking through our best defenses." She pulled out another photo, newer, smuggled in by her contact. Marina at the women's shelter, her smile tentative but real. "Sometimes they break us to save us. Sometimes the ones we think we're using end up being our salvation."

"I'm sorry, baby girl," she whispered to the empty cell. "But some lies are kinder than the truth. And some truths..." She thought of Michael Maddox Johnson's face in his final moments, of Thompsen's panicked phone call afterward, of the evidence she'd carefully buried and the strings she'd meticulously tied. "Some truths are too sharp for anyone to handle."

That night, as her closest allies gathered in the shadows of the prison chapel, Amanda laid out the accelerated plan. Martinez with her guard connections, Prescott with her outside network, each piece carefully positioned over years of patient manipulation. But as she spoke, coordinating movements and contingencies, part of her mind kept drifting to Abby's face. To the way her daughter's expressions shifted between professional skepticism and raw need, between the lawyer she'd become and the abandoned child she'd been.

"The Thompsen Industries revelation changes the timing," she explained, her voice barely above a whisper. "But it doesn't change the endgame. If anything, it gives us more leverage. More pressure points to exploit."

"And your daughter?" Chen asked, her dark eyes shrewd. "You sure she'll play her part once she realizes how deep this goes?"

Amanda's smile was slower this time, less certain than her usual ICE persona. "Abby's smart. Driven. Once she understands what really happened – what Thompson and Johnson did, what they were planning..." She paused, remembering the weight of secrets and the price of revenge. "She'll do what needs to be done. Because underneath all that professional polish, she's still my daughter. Still a survivor."

Later, alone in her cell, Amanda pulled out the worn photo of infant Abby that she'd kept hidden for twenty-five years. The paper was soft with age, the image faded, but those eyes... those eyes still held the same desperate need for love that she'd seen across the prison visiting room.

"You are my sunshine," she sang softly, her voice cracking on the familiar melody. "My only sunshine..."

Amanda tucked the photo away, her movements precise and controlled. These moments of sentiment were becoming a liability. Abby's position as a corporate attorney at Caldwell Ross & Wellington wasn't just coincidence – it was an asset, carefully factored into a plan two decades in the making. The fact that her daughter's need for connection made her vulnerable was simply... convenient.

Still, as she lay on her bunk plotting tomorrow's moves, Amanda found herself calculating angles she'd never considered before. The way Abby's analytical mind picked apart every statement, every gesture. The professional instincts that made her daughter both more valuable and more dangerous as a pawn.

"Sentiment is a weakness," she whispered to the darkness, the words familiar as prison bars. But for the first time in twenty-five years, ICE wasn't entirely sure if she was convincing herself or trying to freeze over a truth, she wasn't ready to face.

After all, ICE hadn't survived this long by letting emotions cloud her judgment. Even if those emotions felt increasingly like spring sunshine, melting away decades of careful calculation, revealing the mother she might have been beneath the legend she'd become.

16 THIRD SESSION

Abby settled into the familiar leather chair in Dr. Chen's office, barely able to contain her excitement. The sunlight streaming through the window caught the dust motes dancing in the air, creating an almost ethereal atmosphere that matched Abby's elevated mood.

"You seem particularly energetic today," Dr. Chen observed, her dark eyes studying Abby's animated expression with careful attention. She adjusted her notepad on her lap, maintaining her usual professional composure despite her client's obvious enthusiasm.

"I am," Abby admitted, her words tumbling out in a rush. "My visit with Amanda was... different. Better. She opened up to me about her time in prison, shared things she's never told anyone else. It felt real, Dr. Chen. Like we were finally connecting as mother and daughter."

Dr. Chen listened thoughtfully, her pen moving across her notepad in precise, measured strokes. When she spoke, her voice carried its characteristic blend of warmth and professional distance. "I'm glad you're feeling positive about the interaction. Can you tell me more about what she shared?"

As Abby recounted the visit's details, Dr. Chen's expression remained attentive but increasingly pensive. She waited for Abby to finish before carefully placing her pen down.

"Abby," she began, her tone gentle but firm, "I hear how meaningful this connection feels to you. And I understand the profound longing you have to build a relationship with your birth mother. But I would be remiss in my duty as your therapist if I didn't express some concerns."

Dr. Chen shifted in her chair, her expression growing more serious. "Let's talk specifically about what Amanda shared with you during this visit. You mentioned she opened up about her time in prison?"

Abby nodded eagerly. "Yes. She told me about her daily routines, the other inmates she befriended, how she worked in the prison library. But more than that, she talked about her emotional journey. How she started to understand the impact of her choices."

"And how did that make you feel, hearing these details?" Dr. Chen probed gently.

"Honestly?" Abby paused, collecting her thoughts. "It was overwhelming. There was this moment when she described reading to other inmates' children during visiting hours. She said it made her think of me, of all the bedtime stories she never got to read to me. She started crying, Dr. Chen. Real tears. Not the manipulative kind you might expect from someone just playing a role."

Dr. Chen made a note on her pad. "You seem very certain about the authenticity of her emotions. What makes you so sure?"

The question caught Abby off guard. She opened her mouth to respond, then closed it again, considering. "I... I guess I just feel it. In my gut. Is that naive?"

"Not naive," Dr. Chen replied carefully. "But it's important to understand that our emotional desires can sometimes cloud our judgment. Tell me about Drake's reaction to these visits."

Abby shifted uncomfortably. "Drake is... supportive. But cautious. He reminds me that Amanda has a history of manipulation, that she's hurt people before."

"And how do you reconcile those two perspectives? Your instinctive trust and Drake's caution?"

"That's what I struggle with," Abby admitted. "When I'm with her, everything feels right. The connection feels genuine. But then I come home, and Drake asks questions that make me doubt myself. Like whether I'm seeing what I want to see rather than what's really there."

Dr. Chen nodded encouragingly. "That's a very insightful observation. Let's explore that feeling of doubt. What specifically triggers it?"

"Well," Abby began, her hands twisting in her lap, "there are moments when Amanda says things that seem... too perfect? Like she knows exactly what I need to hear. She told me this story about keeping a journal all these years, writing letters to me that she never sent. It's beautiful and heartbreaking, but part of me wonders if it's true."

"That's a healthy skepticism," Dr. Chen affirmed. "It doesn't negate the possibility of genuine change, but it acknowledges the complexity of the situation. Have you shared these doubts with Amanda?"

Abby shook her head. "I'm afraid to. What if questioning her sincerity pushes her away? What if I lose this chance at having a relationship with her?"

"That's a valid fear," Dr. Chen acknowledged. "But consider this: if Amanda's change is genuine, wouldn't she understand your need for verification? For time to trust? Real relationships are built on honesty, not just positive emotions."

Silence filled the room as Abby absorbed these words. The excitement that had buoyed her earlier began to settle into something more tempered, more grounded.

"I understand what you're saying," Abby said finally. "But I can't help feeling hopeful. When I'm with her, it's like filling a void I've carried my whole life."

Dr. Chen leaned forward slightly, her expression compassionate but serious. "Let's talk about that void, Abby. It's natural to want to fill it, but it's important to make sure you're not compromising your own well-being in the process."

"What do you mean?"

"Sometimes," Dr. Chen explained, "when we've carried an emptiness for so long, we become vulnerable to anyone who seems capable of filling it. We might overlook red flags or dismiss our own instincts because the promise of wholeness is so alluring."

Abby felt tears welling up in her eyes. "Are you saying I shouldn't trust her at all?"

"No," Dr. Chen said softly. "I'm saying trust should be earned gradually, built on consistent actions over time. It's okay to hope, Abby. It's okay to want this relationship. But let's work on building it slowly, with healthy boundaries and clear eyes."

They spent the next portion of the session discussing practical strategies for maintaining boundaries while nurturing the developing relationship. Dr. Chen helped Abby identify specific behaviors that might indicate manipulation versus genuine change, and they role-played different scenarios that might arise during visits.

"Remember," Dr. Chen emphasized, "you're not just a daughter seeking her mother. You're a strong, independent woman who's built a beautiful life. That life deserves to be protected even as you explore this new relationship."

As their time drew to a close, Dr. Chen suggested an exercise for the coming week. "I'd like you to keep a journal of your visits with Amanda. Not just what happens, but how you feel before, during, and after. Pay attention to any moments that trigger doubt or discomfort. We'll review them together next session."

Abby nodded, already feeling more centered than when she'd arrived. "Thank you, Dr. Chen. For helping me see things more clearly."

"That's what I'm here for," Dr. Chen smiled warmly. "To help you navigate this journey while keeping your feet firmly on the ground."

Walking to her car after the session, Abby felt both lighter and more grounded. The excitement about Amanda remained, but it was now tempered with a healthy dose of caution and self-awareness. Dr. Chen's words echoed in her mind: balance, boundaries, patience.

She knew the road ahead wouldn't be easy, but with Dr. Chen's guidance and her own growing wisdom, she felt better equipped to navigate it. One step at a time, one session at a time, she would find her way through this complex journey of reconciliation and self-discovery.

The afternoon sun painted long shadows across the parking lot as Abby drove home, her mind processing everything from the session. She had come seeking validation for her hopes, but instead had found something more valuable: a framework for building a relationship that could truly last.

In her heart, she still believed in Amanda's capacity for change. But now she understood that belief alone wasn't enough. It needed to be paired with wisdom, with boundaries, with the kind of clear-eyed love that could withstand scrutiny and time.

And perhaps that, more than anything, was the true gift of therapy - not just hope for the future, but tools to build it safely, securely, one carefully considered step at a time.

When Abby arrived home, she found Drake in his home office, surrounded by case files. He looked up at her entrance, immediately noting the thoughtful expression on her face.

"Tough session?" he asked, pushing back from his desk.

Abby sank into the leather armchair by the window, the one they'd bought together when they first moved in. "Not tough exactly. More... illuminating. Dr. Chen helped me see some things I've been avoiding."

Drake closed his laptop, giving her his full attention. "Want to talk about it?"

"She thinks I might be rushing things with Amanda," Abby said slowly. "That I might be so eager to fill this void in my life that I'm not seeing potential red flags."

"And what do you think about that?" Drake's voice was carefully neutral, but Abby could sense the underlying tension.

"I think..." Abby paused, choosing her words carefully, "I think she might be right. Not about Amanda necessarily, but about my own eagerness. Dr. Chen pointed out that real relationships need time to develop, that trust has to be earned."

Drake nodded, relief flickering across his face. "That makes sense. You know I support you in this, Abby, but I've been worried about how quickly everything's been moving."

"I know." Abby reached for his hand. "And I haven't been as receptive to your concerns as I should have been. It's just... when I'm with her, Drake, it feels like filling in this missing piece of myself. Like finally understanding where I came from."

"That's understandable," Drake said softly. "But you're more than just Amanda's daughter, Abby. You're your own person, someone who's built an amazing life despite everything that happened. I don't want to see you lose sight of that."

His words echoed Dr. Chen's so closely that Abby felt tears welling up in her eyes. "That's almost exactly what Dr. Chen said. She wants me to start journaling about my visits with Amanda. Not just what happens, but how I feel before, during, and after."

"That sounds like a good idea," Drake encouraged. "It might help you spot patterns you might miss otherwise."

"Will you..." Abby hesitated, then pressed on. "Will you help me with that? Be another set of eyes? Dr. Chen says it's important to have support systems in place."

Drake pulled her into a tight embrace. "Always. Whatever you need."

That evening, Abby sat at her desk, a new journal open before her. She began writing about her latest visit with Amanda, trying to capture not just the events but the emotional undertones she might have missed in her initial excitement.

As she wrote, patterns began to emerge. The way Amanda seemed to know exactly what to say to touch her heart. How she'd deflect certain questions while emphasizing others. The subtle ways she'd guide conversations away from specific topics, particularly anything involving Drake's father.

Abby's pen hesitated over the page. Was she being too suspicious now, seeing manipulation where there might be only natural conversation flow? Or had she been too trusting before, ignoring signs that should have given her pause?

Her phone buzzed - a text from Amanda: "Thinking of you, sweetheart. Missing our talks already. Can't wait for your next visit."

The message was perfectly innocent, exactly what a mother might send to her daughter. Yet now, with Dr. Chen's words fresh in her mind, Abby found herself analyzing it from different angles. Was the timing coincidental, or had Amanda sensed her pulling back slightly? Was the endearment genuine or calculated?

"Everything okay?" Drake called from the doorway, noticing her furrowed brow.

"Just thinking," Abby replied, showing him the text. "Before today, I would have just been touched by this. Now I'm questioning everything, and I'm not sure if that's healthy either."

Drake pulled up a chair beside her. "Maybe it's not about questioning everything or nothing. Maybe it's about finding a balance - being open to the relationship while staying aware and protective of yourself."

Abby nodded slowly. "Dr. Chen said something similar. She talked about how real change is possible, but it needs to be proven through consistent actions over time." She closed the journal, turning to face her husband fully. "I've been so focused on my relationship with Amanda that I haven't been appreciating the relationships I already have. With you, with Mom, with our friends."

"We understand," Drake assured her. "This is huge for you, discovering your birth mother, trying to build a connection. No one expects you to handle it perfectly."

"But that's just it," Abby said, a new realization dawning. "I've been trying to handle it perfectly. To be the perfect daughter, to make up for lost time. Dr. Chen helped me see that's not realistic or healthy."

She stood up, moving to the window. The street below was quiet, neighborhood houses lit from within, families going about their evening routines. "I need to find a way to integrate Amanda into my life without letting her become my whole life. To build a relationship with her while maintaining all my other relationships."

Drake joined her at the window, wrapping an arm around her shoulders. "That sounds like a good goal. And you don't have to figure it all out at once."

Abby leaned into his embrace, feeling stronger and more centered than she had in weeks. The path ahead was still uncertain, but she no longer felt like she had to rush down it blindly. She had support, she had guidance, and most importantly, she had the wisdom to take it one step at a time.

"Thank you," she whispered to Drake. "For being patient with me through all of this. For supporting me even when I wasn't listening to your concerns."

"That's what family does," Drake replied simply. "We stick together, through all the complicated, messy parts of life."

And that, Abby realized, was perhaps the most important lesson

from today's session with Dr. Chen. True family - whether bound by blood or by choice - was built on a foundation of trust, honesty, and mutual respect. It couldn't be rushed or forced. It had to grow naturally, nurtured by time and understanding.

As she prepared for bed that night, Abby felt a new sense of peace settling over her. The excitement about Amanda was still there, but it no longer felt so desperate, so all-consuming. She had room in her heart for all her relationships, all her roles - daughter, wife, friend, professional - and she didn't have to sacrifice any of them in pursuit of a connection with her birth mother.

That night, she slept more soundly than she had in weeks, her dreams no longer haunted by the shadows of the past. Tomorrow would bring new challenges, new decisions to navigate, but she was ready to face them with clear eyes and a balanced heart.

17 REFLECTIONS AND REVELATIONS

Abby shifted in her chair, aware of Dr. Chen's patient silence as she gathered her thoughts. Through the office window, late afternoon sunlight painted golden rectangles on the carpet, reminding her of how the court light filtered through the high windows of Thompsen Industries' legal department where she'd spent her morning.

"I keep thinking about something that happened at work today," she began, surprising herself with the direction her mind took. "We were negotiating a settlement for a corporate merger, and I found myself reading the room, manipulating the conversation in ways I never really noticed before." She met Dr. Chen's steady gaze. "The thing is, I was good at it. Really good. And it scared me a little."

Dr. Chen tilted her head slightly. "What specifically about it scared you?"

"How natural it felt." Abby's fingers twisted in her lap. "There was this moment when I could see all the angles, all the pressure points. I knew exactly which arguments would land, which compromises would seem generous while actually giving us the advantage." She swallowed hard. "It was like watching Amanda during our visits – the way she reads people, the careful calculation behind every word."

"You're worried about sharing traits with your birth mother?"

"Aren't you?" Abby countered, then immediately softened. "Sorry, that came out wrong. It's just... growing up, I always wondered what parts of me came from her. Now I'm starting to see similarities, and I'm not sure how to feel about that."

Dr. Chen made a note on her pad. "Having similar traits doesn't determine how we use them, Abby. Strategic thinking and emotional intelligence can be powerful tools for helping people, just as they can be used to harm."

The observation triggered a memory from Abby's childhood. "When I was eleven, there was this girl in my class being bullied. Instead of confronting the bullies directly, I spent weeks quietly building alliances, gathering evidence, creating a situation where the bullies exposed themselves to the teachers." A rueful smile crossed her face. "My adoptive mom was horrified at how calculating it all was. But the bullying stopped."

"You used your strategic abilities to protect someone vulnerable," Dr. Chen observed. "That's quite different from using them for personal gain or manipulation."

"But the skills themselves..." Abby trailed off, thinking of the Thompsen Industries files still waiting on her desk. Something about the company's rapid expansion in the early years had caught her attention – patterns that seemed just slightly too perfect. "Sometimes I wonder if I'm drawn to corporate law because it rewards the same kind of strategic thinking Amanda used in her crimes."

Dr. Chen set her notepad aside, leaning forward slightly. "Abby, you've been very open about wanting to know your birth mother. But I sense there's more to it than just understanding why she left. What are you really hoping to learn from this relationship?"

The question hit closer to home than Abby expected. She stood, moving to the window where she could watch the late afternoon traffic below. "I guess... I want to know if it's possible to have her capabilities without becoming her. To understand how someone with so much skill at reading people, at strategic thinking, could end up using those gifts the way she did."

"And what have you observed so far in your visits?"

Abby thought of Amanda's careful revelations, the way each piece of information seemed perfectly timed to draw her closer. "She's brilliant," she admitted. "The way she builds trust, creates emotional connections... Even knowing what I know professionally about manipulation tactics, I still find myself wanting to believe her." She turned back to Dr. Chen. "Is that naive?"

"It's human," Dr. Chen replied gently. "Wanting to connect with our parents is one of our most basic instincts. The challenge is maintaining that openness while staying grounded in reality."

"Reality," Abby echoed, thinking of the Thompsen Industries merger documents. Something about the company's early security contracts had raised red flags – patterns that felt familiar now that she was getting to know Amanda's methods. "Sometimes I think my legal training makes reality harder to see clearly. I'm so used to looking for hidden angles that I second-guess every interaction."

"That awareness can be protective," Dr. Chen noted. "As long as it doesn't prevent you from forming genuine connections."

Abby returned to her chair, feeling more centered. "I don't want to close myself off from knowing her. But I also don't want to be naive about who she is and what she's capable of." She paused, considering her next words carefully. "Yesterday, I was reviewing some old case files, and I noticed something interesting about Thompsen Industries' expansion in the early years. The timing of certain security upgrades, the patterns of corporate acquisition... it was almost too perfect."

"And that observation concerns you?"

"It makes me wonder what else I might find if I look too closely." Abby met Dr. Chen's eyes. "Part of me wants to know the whole truth, but another part wonders if some questions are better left unasked."

Dr. Chen studied her for a moment. "What do you think drives that hesitation? Fear of what you might discover about Amanda, or fear of what those discoveries might reveal about yourself?"

The question hung in the air as Abby considered her response. Outside, the golden afternoon light was fading, shadows lengthening across the carpet. In her mind, she saw the careful stack of Thompsen Industries files waiting on her desk, each one potentially holding pieces of a puzzle she wasn't sure she wanted to complete.

"Maybe both," she finally admitted. "I see these glimpses of her in myself – the way I think, the way I analyze situations – and it's simultaneously fascinating and terrifying. It's like looking into a mirror and seeing not just who I am, but who I could become under different circumstances."

"That's a profound insight," Dr. Chen acknowledged. "How does it affect your approach to building a relationship with her?"

"I want to know her," Abby said slowly, choosing her words with care. "Not just the superficial connection, but the real person beneath the calculation. I want to understand how someone with gifts that could have been used for so much good ended up..." She gestured vaguely. "But I also need to protect myself, my career, my family. There's so much at stake."

As their session drew to a close, Dr. Chen offered a final observation. "It sounds like you're developing a more nuanced understanding of both Amanda and yourself. Remember that sharing certain traits with her doesn't determine your path. Your choices, your values, your commitments — these are what define you."

Abby gathered her things, feeling both lighter and more thoughtful than when she'd arrived. The Thompsen Industries files would still be waiting tomorrow, along with all their uncomfortable questions. But for now, she had a clearer perspective on the delicate balance between knowing her mother and knowing herself.

Walking to her car, Abby reflected on how her professional skills — the very ones that sometimes reminded her of Amanda — could be tools for truth and justice rather than manipulation. Perhaps understanding her inheritance wasn't about rejecting similarities, but about choosing how to use them.

Her phone buzzed with a text from Drake: "Dinner tonight? Dad mentioned something interesting about Thompson's early years."

Abby stared at the message, feeling the weight of uncovered truths and chosen paths. Whatever she discovered in those old files, whatever parts of Amanda she recognized in herself, she would face it with clear eyes and firm boundaries. After all, wasn't that the most important difference between them? The choice to use their shared gifts for truth rather than deception, for protection rather than exploitation?

She typed back a quick reply: "Yes to dinner. And I think it's time we took a closer look at those old Thompsen files."

The sun was setting as she drove home, painting the sky in shades of possibility and warning. Her mind wandered back to that morning's merger negotiations, seeing them in a new light after her therapy session. She had orchestrated the entire meeting like a chess master, anticipating moves, setting up positions, guiding the conversation toward her desired outcome. The realization both thrilled and unsettled her.

Drake was already home when she arrived, kitchen filled with the aroma of his signature pasta sauce. He looked up from chopping herbs, his expression simultaneously warm and concerned. "Productive session?"

"Eye-opening," Abby replied, dropping her briefcase by the kitchen island. "Your dad mentioned something about Thompsen's early years?"

Drake's knife hesitated for a fraction of a second – so brief she might have missed it if she hadn't been watching for it. Another inherited trait from Amanda, perhaps: this instinct for reading micro-expressions, for noticing the smallest tells. "He was reviewing some old security contracts," Drake said carefully. "Found some interesting patterns in the timing of certain upgrades, especially around financial institutions."

Abby's pulse quickened. "What kind of patterns?"

"The kind that make more sense if you assume someone had inside knowledge of security vulnerabilities." Drake set down his knife, meeting her eyes directly. "Dad thinks some of the biggest heists in Wausau during that period might have been connected to security assessments Thompsen Industries performed."

The implications hit Abby like a physical force. She thought of Amanda's careful hints about her past, about connections and consequences. "The prison library," she murmured.

"What?"

"Something Amanda told me about working in the prison library, about having access to newspaper archives." Abby's mind was racing, connecting dots she hadn't even known were there. "She wasn't just passing time – she was researching. Tracking patterns, maybe? Or making sure certain patterns stayed buried?"

Drake abandoned his cooking preparations, moving to stand beside her. "Abby, if there really is a connection between those old heists and Thompsen Industries..."

"It could explain why the company grew so fast," Abby finished. "Perfect security solutions for vulnerabilities they might have helped exploit." She ran a hand through her hair, thoughts spinning. "But why let me see it? Amanda must know I'd eventually notice these patterns, especially with my position at the firm."

"Unless that's exactly what she wants," Drake suggested gently. "You said yourself she's brilliant at manipulation, at seeing all the angles. What if your job at Caldwell & Ross isn't a coincidence?"

The question landed like a stone in still water, ripples of implication spreading outward. Abby thought of Dr. Chen's earlier observations about shared traits, about choices and paths. Was she reading too much into everything now, seeing conspiracy where there might be only coincidence? Or was she finally starting to see clearly, to use her inherited instincts for pattern recognition and strategic thinking to uncover long-buried truths?

"I need to be careful," she said finally. "If there really is a connection, if Amanda is somehow using my position at the firm..." She trailed off, the weight of possibility settling on her shoulders.

Drake wrapped his arms around her from behind, his solid presence grounding her swirling thoughts. "Whatever you decide to do, whatever you find, I'm here. We'll figure it out together."

Abby leaned back into his embrace, grateful for his steadfast support even as her mind continued to race. She was her mother's daughter in so many ways – the strategic thinking, the ability to read people and situations, the instinct for finding patterns in chaos. But she was also her own person, shaped by different choices, different values, different loves.

Tomorrow would bring new challenges, new discoveries, new choices about how much truth to uncover and how to use her inherited talents. But for now, she stood in her kitchen with her husband's arms around her, the scent of herbs and tomatoes filling the air, feeling both the weight and the strength of who she was choosing to be – her mother's daughter, but walking her own path, using her gifts not for deception but for truth, not for personal gain but for justice.

The pasta sauce bubbled on the stove, a homey counterpoint to the complex web of possibilities unfolding in her mind. Whatever Amanda's ultimate game might be, whatever truths lay hidden in those Thompsen Industries files, Abby would face them with clear eyes and firm boundaries, guided by her own moral compass while acknowledging the complicated legacy she'd inherited.

She turned in Drake's arms, meeting his steady gaze. "I think it's time we did more than just look at those files. If there really is a connection between Thompsen Industries' early success and Wausau's biggest unsolved heists..."

"We need to be careful," Drake cautioned. "These aren't just cold cases – they're potentially explosive revelations about one of the city's most powerful companies."

Abby nodded, feeling a familiar surge of strategic energy, but this time tempered by wisdom and purpose. "We'll be careful. We'll be methodical. And we'll use every skill we have – even the ones that remind me of her – to find the truth." She managed a small smile. "After all, isn't that the best way to honor our gifts? By using them for something bigger than ourselves?"

Drake kissed her forehead before returning to his abandoned cooking. As Abby watched him resume chopping herbs with methodical precision, she felt a growing sense of purpose. She might share Amanda's gifts for strategy and manipulation, but she was choosing to use them differently. Whether that choice would protect her or make her vulnerable remained to be seen, but it was her choice to make.

The evening stretched ahead, full of quiet domesticity and simmering revelations. Tomorrow would bring its own challenges, its own tests of character and conviction. But for tonight, Abby was content to be exactly who she was: a woman mapping her own course through the complex legacy of nature and nurture, of inherited traits and chosen paths.

18 FAMILY CONSULTATION

Abby sat at the kitchen table, her hands wrapped around a steaming mug of tea as she looked at the three people who meant the most to her in the world. Her mother, her husband Drake, and her best friend Lily, who had been by her side since they were just kids in grade school.

She had called them all together to talk about her latest session with Dr. Chen, and the new direction that her therapy was about to take. She knew that they would have questions, concerns, and opinions, and she wanted to hear them all before she made any decisions.

"Dr. Chen wants to start a new phase of my therapy," she said, her voice quiet but steady. "She wants to try hypnotherapy, to see if we can uncover any repressed memories from my early childhood, before I was adopted."

Her mother's eyes widened, and she reached out to take Abby's hand in her own. "Oh, sweetheart," she said, her voice filled with concern. "Are you sure you're ready for that? It could be very painful, very traumatic."

Abby nodded, swallowing hard as she tried to find the right words. "I know, Mom," she said, her voice trembling slightly. "But I also know that I need to do this, if I ever want to find peace with my past. The nightmares, the anxiety, the fear... it's all tied up in those early memories, and I need to confront them if I ever want to move forward."

Drake shifted in his chair, his expression troubled. "I understand wanting to explore your early memories, Abby, but the timing concerns me. Especially with what we just discovered about Thompsen Industries."

Lily's head snapped up. "What about Thompsen Industries?"

Abby hadn't planned to share the corporate investigation yet, but perhaps it was all connected – her past, her present, the complicated web of relationships and revelations that seemed to be tightening around her. She took a deep breath and explained about the patterns they'd noticed in the company's early security contracts, the possible connections to historical heists.

Her mother's face paled. "And you think this might be related to... to her?"

"I don't know," Abby admitted. "That's part of why Dr. Chen suggested hypnotherapy. She thinks there might be early memories that could help me understand – not just about Amanda, but about that whole period. About why certain things happened the way they did."

Lily leaned forward, her protective instincts clearly warring with her curiosity. "But if you start remembering things, if you uncover information that's legally sensitive... wouldn't that put you in a difficult position professionally?"

It was a valid question, one that had kept Abby awake the previous night. "Dr. Chen and I discussed that. She's suggested having a legal consultant present during the sessions, someone who can help navigate any potential conflicts of interest."

"That seems wise," Drake said slowly, "but it also makes this feel less like therapy and more like... an investigation."

"Maybe it needs to be both," Abby's mother interjected, surprising everyone. She had been quiet for several minutes, lost in thought. "Abby, sweetheart, I've never told you this, but there was something odd about your adoption. Something that never quite added up."

The kitchen fell silent. Even the usual street noise seemed muffled, as if the world itself was holding its breath. Abby's hands tightened around her mug. "What do you mean?"

"The agency that handled your placement – it closed very suddenly about a year after we got you. There were rumors about irregular paperwork, about corporate donations that couldn't be traced." Her mother's eyes held a mix of concern and determination. "I never wanted to upset you by mentioning it, but with everything that's happening now..."

Drake straightened, his investigator's instincts clearly engaged. "A corporate adoption agency that suddenly closed down, right around the time Thompsen Industries was expanding rapidly?"

"It might be nothing," Abby's mother said quickly. "But if you're going to explore those early memories, Abby, you should know that there might be more to uncover than just your time with... with her."

Lily reached across the table, squeezing Abby's hand. "Okay, now I'm officially worried. This is starting to sound less like therapy and more like opening Pandora's box."

"Maybe it needs to be opened," Abby said quietly. She looked around the table at the people she trusted most in the world. "All my life, I've had these fragments – memories, feelings, intuitions that didn't quite make sense. The strategic thinking that comes so naturally, the way I can read people and situations..." She paused, gathering her thoughts. "What if it's not just inherited traits from Amanda? What if I was somehow aware of things, even as a small child? What if these patterns we're seeing with Thompsen Industries are connected to why she gave me up in the first place?"

Her mother made a small, distressed sound. "Abby, you were just a baby."

"Babies are more perceptive than we give them credit for," Drake pointed out gently. "And if Abby was exposed to certain situations, certain patterns of behavior during her critical developmental period..."

"It could explain a lot," Lily finished. "Like why you went into corporate law instead of criminal defense like you originally planned. Why you're so good at seeing the bigger picture in complex negotiations."

Abby felt a sudden rush of clarity. "That's what Dr. Chen said — that sometimes our earliest experiences shape us in ways we don't consciously remember. She thinks the hypnotherapy might help me understand not just what happened, but why I am the way I am."

"And potentially why Amanda chose now to make contact," Drake added. "If there really is a connection to Thompsen Industries..."

The implications hung heavy in the air. Abby looked around at her family — her real family, the people who had chosen her and whom she had chosen in return. "I need to do this," she said finally. "Not just for me, but for all of us. Whatever the truth is, whatever Amanda's role in all of this might be, I need to understand it."

Her mother reached across the table, taking both of Abby's hands in hers. "Then we'll face it together. But promise me something?"

"Anything."

"Promise me you'll remember who you are. Not who Amanda might have wanted you to be, not what Thompsen Industries might have influenced, but who you've chosen to be. Because that's what matters most — the choices we make, the people we choose to become."

Tears welled in Abby's eyes as she squeezed her mother's hands. "I promise."

As the evening wound down, plans were made. Drake would look into the old adoption agency records through his law enforcement connections. Lily would use her investigative journalism skills to research

Thompsen Industries' corporate history. And Abby's mother would dig through her old papers for any documentation from that period that might help.

But most importantly, they would be there for each other, a united front against whatever truths might emerge from the depths of memory and corporate archives. Because that's what family did – they stood together, protecting each other while supporting the search for truth, no matter how difficult or dangerous that truth might be.

Looking around at her chosen family, Abby felt both terrified and strangely empowered. Whatever memories the hypnotherapy might uncover, whatever connections might emerge between her past and present, she wouldn't face them alone. She had something Amanda had never had – people who loved her for who she was, not what she could do for them.

And maybe that, more than anything, would be her strongest protection against whatever storms lay ahead.

Later that night, after everyone had gone home and Drake had fallen asleep, Abby sat in her home office, surrounded by the comfortable familiarity of her law books and case files. She opened her journal – the one Dr. Chen had suggested she keep – and began to write about the evening's revelations.

The adoption agency connection nagged at her. She'd always assumed her placement with her adoptive parents had been straightforward, if emotionally complicated. But her mother's revelation about corporate donations and sudden closures pointed to something more sinister. Could Thompsen Industries have been involved even then? Had Amanda somehow orchestrated her placement, setting up pieces on a chessboard decades in advance?

"You're overthinking it," she whispered to herself, but the strategic part of her mind – the part that sometimes reminded her so strongly of Amanda – couldn't help seeing patterns, possibilities, connections that seemed too perfect to be coincidental.

She opened her laptop, unable to resist doing a preliminary search on the adoption agency. Most of the information was frustratingly basic, but one detail caught her eye: the agency's former location on North 10th Street, just three blocks from where Thompsen Industries had opened their first major office.

"Of course," Abby murmured, remembering something from her corporate law classes about geographic clustering in business development. Companies often grouped together for efficiency, for shared resources, for...

She stopped, a chill running down her spine. The prison where Amanda was held – wasn't that also on North 10th Street? The coincidence felt too precise, too calculated to be random.

Her phone buzzed with a text from Lily: "Found something interesting in old newspaper archives. Call me tomorrow?"

Abby smiled, grateful once again for her friend's investigative instincts. She typed back a quick reply, then closed her laptop, knowing she needed sleep before tomorrow's challenges.

As she got ready for bed, she caught her reflection in the bathroom mirror. The same green eyes that had stared back at her all her life now seemed to hold new questions, new possibilities. How much of who she was had been shaped by conscious choice, and how much by carefully orchestrated circumstances?

Drake stirred as she slipped into bed beside him. "You okay?" he mumbled sleepily.

"Just thinking," she whispered back, curling into his warmth. "About choices and patterns and who we become."

"Mmm," he responded, pulling her closer. "Remember what your mom said – it's who you choose to be that matters."

Abby closed her eyes, letting his steady breathing calm her racing thoughts. Tomorrow would bring new discoveries, new challenges, new choices to make. The hypnotherapy sessions with Dr. Chen would begin soon, potentially unlocking memories that could change everything. The investigation into Thompsen Industries would continue, possibly revealing connections she wasn't sure she was ready to face.

But for now, she was exactly where she needed to be – surrounded by love, supported by truth, and ready to face whatever revelations awaited. Because that was who she had chosen to be: not just Amanda's daughter, not just a corporate attorney, but a woman brave enough to seek the truth while staying true to herself.

As sleep finally claimed her, Abby's last conscious thought was of patterns – in corporate documents, in childhood memories, in the complicated web of relationships that had brought her to this moment. Whatever she discovered in the days ahead, she would face it with clear eyes and an open heart, guided by the love of her chosen family and the strength of her own convictions.

Her dreams that night were a kaleidoscope of memories and possibilities. She dreamed of the adoption agency's office on North 10th Street, though she couldn't possibly remember it. In her dream, it was connected to Thompsen Industries by a series of underground tunnels, like the corporate equivalent of speakeasies during Prohibition. She saw Amanda moving through these tunnels, younger, carrying folders filled with secrets. She saw herself as a baby, surrounded by paperwork that would shape her future in ways no one could have predicted.

She woke briefly around three AM, the dream fragments slipping away even as she tried to hold onto them. But one image remained crystal clear: a logo she'd seen recently in the Thompsen Industries files, dated from their early years. In her dream, that same logo had been on a folder in Amanda's hands.

Abby reached for her phone, making a quick note before she could forget. Tomorrow she would check those old corporate records again, looking specifically at their branding history. It seemed impossible that her sleeping mind could have made a connection her waking self-had missed, but stranger things had happened.

Drake's arm tightened around her waist as she settled back against the pillows. In the quiet darkness of their bedroom, with the steady rhythm of her husband's breathing beside her, Abby felt an odd sense of peace settling over her. Yes, there were mysteries to unravel, potentially dangerous truths to uncover. But she had something Amanda had never had: a foundation built on love rather than calculation, on trust rather than manipulation.

Maybe that was the key difference between them – not their abilities or their strategic thinking, but the choices they made about how to use those gifts. As sleep reclaimed her, Abby smiled faintly. Tomorrow would bring new challenges, new revelations, new choices to make. But for tonight, she was exactly who and where she needed to be: surrounded by truth, supported by love, and ready to face whatever the future might hold.

19 DOUBTS AND DECISIONS

Abby stared at her computer screen, the HR portal's leave request form waiting for input. The Thompsen Industries files sat in a neat stack to her right, their secrets temporarily relegated to the background of her racing thoughts. She'd spent the morning researching the firm's leave of absence policies, documenting her current cases, and preparing transition memos for each client.

Her fingers hovered over the keyboard as she considered the options: Personal Leave, Medical Leave, Family Medical Leave Act. Each carried different implications, different requirements for documentation. Dr. Chen had offered to provide whatever supporting documentation might be needed, but Abby wanted to handle this properly, professionally.

The previous night's conversation with Drake echoed in her mind. He'd been waiting up when she'd finally left the office, case files and adoption agency research spreading beyond her usual working hours.

"I'm not asking you to stop," he'd said, his voice careful, measured. "But watching you try to handle a full corporate caseload while investigating Thompsen Industries and preparing for hypnotherapy sessions..." He'd paused, choosing his words with obvious care. "I'm worried you're stretching yourself too thin."

She'd started to protest, but the words died in her throat as she realized he was right. The mounting complexity of her investigation into Thompsen Industries demanded full focus. The upcoming hypnotherapy sessions with Dr. Chen would require emotional energy she couldn't spare while juggling client demands. And beneath it all, the growing certainty that Amanda's carefully timed revelations were leading toward something bigger than she'd initially imagined.

Now, sitting at her desk, Abby began filling out the leave request form. Personal Leave, she decided. It offered the most flexibility and required the least external documentation. She detailed her current cases, proposed transition plans for each client, and outlined a tentative timeline: three months, with the option to extend if necessary.

Her office phone buzzed – Margaret from HR. "Do you have a moment to discuss your leave request? We've just received the preliminary notification."

The next hour was a blur of procedural details. Yes, she understood that her billable hours requirement would be prorated. Yes, she would complete all necessary client transition memos before her leave began. No, she wasn't experiencing any workplace issues that HR should be aware of.

"Given your position and case load," Margaret explained, "we'll need two weeks for transition planning. Will that timeline work for you?"

Abby thought of the Thompsen Industries logo from her dream, of the geographic clustering along North 10th Street that seemed too perfect to be coincidental. "Yes, two weeks are fine. I want to ensure smooth transitions for all my clients."

She spent the afternoon drafting detailed handoff documents, her legal training turning personal chaos into an orderly procedure. Each memo was a masterpiece of professional documentation, revealing nothing of the emotional turbulence beneath.

When Marcus Wellington, the Chief Managing Partner, requested a brief meeting, Abby was prepared. She brought a concise summary of her transition plans, her pending cases organized by priority and complexity.

"I won't pry into your personal matters," Marcus said, studying her with genuine concern. "But I want you to know that taking time for yourself isn't a sign of weakness. The firm will support whatever you need."

"Thank you," Abby replied, maintaining her professional composure. "I've prepared detailed transition plans for each case. Anderson can take point on the merger negotiations, and I've spoken with Patricia about handling the regulatory compliance reviews."

Marcus nodded approvingly at her thoroughness. "We'll have formal correspondence for your files by end of day. Take care of yourself, Abby. The firm will be here when you're ready to return."

Later that evening, she finally called Dr. Chen. "I've submitted the leave paperwork," she reported, settling onto her home office couch. "Two weeks for client transitions, then three months of personal leave."

"How are you feeling about the decision?" Dr. Chen's voice carried its usual careful balance of support and inquiry.

"Relieved," Abby admitted. "And terrified. What if what we uncover during hypnotherapy affects my ability to return to work? What if the Thompsen Industries connection goes deeper than we suspect?"

"One step at a time," Dr. Chen counseled. "You've handled this decision with characteristic thoroughness. Let's apply that same careful approach to our exploration of your memories."

After hanging up, Abby found Drake in their kitchen, preparing dinner. The domestic normalcy of the scene nearly brought tears to her eyes.

"I did it," she said simply.

He turned from the stove, enfolding her in a tight embrace. "I'm proud of you," he murmured into her hair. "Taking time to handle this properly, to take care of yourself – that's not weakness, Abby. That's wisdom."

She breathed in his familiar scent, letting herself lean into his strength. "There's so much we still need to investigate. The adoption agency, Thompsen Industries, Amanda's connections to everything..."

"And we'll investigate all of it," Drake assured her. "But we'll do it right, with clear heads and proper support. Together."

Abby nodded against his chest, feeling some of her tension ease. She had followed all the proper procedures, documented everything meticulously, created a professional framework for her personal journey. Now came the harder part: facing whatever truths lay waiting in her earliest memories, in corporate archives, in the careful web Amanda might have been weaving for decades.

But first, dinner with her husband. First, the quiet comfort of their shared life. First, the foundation of love and trust she had built, so different from the calculations and manipulations that seemed to define her birth mother's world.

The formal letter from Marcus Wellington arrived in her inbox just as she was leaving the office. His words were kind, supportive, perfectly appropriate for her personnel file. What he couldn't know, what no one at the firm could know, was that this leave of absence might uncover truths that would shake the corporate world to its foundations.

For now, though, Abby had done everything by the book. Her cases would transition smoothly, her clients would be well served, her professional reputation would remain intact. Whatever storms lay ahead, she had created a solid harbor from which to weather them.

The next morning, Marcus Wellington's assistant requested another meeting. When Abby entered his corner office, she found him standing by the floor-to-ceiling windows, gazing out at the Wausau's skyline. He turned as she entered, his expression thoughtful.

"Please, sit down, Abby," he gestured to one of the leather chairs facing his desk. Instead of taking his usual position behind it, he chose the chair next to hers. The informality of the gesture wasn't lost on her.

"I've been reviewing your case files," he began, "particularly your work on the Thompsen Industries accounts." Abby felt her pulse quicken, but kept her expression neutral. "Your attention to detail, your ability to see patterns others miss – it reminds me of myself at your age."

He paused, seeming to choose his next words carefully. "I've been in corporate law for over thirty years, Abby. I've seen brilliant young attorneys burn out trying to prove themselves. But I've also seen something different in you. A depth of understanding, an ability to see beyond the surface of things."

"Thank you, sir," Abby replied, wondering where this was leading.

"When I received your leave request, I did something I rarely do. I looked back at your interview file from when we first hired you." He pulled out a familiar-looking folder. "Do you remember what you said when I asked you why you chose corporate law instead of criminal defense?"

Abby remembered the interview clearly. It had been just after passing the bar, when she was still trying to reconcile her natural talents with her chosen path. "I said that corporate law was where patterns matter most – that understanding the relationships between companies, the flow of power and influence, could affect more lives than individual criminal cases."

Marcus nodded, a slight smile playing at the corners of his mouth. "Most young lawyers talk about career advancement or financial rewards. You talked about patterns and relationships. It struck me then, as it strikes me now, that you see this work differently than most."

He leaned forward slightly. "Which is why I want you to know something. Whatever you're dealing with, whatever you need to explore during this leave of absence – your position here is secure. Not just because of your exceptional legal skills, but because we need more attorneys who understand that corporate law isn't just about contracts and mergers. It's about understanding the deeper patterns that shape our world."

The words hit uncomfortably close to home. Did he somehow suspect her investigation into Thompsen Industries? Her connection to Amanda? But his expression remained open, genuinely concerned.

"The firm will support you fully during your leave," he

continued. "Your benefits will remain intact, your clients will be well-cared for, and your office will be waiting when you return. Take whatever time you need to handle your personal matters. Some journeys can't be rushed."

As if sensing her unasked questions, he added, "Years ago, I took my own leave of absence. Three months turned into six. I needed to resolve some... family matters." Something in his tone made Abby wonder if he knew more than he was letting on. "When I returned, I was a better lawyer for it. Sometimes stepping away helps us see the bigger picture more clearly."

He stood, signaling the end of their conversation, but paused before opening his office door. "One more thing, Abby. If during your leave you discover anything that requires... legal consultation, my door is always open. Off the record, of course."

The implication was clear enough. Whatever she might uncover about Thompsen Industries, about her past, about the complex web of connections she was just beginning to understand – she had an ally in Marcus Wellington. Whether that was reassuring or concerning, she wasn't quite sure.

Walking back to her office, Abby felt the weight of everything shifting slightly. She followed all the proper procedures, created a professional framework for her personal journey. But Marcus's words suggested layers of understanding she hadn't anticipated. Like the geographic clustering along North 10th Street, like the patterns in Thompsen Industries' early security contracts, like the careful orchestration of her own career path – everything seemed connected in ways she was only beginning to grasp.

Back at her desk, she found the formal letter from Marcus had already arrived in her inbox. The language was perfectly appropriate for her personnel file, the support and appreciation genuine. But now she understood it as what it was: not just a professional courtesy, but a message. Whatever storms lay ahead, she had more allies than she'd realized.

The spring rain tapped against their bedroom window as Abby reviewed case files late into the night. Drake watched her from their bed, a familiar ache of loneliness settling in his chest despite her physical presence just feet away. "Abby," he said softly, "do you ever think about our future? Beyond cases and careers?" She looked up, distracted. "What do you mean?" Drake hesitated. "Family. Children. A legacy that's more than just legal victories." Abby's expression softened as she set aside her work. "With everything happening with Amanda... it just hasn't seemed like the right time." "I wonder if there ever will be a right time," Drake replied, the words carrying more weight than he'd intended. "Sometimes I feel like I'm competing with your mother for whatever attention isn't already claimed by your cases." The truth of his words hung between them, unexpected but impossible to ignore.

20 PATTERNS IN MEMORY

Rain tapped against Dr. Chen's office window in an irregular rhythm that Abby's mind couldn't help trying to decode. The droplets formed trails down the glass, merging and splitting in patterns that reminded her of corporate organizational charts – of Thompsen Industries' early expansion maps along North 10th Street.

"You seem preoccupied today," Dr. Chen observed, adjusting the lamp beside her chair until the room held just the right balance of light and shadow. "Where are your thoughts?"

"Everywhere. Nowhere." Abby shifted into the familiar leather chair. "I keep thinking about what Marcus Wellington said – about taking his own leave of absence years ago to handle 'family matters.' The way he emphasized it..." She traced a raindrop's path down the window with her eyes. "It feels connected somehow."

"To the memories we'll be exploring today?"

"To everything. The adoption agency's location, the Thompsen Industries contracts, Amanda's careful revelations." Abby turned back to Dr. Chen. "I can't help looking for patterns. It's what I do, what I've always done. Maybe what I was taught to do before I could even form words."

Dr. Chen nodded thoughtfully. "Then let's use that. Instead of fighting your analytical mind, we'll let it guide us — but through memory rather than strategy." She leaned forward slightly. "As you go under, focus on any patterns you notice. Colors, sounds, repeated words or gestures. Whatever draws your attention."

Abby closed her eyes, letting Dr. Chen's voice guide her through the familiar relaxation sequence. The rain's rhythm seemed to slow, each drop falling with deliberate purpose, like pieces being positioned on a chess board. She felt her consciousness drift, memories rising like bubbles through dark water.

The first image came with startling clarity: industrial carpet in a distinctive shade of blue-gray, with a repeating diamond pattern that her three-year-old self had been tracing with one finger. The texture was rough against her skin, but the pattern was soothing, predictable. She could feel the vibration of adult voices above her.

Amanda's voice cut through the haze, not with the careful modulation of their prison visits, but sharp and focused. "The timing has to be perfect. If the security upgrades don't align exactly with the schedule..."

A man's voice responded, too low to make out the words. But his cufflinks caught her attention — golden squares with a geometric design she recognized from old Thompsen Industries marketing materials, before their current corporate logo. The same design she'd seen in the files on her desk just last week.

The memory shifted, fragments realigning. She was being carried down a hallway, the diamond-pattern carpet stretching endlessly ahead. Over the shoulder of whoever held her, she could see Amanda speaking with another man in an expensive suit. His desk held a folder in that particular shade of green that major financial institutions used for sensitive documents.

"The adoption records will be sealed," the man was saying, his tone careful but confident. "But if anything ever comes to light..."

Amanda's laugh was cold, calculated. "By then the statute of limitations will have expired. And she'll be positioned perfectly."

Something about the way Amanda said "positioned" sent a chill through even the memory. On the wall behind them, a calendar showed a date that made Abby's legal mind snap to attention: two weeks before her official adoption, three days before Thompsen Industries announced their revolutionary new security system, and exactly one day after Wausau's largest unsolved bank heist.

"Abby?" Dr. Chen's voice drew her gently back to the present. "What did you see?"

Rain still fell against the window, but the patterns had changed — or perhaps she was finally seeing them clearly. "I saw proof," she said quietly, her attorney's mind already cataloging details, building connections. "Amanda didn't just give me up for adoption. She placed me strategically – with a family that would encourage my natural abilities, in a city where I'd eventually be positioned to..." She stopped, the implications hitting her full force.

"To what?"

"To either expose everything or protect it." Abby sat up straighter, hands gripping the chair arms. "The adoption agency's location, Thompsen Industries' expansion, Marcus Wellington's cryptic warnings – it's all connected. Amanda didn't just plan her heists. She planned decades ahead, positioning pieces..." Her hands shook slightly as she pulled out her phone, texting Drake: "Need you to check something. Thompsen Industries' original security patent. Look for geometric square design in documentation. Then cross-reference with bank robbery reports, North 10th Street, one day prior."

Dr. Chen watched her with careful consideration. "What will you do with this information?"

"That depends on what Drake finds." Abby stood, moving back to the window. "And on whether Marcus Wellington's own family leave years ago means what I think it might." She watched the rain create new patterns on the glass. "Amanda positioned me to make a choice. Now I just have to figure out what she thought that choice would be."

Her phone buzzed – Drake's response was immediate: "Found something. Wellington's family leave coincided with major security overhaul at three banks. All on North 10th. Call me ASAP."

The pieces were falling into place with a clarity that both thrilled and terrified her. Amanda hadn't just planned a series of heists – she'd orchestrated a decades-long strategy that included everything from Abby's childhood development to her eventual career placement. The adoption agency's sudden closure, Thompsen Industries' rapid expansion, even Marcus Wellington's cryptic support – all formed a pattern so intricate it could only be fully appreciated from a distance.

"Time's almost up," Dr. Chen noted softly. "What's your next step?"

Abby gathered her things, mind already mapping out possibilities. "I need to understand the full pattern – not just the parts Amanda wants me to see, but everything. Including the pieces she might have missed." She paused at the door. "Because that's the real difference between us, isn't it? She sees patterns as tools for control. I want to see them as paths to truth."

The rain followed her to her car, but its rhythm no longer seemed like something to decode. Instead, it felt like an accompaniment to her racing thoughts, to the plans already forming. Drake would be waiting with his discoveries, and together they would begin mapping out the true scope of Amanda's long game – not to play it, but to transcend it.

As she drove home, Abby couldn't shake the memory of that green folder on the desk. Something about its placement, its particular shade, nagged at her. She needed to check the Thompsen Industries files again, this time looking not just for what was there, but for what might have been deliberately left out. Because if Amanda had planned this far ahead, there had to be more – more connections, more breadcrumbs, more choices waiting to be made.

Late April 2015

The pregnancy test's two pink lines appeared just before Drake had called with his findings about Wellington, and she hadn't found the right moment to share her news. The dogwood trees outside were in full bloom, their white petals occasionally drifting past the window – nature's reminder of renewal and new beginnings. "Drake," she said softly, her voice steady despite her racing heart. "There's something else we need to discuss." He looked up from the documents, his investigator's focus shifting instantly at her tone. "What is it?" "I'm pregnant." The words hung in the air between them, transforming the space from investigation headquarters to intimate sanctuary. Drake's eyes widened, joy and concern battling across his features. "Are you... are you sure?" Abby nodded, managing a small smile. "Confirmed it this afternoon. About six weeks along, according to the doctor's estimate. Right before you called about Wellington."

21 NEW COMPLICATIONS

Late April 2015

As spring gave way to early summer, Abby's pregnancy remained their secret treasure, shared only with Dr. Chen and carefully concealed from everyone else – especially Amanda. Her stomach remained flat, though the persistent morning sickness left her exhausted in ways her demanding legal career never had. Drake had transformed since the announcement, his earlier feelings of neglect replaced by protective devotion. Each morning, he prepared her ginger tea before she could even ask, anticipating her needs with a tenderness that made her heart ache. "You know we'll have to tell her eventually," Abby said one evening as they sat on the porch, watching fireflies emerge in the twilight. The summer heat made her skin flush despite the ceiling fan spinning lazily above them. Drake's hand found hers, squeezing gently. "I know. But let's just have this for ourselves a little longer. Before it becomes part of... everything else." The unspoken "everything else" hung between them – Amanda's manipulation, the Thompsen Industries investigation, the growing complexity of their intertwined histories.

Drake's evidence about Wellington lay scattered across their coffee table - bank records, security upgrade timelines, and property documents all pointing to a pattern too precise to be coincidence. Abby stared at the papers, her analytical mind trying to reconcile these discoveries with the even more personal revelation she'd confirmed just hours ago.

"The timing matches perfectly," Drake said, highlighting another document. "Wellington's family leave coincided with not just the bank renovations, but with three major security system installations. All within a two-block radius of the adoption agency."

Abby nodded, her hand unconsciously drifting to her still-flat stomach. The pregnancy test's two pink lines had appeared just before Drake had called with his findings, and she hadn't found the right moment to share her news. "And the geometric pattern from my memory?"

"Shows up in the original patent applications." Drake pulled out a yellowed document. "But here's where it gets interesting - the design firm that created it went defunct three days after the patent was approved. Just like the adoption agency's sudden closure."

The familiar thrill of connecting pieces tingled through Abby's mind, but it mixed now with a new, fierce protective instinct. She thought of Amanda's careful orchestration, of positions and patterns laid out decades in advance. Would her own child inherit this same strategic mind? Would they too be pieces in Amanda's long game?

Drake moved around the coffee table, gathering her into his arms. His embrace was gentle but fierce, protective. When he pulled back, his eyes were shining but serious.

"This changes things," he said quietly.

"Does it?" Abby challenged, her analytical mind already racing ahead. "Or does it make understanding Amanda's choices even more crucial? This child will inherit her genetic legacy too, Drake. Her patterns of thinking, her capabilities..."

"But not her choices," Drake insisted. "You're proof of that. You use those same gifts for justice, for truth."

Abby stood, moving to the window. Outside, the city lights sparkled like data points waiting to be connected. "Do I? Look at what we've uncovered - decades of corporate manipulation, strategic positioning, lives arranged like pieces on a chess board. What if understanding Amanda isn't just about the past? What if it's about protecting our child's future?"

Drake was quiet for a moment, processing. When he spoke, his voice held both compassion and determination. "Then we face it together. But Abby, we have to be smart about this. The timing..."

"I know." She turned back to him, one hand still resting protectively over her stomach. "If Wellington's involvement goes as deep as we suspect, if Thompsen Industries' early success really was built on insider knowledge of security vulnerabilities..."

"Then we're dealing with people who've successfully buried these secrets for decades," Drake finished. "People who might not appreciate them being uncovered now."

Abby moved back to the coffee table, studying the documents with renewed purpose. "The hypnotherapy sessions have been revealing more than just memories. They've been showing me patterns - connections I might have noticed as a child but couldn't understand until now."

"Are you thinking of stopping them?"

"No." Her voice was firm. "But I need to be strategic about how we proceed. Dr. Chen should know about the pregnancy - it might affect how we approach the sessions. And Amanda..."

Drake tensed slightly. "You still want to continue the prison visits?"

"More than ever." Abby met his concerned gaze steadily. "But not just as her daughter now - as a mother protecting her own child. I need to understand not just what she did, but why. What she was trying to protect or prevent."

She gathered the documents into neat piles, her organizational instincts kicking in. "We have three main threads: Wellington's involvement, the adoption agency's connection to Thompsen Industries, and whatever Amanda was trying to position me to discover. They all intersect somewhere."

Drake wrapped his arms around her from behind, his hands coming to rest protectively over hers on her stomach. "Then we follow the threads carefully. Together. But promise me something?"

"Anything."

"Promise me that protecting yourself - and our baby - comes first. Before any investigation, any revelation."

Abby leaned back into his embrace, letting herself feel the full weight of both her joy and her responsibility. "I promise. This child will never be a piece in someone else's game. Even Amanda's."

They stood together, surrounded by evidence of past secrets and future possibilities. Tomorrow would bring new challenges - telling Dr. Chen, adjusting their investigation strategy, navigating the delicate balance between truth-seeking and protection. But for now, Abby let herself simply be held, supported by Drake's strength as their world shifted on its axis.

The papers on the coffee table still beckoned with their half-revealed secrets, but they could wait. Tonight was for embracing new dreams while holding firm to old promises - of justice, of truth, of love strong enough to break generations-old patterns and forge new ones.

As if sensing her thoughts, Drake gently turned her to face him. "What are you thinking?"

"About patterns," Abby said softly. "Not just the ones we're investigating, but the ones we create ourselves." She moved to gather her laptop, pulling up the calendar where she tracked her meetings with Amanda. "Each visit, each revelation - they're all carefully timed. But now I wonder if I've been unconsciously creating patterns too, seeking answers about my past just as I'm about to create a new future."

Drake sat beside her, studying the calendar. "Like mother, like daughter?" His tone held no judgment, only understanding.

"But with a crucial difference," Abby said, closing the laptop. "Everything Amanda did was about control - controlling outcomes, controlling people, controlling the future itself. What we're doing, what we're creating..." She placed her hand over her stomach again. "It's about freedom. Freedom to know the truth, freedom to choose our own path."

She leaned into Drake's embrace, feeling the steady rhythm of his heartbeat. Tomorrow they would dive back into the investigation, armed with new purpose and new caution. They would carefully trace the threads of corporate misconduct and family secrets, always mindful now of the precious new life that gave their quest both urgency and limits.

But tonight was for acknowledging that some patterns were worth embracing - like love, like family, like the unshakeable bond between two people facing an uncertain future with courage and conviction.

"But I need you to promise me something," he said softly, his voice muffled slightly by her hair. "I need you to promise me that you'll be careful, that you'll take care of yourself and our baby first and foremost. And I need you to promise me that if it ever becomes too much, if you ever feel like you're losing yourself in this search, that you'll come to me, that you'll let me help you find your way back."

Abby nodded, her face still pressed against his chest. "I promise," she whispered, her voice choked with emotion. "I promise, Drake. You and this baby, you are my everything. And I will never let anything come between us, not even my own past."

They held each other for a long time, their hearts beating in unison, their love for each other a palpable force in the room. And as they sat there, wrapped in each other's arms, Abby knew that no matter what the future held, no matter what challenges lay ahead, she would always have Drake by her side, her rock, her anchor, her true north.

With a soft, contented sigh, she pulled back slightly, looking up at him with shining eyes. "Thank you," she whispered, her voice filled with love and gratitude. "Thank you for being you, for loving me, for supporting me through everything."

Drake smiled, his hand coming up to cup her cheek gently. "Always," he said softly, his voice a promise. "Always and forever, my love."

And with those words, they sealed their love with a kiss, their hearts and their lives intertwined, their future stretching out before them like a shining path, filled with hope and possibility and the unshakable certainty that together, they could face anything, overcome anything, as long as they had each other.

22 THE PURSUIT OF ANSWERS

May 2015

Abby sat in the familiar comfort of Dr. Chen's office, her hand resting gently on the slight swell of her belly. She was in her second month of pregnancy, and the reality of the life growing inside her had only intensified her desire to uncover the secrets of her past.Dr. Chen sat across from her, her face warm and welcoming, but her eyes filled with a hint of concern. "Abby," she said softly, her voice gentle but firm. "It's wonderful to see you again, and I'm so happy for you and Drake, congratulations on your pregnancy."

Abby smiled, her hand rubbing small circles on her stomach. "Thank you, Dr. Chen," she said, her voice filled with a mixture of joy and determination. "I know it's been a while since our last session, but I'm ready to dive back in, to keep exploring my memories and my past."

Dr. Chen nodded, her face growing serious. "I understand your determination, Abby," she said softly. "But I want to remind you that the mind is a delicate thing, especially during pregnancy. The hormonal changes, the physical and emotional demands of growing a new life, can make the process of uncovering trauma even more challenging."

Abby leaned forward, her eyes intense. "I know that, Dr. Chen," she said, her voice firm. "But I also know that I can't let this pregnancy stop me from pursuing the answers I need. I want to be the best mother I can be, and I believe that means facing my past head-on, no matter how difficult it may be."

Dr. Chen was silent for a long moment, her eyes searching Abby's face. "I admire your courage and your determination, Abby," she said finally, her voice filled with respect. "But I also want to caution you against trying to rush the process. The mind reveals trauma in its own time, and trying to force it can be counterproductive, even harmful."

Abby nodded, her jaw set with determination. "I understand that, Dr. Chen," she said, her voice unwavering. "But I also know that I'm not the type of person who can just sit back and wait for answers to come to me. I need to be proactive, to take control of my own healing. And I believe that hypnotherapy is the key to unlocking the memories and the emotions that I've buried for so long."

Dr. Chen leaned back in her chair, her face pensive. "If this is truly what you want, Abby," she said softly, "then I will support you every step of the way. But I need you to promise me that you will be honest with me, and with yourself, about how you're feeling. If at any point the process becomes too much, if you feel like you're pushing yourself too hard, I need you to tell me."

Abby nodded, her eyes filled with gratitude. "I promise, Dr. Chen," she said, her voice filled with conviction. "I trust you, and I know that you have my best interests at heart. But I also know that I need to do this, for myself and for my baby. I need to find the peace and the closure that I've been searching for my whole life."

With those words, Abby settled back into the soft cushions of the couch, her eyes fluttering closed as Dr. Chen began to guide her into a deep, hypnotic state. She felt herself drifting, her mind letting go of the conscious world and sinking into the depths of her subconscious.

And as she traveled deeper and deeper into the recesses of her mind, Abby knew that she was on the right path, that every step she took, every memory she uncovered, was bringing her closer to the truth, to the understanding and the healing that she so desperately craved.

She thought of the tiny life growing inside her, of the love and the hope and the possibility that it represented. And she knew that no matter how difficult the journey ahead might be, no matter what painful truths she might uncover, she was doing it all for her child, for the chance to give them a life free from the shadows of the past.

With a deep, steadying breath, Abby surrendered herself to the process, her mind opening like a flower to the gentle probing of Dr. Chen's voice. And as she delved deeper and deeper into the mysteries of her own psyche, she felt a sense of peace and purpose wash over her, a certainty that she was exactly where she needed to be, doing exactly what she needed to do.

For Abby, the pursuit of answers was more than just a personal quest. It was a mission, a calling, a sacred duty to herself and to her unborn child. And as she navigated the twists and turns of her own mind, she knew that she would stop at nothing to uncover the truth, to heal the wounds of her past and build a brighter, more hopeful future for herself and for her family.

With a small, secret smile, Abby let herself sink even deeper into the trance, her mind and her heart open and ready for whatever revelations lay ahead. She was a woman on a mission, a seeker of truth and healing, and nothing, not even the challenges of pregnancy or the fears of her own subconscious, would stand in her way.

23 STRATEGIC ADJUSTMENTS

Abby checked her watch for the third time in five minutes, the leather chairs in Dr. Chen's waiting room doing little to ease her anxiety. Behind the closed door, her mother was delving into memories that had been buried for decades. What truths would emerge? And was Abby ready to hear them?.

She traced an invisible pattern on the window's scratched surface, mimicking the organizational charts she'd memorized from Thompsen Industries' early days. Every position, every movement had been calibrated with precision. Abby's career path, her analytical abilities, even her choice of law firm – all pieces arranged with the patience of a master strategist. But this pregnancy introduced an element of chaos that even Ice's careful planning hadn't accounted for.

"Maternal instinct," she murmured, testing the words like an unfamiliar language. She'd weaponized her own maternal connection, using it to draw Abby closer, to position her for the eventual endgame. But now her daughter had found a different kind of maternal purpose, one that threatened to rewrite all of Ice's carefully constructed scenarios.

The guard's footsteps echoed down the corridor, a rhythm Ice had learned to read like a metronome. Jenkins, working an extra shift, his pace slightly slower than usual – details that could matter someday. Everything mattered in the long game.

"Still expecting your daughter?" Jenkins asked, his tone carrying that mixture of professional distance and casual cruelty that defined prison relationships.

Ice turned from the window, her face composed in the mask she'd perfected over years of incarceration. "Expectations are for amateurs," she replied smoothly. "I deal in certainties."

But alone again in her cell, she allowed herself to acknowledge the miscalculation. She'd assumed Abby's drive for answers would override everything else, that the carefully laid breadcrumbs about Thompsen Industries and the adoption agency would consume her investigative focus. The pregnancy changed that equation. Now every revelation would be filtered through the lens of maternal protection – Ice recognized this because she'd once made decisions through that same lens, though for very different ends.

She moved to her small desk, where a stack of permitted papers lay in precise order. Between the lines of approved correspondence, hidden in plain sight, were the threads of plans within plans. Ice began to review them systematically, her mind adapting and adjusting like the security systems she'd once learned to circumvent.

The Thompsen Industries connection was still viable – perhaps even more so now. Abby's protective instincts toward her unborn child might make her more, not less, interested in understanding the corporate machinations that had shaped her own childhood. But the timing would need to be perfect, the pressure precisely calibrated.

Ice thought of Marcus Wellington's careful hints, the breadcrumbs he'd left for Abby to follow. She'd anticipated that connection years ago, had factored his own family history into her calculations. Now she needed to understand how Abby's pregnancy might affect his willingness to reveal what he knew about the past.

"Patterns within patterns," she whispered, echoing words she'd once used to teach a young As the minutes ticked by, Abby found herself drifting into her own fragmented memories—a lullaby whose melody she could almost grasp, the sensation of being held by unfamiliar arms, a blue-gray carpet with a diamond pattern. Were these real memories or constructions built from the stories she'd been told? And which version would emerge from behind that door—the truth, or whatever version of it Amanda chose to share?

Ice closed her eyes, visualizing the complex web of relationships and revelations she'd constructed over decades. Like a master chess player, she began to see new possibilities in what had first appeared to be a setback. Abby's pregnancy didn't have to derail the plan – it simply required adjusting the strategy, recalibrating the pressure points.

A slight smile played across her lips as new patterns emerged in her mind. Perhaps this development could be turned to advantage. After all, what better motivation for understanding the past than protecting the future? The game wasn't over; it was simply entering a new phase, with stakes higher than even Ice had originally planned.

She returned to the window, her reflection ghostly against the darkening sky. Behind that carefully composed face, her mind continued its relentless calculation of moves and countermoves, each adjusted to account for the precious new variable growing inside her daughter. The endgame remained the same – only the path to reaching it needed to change.

When the door finally opened, Amanda appeared transformed. Her typically composed features were tear-stained, her hands trembling as she clutched a tissue. Abby rose, her lawyer's instincts automatically analyzing the display of emotion—was it genuine vulnerability or carefully crafted performance? "Mom? Are you okay?" The word 'Mom' still felt new on her tongue when addressing Amanda. "It was... intense," Amanda whispered, her voice breaking. "I remembered holding you, Abby. Your tiny hand wrapped around my finger..."

That night, as Drake slept beside her, Abby stared at the ceiling, turning over every detail of Amanda's post-hypnotherapy revelations. The stories aligned with her own fragmented memories—the hospital, the lullaby, the sense of being deeply loved and then abruptly abandoned. But something nagged at her, a sense that pieces were still missing. "What aren't you telling me, Mom?" she whispered into the darkness. As an attorney, she'd learned that the most important details were often the ones deliberately omitted. And Amanda, despite her apparent vulnerability, seemed to be editing her revelations with careful precision.

24 CALCULATED REVELATIONS

The autumn morning mist clung to County Road K as Abby and Drake approached Taycheedah Correctional Institution. The stark institutional architecture emerged gradually through the haze, its security fencing and guard towers a reminder of the careful choreography required for every interaction within its walls. Abby sat in the passenger seat, one hand resting lightly on her growing belly while the other held the visitor registration form they'd need to present at intake.

"You're certain about this?" Drake asked, his voice carrying the careful neutrality he reserved for their most sensitive investigations. They both knew this wasn't just about sharing pregnancy news – it was about testing Amanda's reaction, watching for the subtle tells that might reveal how this development fit into her larger schemes.

"Dr. Chen thinks the timing is significant," Abby replied, thinking of their last session. "The way the memories are surfacing now, just as I'm creating my own family narrative..." She trailed off, remembering the blue-gray carpet, the geometric patterns that had seemed so soothing to her three-year-old self. "Nothing in Amanda's world is ever purely coincidental."

The intake procedures at TCI felt mechanical, routine, but Abby noticed new details today – the way the guard's eyes lingered on her slight baby bump, the subtle shift in how they handled her processing. Already, motherhood was changing how the world perceived her, adding new layers to every interaction. She recognized Officer Peterson at the desk, noting how he checked her ID against the approved visitor list with the same methodical precision she'd come to expect from everything in Amanda's orbit.

Amanda was waiting in the visitation room, her posture relaxed but alert, like a chess master preparing for an unexpected opening move. The moment their eyes met, Abby saw it – the flash of calculation behind her mother's warm smile, the rapid assessment of what this visit might mean.

"Abby," Amanda rose, her embrace perfectly calibrated – warm enough to seem genuine, controlled enough to maintain the power dynamic she preferred. "This is an unexpected pleasure."

"Life is full of unexpected developments," Abby replied, settling into her chair as Drake took his position slightly behind her, a subtle reminder of the protective barriers now in place. "Some of them actually welcome."

Amanda's eyes flickered briefly to Abby's midsection, then back to her face. A smile spread across her features, one that reached her eyes but didn't quite soften the analytical gleam within them. "You're pregnant."

It wasn't a question. Of course it wasn't – Amanda had likely read the signs before Abby had even spoken, had probably already begun recalculating her long-term strategies.

"Four months," Abby confirmed, watching her mother's face with the same careful attention she'd learned to apply to corporate documents and security protocols. "Drake and I are expecting."

"A new generation," Amanda mused, her voice carrying layers of meaning that Abby had learned to decode over months of visits. "How wonderful to see patterns repeating, evolving..." She reached across the table within the strict limits allowed by TCI's visitation rules, her hand hovering near Abby's. "Though hopefully some patterns are meant to be broken."

Abby caught the double meaning, heard the subtle probe beneath the maternal warmth. "I've been thinking a lot about patterns lately," she said, letting her analytical mind guide the conversation. "About how they shape us, how they connect seemingly unrelated events – like adoption agencies and security systems, family leaves and corporate expansions."

Amanda's smile didn't waver, but something shifted in her eyes – appreciation, perhaps, for how her daughter could weave investigation and intimacy into the same conversation. "Motherhood has a way of clarifying things," she offered. "Of helping us see connections we might have missed before."

"Or questioning connections we thought we understood," Abby countered softly, thinking of the green folder from her memories, of

Wellington's carefully timed absences. "A child changes everything – priorities, perspectives, the weight we give to past decisions."

When their allowed visiting time drew to a close, Abby studied her mother's face one last time, searching for any crack in the careful facade. But Amanda had spent too many years in places like this, had learned to turn every regulation, every restriction into another layer of her intricate strategies.

As they drove away from TCI, following County Road K back toward Fond du Lac, Abby found herself mapping patterns within patterns – the guard rotations, the visiting hour schedules, the careful orchestration of every movement within those walls. Her mother had mastered these rhythms, had learned to work within and around them with the same precision she'd once applied to security systems.

"She'll use this," Abby said quietly, watching the facility recede in the side mirror. "The pregnancy, the new visiting restrictions it'll bring, the changed security protocols – she'll fold it all into whatever game she's playing."

Drake reached over to squeeze her hand, his touch grounding her racing thoughts. "Then we stay ahead of her," he said simply. "We use the same patterns to understand what she's planning."

Abby nodded, feeling another flutter of movement from the baby. In that moment, she made a silent promise to her child – to unravel these patterns not just for herself, but for the next generation. To understand Amanda's games not to play them, but to finally, irrevocably break free of them.

    The mist was lifting as they turned onto Highway 151, revealing a landscape of possibilities that extended far beyond TCI's carefully controlled boundaries. Abby had nine months to decode her mother's long game – and this time, she had something Amanda had never truly understood: a reason to seek truth that transcended strategy itself.

25 INHERITED INSTINCTS

Abby stood on her childhood home's front porch, her hand hovering over the doorbell as she processed the morning's revelations from her therapy session with Dr. Chen. The geometric patterns from her memories seemed to overlay everything now - even the familiar arrangement of her mother's potted plants held hints of calculated positioning she'd never noticed before.

Liz opened the door before Abby could ring, mother's intuition as keen as ever. She took one look at her daughter's face and her expression shifted from welcome to careful assessment. "You've remembered something."

The kitchen, with its warm familiarity, felt like neutral ground. Liz moved through their old routine - coffee for herself, herbal tea for Abby's pregnancy - while Abby traced the wood grain patterns on the table she'd done her homework on for years. The same table where she'd first shown her adoptive mother her law school acceptance letter, where they'd planned her wedding to Drake.

"Amanda knew," Abby said finally, her analytical mind still piecing together the implications. "She knew exactly which family would adopt me, didn't she? It wasn't just chance that I ended up with parents who would nurture my particular... abilities."

Liz set their mugs down with deliberate care, her movements measured. "What makes you say that?"

"The patterns are too precise." Abby pulled out her tablet, bringing up the documents Drake had compiled. "Look at this - Dad's position at the university gave him security clearance for government contracts. Your background in child psychology meant you'd recognize and support my analytical tendencies. The adoption agency's location, the timing of everything..." She looked up at her mother. "It wasn't coincidence. It was choreography."

Liz studied the documents, and Abby saw the same sharp intelligence that had helped guide her development now turned to understanding Amanda's long game. "You think she positioned you with us specifically? After all these years, I wondered..."

"Mom," Abby hesitated, then pressed on. "Did you ever suspect? During the adoption process, did anything feel... orchestrated?"

"Not at the time." Liz's voice carried decades of careful consideration. "But later, after you started showing such specific talents, after the first signs of your pattern recognition abilities..." She paused, choosing her words with precision. "I started to notice patterns of my own. The way certain doors opened for you, how your path seemed...

prepared."

"Like Thompsen Industries," Abby said softly. "The internship that fell into place so perfectly. Wellington's mentorship. Even my specialization in corporate security law..." She felt the baby move and pressed a hand to her stomach. "She wasn't just giving me up for adoption. She was positioning me for something specific."

Liz reached across the table, her hand covering Abby's. "Does Drake know you're here? That you're putting these pieces together?"

"He's following up on some bank records from the period around my adoption. The timing of certain security system upgrades, property transfers..." Abby met her mother's gaze. "Mom, I need to ask you something, and I need you to be completely honest with me."

"Always."

"When you and Dad were going through the adoption process, did anyone ever mention Thompsen Industries? Any connection at all, no matter how small?"

Liz was quiet for a long moment, and Abby saw her mother's mind working with the same methodical precision that had helped shape her own analytical abilities. "There was a lawyer," she said finally. "Not directly involved with the adoption, but he facilitated some of the paperwork. He had cufflinks with a geometric pattern - I remember because you were fascinated by them, even as a baby. Always reaching

172

for them when he was near."

Abby felt her heart rate quicken. "Golden squares? With an interlocking design?"

"Yes." Liz's eyes sharpened. "How did you...?"

"It's the original Thompsen Industries logo. Before they rebranded." Abby pulled up another document. "Mom, that lawyer - did he ever mention Marcus Wellington? Or any connection to banking security systems?"

"Not directly, but..." Liz stood suddenly, moving to the old filing cabinet in the corner. "I kept everything from that period. Every document, every business card..." She pulled out a thick folder, its edges worn with age. "I always had a feeling they might be important someday."

As they spread the documents across the table, Abby felt the familiar thrill of patterns emerging. Her mother's meticulous record-keeping, combined with her own trained eye for corporate connections, revealed thread after thread of carefully hidden links.

"She didn't just choose you as my parents," Abby whispered, the full scope of Amanda's strategy becoming clear. "She chose this whole community. The school district with the advanced math programs, the proximity to Thompsen Industries' early expansion sites..." She looked up at her mother. "She built a whole ecosystem around me."

"The question is why." Liz's voice was gentle but firm. "And more importantly, what does she expect from you now?"

"That's what scares me." Abby rested both hands on her belly, feeling her daughter move. "Especially now, with the baby coming. If she planned this far ahead for me, what plans might she have for her granddaughter?"

Liz moved around the table, wrapping her arms around Abby from behind. "Listen to me very carefully," she said, her voice carrying the weight of years of protective love. "Amanda may have orchestrated your placement with us, but she couldn't control how we raised you. The moral compass you developed, the choices you've made - those are yours. And this baby?" She placed her hands over Abby's. "This little one will have something you didn't: a mother who sees the patterns for what they are."

Abby leaned back into her mother's embrace, letting years of careful guidance and unconditional love steady her racing thoughts. "I need your help, Mom. Not just as my mother, but as someone who understands child psychology. If Amanda was able to recognize and position me for my abilities at such a young age..."

"You want to know how to protect your daughter from the same kind of manipulation," Liz finished. "Without stifling her natural gifts."

"Exactly." Abby turned to face her mother. "Because these

abilities - the pattern recognition, the analytical thinking - they're not just learned skills. They're inherited. And if my daughter has them..."

"Then we make sure she uses them for good, just like you do." Liz's voice was firm. "We teach her to see manipulation for what it is, to understand that patterns can be observed without being exploited." She smiled softly. "And we surround her with so much love and stability that no amount of strategic positioning can override her own moral compass."

They spent the next few hours going through old documents, Abby's trained legal mind combining with her mother's psychological insight to uncover layers of connection they'd never seen before. Each revelation made Amanda's long game clearer, but also highlighted the strength of the family bonds that had shaped Abby's true path.

As the afternoon light began to fade, Abby gathered the documents they'd identified as most significant. "Drake needs to see these," she said, carefully organizing them. "Especially the connections to Wellington's early career. There's something there, something about the timing of his own family leave..."

"Abby." Liz's voice stopped her. "Promise me something."

"Anything."

"As you unravel all this, as you follow these patterns to whatever end Amanda planned... remember that the strongest pattern in your life isn't her strategic positioning. It's love. Real, unconditional, unmanipulated love."

Abby hugged her mother tightly, feeling the baby move between them - three generations of women, bound by something far stronger than strategic calculation. "I promise," she whispered. "And Mom? Thank you. Not just for today, but for all of it. For being exactly the mother I needed, whether Amanda planned it or not."

As she drove home, the folder of documents secure beside her, Abby felt a new clarity emerging from the complicated web of revelations. Amanda might have orchestrated her placement, might have positioned every piece of her early life with calculated precision. But it was Liz - steady, loving, insightful Liz - who had given her the tools to see those patterns and choose her own way of using them.

Her daughter would have the same choice, protected by the combined insight of both her mothers - one who had learned to see patterns as tools for justice, and one who had taught her that the most important patterns were the ones woven from love.

The sun was setting as Abby pulled into her driveway, casting long shadows that reminded her of the prison visiting room at Taycheedah. She sat in her car for a moment, one hand on her belly, the other still resting on the folder of documents they'd uncovered. The revelations from her mother's records had illuminated patterns she'd missed before, but they'd also raised new questions about Amanda's ultimate endgame. The careful positioning, the strategic placement - it all suggested a plan far more intricate than simple manipulation or control.

Drake met her at the door, his investigator's instincts immediately registering the weight of new discoveries in her expression. "Your mom found something," he said, not really a question. Abby nodded, following him to their home office where his own research was spread across the desk - bank records, security system specifications, and a timeline of Wellington's career movements that now seemed even more significant in light of Liz's documents. "The lawyer with the Thompsen Industries cufflinks," she began, laying out the adoption papers. "He wasn't just facilitating paperwork. Look at the dates of his visits compared to the security system installations at these three banks." She pointed to a series of timestamps that formed a pattern so precise it could only have been intentional. Drake leaned in, his eyes narrowing as he saw the connections. "Amanda wasn't just planning your future," he said slowly. "She was building a network. Using the adoption process to position pieces for something bigger."

They worked late into the night, cross-referencing Liz's meticulous records with Drake's investigative findings. The picture that emerged was both fascinating and disturbing - a web of connections that stretched from Abby's earliest days through to her current position, all orchestrated with a precision that seemed almost impossible. Yet as she felt her daughter move within her, Abby found herself drawing strength from her mother's words about love being the strongest pattern. Whatever Amanda had planned, whatever web she had woven, she hadn't accounted for the power of real family bonds, of choices made from love rather than calculation. As she finally headed to bed, leaving Drake still piecing together the timeline of Wellington's involvement, Abby made a silent promise to both her mother and her unborn child. She would use these revelations not to fulfill whatever role Amanda had designed for her, but to protect the future - a future where patterns could be understood without being exploited, where strategic thinking could serve justice rather than manipulation, and where love remained the strongest force in shaping a life's direction.

ABBY

26 STRATEGIC ANALYSIS AFTER DARK

July 2015

Abby sat in the familiar comfort of Dr. Chen's office, her hand resting gently on the slight swell of her belly. She was four months pregnant now, the summer heat making her newly fitted maternity clothes feel particularly restrictive. Outside, cicadas hummed their relentless summer chorus, creating a natural white noise beyond the office windows. "Abby," Dr. Chen said softly, her face warm and welcoming, "it's wonderful to see you again, and I'm so happy for you and Drake. Congratulations on your pregnancy." Abby smiled, her hand rubbing small circles on her stomach. "Thank you, Dr. Chen. I know it's been a while since our last session, but I'm ready to dive back in, to keep exploring my memories and my past."

The soft glow of Abby's laptop screen illuminated the bedroom as she cross-referenced the documents from her mother's filing cabinet against Drake's latest findings. Her husband sat propped against the headboard beside her, his own tablet displaying Wellington's newly uncovered financial records from the period surrounding her adoption.

"Look at this," Drake said softly, angling his screen toward her. "Three days before the Thompsen Industries security patent was filed, Wellington made a series of transfers to offshore accounts. The amounts match the pattern we found in the adoption agency's records."

Abby nodded, her hand absently resting on her growing belly as she traced the connections. "And the geometric progression in the numbers - it's the same one that appears in Amanda's early bank jobs. The ones that were never solved."

Drake set his tablet aside, turning to study his wife's face in the dim light. "Today with your mom - you found something else, didn't you? Something beyond the lawyer's cufflinks."

"She kept everything, Drake." Abby closed her laptop, but the patterns she'd discovered continued to dance behind her eyes. "Every document, every business card, every seemingly random interaction during the adoption process. When you map it all against the Thompsen Industries expansion timeline..."

"It shows premeditation," Drake finished. "Long-term strategic positioning."

"Not just positioning." Abby shifted to face him fully. "Programming. The advanced math programs in my school district, the specific teachers I was assigned to, even the extracurricular activities that were 'suggested' by the guidance counselor - they all traced back to connections with either Thompsen Industries or Wellington's sphere of influence."

Drake was quiet for a moment, his investigator's mind working through the implications. "She wasn't just placing you with a family that would nurture your abilities," he said slowly. "She was creating an entire ecosystem to shape how you'd use them."

"For what though?" Abby felt the baby move and pressed her hand more firmly against her belly, as if trying to protect her daughter from the weight of these revelations. "What's the endgame here, Drake? Because every pattern we uncover suggests this goes beyond simple manipulation or control."

Drake reached out, covering her hand with his own where it rested on her stomach. "Maybe that's what scares me most," he admitted. "The level of calculation involved, the decades of careful maneuvering. And now, with the baby coming..."

"You think she has plans for her too." It wasn't a question. They'd both seen how Amanda's eyes had changed during their last visit at Taycheedah, that flash of strategic assessment when she'd learned of the pregnancy.

"I think we need to be very careful," Drake said, choosing his words with precision. "The patterns you and your mom uncovered today - they show Amanda thinking in generational terms. Planning moves that wouldn't play out for decades."

Abby leaned into his shoulder, drawing strength from his solid presence while her mind continued to process. "Dr. Chen says that's part of why the memories are surfacing now. The pregnancy isn't just triggering maternal instincts; it's making me see patterns I might have missed before. Understanding Amanda's strategies from a mother's perspective."

"And from that perspective?"

"I see how she used love - real love - as part of her calculation." Abby's voice caught slightly. "She chose Liz and Dad precisely because they would love me unconditionally, would nurture not just my abilities but my moral compass. It's like she wanted to ensure I'd use these gifts for good, even as she was positioning me for... whatever this is."

Drake pulled her closer, his investigator's instincts never dulling his capacity for emotional support. "That tracks with what we found in Wellington's records. The way he positioned certain opportunities, always just slightly offset from any direct connection to the original security breaches."

"Creating a path for me to discover the truth," Abby murmured. "But discover it as someone shaped by love and ethics rather than pure strategy." She felt another flutter of movement from the baby. "The question is, what do we do with these revelations? How do we protect our daughter while still unraveling whatever game Amanda's playing?"

Drake was quiet for a long moment, his hand still joined with hers over their growing child. "We use what we know," he said finally. "The patterns you've uncovered, the strategies you've identified -

we turn them to our advantage. We stay ahead of her manipulations by understanding how she thinks, how she plans."

"While making sure our daughter has what I had," Abby added softly. "A foundation of real love, of ethical certainty strong enough to withstand any strategic positioning."

"Exactly." Drake shifted to face her fully. "And we keep building the case, following the threads between Thompsen Industries, Wellington, and these early security system installations. Because understanding Amanda's long game isn't just about protecting our family anymore - it's about finally uncovering the truth behind decades of corporate manipulation."

Abby nodded, her analytical mind already mapping next steps even as exhaustion began to creep in. "We'll need to dig deeper into those offshore accounts, trace the geometric progressions in Wellington's transfers. And I want to review my old school records, look for any other 'suggested' activities that might connect to Thompsen Industries' development timeline."

"Tomorrow," Drake said firmly, gently closing her laptop and setting it aside. "Tonight, we rest. We process. We remember that while Amanda may have orchestrated certain aspects of your life, she couldn't control the most important outcome."

"What's that?"

"That you became someone who uses pattern recognition for justice rather than manipulation. Someone who sees connections as a way to protect rather than exploit." His hand tightened over hers. "Someone who will teach our daughter to do the same."

As they settled into sleep, Abby's mind continued to work, fitting new pieces into the complex puzzle of her past. But Drake's steady presence and their shared determination to protect their child's future provided an anchor against the dizzying depth of Amanda's strategies.

The patterns were there, intricate and far-reaching. But they were no longer just Amanda's to manipulate. With every revelation, every connection uncovered, Abby and Drake were building their own strategy - one founded on love, justice, and the unshakeable bond between them.

Their daughter would inherit these gifts of pattern recognition and strategic thinking. But she would inherit something else too: the strength to use them for good, guided by parents who understood both the power and the responsibility of seeing such patterns clearly.

As Abby drifted on the edge of sleep, a new pattern emerged in her thoughts - something about the timing of Wellington's family leave and the geometric progression in those offshore transfers. She sat up suddenly, reaching for her laptop.

"What is it?" Drake asked, instantly alert despite his fatigue.

"The progression wasn't just in the numbers," Abby said, her fingers flying across the keyboard. "It was in the timing too. Look at this - Wellington's leave coincided perfectly with three major security system upgrades, but there's another pattern hidden in the dates."

Drake leaned over, fully awake now. "The Fibonacci sequence?"

"Not exactly, but similar. It's a variant, one I've seen before." Abby pulled up another document. "Here - in Amanda's earliest known jobs. The time intervals between security breaches followed the same progression. But in Wellington's case, he was installing the upgrades that would supposedly prevent such breaches."

Drake's investigator instincts kicked into high gear. "Unless he wasn't preventing them at all. What if he was creating deliberate vulnerabilities, ones that could only be exploited by someone who understood this specific pattern?"

"Someone like Amanda," Abby whispered. "Or someone she trained to recognize these patterns from childhood." Her hand went to her belly again, a protective gesture that had become instinctive. "Someone like me."

Drake covered her hand with his own. "But you chose a different path. You use these patterns to protect, to prevent exploitation."

"Because of Liz and Dad," Abby said softly. "Because they gave me something Amanda might not have anticipated in all her calculations - a moral framework strong enough to withstand strategic manipulation." She paused, a new thought forming. "What if that was part of her plan too? What if she chose them not just for their ability to nurture my skills, but for their strong ethical foundation?"

Drake considered this, his analytical mind engaging with the psychological implications. "A failsafe," he suggested. "Ensuring that even if her larger strategy succeeded, the power would be in the hands of someone with a strong moral compass."

"It fits the pattern," Abby acknowledged, pulling up her notes from recent therapy sessions. "Dr. Chen and I have been exploring this idea that Amanda's strategic thinking operates on multiple levels. The surface level appears manipulative, self-serving, but underneath..."

"There's a longer game," Drake finished. "One that might actually serve justice, if played out through someone who would use these abilities ethically."

Abby nodded, feeling another flutter of movement from the baby. "Which brings us back to our daughter. If these abilities are inherited, if she has the same capacity for pattern recognition..."

"Then we make sure she has what you had," Drake said firmly. "A strong ethical foundation, unconditional love, and the freedom to choose her own path." He paused, considering. "But we also teach her to recognize manipulation, to understand these patterns for what they are."

"Balance," Abby murmured. "Just like Liz was talking about today. Teaching her to use her gifts without being used by them." She looked down at her laptop screen, where the geometric progression glowed like a roadmap to understanding. "We need to document all of this. Not just the evidence we're gathering about Thompsen Industries and Wellington, but the patterns themselves. The way Amanda thinks, the layers of strategy in her planning."

Drake reached for his own notebook, where he'd been tracking their investigation. "We create a guide," he suggested. "Something that can help our daughter understand her inheritance - both the abilities and the ethical framework to use them responsibly."

"A legacy of truth rather than manipulation," Abby agreed. She began typing, organizing their discoveries into a coherent narrative. "We start with the basic patterns - the geometric progressions, the timing sequences. Then we layer in the psychological elements, the way Amanda uses these patterns to create long-term strategies."

"And we include the counterbalance," Drake added. "The ways love and ethics can guide the use of these abilities. The importance of choosing justice over advantage, protection over exploitation."

They worked together in the quiet darkness, documenting patterns and principles, creating a guidebook for their daughter's future. It wasn't just about protecting her from Amanda's manipulation anymore - it was about empowering her to understand and use her inherited gifts wisely.

"There's something beautiful about it," Abby said finally, saving their work. "The way these patterns flow through generations, evolving from tools of manipulation into instruments of justice. It's like watching the progression itself transform into something more ethical, more purposeful."

Drake wrapped his arm around her shoulders, drawing her close. "That's your influence," he said softly. "You're the inflection point where the pattern changes direction. And our daughter will benefit from that transformation."

As they settled back into bed, Abby felt a deep sense of purpose settling over her. The weight of Amanda's long-term strategies remained, but it felt less threatening now, more like a complex inheritance that could be understood and redirected rather than a trap to be feared.

"Tomorrow," she murmured, sleep finally beginning to claim her, "we need to look deeper into those security system specifications. The geometric progression might appear in the actual code, not just the timing of the installations."

"Tomorrow," Drake agreed, his voice already heavy with sleep. "For now, rest. Our daughter needs her mother's strength for all the pattern recognition ahead."

Abby smiled in the darkness, feeling the baby move one more time before stillness settled over them. In her mind, patterns continued to shift and align, but they were no longer just Amanda's strategic web. They were becoming something new - a bridge between generations, a tool for understanding and protecting rather than manipulating and controlling.

As she drifted off, Abby held onto that transformation, that promise of turning inherited abilities into forces for good. Their daughter would face her own challenges, her own patterns to decode, but she would do so armed with truth, love, and the wisdom of those who had navigated these waters before her.

In the moments before sleep fully claimed her, Abby's mind made one final connection - something about the layout of her old elementary school, the way certain classrooms had been arranged in a pattern that mirrored early Thompsen Industries' security configurations. She forced her eyes open long enough to make a note on her phone: "Check school blueprints against TI security grid - possible spatial correlation?" The revelation could wait until morning, but she knew from experience how such insights could slip away in the night, like patterns in snow melting under the morning sun.

Drake's steady breathing beside her provided a rhythm to anchor her racing thoughts. She thought about how their investigation had evolved, from trying to understand Amanda's past crimes to uncovering a decades-long strategy that encompassed architecture, education, corporate expansion, and now, potentially, genetic inheritance. The scope was dizzying, yet somehow the pattern felt more coherent with each new piece they uncovered. Like a fractal design, each small detail reflected the larger structure, creating a map of intention that stretched across time and generations. Their daughter moved again, as if responding to her mother's active mind, and Abby wondered if the pattern recognition ability was already active in her developing brain, already beginning to make sense of the rhythms and sequences of the world around her.

Finally, as exhaustion overcame her analytical drive, Abby let herself sink into sleep, one hand still resting protectively over her belly, the other intertwined with Drake's. Tomorrow would bring new revelations, new patterns to decode, new strategies to understand. But for now, she could rest in the knowledge that they were building something powerful: a framework of understanding that would help their daughter navigate the complex legacy she would inherit. Not just the ability to see patterns, but the wisdom to use that gift for justice, the strength to resist manipulation, and the love that would always guide her toward truth. As consciousness faded, Abby's last thought was of three generations of women - Amanda, herself, and her unborn daughter - each connected by an extraordinary ability, but each choosing their own path in how to use it.

27 SHADOWS OF ICE

Amanda sat in her room at the Johnson house, methodically reviewing her journals. Her hand trembled slightly as she wrote - a weakness she'd been carefully concealing from the family. The facade of the doting grandmother had served her well, but ICE knew time was growing short.

Through her window, she could see Mandy playing in the backyard, the girl's movements displaying an unconscious grace that reminded Amanda of herself at that age. The child had inherited more than just her looks - there was a sharpness in those eyes, a calculating intelligence that thrilled and concerned ICE in equal measure.

"Grandma!" Mandy's voice carried through the window. "Come watch me on the monkey bars!"

Amanda smiled, the expression genuine despite herself. She'd grown to care for the child more than she'd intended - a weakness ICE hadn't anticipated. Still, it could serve her purposes.

As she made her way downstairs, fighting to keep her steps steady despite the growing pain in her chest, Amanda reflected on her position within the family. Abby and Drake trusted her completely now, their initial suspicions long buried under years of carefully orchestrated devotion. Even Liz had warmed to her, though Amanda noticed the occasional sharp glance when she thought no one was looking.

In the backyard, Mandy demonstrated her latest feat of acrobatics. Amanda watched closely, noting how the girl assessed each move before attempting it, planning her path with instinctive strategy.

"Very good," Amanda praised, her voice warm but her eyes calculating. "You know, success is all about understanding patterns, seeing the connections others miss."

Mandy dropped from the bars, landing with perfect balance. "Like you taught me with chess?"

"Exactly." Amanda settled onto the garden bench, gesturing for Mandy to join her. The pain in her chest flared, but she kept her expression serene. "Life is like chess - every move matters, every piece has its purpose."

As they sat together in the late afternoon sun, Amanda began another careful lesson in strategy, wrapped in the guise of grandmotherly wisdom. She'd been planting these seeds for years, preparing the ground for what was to come.

That evening, as the family gathered for dinner, Amanda felt the familiar pressure building in her chest. She'd known about the condition for months but had chosen to keep it private. ICE didn't believe in showing weakness, and besides, this too could be turned to advantage.

"Are you feeling alright, Mom?" Abby asked, noticing Amanda's pallor. "You seem tired lately."

"Just age catching up with me," Amanda deflected smoothly. But she caught Mandy watching her intently, those sharp eyes missing nothing. The girl was nearly ready, Amanda realized. Soon, it would be time for the final lessons, the truths that would ensure ICE's legacy lived on.

Later, alone in her room, Amanda recorded her observations in a special journal - one meant for Mandy's eyes only, when the time was right. Her hand shook more pronouncedly now, but she forced herself to write clearly:

"My darling granddaughter, you who see so much more than they think. There are truths you'll need to know, patterns you'll need to understand. ICE is more than just a person - it's a way of seeing the world, of moving through it unseen until the moment of strike..."

She closed the journal carefully, hiding it in its usual spot. The chest pain was worse tonight, but it didn't matter. Everything was proceeding according to plan, even this final weakness would serve her purpose. ICE's legacy would survive, transformed but undiminished, in the sharp eyes and calculating mind of a child who understood patterns all too well.

In the darkness, Amanda smiled. Some fires, after all, burned coldest just before they spread.

28 Echoes of Doubt

The afternoon light filtering through Dr. Chen's office windows cast long shadows across the floor, mirroring the dark thoughts weighing on Abby's mind. She settled into the familiar leather chair, noting how the usually comforting scent of lavender seemed oddly cloying today.

Dr. Chen studied her long-time patient with careful consideration. "You seem troubled, Abby. More so than usual."

"Amanda wants to move in with us," Abby said without preamble, her fingers twisting in her lap. "She says she's changed, that she wants to be part of our lives. But..." She trailed off, the words catching in her throat.

"But you're remembering the patterns," Dr. Chen finished gently. "The manipulation, the calculated moves."

"Yes." Abby stood abruptly, moving to the window. Outside, life continued its normal rhythm - people walking, cars passing, all unaware of the storm raging within these walls. "Drake thinks I'm being too suspicious. He says everyone deserves a second chance. Even Liz seems to be warming to the idea."

"And what does your instinct tell you?" Dr. Chen's voice remained neutral, but her pen moved across her notepad with deliberate strokes.

Abby pressed her forehead against the cool glass. "That's just it - I don't trust my instincts anymore. Every time I think I understand Amanda, every time I start to believe in her change..." She turned back to face Dr. Chen. "Did I tell you about the look I caught in her eyes last week? Just for a moment, when she thought no one was watching. It was like seeing a mask slip."

Dr. Chen set her notepad aside, leaning forward. "Abby, you've made tremendous progress in understanding your relationship with Amanda. But progress doesn't mean you have to ignore your protective instincts."

"But what if those instincts are just fear? What if I'm letting past trauma cloud my judgment?" Abby returned to her seat, feeling the weight of responsibility pressing down on her. "We have a good life, Dr. Chen. Drake, our home, my career - everything's finally in balance. Having Amanda move in would change all of that."

"Change isn't inherently negative," Dr. Chen observed. "But it does require careful consideration, especially when it involves someone with Amanda's history."

Abby nodded, remembering countless therapy sessions dissecting that history. "She's different now, supposedly. The prison counselors say she's made real progress. But sometimes..." She hesitated, voicing a fear she'd barely admitted to herself. "Sometimes I wonder if she's just gotten better at hiding who she really is."

"That's a valid concern," Dr. Chen acknowledged. "Perhaps we should explore what concrete boundaries would need to be in place if Amanda were to move in. What safeguards would help you feel secure?"

As they discussed practical considerations - separate living spaces, clear expectations, exit strategies - Abby felt some of her anxiety begin to ease. Yet beneath the rational planning, a nagging doubt persisted.

"There's something else," she admitted finally. "Something I haven't told anyone, not even Drake." She took a deep breath, forcing herself to maintain eye contact with Dr. Chen. "Last month, I found some old case files at the firm. They mentioned Amanda - her early cases, before... everything. The patterns I saw there, the way she operated..." Abby's voice dropped to barely above a whisper. "They're the same patterns I'm seeing now."

Dr. Chen's expression remained carefully neutral, but her pen stilled on the page. "Have you verified these files?"

"They disappeared before I could dig deeper. When I asked about them, no one seemed to know what I was talking about." Abby laughed humorlessly. "I'm probably being paranoid."

"Or perhaps you're recognizing something others have missed," Dr. Chen suggested quietly. "Your intuition has been honed by experience, Abby. Don't dismiss it too quickly."

As their session drew to a close, Abby felt both clearer and more troubled. The practical strategies they'd discussed provided a framework for moving forward, but the deeper questions remained unanswered.

"Same time next week?" Dr. Chen asked, walking her to the door.

Abby nodded, gathering her coat. "Thank you. For everything."

In the elevator, Abby checked her phone. Three missed calls from Amanda via CenturyLink. As she stared at the notification, she remembered something Dr. Chen had said in an earlier session: "Sometimes the most dangerous patterns are the ones that feel most familiar."

The elevator doors opened, and Abby stepped out into the gathering dusk, her mind already turning over plans within plans. If Amanda was playing a long game, perhaps it was time to start one of her own.

29 FROST AND FIRE

The concrete walls of Amanda's cell seemed to close in as she processed the implications of Abby's pregnancy announcement. A grandchild. The word felt foreign, dangerous - a complication she hadn't anticipated in her carefully constructed plans. She moved to the window, watching shadows lengthen across the prison yard as the day's light faded.

The initial surge of genuine emotion that had coursed through her during Abby's visit disturbed ICE more than she cared to admit. For a brief moment, she had felt real joy, true maternal pride - feelings that threatened the careful walls she'd built around her heart. Such weakness couldn't be tolerated, not when she was so close to achieving her goals.

"Congratulations, Cole," Officer Martinez called during evening rounds. "Heard you're going to be a grandmother."

ICE's response was perfectly calibrated - a tremulous smile, eyes bright with seemingly genuine tears. "Yes, isn't it wonderful?" The performance earned her a sympathetic nod as the guard moved on. Alone again, the mask slipped away, replaced by cold calculation.

She pulled out her notebook, the pages filled with meticulous observations of Abby's visits, every reaction catalogued, every weakness noted. This pregnancy changed the dynamics significantly. Abby would be more protective now, more cautious about potential threats to her growing family. But she would also be more vulnerable, her emotions heightened, her natural instincts to nurture and connect amplified.

ICE began to write, her pen scratching against paper with predatory precision. She would need to adjust her approach, recalibrate her manipulation to account for Abby's maternal instincts. Perhaps even use them to her advantage. After all, what expectant mother wouldn't want her child to know their grandmother?

"Family is everything," she whispered, practicing the line that would become her new mantra. The words tasted bitter, but she knew they would resonate with Abby's desperate desire for connection, for wholeness.

A memory surfaced unbidden - Abby as an infant, tiny fingers gripping Amanda's hand before they took her away. ICE ruthlessly suppressed the image. Sentiment was a luxury she couldn't afford, not with freedom so tantalizingly close.

She reviewed her legal files, notes accumulated over years of studying case law from the prison library. There were precedents for early release based on family circumstances, particularly when strong support systems could be demonstrated. Abby's position as a respected attorney, her stable home life, the impending arrival of a grandchild - all could be leveraged in the right appeal.

"Playing the long game has served me well," ICE mused, adding another note to her growing strategy. She would need to be patient, to let Abby's pregnancy progress while slowly planting seeds of doubt about the original conviction. A carefully timed revelation here, a seemingly accidental discovery there - breadcrumbs leading her daughter down the path ICE had chosen.

The night deepened around her cell, but ICE continued planning. She mapped out contingencies, anticipated obstacles, calculated risks. The pregnancy had thrown her original timeline into disarray, but perhaps that was for the best. A more subtle approach might prove more effective in the end.

As lights-out approached, ICE carefully stored her notes in their hiding place. Tomorrow, she would begin implementing her revised strategy. More demonstrations of maternal concern, more subtle hints about past injustices, more carefully crafted moments of vulnerability - all designed to draw Abby closer, to cement her role in her daughter's expanding family.

"Sleep well, little one," she whispered into the darkness, the words carrying a double meaning - both for her unborn grandchild and for the last remnants of Amanda's maternal heart, which ICE was determined to freeze solid once and for all.

The night watch passed her cell, flashlight beam briefly

illuminating her face. ICE presented the perfect picture of a grandmother-to-be, peaceful in sleep. But behind her closed eyes, calculations continued, plans within plans spinning out like frost patterns on glass. She would have her freedom, no matter the cost. And if that meant exploiting her own daughter's deepest desires for family and connection, then so be it.

After all, ICE had learned long ago that love was just another tool in her arsenal, another weapon to wield in her endless quest for control. And now, with a grandchild on the way, she had been handed the perfect instrument for her most ambitious manipulation yet.

30 "FAMILY PHOTO"

Drake stood frozen in Abby's office, staring at the yellowed newspaper clipping she'd handed him. His fingers traced the edge of the photo, lingering on his father's familiar smile. But it was the woman beside him that made his chest tighten – Amanda Cole. No, he corrected himself, Amanda Johnson. His aunt.

"I remember this day," he whispered, the words catching in his throat. "I was there, behind the camera. Dad had just gotten the new storefront sign..." His voice trailed off as fragments of memory surfaced like debris after a storm.

Abby touched his arm gently. "You never mentioned your aunt before."

Drake sank into the chair, the photo trembling in his hands. "I didn't... I thought..." He pressed his palm against his forehead. "After Dad died, Mom got rid of everything. Every photo, every reminder. She said it was too painful, but now I wonder if she was trying to erase Amanda too."

Memories began flooding back: summer barbecues with his aunt's laughter ringing across the yard, Christmas mornings where she'd sneak him extra cookies, heated arguments between her and his father that went silent when they noticed him watching.

"The trial," he said suddenly. "I wasn't allowed to attend. Mom said I was too young, but she went every day. When it was over, she told me we didn't have any other family left." His voice hardened. "She lied."

Abby knelt beside him, her legal pad balanced on her knee. "Drake, I have to tell Amanda about our connection. Ethically, I need her informed consent to continue representing her."

Drake looked up sharply. "You're still going to help her? After what she did to Dad?"

"If she wants me to," Abby said softly. "The law recognizes that even people who've done terrible things deserve representation. And Drake... there might be more to the story than we know."

31 THE WEIGHT OF LOVE

July 2015

Liz paced the length of her living room, each step echoing with the weight of maternal concern. The antique clock on the mantel seemed to mock her with its slow progression, marking the minutes until Abby and Drake returned from their prison visit with Amanda. Outside, the late summer heat shimmered above the asphalt, creating mirages that distorted the view.

The sound of a car door finally broke the silence. Liz moved to the window, watching as Abby emerged from the passenger side, one hand protectively cradling her visibly pregnant belly. At twenty-two weeks, there was no hiding the pregnancy anymore – especially from Amanda. Even from this distance, Liz could read the complex emotions playing across her daughter's face - joy warring with uncertainty, hope shadowed by doubt.

"Mom?" Abby's voice carried through the front door before it fully opened. "We're back."

Liz met them in the entryway, her arms automatically opening to enfold her daughter. The embrace felt different now, careful of the precious life growing within. "How did it go, sweetheart?" she asked, studying Abby's face for any signs of distress.

"Amanda was...happy," Abby said, her voice carrying a note of surprise. "Really happy about the baby. She cried, Mom. Actually cried."

Drake hung back slightly, his expression guarded. Liz caught his eye, seeing her own concerns reflected there. They had both witnessed Amanda's performances before, her carefully orchestrated displays of emotion designed to draw Abby closer.

"That's wonderful," Liz managed, guiding them into the living room. The afternoon light painted soft shadows across the family photos lining the walls - twenty-five years of memories, of scraped knees and graduation gowns, of birthday cakes and wedding flowers. Each image a testament to the life they'd built together, the love that had nothing to do with biological connections.

"She talked about wanting to be part of the baby's life," Abby continued, settling onto the couch. "About making up for lost time, about being the grandmother she never had the chance to be with me."

Liz felt her heart constrict. She remembered those early days after adopting Abby, the sleepless nights spent rocking her colicky baby, the first steps, first words, first everything. Where had Amanda been then?

"Abby," she began carefully, choosing her words with practiced precision, "I know you want to believe in Amanda's change. And maybe she has changed. But pregnancy..." She paused, gathering her thoughts. "Pregnancy makes us vulnerable. Our emotions are heightened, our natural instincts to connect and nurture are amplified. I just want you to be careful about the decisions you make during this time."

"Mom-" Abby started, but Liz pressed on.

"Let me finish, please. I'm not trying to come between you and Amanda. I understand that she's part of who you are, part of your story. But my job - my privilege - as your mother is to protect you, even now. Especially now."

Drake moved to sit beside Abby, his hand finding hers. "Your mom's right about being careful," he said softly. "We can maintain contact with Amanda without rushing into anything."

Tears welled in Abby's eyes, spilling over as she looked between her husband and the woman who had raised her. "I feel so torn," she whispered. "When I'm with Amanda, everything she says makes sense. She seems so sincere, so desperate to make amends. But then I come home, and I remember..."

"Remember what, sweetheart?"

"All the times you were there. The nightmares, the skinned knees, the broken hearts. Every moment that made me who I am - you were there for all of it. Amanda... she's trying to claim a role she gave up. And part of me wants to let her, wants to believe she deserves that chance. But another part..."

Liz knelt before her daughter, taking both her hands. "Listen to that other part, Abby. Not out of anger or resentment, but out of wisdom. You're not just protecting yourself anymore. This baby-" she touched Abby's stomach gently "-deserves to be surrounded by love that's proven, love that's weathered storms and stood the test of time."

The room fell silent save for the ticking of the mantel clock and the distant rustle of wind through trees. Finally, Abby spoke, her voice stronger. "I won't cut Amanda out completely. I can't. But I promise to be careful, to put my baby's wellbeing first."

Liz felt tears of pride and relief fill her eyes. This was the daughter she'd raised - compassionate but strong, willing to see the best in others while maintaining healthy boundaries.

"That's all I ask," she said, rising to pull Abby into another embrace. Over her daughter's shoulder, she caught Drake's eye again, seeing the same mixture of love and protective concern she felt in her own heart.

As the afternoon light began to fade, they remained together in the living room, three people bound by choice rather than blood, united in their determination to protect the new life that would soon join their family. Outside, the wind continued to blow, carrying with it the promise of change and the whispered prayers of a mother's endless love.

Liz knew the challenges ahead would test them all. But watching Abby now, seeing the strength and wisdom in her daughter's eyes, she felt a surge of fierce pride. Whatever Amanda's true intentions might be, she had not reckoned with the power of a mother's love - not the biological connection she claimed, but the deep, unshakeable bond forged through years of shared life, of joy and tears, of unwavering presence and unconditional acceptance.

That was the true meaning of motherhood, and Liz would defend it with every breath in her body.

32 THE PATH FORWARD & PLAYING REFORM

The courthouse air felt thick with tension as Amanda stood before Judge Ramírez. Her prison uniform, worn thin at the edges from countless washings, seemed to hang differently on her frame now – less like armor, more like a chrysalis she was ready to shed.

Abby rose from the defense table, her voice steady despite the weight of new knowledge between her and her client. The disclosure of their relationship had led to tears, then to a deeper understanding that somehow strengthened their attorney-client bond rather than severing it.

"Your Honor, Ms. Cole has not only completed every rehabilitation program available at Taycheedah, she has created new ones." Abby gestured to the stack of testimonials on her desk. "The art therapy program she developed has been adopted by three other correctional facilities. Her work with at-risk youth through the prison outreach program has directly impacted over fifty young lives."

ICE maintained perfect stillness as her lawyer presented the documentation - certificates of completion, glowing reports from instructors, carefully crafted letters from fellow inmates she'd helped mentor. Each piece of paper represented months of calculated performance, every positive review earned through precise manipulation of perceptions. From her position in the front row, Abby was watching intently, her face a perfect study of hope and cautious optimism. ICE could read the attorney's training warring with the daughter's desperate desire to believe. Perfect. Everything was unfolding exactly as planned.

"Your Honor," Amanda's lawyer began, "I'd like to present evidence of my client's extraordinary progress. Over the past year, Ms. Cole has not only participated in but excelled at Taycheedah's innovative rehabilitation program."

Judge Ramirez leaned forward, reading glasses perched on the edge of her nose as she studied Amanda's file. "Ms. Cole, you've served twenty-five years of your sentence. In that time, you've shown remarkable transformation. However, I need to be convinced that this change is genuine and sustainable."

Amanda rose deliberately; her hands clasped in a gesture that conveyed humility rather than her usual control. "Your Honor, this program has provided me with more than merely job skills. It has helped me comprehend the consequences of my choices, not just for myself but also for my family." Her voice faltered slightly, a well-timed display of emotion. "My daughter Abby has been immensely supportive of my rehabilitation. With her assistance, I am learning to become not only a better individual but also a better mother."

Amanda stepped forward, her hands tightly clasped. "Your Honor, when I arrived at Taycheedah, I was angry, lost, and convinced that I was a victim of my circumstances. Through therapy and honest self-reflection, I have come to recognize the true impact of my actions—not only on Jasmine's family but also on my own." Her eyes briefly flickered to where Drake sat at the back of the courtroom before returning to the judge. "While I cannot undo what I have done, I am committed to dedicating whatever time I have left to helping others make different choices."

ICE noted how the judge's expression softened at the mention of family reconciliation. Everything was proceeding according to plan. The rehabilitation program had provided exactly the framework she needed to orchestrate this performance.

"Ms. Thompson - Abby," the judge turned to address her daughter, "would you like to speak on your mother's behalf?"

The judge nodded slowly, considering. "Given the comprehensive rehabilitation plan presented by counsel, including secured employment, housing at New Horizons Halfway House, and continued therapy, I am inclined to grant this petition for supervised release..."

Abby stood, and for a moment, ICE felt an unexpected crack in her careful facade. Her daughter looked so professional in her court attire, so much like the powerful woman ICE had calculated she would become.

"Your Honor, I've witnessed my mother's transformation through this program firsthand," Abby said, her voice steady despite the emotion ICE could detect beneath it. "Her commitment to change, her willingness to engage in both job training and family counseling... it's shown me a side of her I never knew existed."

Perfect. ICE had trained her well, even if Abby didn't realize it. Every word reinforced the narrative they'd carefully constructed together - the prodigal mother, the forgiving daughter, the power of rehabilitation to heal broken families.

The judge made her final notes before looking up. "Ms. Cole, your participation in Taycheedah's job training initiative and your efforts at family reconciliation are commendable. I'm approving your transfer to the halfway house program, with continued supervision and mandatory counseling..."

ICE maintained her pose of grateful humility while internally calculating her next moves. The rehabilitation program had served its purpose - providing documented evidence of reform while creating opportunities for deeper manipulation of both system and family.

After the hearing, Abby hugged her mother tightly. "I'm so proud of you, Mom."

Amanda returned the embrace, allowing genuine warmth to color her performance. After all, the best cons were the ones where everyone got what they wanted - even if what they wanted was just a beautiful lie.

As they left the courthouse together, ICE was already documenting the day's success in her mental notebook. The job training program had been the perfect tool, its timing exquisitely suited to her needs. Sometimes the system provided exactly the props required for a flawless performance.

The halfway house waited ahead, another stage for her carefully choreographed transformation. But for now, ICE allowed Amanda to smile, to accept her daughter's joy, to play the role of reformed mother to perfection.

The game was evolving, and so was her performance.

33 A CAREFUL REQUEST

September 2015 The late summer sun cast long shadows across the driveway as Drake helped Abby from the car. At six months pregnant, her movements had begun to slow, her body adjusting to accommodate their growing daughter. The air still held the warmth of summer, though the first few maple leaves had started to turn, hints of gold appearing at the edges of their green canopy.

"Amanda's called three times today," Drake said, his voice carefully neutral as he supported Abby up the front steps. "She wants to help with the nursery this weekend."

Abby paused, one hand pressed against her lower back. "And how do you feel about that?"

Drake was quiet for a moment, the only sound the distant buzz of cicadas clinging to the last days of summer. "I'm trying, Abby. For you. For our daughter." He placed his hand gently on her rounded belly. "But sometimes I wonder if we're being naive. The way she's inserted herself into every aspect of the pregnancy, the nursery plans, the doctor appointments..."

"She's excited about being a grandmother," Abby said, but even to her own ears, the words sounded incomplete. Amanda's enthusiasm had an intensity that occasionally felt calculated rather than genuine.

"Maybe," Drake conceded. "Or maybe she's playing the longest game of all."

The crisp November air carried the scent of fallen leaves as Amanda stepped out of the halfway house, a small bag containing her meager possessions clutched in her hand. After months of careful maneuvering and perfectly timed displays of reformation, she had finally secured approval for transition to less restrictive housing.

Relief flooded her features - a genuine emotion that surprised even her. The halfway house, with its rigid schedules and constant supervision, had begun to feel suffocating. Yet beneath that authentic relief, ICE's calculating mind was already spinning possibilities, mapping out the next phases of her carefully orchestrated plan.

Amanda paced the small confines of her room at the halfway house, rehearsing the conversation to come for the hundredth time. Every word, every gesture had to be perfectly calibrated - vulnerable enough to evoke sympathy, but not so desperate as to raise suspicion. After all, ICE hadn't survived this long by being sloppy.

She glanced at her watch—2:15 PM. Visiting hours had started at 2:00, which meant Abby should be through the visitor check-in process by now. Amanda had specifically requested this meeting during her weekly case management session, careful to frame it as part of her "family reunification goals" that looked so good on progress reports.

The afternoon sun cast long shadows through the barred windows, turning the institutional beige walls into a canvas of light and shadow. The shared bathroom down the hall flushed, followed by the sound of her roommate Sandra returning to their neighboring room before her mandatory job-search workshop at 3:00. Amanda was grateful for the temporary privacy—so hard to come by in a place where personal space was a luxury.

She heard Abby's familiar footsteps approaching down the hallway, accompanied by the distinctive squeak of her professional heels on the worn linoleum. A staff member's voice—probably Ms. Winters—directed her to Room 14. Amanda quickly settled into the room's only chair, deliberately choosing the less comfortable position - a small sacrifice that would subconsciously put her daughter at ease.

"Mom?" Abby's voice carried that mixture of hope and wariness that Amanda had come to expect. Always wanting to believe in her mother's redemption, always afraid of being disappointed again.

Amanda took a deep breath, letting a carefully measured tremor enter her voice. "Abby... thank you for coming. There's something I need to ask you, but I'm afraid..."

She watched her daughter's face soften with concern. Abby moved into the room, perching on the edge of the bed. Perfect - exactly where Amanda had hoped she would sit, close enough for intimacy but far enough to maintain a sense of safety.

"What is it, Mom? You know you can talk to me about anything."

Amanda's hands twisted in her lap, a deliberate show of vulnerability. "I know this is a lot to ask, but... do you think there's any way I could move in with you and Drake? Just for a little while, until I can find a job and get back on my feet?"

She saw the shock register on Abby's face, followed by a rapid succession of emotions - sympathy, uncertainty, fear. Amanda forced herself to remain still, fighting the urge to press her advantage. Let Abby work through it on her own, let her convince herself.

"Mom, I..." Abby's voice trembled slightly. "I don't know. It's not that I don't want to help you, but I have to think about my family too. Drake and I, we've just found our rhythm with the baby, and I'm not sure how he would feel about this."

Amanda nodded, allowing a flicker of disappointment to cross her features. "I understand," she said softly. "I don't want to disrupt your life. I just thought, perhaps being closer to you and the baby, it would help me stay on track. Help us grow stronger, as a family."

She watched the words land, saw them take root in Abby's consciousness. Her daughter had always craved family connection, had always wanted to believe in the possibility of redemption. It was her greatest strength - and her greatest vulnerability.

"It's not just about what Drake and I want," Abby explained, her legal training evident in her careful choice of words. "There are legal issues too. Your living situation, it's part of your parole conditions, right? Any changes would have to be approved by the court, by your parole officer."

Amanda sighed, infusing her voice with just the right mix of resignation and hope. "I know. But is it possible you could check into it? Talk to Drake, talk to my parole officer? See if there's any way we could make it work?"

She could see Abby wrestling with the decision, her natural caution warring with her desire to help. The silence stretched between them, heavy with unspoken hopes and fears.

"I can't make any promises," Abby finally said, her voice hesitant. "But I'll talk to Drake. We'll see what our options are, what the next steps would be. But Mom, you have to understand, if it's not possible, if it's not what's best for everyone involved..."

"I know," Amanda interjected quickly, careful not to appear too eager. "I know, and I'll respect that. I'm not trying to force anything. I just... I just want a chance to be closer to you, to make up for lost time."

Abby reached out, taking Amanda's hand in a gesture of comfort. ICE noted the warmth of her daughter's skin, the slight tremor in her fingers that betrayed her emotional state. So trusting, so desperate to believe.

"We'll find a way," Abby promised. "Perhaps it won't be living together, but we'll find a way to keep growing, to keep healing. As a family."

Amanda nodded, blinking back tears that weren't entirely fabricated. "Thank you," she whispered. "Thank you for not shutting me out, for being willing to try."

As Abby prepared to leave, Amanda stood, opening her arms in invitation. "Before you go, can I... can I have a hug?"

She felt Abby hesitate, surprised by the request. Physical affection had never been part of their relationship, and the novelty of it caused a momentary flash of suspicion in her daughter's eyes. But Abby's innate kindness won out, and she stepped forward into her mother's embrace.

For a moment, it felt genuine. Comforting, even. But then Amanda felt Abby stiffen slightly, perhaps sensing something in the embrace that triggered her instincts. ICE mentally cursed - had she held on too long? Too tight?

A sharp knock at the door disrupted the moment. "Five minutes until the end of visiting hours, ladies," came the voice of Mr. Reyes, one of the stricter staff members.

Abby pulled back, masking her discomfort with a smile that didn't quite reach her eyes. "Mom, regardless of whether we can get you out of here, I want you to know that I'm committed to building our relationship. There's still so much I want to know about you, about us."

Amanda's brow furrowed slightly as she worked to interpret Abby's tone. "Us?" she repeated, keeping her voice light, casual. "Of course, sweetie. We can discuss anything you like."

The endearment felt wrong even as she said it, and she saw Abby notice the slight grimace that crossed her face. Sloppy, ICE chided herself. Too much, too fast.

Later, after the mandatory 6 PM house meeting where she'd sat through announcements about job fair opportunities and the new sign-out procedures, Amanda retreated to her room. She had fifteen minutes before she needed to report to the common area for communal dinner—another requirement that she found both tedious and useful for studying the behaviors of other residents.

She replayed every moment of the conversation with Abby, analyzing each word, each gesture. She had laid the groundwork, planted the seeds of her request in fertile soil. Now she just had to wait, to let Abby's natural inclination toward family connection work in her favor.

But something nagged at her. That moment during the hug, that flash of awareness in Abby's eyes... Her daughter was more perceptive than she'd anticipated. She would need to be more careful, more precise in her manipulations.

The intercom crackled to life: "All residents to the dining hall. Dinner service begins in five minutes."

Amanda sighed and tucked her journal—the one they'd encouraged her to keep as part of her "emotional processing"—under her thin mattress. Her roommate Sandra was already gone, probably eager to get first choice of the mediocre dinner options. Amanda took a moment to make her bed, smoothing the government-issue blanket with precision. The staff conducted random room inspections, and she'd always ensured hers was immaculate—another small way to build her reputation as a model resident.

As she walked down the corridor, she nodded politely to Mrs. Peterson, the night supervisor who was just beginning her shift. The older woman smiled back warmly. "How was your visit today, Amanda? Family doing well?"

"Very well, thank you for asking," Amanda replied, the perfect mix of gratitude and humility in her voice. "My daughter is such a blessing."

Mrs. Peterson patted her arm. "That's wonderful. Family support makes all the difference in success rates, you know."

"I'm counting on it," Amanda said with a smile that didn't quite reach her eyes.

After dinner came the evening chore rotation. Amanda had strategically volunteered for kitchen cleanup months ago—it was one of the less desirable duties, which made her seem selfless, but it also gave her access to potential resources: people's food preferences, kitchen tools, and most importantly, conversations. People talked freely while doing dishes, revealing weaknesses and connections that might prove useful.

As night fell over the halfway house, Amanda finally returned to her room for the last hour before the 10 PM curfew check. She stood at her window, watching the shadows lengthen across the exercise yard, where a few residents were getting in their last cigarettes of the day before being locked in for the night.

Soon, she told herself. Soon she would be free of this place, installed in the heart of her daughter's home, perfectly positioned to execute the next phase of her plan.

But as she turned away from the window, a small voice in the back of her mind whispered a warning. Was she underestimating Abby? Had years of legal training and therapy made her daughter more adept at spotting manipulation? Only time would tell.

For now, ICE would wait, would watch, would plan. After all, patience had always been her greatest weapon.

The quiet of evening settled over the halfway house, broken only by the distant sound of a guard's radio crackling. The 10 PM room check completed, Amanda sat on her narrow bed, forced to keep her light on until Sandra finished her shower—one of the few privileges of "Phase 2" status that they'd both earned through good behavior and program compliance.

Her mind raced through contingency plans. She had learned long ago that success required anticipating every possibility, preparing for every potential obstacle. And right now, the biggest variable in her equation was Drake.

She had watched her son-in-law carefully over the months, noting his protective instincts toward Abby, the way his shoulders tensed slightly whenever Amanda's past was mentioned. He would be the hardest to convince, the most resistant to having her in their home. But everyone had pressure points, vulnerabilities that could be exploited. For Drake, it was his deep love for Abby and his desire to support her healing journey. That would be the key - making him believe that having Amanda closer would help Abby process her trauma, strengthen their family bonds.

She'd need to bring it up with her case manager, Mrs. Donovan, during their weekly meeting tomorrow. Frame it as part of her reintegration plan, emphasize how living with family would provide stability, structure, accountability. And of course, she'd need to address how she'd continue to meet the conditions of her parole—regular check-ins, drug testing, employment efforts. Perhaps she could suggest some compromises: ongoing residency requirements but with approved overnight stays as a stepping stone. Amanda knew the system well enough to work within it.

The sound of footsteps in the corridor drew Amanda from her thoughts. The night guard, Marcus, was making his final rounds before lights-out at 11. She had made a point of being a model resident, earning the trust and goodwill of the staff. It was amazing how far a few kind words and a consistently pleasant demeanor could go toward making people lower their guards. Even now, she could hear Marcus pause briefly outside her door - he often stopped to check on her, worried about the "poor grandmother" trying to reconnect with her family.

"Everything okay in there, ladies?" he called through the door.

"All good, Marcus," Sandra replied, returning from her shower in a cloud of cheap drugstore body spray.

"Sleep well, then. Remember, AA group meets at 9 AM sharp for those on the sign-up sheet."

"I'll be there," Amanda called, the perfect amount of determination in her voice. She had never touched alcohol in her life, but the AA meetings were an excellent source of information and building rapport.

Amanda allowed herself a small smile in the darkness after lights-out. People were so eager to believe in redemption stories, in the power of love to change even the hardest hearts. They wanted to think that time and regret could sand down the sharp edges of a person, transform a predator into a grandmother. What they failed to understand was that some people didn't change - they simply got better at hiding their true nature.

Still, as she lay back on her thin mattress, listening to Sandra's soft snoring from across the room, Amanda felt an unexpected twinge of... something. Not quite guilt - ICE had frozen that emotion out of her system long ago. But perhaps a kind of wistfulness, a faint echo of what might have been if things had been different. She thought of Abby's face when she'd pulled away from their hug, that moment of instinctive wariness. Her daughter had grown into a perceptive woman, sharp enough to sense the currents moving beneath the surface. In another life, under different circumstances, Amanda might have felt proud of that.

But such thoughts were dangerous, a weakness she couldn't afford. ICE had survived this long by maintaining absolute control, by never letting sentiment cloud her judgment. As she drifted toward sleep, Amanda pushed away the whispers of what-ifs and might-have-beens. Tomorrow would bring new challenges, new opportunities to advance her plans: another house meeting to sit through, her weekly case management session, two hours of mandatory employment counseling, and the tedium of communal living to navigate.

And she would face them as she always had - with calculation, precision, and the ice-cold clarity that had become her trademark. After all, she hadn't chosen her nickname by accident. In this world, only the coldest hearts survived intact.

34 ABBY'S NEW BABY

December 2015

The hospital room was bathed in the soft glow of afternoon sunlight filtering through half-drawn blinds. Abby lay propped against starched white pillows, her face glowing with exhaustion and joy as she cradled her newborn daughter. Despite her fatigue, she couldn't take her eyes off the tiny, perfect features of Amanda Abigail Thompson, born just hours earlier at 9 pounds, 13 ounces.

Drake stood beside the bed, one hand resting protectively on Abby's shoulder while the other gently stroked his daughter's downy head. The wonder in his eyes matched Abby's as they both marveled at the miracle they had created.

"She's perfect," Drake whispered, his voice thick with emotion. His fingers trembled slightly as they traced the delicate curve of the baby's cheek. "Just like her mother."

Abby looked up at him, tears of happiness shimmering in her

eyes. After everything they'd been through - the complications of their family history, the careful dance of integrating Amanda into their lives - this moment felt like a fresh start, a new chapter filled with possibility.

"I can't believe she's really here," Abby murmured, adjusting the soft blanket around her daughter's shoulders. "After all the waiting, all the preparation... she's finally in our arms."

The baby stirred slightly, her tiny rosebud mouth forming a perfect 'O' as she yawned. Her eyes, that deep newborn blue that held all the mysteries of new life, fluttered open briefly before closing again in contentment.

"She has your nose," Drake observed, perching carefully on the edge of the bed. "But I think I see some of my mother in her chin." He paused, then added softly, "And maybe a bit of Amanda in her eyes."

The mention of Amanda brought a complex wave of emotions to Abby's face. Her birth mother had been a constant presence throughout the pregnancy, offering support and guidance while carefully maintaining the boundaries they'd established. It had been a delicate balance, but one that seemed to be working.

"Speaking of Amanda," Abby said, glancing at the clock on the wall, "she should be here soon. The nurses said they'd let her up as soon as visiting hours started."

Drake nodded, his expression thoughtful. He had watched his

wife navigate the complicated waters of her relationship with Amanda over the past months, proud of how she'd maintained both compassion and caution. "How are you feeling about that? About her meeting the baby?"

Abby considered the question carefully, her fingers absently stroking her daughter's tiny hand. "Honestly? I'm nervous. But also hopeful. She's been so different lately - more open, more genuine. Maybe becoming a grandmother will help continue that growth."

Just then, a soft knock at the door drew their attention. Amanda stood in the doorway, her face a mixture of anticipation and uncertainty. She held a small wrapped package in her hands, twisting the ribbon nervously.

"Is this a good time?" she asked, her voice uncharacteristically hesitant. "I can come back later if you need more rest."

"No, please come in," Abby smiled, gesturing her mother forward. "There's someone very special we'd like you to meet."

Amanda approached the bed slowly, her eyes fixed on the tiny bundle in Abby's arms. As she drew closer, her carefully maintained composure began to crack. Tears welled in her eyes as she got her first glimpse of her granddaughter.

"Oh, Abby," she breathed, one hand rising to cover her mouth. "She's beautiful. Absolutely beautiful."

Drake pulled a chair close to the bed, positioning it perfectly for Amanda to sit and get a better view. It was a small gesture, but one that spoke volumes about how far they'd all come in their complicated family dynamic.

As Amanda settled into the chair, Abby carefully shifted the baby, preparing to pass her to her grandmother. "Would you like to hold her?"

Amanda's hands trembled as she reached out, accepting the precious bundle with infinite care. "Hello, little one," she whispered, her voice catching. "I'm your grandma. I've been waiting so long to meet you."

The room fell silent save for the soft sounds of the newborn's breathing and the distant bustle of hospital activity. In that moment, watching her mother cradle her daughter, Abby felt a sense of completion she hadn't known she was missing.

The baby stirred in Amanda's arms, one tiny fist escaping the blanket to wave in the air. Amanda caught the small hand gently between her fingers, marveling at the perfection of each miniature nail.

"She has your chin," Amanda said softly, looking up at Abby. "And that determined little crease between her eyebrows - that's all you. I remember seeing that same expression on your face when you were just hours old."

The words hung in the air, heavy with meaning. It was the first time Amanda had ever spoken of Abby's birth, of those precious few days before the adoption. Abby felt Drake's hand tighten slightly on her shoulder, offering silent support.

"Did you..." Abby hesitated, then pressed on. "Did you hold me like this? When I was born?"

Amanda's eyes clouded with memory, her fingers still gentle on the baby's hand. "Yes," she whispered. "For three days, I held you just like this. I memorized every detail of your face, knowing I wouldn't..." She stopped, swallowing hard. "Knowing our time was limited."

The baby chose that moment to let out a small cry, breaking the tension in the room. Amanda immediately began to rock gently, humming a soft melody that seemed to emerge from some deep, forgotten place.

"You are my sunshine," she sang quietly, "my only sunshine..."

Abby's breath caught in her throat. The lullaby - the one that had haunted her dreams, that had surfaced during hypnotherapy with Dr. Chen. Here was proof that those memories were real, that some part of her had held onto those first precious days of life.

Drake moved closer, wrapping an arm around his wife as they watched Amanda soothe their daughter. The scene felt surreal - ICE, the woman whose cold calculation had caused so much pain, now melting in the presence of this innocent new life.

"What do you think, Mom?" Abby asked softly. "About her name? About us calling her Amanda?"

Amanda looked up, surprise and something deeper flickering across her face. "You're really naming her after me?"

"After both of you," Drake said, his voice gentle but firm. "Amanda Abigail Thompson. A name that honors the past while looking toward the future."

Fresh tears spilled down Amanda's cheeks as she looked back at her namesake. "Thank you," she whispered. "For giving me this chance. For letting me be part of her life. I promise you both, I'll spend every day trying to be worthy of this trust."

As if in response, baby Amanda's eyes fluttered open, fixing on her grandmother's face with that unfocused newborn gaze. Amanda gasped softly at the connection, at the weight of possibility contained in that innocent look.

The moment was interrupted by a nurse entering to check Abby's vitals. Amanda carefully returned the baby to her mother's arms, her movements betraying a reluctance to let go.

"I should let you rest," she said, rising from the chair. "But may I... may I come back tomorrow?"

"Of course," Abby smiled. "You're family, Mom. This little one is going to need her grandmother."

As Amanda left the room, pausing for one last look at the peaceful tableau of mother and child, neither Abby nor Drake could know the complex calculations already forming behind her eyes. For even in this moment of genuine emotion, ICE was never fully absent. The baby represented not just a chance at redemption, but an opportunity - one that would require careful planning and infinite patience to realize.

But for now, in the gentle quiet of the hospital room, love held sway over calculation. A new chapter had begun, its pages yet to be written, its story yet to unfold. Baby Amanda slept peacefully in her mother's arms, unaware of the complicated legacy she carried in her very name, or the profound impact her arrival would have on all their lives.

35 FAMILY EVOLUTIONS

Her first days of relative freedom brought a mix of triumph and unexpected challenges. The small apartment she'd been assigned felt simultaneously liberating and confining - more space than her cell, less control than she was used to. Amanda found herself struggling to adapt to the sudden abundance of choices: when to eat, when to sleep, how to structure her days.

But the greatest challenge came in mid-December, when she received the call from Abby that she had gone into labor. The baby, a week early but healthy, had arrived after fourteen hours of labor. Little Amanda, a name choice that had both pleased and strategically benefited the grandmother, was a perfect 9 pounds, 13 ounces., with a dusting of dark hair and her mother's determined chin.

Her first visits with her newborn granddaughter had an unsettling effect on her namesake. Each time she held the baby, Amanda felt ICE's carefully constructed walls beginning to crack, genuine warmth seeping through the fissures.

"Who's grandma's precious girl?" she would coo, cradling the tiny infant. The words emerged naturally, startling her with their sincerity. Little Amanda would blink in response, tiny fingers reflexively grasping her grandmother's offered finger with complete trust, unknowingly wielding more power to destabilize ICE than any prison guard ever had.

Drake watched these interactions carefully, his protective instincts warring with his desire to support Abby's hope for family healing. He noticed how Amanda's entire demeanor would shift when holding the baby - her shoulders softening, her smile reaching her eyes in a way it rarely did otherwise.

"She's good with her," he admitted to Abby one evening after Amanda had left. "Better than I expected."

Abby, exhausted from the demands of new motherhood but glowing with happiness, looked up at her husband. "I know. Sometimes when I watch them together, I see glimpses of who she might have been... who she might still become."

But Amanda's transformation wasn't without its complications. Some days, when the pressure of maintaining her reformed persona became too much, ICE would resurface with frightening clarity. She would catch herself calculating how to use her growing bond with the baby to further secure her position in the family, how to leverage Abby's maternal instincts and postpartum vulnerability to deepen her dependence.

These moments of cold clarity were becoming more infrequent, though, displaced by genuine moments of connection. By March, when little Amanda reached three months old and began to smile responsively, Amanda felt a surge of pride untainted by calculation. When the baby first turned her head specifically at the sound of "Gamma" in June, Amanda's tears of joy were real, surprising her with their intensity.

As spring turned to summer, Amanda found herself spending more time at Abby and Drake's home, her presence becoming an increasingly natural part of their family routine. She learned little Amanda's favorite songs, memorized the exact way she liked her stuffed elephant positioned for naps, discovered the specific bounce that would soothe her teething cries.

One particularly challenging evening in July, when little Amanda was fussy with a summer cold, Amanda paced the living room for hours, softly singing the same lullaby she'd once sung to Abby. The baby finally drifted off to sleep on her shoulder, one tiny hand curled trustingly around her grandmother's finger.

Looking down at her sleeping granddaughter, Amanda felt the familiar war within herself - ICE's strategic mind noting how this display of devotion would further cement her position in the family, while another part of her, a part she'd thought long dead, simply marveled at the perfect weight of the sleeping child, the soft puffs of breath against her neck.

"You're a natural with her," Abby said quietly from the doorway, startling Amanda from her reverie. "It's like you've been doing this forever."

Amanda turned carefully, mindful of her precious burden. "I missed this with you," she admitted, the words emerging before ICE could censor them. "All of it. The midnight cuddles, the first steps, the little daily miracles."

Abby moved closer, gently brushing a wisp of hair from her daughter's forehead. "Maybe this is your second chance," she suggested. "A chance to do things differently."

The words hung in the air between them, heavy with possibility and unspoken fears. Amanda looked down at her granddaughter's peaceful face, feeling the familiar tug-of-war in her heart. ICE whispered strategies and calculations, but for once, those cold assessments seemed less compelling than the simple warmth of the baby in her arms.

Later that night, alone in her apartment, Amanda stood at the window watching summer lightning flicker in the distance. She thought about second chances, about redemption, about the unexpected power of a baby's unconditional love to thaw even the coldest heart. For the first time in decades, ICE's voice seemed less certain, less dominant in her mind.

Yet even as she acknowledged this change, Amanda knew the path ahead would not be simple. The habits of a lifetime couldn't be undone by a few months of domestic bliss, no matter how genuine. The question that kept her awake at night was whether she could find a way to integrate both parts of herself - to maintain the strength and survival instincts that ICE had given her while allowing space for the warmer, more genuine emotions her granddaughter evoked.

As she finally turned away from the window, Amanda caught her reflection in the darkened glass. The face that looked back at her seemed somehow softer than it had in years, yet no less determined. Perhaps that was the real transformation taking place - not a complete thaw, but a gradual tempering, ice learning to coexist with warmth.

By December 2016, little Amanda's first birthday approached, and with it came new challenges and revelations. Amanda found herself helping prepare for the milestone celebration, watching with mingled joy and calculation as her granddaughter discovered the magic of twinkling Christmas lights and shiny wrapping paper.

"Just wait until she's old enough to really understand Santa," Drake remarked one evening as they watched the baby bat at low-hanging ornaments on the Christmas tree. His voice held a warmth that surprised Amanda - he'd been gradually letting his guard down around her, though she knew his protective instincts remained razor-sharp.

"I remember Abby's first real Christmas," Liz found herself saying, the memory surfacing unbidden, her voice warming with maternal tenderness. "She was barely walking, but somehow she managed to climb halfway up the tree trying to catch the lights." A gentle smile spread across her face as she relived the precious moment, still so fresh in her mind. As a new mother, Liz found herself constantly amazed by these small moments that filled her heart with unexpected joy.

From across the room, Amanda watched with a carefully neutral expression, though internally ICE was calculating. These personal anecdotes were territory she couldn't claim - memories from before she had entered their lives.

Liz felt a flutter of emotion - the natural protectiveness of a mother, alongside a subtle urge to stake her claim as the primary maternal figure. "It was before... before we even had the tree fully decorated. You were fearless even then, always reaching for the brightest thing in sight."

Amanda shifted slightly, recognizing the subtle territorial marking in Liz's words. ICE advised patience - there would be other opportunities to assert influence.

The moment hung between them, fragile as a soap bubble. Then little Amanda broke the tension by successfully grabbing a glass ball from the tree, prompting all three adults to lunge forward in unified protective instinct.

As both women reached for the ornament, their hands briefly touched. Liz extracted it from her daughter's surprisingly strong grip, noticing how Amanda had pulled back just slightly, allowing her this small victory. The gesture wasn't lost on Liz, who offered a small appreciative nod.

Amanda observed how naturally they had all moved together, while noting that Liz had positioned herself as the primary protector. It was the sort of integration she had hoped for - yet the reality of sharing maternal authority felt different than she had anticipated.

The days leading up to Christmas and little Amanda's first birthday brought a flurry of activity. Liz orchestrated holiday preparations with confident efficiency, while Amanda found herself carefully navigating the balance between helpful grandmother and overstepping boundaries.

"You're doing it wrong," Liz told Drake one afternoon, watching him struggle with a particularly awkward package. Her words were teasing, not critical. "Here, let me show you."

Before she could demonstrate, Amanda interjected smoothly. "Actually, I might have a trick for that particular shape." She displayed the proper technique for wrapping odd-shaped gifts, a skill she'd perfected during her years of creating convincing packages for less innocent purposes.

Drake watched her efficient movements with admiration. "Where did you learn to wrap like that?"

ICE immediately supplied a plausible lie, but Amanda found herself telling a partial truth instead. "I had lots of practice over the years. When you don't have much, you learn to make the presentation special."

Liz watched the exchange, feeling a momentary flicker of insecurity at how easily Amanda had claimed this small spotlight. Yet when she caught the genuine warmth in Amanda's eyes as she glanced at little Amanda, Liz felt her defensiveness soften slightly. Perhaps there was room for both of them in this child's life after all.

Later that night, after the baby was asleep and Drake had retired to his home office to finish some work, Abby approached Amanda with a small, carefully wrapped package.

"I know we're supposed to wait until Christmas morning," she said hesitantly, "but I wanted to give you this privately."

Amanda accepted the package, noting its weight and dimensions with instinctive assessment. When she opened it, she found a beautiful leather-bound photo album. Inside were dozens of pictures of little Amanda, from her first moments in the hospital through her recent adventures in early mobility.

"I thought you might like to have copies of these," Abby explained, her voice soft. "To make up for some of what you missed with me."

The gesture hit Amanda with unexpected force. ICE's voice tried to analyze it for strategic value, but for once, those cold calculations were drowned out by a wave of genuine emotion. Her hands trembled as she turned the pages, taking in each captured moment of her granddaughter's young life.

"Thank you," she managed, her voice rough. "This is... this means more than I can say."

Abby reached out and squeezed her hand. "Merry Christmas, Mom. And thank you for being here for Amanda's first birthday."

The holiday itself passed in a blur of torn wrapping paper, excited squeals, and moments that tested Amanda's ability to maintain her composure. Little Amanda, overwhelmed by the excitement, alternated between bouts of joy and overtired meltdowns. Amanda found herself naturally stepping in to help, offering experienced support without being asked.

"How do you always know exactly what she needs?" Abby asked wonderingly, watching her mother successfully settle the overtired baby for a nap amid the chaos.

Amanda looked down at her sleeping granddaughter, considering the question. "I think... I think maybe I'm finally learning to listen. To pay attention to what others need instead of just calculating what I can gain."

The admission surprised them both. It was perhaps the most honest thing Amanda had said about her own transformation, acknowledging both her manipulative past and her genuine efforts to change.

As winter melted into spring of 2017, Amanda found herself facing new challenges. Little Amanda was becoming more mobile, more verbal, more of a distinct personality. Her demands for "Gamma" became more frequent and specific. She wanted stories read in exactly the right voice, songs sung in precisely the right order, comfort offered in particular ways.

These rigid requirements might once have frustrated Amanda, might have triggered ICE's impatience with anything that couldn't be controlled. Instead, she found herself adapting, learning her granddaughter's preferences, delighting in the small victories of perfectly executed routines.

One rainy April afternoon, as she sat in the rocking chair with little Amanda finally asleep on her chest, Amanda caught sight of their reflection in the nursery window. The image gave her pause - the notorious ICE, feared and respected in the darkest corners of society, now completely at peace serving as a human pillow for a drooling toddler.

The irony might have amused her, but instead it prompted a deeper reflection. She had spent decades building ICE's reputation, crafting an persona of impenetrable calculation and control. Now, without quite meaning to, she was building something else - a legacy of love, of genuine connection, of the kind of influence that came not from fear but from trust.

That evening, after Abby and Drake had returned from work and little Amanda was engaged in her favorite game of "cooking" with plastic vegetables, Amanda found herself observing the domestic scene with new eyes. ICE's voice still whispered assessments and strategies, but it was no longer the only voice she heard. There was another perspective emerging, one that valued these simple moments not for their strategic potential, but for their inherent worth.

"Gamma, look!" Little Amanda held up a plastic carrot with profound seriousness. "It's soup!"

Amanda accepted the imaginary offering with equal gravity, pretending to sip from the empty toy pot. "Delicious," she declared, earning a delighted giggle from her granddaughter.

Across the room, she caught Abby watching them, a complex mix of emotions playing across her daughter's face. In that moment, Amanda realized that perhaps the greatest manipulation of all had been the one she'd practiced on herself - the belief that ICE's calculating coldness was the only way to survive.

As spring progressed into summer, bringing with it little Amanda's approaching eighteen-month milestone, Amanda found herself at a crossroads. The person she had been and the person she was becoming seemed increasingly at odds. Yet somehow, in the warm chaos of family life, in the unconditional love of a toddler who cared nothing for past sins or carefully maintained facades, she was finding a way forward.

It wasn't the complete thaw she had once feared and Abby had hoped for. Rather, it was something more complex - an integration of ICE's strength and survival instincts with the warmer, more genuine emotions her granddaughter evoked. Like the changing seasons themselves, it was a gradual transformation, marked not by sudden dramatic changes but by small, daily choices to let love in.

36 HEART TO HEART

The autumn wind rustled through the trees outside Le Petit Café, where Amanda had insisted they meet rather than the modest confines of her apartment, where she had been living for about 5 months now. She'd chosen this place carefully - intimate enough for private conversation but public enough to seem non-threatening. The morning rush had passed, leaving the café half-empty, the remaining patrons absorbed in laptops or newspapers.

ICE had prepared meticulously for this performance. The slightly trembling hands, the occasional darting glances toward the exit, the way she twisted her paper napkin - all calculated to project vulnerability. She'd even forgone makeup, letting the fluorescent lighting emphasize the shadows under her eyes, evidence of sleepless nights that were more strategic than genuine.

Abby watched her mother from across the small table, her lawyer's instincts noting every detail. The way Amanda's shoulders hunched protectively, how she'd positioned herself with her back to the wall, the slight tremor in her voice when she ordered her coffee. After months of regular visits, Abby had learned to read her mother's tells, but today felt different. The anxiety seemed deeper, more genuine - or perhaps just more skillfully performed.

"Mom," Abby said softly, reaching across the table to touch

Amanda's restless hands. "Whatever it is, you can tell me. I'm here for you."

The touch sent an unexpected jolt through ICE's carefully maintained composure. Physical contact was always tricky - too much tension would seem defensive, too little would undermine the vulnerability she needed to project. She let her hands tremble slightly beneath Abby's, allowing a flicker of genuine response to enhance her performance.

"Abby," she began, her voice barely above a whisper, calibrated to draw her daughter closer, to create an intimate bubble in the public space. "There's something I need to tell you. Something I've only just begun to remember myself."

A server passed nearby, the scent of fresh coffee and warm pastries momentarily overwhelming the tension between them. ICE used the interruption to gather herself, to check her daughter's reaction. Abby's professional mask had slipped, revealing the concerned daughter beneath. Perfect.

"My childhood," Amanda continued, letting her voice crack slightly. "There's so much I don't remember. So much I think I blocked out. But lately, pieces have been coming back. Flashes of... of pain, of violation..."

The café's gentle background music seemed to fade away as Abby's eyes widened with understanding. ICE noted the slight pallor that crept into her daughter's cheeks, the way her fingers tightened unconsciously around her coffee cup. The lawyer was giving way entirely to the daughter now - exactly as planned.

"I think I was raped, Abby." Amanda delivered the words in a broken whisper, each syllable weighted with carefully crafted pain. "I think... I think I got pregnant. And my mother, your grandmother... I think she gave the baby... you.... away."

The confession hung in the air between them, heavy as storm

clouds. Through lowered lashes, ICE watched her daughter process the information. Abby's legal training was evident in the way she controlled her initial reaction, in how her eyes flickered briefly to the side - accessing memory, searching for inconsistencies. But maternal instinct overrode professional skepticism, just as ICE had counted on.

Abby moved to the chair beside her mother, pulling Amanda into a tight embrace. The scent of her daughter's shampoo - something floral and expensive - mingled with the café's coffee aroma. ICE allowed herself to shake slightly, letting out carefully measured sobs against Abby's shoulder.

"Mom," Abby whispered, her voice thick with emotion, "I'm so sorry. I'm so sorry you went through that, that you've carried this pain alone for so long."

Inside her mind, ICE smiled coldly at how perfectly it was all playing out. Every tear, every tremor, every broken word was achieving its intended effect. The story she'd crafted contained just enough truth to be verifiable, just enough ambiguity to be safe from detailed investigation. The perfect foundation for the next phase of her plan.

"I didn't even know I was carrying you," Amanda managed, her voice muffled against Abby's shoulder. "It was just... a surprise. But now, you're all I can think about. My child, right here. And the things that were done to me, the reasons I am the way I am..."A barista dropped something in the kitchen, the sudden clatter making Amanda jump - a genuine startle that served her performance beautifully. Abby's arms tightened around her, protective and fierce.

"We'll get through this, Mom," she promised, conviction burning in every word. "You're not alone anymore. We'll face this together, and we'll find a way to heal. I'm here, no matter what."

They sat in silence for a moment, the café's ambient sounds washing over them - the hiss of the espresso machine, the quiet conversations of other patrons, the gentle clink of cups against saucers.

ICE used the time to regulate her breathing, to let her daughter see her gradually composing herself.

"There's something else," Amanda said finally, her voice steadier now but still vulnerable. "My apartment... it's so empty. So lonely. And I've been thinking..."

She paused, allowing uncertainty to flicker across her face, knowing it would make what came next more believable.

"I want to be closer to you, to little Amanda. I miss so many moments with her, and she's growing so fast." A carefully constructed smile wavered on her lips. "I've been wondering if... if it might make sense for me to move in with you and Drake. Just temporarily, of course. To help with the baby, to be there for those little moments that matter so much."

Abby's expression shifted slightly, a barely perceptible tension appearing at the corners of her eyes. ICE noted it immediately - the suggestion had landed as expected, with both appeal and caution.

"Mom," Abby said gently, "that's a big step. For all of us."

"I know," Amanda replied quickly, allowing a note of earnest hope to color her voice. "And I wouldn't suggest it if I didn't think I could be helpful. Little Amanda lights up when she sees me. And with everything I'm processing now... being surrounded by family, by love, it could make all the difference."

The sun slanted through the café's windows, casting patterns across their table. Abby's face showed the internal struggle - compassion warring with caution, hope tempering reservation. "Let me talk to Drake," she said finally. "This isn't just my decision to make." ICE nodded, the perfect picture of understanding, while inwardly counting this as the first victory in her carefully orchestrated campaign. The seed had been planted. Now she just needed to nurture it carefully, to guide it toward the outcome she desired. "Of course," she said, reaching out to squeeze her daughter's hand gratefully. "Take all the time you need. I just... I just want to be there for you both. For all of you." Abby's smile was warm, if still tinged with uncertainty. "I know, Mom. I know you do."

Three days later, Abby found herself in a different café, this one closer to Amanda's apartment. The conversation with Drake had been difficult but ultimately productive. He'd been skeptical at first, his natural protectiveness flaring, but eventually agreed that they needed to understand what had happened in the past if they were ever going to move forward with any semblance of trust.

"I'll be standing by," he'd told her. "But you're right—Amanda might be our best window into understanding what we're dealing with here."

Now, waiting for Amanda to arrive, Abby rehearsed what she would say. This wasn't just about ICE anymore—it was about healing wounds that had festered too long in darkness. She spotted Amanda pushing through the door, her dark hair windblown, eyes scanning the room until they found Abby.

"Sorry I'm late," Amanda said, sliding into the seat across from her. "Transit was a nightmare."

"No problem," Abby replied, sliding a chai latte—Amanda's favorite—toward her. "Thanks for meeting me."

Amanda wrapped her hands around the warm cup. "You sounded serious on the phone. Is everything okay?"

Abby took a deep breath. This was the moment of truth.

"I wanted to talk to you about something that might help us all—including you—make sense of what's happening with our daughter."

Abby watched Amanda carefully, noting how she seemed to fold inward, her shoulders hunching slightly as if bracing against an unseen weight. The café around them hummed with afternoon activity, but they might as well have been alone for all the attention they paid to their surroundings.

"I know it sounds intimidating," Abby said, her voice gentle but firm. "But Dr. Chen helped me work through some of my own... complications. She has this way of making you feel safe, even when you're exploring difficult memories."

Amanda traced the rim of her untouched coffee cup. "I don't know what good it would do. Those memories are buried for a reason, aren't they?"

"Maybe," Abby acknowledged. "But they're still affecting you, whether you access them or not. Think about your reaction whenever your mother is mentioned, how you freeze up. Those aren't just emotional responses—they're protective mechanisms."

"And hypnosis?" Amanda's voice carried a note of skepticism. "Isn't that just parlor tricks?"

Abby shook her head. "Not the way Dr. Chen practices it. It's more like... guided meditation. She helps create a space where your mind feels secure enough to examine those locked rooms." She reached across the table, her hand stopping just short of Amanda's. "You don't have to decide right now. But sometimes understanding where we've been is the only way to choose where we go next."

Amanda's gaze drifted to the window, watching pedestrians navigate the sidewalk with determined purpose. When she finally looked back at Abby, there was something new in her expression—a fragile resolve taking shape behind the fear.

"You really think it could help?" she asked, her voice barely audible above the café's ambient noise.

"I do," Abby replied without hesitation. "And I'd go with you, wait for you... whatever you need."

Amanda allowed herself a brief, hesitant smile. "Very well," she whispered. "I will make an effort. If you believe it could be beneficial and you have confidence in Dr. Chen, I am willing to attempt it."

The tension in Abby's shoulders eased slightly. This was just a first step, but sometimes the first step was the hardest part of any journey. Whatever Amanda discovered about her mother, about herself—at least she wouldn't be facing it alone.

ICE allowed herself a brief, hesitant smile. "Very well," she whispered. "I will make an effort. If you believe it could be beneficial and you have confidence in Dr. Chen, I am willing to attempt it."

The joy that spread across Abby's face was almost painful to watch. Such pure emotion, such complete belief in the possibility of healing and redemption. ICE felt a momentary twinge of... something. Not quite guilt - she'd frozen that emotion out of her system long ago. But perhaps a flicker of recognition, an acknowledgment of the pain her performance would eventually cause.

She pushed the feeling aside, focusing instead on her next moves. The therapist would need to be managed carefully, her revelations parceled out in just the right measure to maintain credibility while advancing her agenda. But for now, she had achieved her primary objective - deepening Abby's emotional investment, creating another layer of dependency and trust.

As they prepared to leave the café, Amanda allowed herself to be helped into her coat, accepting Abby's solicitous attention with just the right mix of gratitude and lingering fragility. The cool autumn air hit her face as they stepped outside, and she took a deep breath, as if drawing strength from the crisp morning.

"Thank you, Abby," she murmured, her voice still carefully modulated. "Thank you for being here, for believing in me. It means more than I can say."

And as they walked to Abby's car, ICE was already planning her next performance, calculating how to use this new development to maximum advantage. The therapist, the trauma narrative, the deepening bond with Abby - all pieces in her intricate game, moves on a board that only she could see.

Let them believe in healing, in redemption, in the power of love to overcome trauma. ICE would play her role perfectly, every tear and trembling smile another step toward her ultimate goal. After all, the best cons were the ones where everyone got what they wanted - even if what they wanted was just a beautiful lie.

37 YOU GET WHAT YOU PAY FOR

The soothing beige walls of Dr. Chen's office seemed to close in around Amanda as she stepped inside, her practiced eyes immediately cataloging every detail. Two exits - the main door and what appeared to be a private entrance behind the therapist's desk. A white noise machine humming discretely in the corner. Certificates and diplomas arranged with careful precision on the walls. The room was designed to project both professionalism and comfort, much like the woman who now rose to greet her.

ICE had researched Dr. Chen thoroughly before this meeting. Harvard-educated, twenty years of experience specializing in trauma and family reconciliation. The therapist's reputation for insight and empathy could make her either an invaluable ally or a dangerous obstacle, depending on how well ICE played this performance.

"Please, have a seat," Dr. Chen said warmly, gesturing to the plush armchair across from her own. Her voice carried just the right mix of professional authority and maternal warmth. "I'm so glad you've decided to come in today."

Amanda perched carefully on the edge of the chair, allowing her hands to fidget in her lap - a calculated display of nervousness. The lavender scent diffusing through the room was meant to be calming, but ICE used it to fuel her performance, letting her breathing quicken slightly as if fighting anxiety.

"Thank you for seeing me," she said softly, perfectly calibrating uncertainty in her voice. "Abby speaks very highly of you."

Dr. Chen smiled, crow's feet crinkling at the corners of her eyes. ICE noted how the expression seemed genuinely warm while maintaining professional distance - a skill she could appreciate. "Abby is a remarkable young woman," the therapist agreed. "And I'm honored that she trusts me enough to recommend me to you. But today is about you, Amanda. About your journey and what you hope to gain from our time together."

ICE let Amanda nod, drawing a shaky breath that made her shoulders tremble slightly. She had practiced this performance in her apartment, testing different levels of vulnerability until she found the perfect balance. "I... I don't even know where to start," she admitted, dropping her gaze to her twisting hands. "There's so much I've kept buried for so long. So much I'm just starting to remember."

Dr. Chen leaned forward, her posture open and attentive. Even in this simple movement, ICE could read years of training and experience. "That's very common for survivors of trauma," she said gently. "The mind has a way of protecting itself by blocking out painful memories. But those memories, those experiences, they still impact us, even when we're not consciously aware of them."

Amanda looked up, allowing carefully measured tears to gather in her eyes. The morning light filtering through the office windows caught them perfectly, creating a shimmer of vulnerability. "I want to remember," she whispered, letting her voice crack on the last word. "I need to understand what happened to me, how it's shaped me. But I'm scared. Scared of what I might uncover, of how it might change everything."

Through lowered lashes, ICE watched Dr. Chen's reaction. The therapist's expression showed compassion without pity - another skilled performance, though presumably more genuine than her own. "That fear is completely understandable," Dr. Chen affirmed. "Facing our trauma is one of the bravest things we can do. And I want you to know that you're not alone in this. I'm here to support you, to provide a safe space for you to explore your experiences and emotions at your own pace."

ICE allowed Amanda's posture to relax incrementally, as if responding to the therapist's warmth. Each minute shift was calculated to show gradual trust-building, the kind of response Dr. Chen would expect from a genuine trauma survivor. "Thank you," she murmured, softening her voice. "I think... I think I'm ready to start. To start unpacking all of this."

The session continued, a delicate dance of revelation and response. ICE carefully parceled out hints of Amanda's traumatic past, never giving too much detail but leaving enough breadcrumbs for Dr. Chen to follow. The story she'd crafted was masterful in its ambiguity - enough truth to be verifiable, enough uncertainty to be clinically interesting.

Dr. Chen responded with exactly the kind of professional compassion ICE had anticipated, offering support and validation while gently probing for deeper understanding. "It's important to remember that healing is a process," she explained, her voice carrying that perfect note of practiced empathy. "There may be setbacks, moments of pain and confusion. But with time, with compassion for yourself and the support of those who care about you, it is possible to find peace, to build a life beyond the trauma."

Amanda let a tear slip down her cheek, carefully timed to emphasize her emotional vulnerability. "I want that," she said softly, her voice trembling but determined. "I want to find that peace, that life. For myself, and for Abby. I don't want my past to define me anymore."

Inside, ICE smiled coldly at how perfectly it was all playing out. Dr. Chen was exactly the kind of therapist she needed - skilled enough to help craft a convincing narrative of recovery, but not so sharp as to see through the performance. Each session would build her credibility, create another layer of professional documentation supporting her reformation.

As the session drew to a close, Dr. Chen leaned forward, offering a tissue box with practiced grace. "You've taken an important first step today, Amanda," she said warmly. "I know it wasn't easy to share these feelings, these memories. But I want you to know that you're not alone in this journey. We'll work together at your pace, building trust and understanding as we go."

Amanda dabbed at her tears, letting her hands shake slightly. "Thank you, Dr. Chen," she whispered. "I... I feel safer already, just knowing I have someone to talk to. Someone who understands."

The words were perfectly chosen, calculated to appeal to both the therapist's professional pride and maternal instincts. ICE watched with satisfaction as Dr. Chen's expression softened further, the careful professional mask slipping just slightly to reveal genuine concern.

"That's what I'm here for," Dr. Chen assured her. "To provide a safe space for you to explore these memories and emotions. We'll take it one step at a time, working together to help you process your experiences and build a stronger future."

As Amanda gathered her purse to leave, she allowed her movements to be slightly unsteady, as if emotionally drained by the session. It was another calculated detail, one that would stick in Dr. Chen's mind as she wrote up her session notes.

In the waiting room, Abby stood immediately, concern evident on her face. ICE let Amanda stumble slightly, allowing her daughter to steady her with protective hands. "Are you okay, Mom?" Abby asked softly, her voice thick with worry.

"Yes," Amanda managed a tremulous smile. "Yes, I think I am. Dr. Chen is... she's everything you said she would be."

The drive home was quiet, Abby shooting concerned glances at her mother while Amanda stared out the window, apparently lost in emotional reflection. Inside, ICE was already planning her next sessions, calculating how to build on this foundation of vulnerability and trust.

Let Dr. Chen think she was helping a traumatized woman heal. Let Abby believe her mother was finally facing her demons. ICE would play this role perfectly, using their compassion and expertise to further her own ends. After all, therapy was just another kind of performance, and she had always been an excellent actress.

The autumn sun was setting as they pulled up to the apartment, painting the sky in shades of gold and shadow. Amanda turned to her daughter with carefully crafted gratitude in her eyes. "Thank you," she whispered. "For believing in me, for helping me find Dr. Chen. I couldn't do this without you."

Abby's eyes filled with tears as she pulled her mother into a fierce hug. ICE allowed Amanda to relax into the embrace, even as her mind continued calculating, planning, refining her performance for the sessions to come.

After all, therapy was an investment, and ICE intended to get exactly what she paid for - another witness to her reformation, another professional voice to validate her change. Dr. Chen would be her most convincing audience yet, and ICE was ready to give the performance of a lifetime.

Back in her room at the halfway house, ICE began methodically reviewing the session, documenting every reaction, every nuance of Dr. Chen's responses. The therapist's background in trauma work would make her expectations predictable - the careful establishment of trust, the gradual revelation of memories, the expected resistance and breakthrough moments. ICE could map out the entire therapeutic journey, crafting each session to build perfectly on the last.

She pulled out her hidden notebook, the one containing her real plans rather than the sanitized version she would share in therapy. Dr. Chen's office layout, her mannerisms, her preferred therapeutic techniques - every detail could be useful. ICE had learned long ago that the most convincing lies were built on foundations of truth, and she intended to use her genuine understanding of trauma to make her performance unquestionable.

She would need to carefully calibrate her progress - not too fast to seem suspicious, not too slow to maintain interest. Each session would reveal another carefully crafted piece of her past, building toward a narrative that would cement her position in Abby's life.

ICE tucked away her notebook and arranged herself on the bed, letting exhaustion show in her posture. "Just tired," she called back, her voice deliberately weak. "It was... it was a lot to process."

She would need to appear slightly shaken for the next few days.

Tomorrow, she would call Abby, her voice carefully balanced between fragility and determination. She would express gratitude for finding Dr. Chen, share carefully selected insights from the session, reinforce their growing bond. Every interaction was an opportunity to deepen Abby's emotional investment, to strengthen her belief in her mother's journey toward healing.

The night deepened around her as ICE continued planning, mapping out the intricate dance of therapy and manipulation that would unfold over the coming months. Dr. Chen would become an unwitting ally, her professional expertise lending weight to ICE's carefully constructed narrative of trauma and recovery.

Let them all believe in redemption, in the healing power of therapy and family love. ICE would play her role to perfection, each vulnerable moment and tearful breakthrough another step toward her ultimate goal. The performance had begun, and she intended to make every session worth its weight in gold.

Outside her window, the lights cast harsh shadows across the exercise yard, their unblinking gaze a reminder of the constraints she still needed to navigate. But ICE felt more in control than ever. With Dr. Chen's unwitting help, she would craft a story of recovery so compelling that even the most skeptical observer would be convinced.

After all, the best therapy was about transformation - and ICE was about to give them a transformation they would never forget.

38 THE LONG GAME

The fluorescent lights in Dr. Chen's waiting room cast a clinical glow as Amanda emerged from her session, each step a carefully measured performance of emotional exhaustion. The cream-colored walls seemed to pulse slightly, a effect she'd deliberately cultivate by controlling her breathing throughout the session's "breakthrough" moment.

Abby rose from her chair, concern etched across her features in a way that ICE had learned to read like a master cartographer mapping familiar terrain. "Hey, Mom," her daughter said softly, reaching out with that characteristic hesitancy that always preceded their deeper moments. "How did it go?"

ICE let Amanda's hands tremble slightly as she accepted her daughter's embrace, timing a small sob to catch in her throat. The performance had to be perfect - not too dramatic to seem artificial, but raw enough to suggest real therapeutic progress. She'd spent hours practicing this moment in her halfway house room, calibrating each micro-expression.

"It was... intense," she managed, her voice cracking on the second word. Inside, ICE savored the flicker of protective concern that crossed Abby's face. "Dr. Chen really knows how to... how to get to the heart of things."

The therapist's office door clicked shut behind them, and ICE used the sound to trigger a small flinch - another calculated detail that wouldn't escape Abby's notice. She'd learned that her daughter cataloged these reactions with an attorney's precision, building her own case file of her mother's supposed recovery.

"She said we'd meet weekly," Amanda continued, letting exhaustion seep into her tone. "She wants me to try some grounding exercises when the... when the memories start feeling too intense." The hesitation was perfectly timed, suggesting depths of trauma still too raw to voice.

Abby's hand found hers, squeezing gently. "I'm so proud of you, Mom. I know how hard this must be, facing everything head-on like this."

ICE allowed Amanda's posture to soften at the praise, even as her mind calculated the impact of each response. The session had gone exactly as planned - Dr. Chen picking up on the carefully planted hints about childhood trauma, making the connections ICE had meticulously laid out. The therapist's own expertise would fill in the blanks, creating a narrative more convincing than anything ICE could explicitly state.

"There's something else," Amanda said softly as they walked toward the elevator. She kept her gaze fixed on the floor, using her peripheral vision to monitor Abby's reaction. "Dr. Chen thinks... she thinks my relationship with you might be triggering some of the deeper memories. About my own mother, about what happened when I was young."

The elevator arrived with a gentle chime, and ICE used the moment of transition to let Amanda's hands shake more visibly. Abby's sharp intake of breath told her the detail hadn't gone unnoticed.

"Oh, Mom," Abby's voice cracked with emotion. "Whatever you need, whatever helps you heal - I'm here. We can take things slower if that would help."

ICE felt a familiar twist of satisfaction beneath Amanda's

vulnerable exterior. This was exactly the response she'd been orchestrating - Abby offering to create distance even as her protective instincts drew her closer. The push-pull dynamic would serve ICE's purposes perfectly, creating opportunities for carefully staged moments of connection and revelation.

The autumn air hit them as they exited the building, and ICE let Amanda pull her light jacket closer, a subtle reminder of her fragility. "Actually," she said, timing a slight catch in her voice, "Dr. Chen thinks our relationship might be key to my healing. Something about... about breaking the cycle of trauma."

They reached Abby's car, and ICE watched her daughter process this information, noting how her professional mask slipped to reveal raw hope beneath. The manipulation was masterful - using therapeutic language to justify increased contact while playing to Abby's deepest desires for connection.

"Whatever you need, Mom," Abby repeated, her voice thick with emotion. "Whatever it takes to help you heal."

As they drove the apartment, ICE began laying groundwork for future sessions. She let Amanda speak hesitantly about the grounding exercises, the breathing techniques, the journal Dr. Chen had suggested she keep. Each detail was another strand in the web she was weaving, another piece of evidence for her eventual redemption.

The security lights of the apartment came into view, and ICE prepared Amanda's final performance of the day. "Thank you, Abby," she whispered, letting tears gather but not fall. "For believing in me, for not giving up even when I gave you every reason to."

Abby pulled into the parking spot, her own eyes glistening. "You're my mother," she said simply. "And I'm not going anywhere."

ICE let Amanda smile tremulously as she exited the car, maintaining the fragile expression until she was safely inside the building.

Only then, in the privacy of her room, did she allow her true face to emerge. She pulled out her notebook, documenting every reaction, every nuance of the day's performance.

The game was proceeding perfectly. Dr. Chen would become another unwitting ally, her professional expertise lending credibility to ICE's carefully constructed narrative. And Abby, sweet, hopeful Abby, would continue to see exactly what she needed to see - a mother fighting her demons, reaching for redemption.

Let them believe in healing, in the power of therapy to unlock buried truths. ICE would play this role to perfection, each vulnerable moment another step toward her ultimate goal. After all, the most convincing lies were the ones wrapped in therapeutic insight, validated by professional expertise.

The night deepened around her as ICE continued planning, mapping out future sessions with the precision of a master strategist. Every tear, every trembling confession, every breakthrough would be carefully choreographed to advance her agenda while appearing completely genuine.

After all, therapy was just another kind of long con, and ICE was playing for keeps.

39 WHERE IT ALL STARTED

December 2017

Amanda settled into the now-familiar chair in Dr. Chen's office, her posture carefully calibrated to project the right mix of nervousness and determination. Over the past two weeks, ICE had been meticulously documenting the therapist's patterns, noting how Dr. Chen responded to different displays of emotion, which therapeutic techniques seemed to excite her professional interest the most. The office's lavender scent diffuser, the carefully arranged degrees on the wall, the strategic placement of tissues - every detail factored into ICE's ongoing assessment.

"How are you feeling today, Amanda?" Dr. Chen's warm smile carried the same maternal energy that ICE had observed in their previous sessions. Even the therapist's body language followed predictable patterns - the slight forward lean when showing interest, the calculated pauses before deeper questions.

"Nervous," Amanda admitted, allowing her hands to tremble slightly in her lap. "But also curious, I guess. About what we might uncover." The words were chosen carefully, designed to suggest both vulnerability and a willingness to engage with the therapeutic process. ICE had spent hours practicing this particular mix of hesitation and hope.

Dr. Chen leaned forward, her expression brightening with professional enthusiasm. "That's a very normal reaction. Today, I'd like to discuss a technique that could potentially help us access some of those deeper memories and emotions you've been struggling with. Have you ever heard of hypnotherapy?"

ICE felt a flicker of satisfaction beneath Amanda's uncertain exterior. She'd researched Dr. Chen's specialties extensively, calculating that hypnotherapy would likely be suggested around their third session. The technique's reputation for accessing repressed memories made it perfect for ICE's carefully constructed narrative of trauma and recovery. More importantly, it would provide a framework for introducing memories that could never be definitively verified.

"Like, being hypnotized?" Amanda's voice carried just the right note of skepticism. "I thought that was just for entertainment, for making people cluck like chickens or something." The naive response was designed to let Dr. Chen feel professionally superior while establishing Amanda's lack of prior knowledge about the technique.

Dr. Chen's chuckle was exactly what ICE had anticipated - warm, professionally indulgent. "That's a common misconception. Clinical hypnotherapy is actually a well-established therapeutic technique. It's a state of focused attention and heightened suggestibility that can help us access parts of the mind that are usually hidden from our conscious awareness."

As the therapist explained the process, ICE rapidly assessed the opportunities and risks. Hypnotherapy would require a delicate balance - appearing to access genuine trauma while maintaining enough control to avoid revealing anything truly damaging. But if played correctly, it could provide powerful validation for her manufactured narrative of recovery. The key would be selecting which real memories to share and which to fabricate.

"And you think this could help me remember... everything?" Amanda's whispered question was perfectly pitched to suggest both hope and fear. ICE had practiced the tone extensively, knowing the importance of this moment in setting up future sessions.

Dr. Chen's expression grew appropriately serious. "It's not about forcing memories to surface, Amanda. It's about creating a safe space where your mind can explore and process at its own pace. We would work together to ensure you feel in control throughout the entire process."

ICE noted how the therapist emphasized control - a common approach with trauma survivors. She let Amanda nod slowly, vulnerability evident in every movement. "I think... I think I'd like to try it." The slight catch in her voice was calculated to suggest courage emerging through fear.

As they began the session, ICE maintained careful awareness even as Amanda appeared to relax into a trance state. Years of cons had taught her the value of maintaining multiple levels of consciousness - appearing completely vulnerable while remaining sharply alert. Dr. Chen's soothing voice guided them deeper, and ICE began feeding carefully selected memories through Amanda's consciousness.

The memories she chose to reveal were a masterpiece of manipulation - fragments of real trauma artfully combined with manufactured details, each one designed to support her larger narrative. The small, dark room from her childhood became a staging ground for suggesting deeper abuse. The blur of her mother's alcoholic rage was allowed to surface, but the specific incidents remained conveniently vague. Each detail was chosen to create maximum emotional impact while remaining impossible to verify.

"I'm... I'm little," Amanda murmured, her brow furrowing in a practiced display of distress. "Maybe four or five. I'm alone a lot. The house is always dark." ICE carefully layered in sensory details - the musty carpet smell, the grimy windows - knowing they would add authenticity to the memories.

Through half-closed eyes, ICE watched Dr. Chen's reactions, noting which details drew the strongest response. The therapist's slight intake of breath at mentions of abandonment, the subtle lean forward during descriptions of physical abuse - each reaction was cataloged for future reference.

"My mother," Amanda whispered, timing a tremor in her voice

perfectly. "She's angry. She's always angry." The memory was real enough, but ICE carefully edited the details, creating spaces where Dr. Chen's own professional knowledge would fill in the blanks with exactly what she expected to hear.

A man's voice was introduced into the narrative - carefully ambiguous, threatening without being specific. ICE watched Dr. Chen's professional mask slip slightly, revealing the emotional investment she was developing in Amanda's story. Perfect.

As the session progressed, ICE orchestrated a symphony of trauma and resilience. Amanda's tears were real - a physical response ICE had learned to trigger on command - but every sob was strategically timed for maximum impact. The memories flowed in a carefully choreographed sequence: the dingy school bathroom where young Amanda washed her clothes, the park where she watched other families living normal lives, the teenage years of self-harm and substance abuse.

Each revelation was chosen to reinforce Amanda's victim narrative while simultaneously explaining her criminal history. The progression from abused child to troubled teen to desperate young mother was presented with perfect theatrical timing, building to the pivotal moment - Abby's birth.

"I didn't want to let her go," Amanda sobbed, her whole body shaking with seemingly uncontrollable emotion. "But I knew... I knew I couldn't be what she needed. I was too broken." The confession was delivered with exactly the right mix of pain and self-awareness, designed to cement Dr. Chen's investment in Amanda's redemption story.

Throughout it all, ICE maintained absolute control, monitoring Dr. Chen's reactions while simultaneously managing Amanda's physical responses. When the therapist began guiding Amanda back to full awareness, ICE was already calculating how to leverage the session's revelations in future conversations with Abby.

"You're doing wonderfully, Amanda," Dr. Chen soothed, her voice thick with professional satisfaction. "Now, I want you to imagine all of those painful memories being enclosed in a protective bubble. They're still there, but they can't hurt you anymore. You're safe now, and you're strong enough to face them."

As Amanda's breathing steadied, ICE began preparing the final act of today's performance. The transition back to consciousness needed to appear gradual, with just the right mix of disorientation and emotional rawness. She let Amanda's hands shake as she accepted a tissue, allowing tears to continue falling even as her breathing normalized.

"How are you feeling?" Dr. Chen asked gently, radiating therapeutic concern.

Amanda took a shaky breath, wiping at her tear-stained cheeks. "Like I've been hit by a truck," she admitted with a weak laugh - a calculated moment of humor to show resilience. "But also... I don't know. Like maybe I understand myself a little better now."

Inside, ICE catalogued the session's successes. The hypnotherapy had provided a perfect opportunity to establish her childhood trauma narrative, laying groundwork for future revelations.

Dr. Chen's obvious satisfaction with the breakthrough would make an excellent addition to her progress reports. More importantly, the session had created a framework for introducing more strategic "memories" in future sessions.

As they began to process what had surfaced, ICE carefully guided Amanda's responses to reinforce the therapeutic narrative. Each insight was crafted to show just enough progress to be convincing while leaving plenty of room for future "breakthroughs." The goal was to keep Dr. Chen invested in Amanda's recovery while maintaining control over what memories would "surface" next.

The session concluded with Dr. Chen practically glowing with professional satisfaction, clearly convinced she had facilitated a major breakthrough. As Amanda gathered her things, appearing emotionally drained but hopeful, ICE was already planning the next phase of her performance.

The sunlight streaming through the office windows seemed to highlight Amanda's vulnerability, her emotional exhaustion. But beneath this carefully crafted exterior, ICE was already mapping out how to use today's revelations to maximum advantage. The hypnotherapy session had opened new possibilities for manipulation, new avenues for cementing her position in Abby's life.

Let them believe in the power of hypnotherapy to unlock buried truths. Let them see a wounded woman finally facing her demons. ICE would continue crafting her performance with surgical precision, each revelation another step toward her ultimate goal. The battle between Amanda's apparent journey toward healing and ICE's cold manipulation was intensifying, but only one of them truly knew the rules of this game. And ICE never played to lose.

The walk to the parking lot provided an opportunity for one final display of emotional vulnerability - a slight stumble, quickly corrected, that would reinforce Dr. Chen's perception of Amanda's fragile state. Every detail mattered in maintaining the perfect illusion of a trauma survivor beginning to heal.

As she drove away from the office, ICE allowed herself a moment of cold satisfaction. The foundation had been laid perfectly. Future sessions would build on today's revelations, each carefully crafted memory adding another layer to her manipulation. Dr. Chen, Abby, the entire system - they would see exactly what they wanted to see: a woman fighting her way back from darkness toward redemption.

But the truth remained frozen at ICE's core, unchanged by all the tears and revelations. This was just another long con, perhaps her most masterful yet. And like all her best performances, it would succeed because everyone involved wanted so desperately to believe in the possibility of healing, of change, of redemption.

They would never suspect that the very process meant to heal Amanda's fractured psyche was being used to perfect her deception. After all, the best lies were the ones wrapped in therapeutic insight, validated by professional expertise, and delivered with exactly the right amount of hard-won hope.

But the truth remained frozen at ICE's core, unchanged by all the tears and revelations. This was just another long con, perhaps her most masterful yet. And like all her best performances, it would succeed because everyone involved wanted so desperately to believe in the possibility of healing, of change, of redemption.

Back in her apartment, ICE began her meticulous post-session documentation. She pulled out her hidden notebook, the one concealed behind the loose baseboard where even the most thorough room searches wouldn't find it. The pages were filled with detailed observations about Dr. Chen's therapeutic techniques, her patterns of response, her professional vulnerabilities.

Today's hypnotherapy session had provided a wealth of new information. ICE noted how the therapist's breathing had changed during certain revelations, the slight shifts in her posture that betrayed emotional investment. Most importantly, she documented exactly which types of memories had drawn the strongest reactions - the moments of childhood abandonment, the suggestions of physical abuse, the heart-wrenching scene of giving up baby Abby.

"Hypnotherapy provides perfect deniability," ICE wrote in her precise handwriting. "Memories surfacing through trance state can't be verified but carry weight of therapeutic validation. Build on mother/alcohol theme - Dr. C responds strongly to addiction narrative. Save sexual trauma hints for later sessions - more impact after trust fully established."

She paused in her writing, considering the delicate balance required for her next moves. The hypnotherapy had opened up new possibilities, but it also presented risks. Too many dramatic revelations too quickly would seem suspicious. The key would be pacing the discoveries, letting each new memory surface organically within the therapeutic framework Dr. Chen had established.

"Physical responses during trance state highly effective - tears, trembling, muscle tension. Dr. C particularly affected by somatic manifestations of trauma. Develop more physical symptoms for future sessions?"

She turned to a fresh page, beginning to map out the memories she would allow to "surface" in their next session. Each one would need to be carefully crafted - enough truth to feel authentic, enough ambiguity to avoid verification, enough emotional impact to maintain Dr. Chen's professional interest.

Her thoughts turned to Abby, who would be anxiously waiting to hear about today's breakthrough session. ICE began drafting the conversation in her mind, planning exactly how Amanda would describe the hypnotherapy experience. She would need to seem shaken but hopeful, vulnerable but determined to heal. The perfect combination to deepen Abby's emotional investment while reinforcing the narrative of maternal redemption.

A memory surfaced - unexpected, unwanted - of Abby as a newborn, her tiny hand curled around Amanda's finger. ICE pushed it aside ruthlessly. Real memories were dangerous, especially now. They could contaminate the carefully constructed narrative she was building, introduce genuine emotions that might disrupt her performance.

Instead, she focused on reviewing the progressive backstory she was creating through the therapy sessions. Each revelation had been chosen to serve multiple purposes: explaining her criminal history, justifying her abandonment of Abby, creating sympathy while maintaining an air of mystery that would keep Dr. Chen intrigued.

"Key elements to develop," she wrote, underlining the heading twice:

- Mother's alcoholism (foundation for addiction narrative)

- Childhood abandonment (explains attachment issues)

- Physical abuse (justifies criminal survival tactics)

- Teenage self-destruction (bridges victim/perpetrator gap)

- Pregnancy trauma (reinforces maternal redemption arc)

ICE reviewed her notes from previous sessions, ensuring that today's revelations aligned perfectly with the groundwork she'd already laid. Consistency was crucial - the slightest contradiction could unravel the entire performance. She'd learned that lesson the hard way in previous cons, when a single misaligned detail had shattered carefully constructed deceptions.

The evening medication call echoed through the hallway. ICE quickly tucked away her notebook and arranged herself on the bed, letting exhaustion show in her posture. When the nurse peered in, she would see exactly what she expected - a woman emotionally drained from an intense therapy session, taking refuge in the solitude of her room.

"Amanda?" The nurse's voice was gentle, concerned. "Everything okay? You missed dinner."

"Just tired," Amanda replied, her voice carefully modulated to suggest emotional fatigue. "The therapy session today... it was intense. Dr. Chen used hypnosis to help me access some old memories."

The nurse's expression softened with understanding. "That must have been difficult. Would you like me to bring you some tea? Maybe something light to eat?"

ICE let Amanda's hands tremble slightly as she accepted the offer. Every interaction was an opportunity to reinforce her narrative, to add another witness to her apparent transformation. The nurse would note her emotional state in the evening report, creating another official record of her therapeutic progress.

The hypnotherapy sessions would need to build gradually, each revelation carefully timed for maximum impact. She began sketching out a timeline, mapping the progression of memories that would surface over the next few months:

Session 4: Expand on mother's alcoholism, introduce hints of boyfriends' abuse

Session 5: First memories of self-medicating, beginning of addiction spiral

Session 6: Teenage years - cutting, drugs, early criminal behavior

Session 7: Meeting Abby's father (keep details vague, unreachable)

Session 8: Pregnancy, birth, agonizing decision to give up baby

Each session would add another layer to her narrative, another piece of evidence supporting her journey toward redemption. Dr. Chen would see exactly what she expected to see - a trauma survivor gradually accessing and processing buried memories, working through layers of pain toward healing.

The night deepened around her as ICE continued refining her strategy. She reviewed her notes on Dr. Chen's therapeutic approaches, identifying opportunities to guide the therapy in directions that would serve her purposes. The therapist's emphasis on maternal attachment and intergenerational trauma played perfectly into ICE's planned narrative.

A memory tried to surface again - this time of Abby in the courtroom, eyes shining with hope as the judge ordered family counseling. ICE froze it out, encasing it in the same emotional ice that had preserved her through years of cons and captures. Sentiment was a luxury she couldn't afford, not when she was so close to achieving her goals.

The security lights outside cast harsh shadows across her desk as she made her final notes for the night. Tomorrow would bring new challenges - Abby's questions about the session, the halfway house staff's concerned observations, the ongoing performance of a woman gradually confronting her traumatic past.

But ICE was ready. She had played many roles in her criminal career, but this might be her masterpiece - the ultimate con, using the very tools of healing and redemption to achieve her ends. Let them all believe in the power of therapy to unlock buried truths. Let them see a wounded woman finally facing her demons.

The truth remained as cold and hard as her namesake: every tear, every trembling confession, every breakthrough moment was just another calculated step toward her true objective. And as she finally allowed herself to rest, ICE smiled in the darkness, knowing that her performance was only beginning.

The night seemed to deepen around her, but sleep remained elusive. ICE pulled out her third notebook - the one where she tracked the broader game beyond the therapy sessions. Dr. Chen was just one piece of a larger performance, and every element needed to work in perfect synchronization.

She began mapping out the expanding web of relationships and manipulations that would secure her position in Abby's life. The halfway house staff, Dr. Chen, Abby's adoptive mother Liz, even the other residents - each one needed to see a slightly different version of Amanda's transformation, all building toward the same ultimate goal.

For the halfway house staff, she was crafting the image of a model resident struggling with emotional breakthroughs. Their incident reports would document her progress: the nights spent in apparent emotional turmoil after therapy, the careful way she now handled confrontations, the increasing engagement in house activities. Every detail would support her narrative of rehabilitation.

For Liz, the performance required an especially delicate touch. ICE had observed how Abby's adoptive mother watched her during their family dinners, noting the slight tension in her smile, the way her hands tightened on her silverware when Abby called Amanda "Mom." There was leverage there, in that maternal jealousy, but it would need to be handled carefully.

"Build Liz's trust through deference," ICE wrote in her precise handwriting. "Acknowledge her primary role in Abby's life. Show gratitude for her willingness to share family moments. Never challenge her position - let her see Amanda as a supplement to, not replacement for, maternal bond."

She turned to a fresh page, beginning to sketch out the next phase of her plan. The hypnotherapy sessions would provide a foundation, but she needed to build multiple layers of verification. Perhaps it was time for Amanda to join a trauma survivors' support group? The additional witnesses to her "recovery" could prove valuable.

A sound in the hallway caught her attention - likely a neighbor returning home late. ICE quickly noted the time. Understanding her apartment building's rhythms was crucial; these quiet hours provided the perfect opportunity for maintaining her various journals and planning her next moves.

Her thoughts turned to Abby again, this time strategically rather than emotionally. Tomorrow, her daughter would want details about the hypnotherapy session. ICE began crafting the conversation in her mind, planning exactly how to describe the "memories" that had surfaced.

"Lead with vulnerability," she wrote. "Share enough details to satisfy curiosity but maintain mystery. Emphasize emotional impact over specific memories. Build anticipation for future revelations."

The key would be balancing Abby's natural protective instincts with her professional curiosity. As a lawyer, she would want to understand, to analyze. ICE would need to provide enough substance to engage that analytical mind while ensuring the emotional narrative remained primary.

She began listing potential conversation points:

- Initial skepticism about hypnotherapy (shows honesty)

- Emotional difficulty of accessing memories (creates sympathy)

- Specific memory of watching other families in park (safe, verifiable)

- Vague hints about darker memories (maintains intrigue)

- Expression of gratitude for Abby's support (reinforces bond)

Each element would be carefully calibrated to deepen Abby's emotional investment while avoiding any details that might trigger her legal instincts for investigation.

The midnight medication call echoed through the hallway. ICE paused in her writing, listening to the familiar routine of institutional life. These interruptions had become useful markers in her planning, helping her track time without drawing attention with too many glances at the clock.

She returned to her notes, this time focusing on Dr. Chen's likely next moves. The therapist's enthusiasm for the hypnotherapy breakthrough would need to be carefully managed. Too much success too quickly might raise professional suspicions.

"Potential complications to plan for," she wrote:

- Dr. Chen suggesting EMDR or other trauma therapies

- Questions about specific dates/locations of memories

- Attempts to contact original family members

- Interest in police reports or medical records

- Suggestion of group therapy with other survivors

Each potential challenge would need a prepared response, a way to redirect or delay without appearing resistant to treatment. ICE began crafting explanations and deflections, each one designed to maintain control while appearing to embrace the therapeutic process.

The night air grew cooler, seeping through the poorly insulated windows. ICE pulled her thin blanket around her shoulders as she continued planning. The sensation reminded her of countless nights in prison, where cold and discomfort had been constant companions. But those experiences, like everything else in her past, could be turned to advantage - proof of her endurance, her survival instincts.

She turned back to her primary notebook, the one containing her master strategy. The hypnotherapy sessions had opened new possibilities, but they also required adjustments to her timeline. She began revising her projected benchmarks:

Month 1-2: Establish trauma narrative through hypnotherapy

Month 3-4: Begin processing "recovered" memories in regular sessions

Month 4-5: Show measurable progress in emotional regulation
Month 5-6: Start addressing relationship with Abby more directly

Month 6-7: Demonstrate improved family dynamics

Month 7-8: Begin discussing future plans, education goals

Month 8-9: Show concrete steps toward rehabilitation goals

Month 9-10: Position for early release consideration

Each phase would need to show clear progress while maintaining room for setbacks - the occasional emotional regression or triggered response that would make her transformation more believable.

The sound of early morning birds began to filter through her window. ICE glanced at her watch, noting that she'd spent another night fine-tuning her performance. But sleep was secondary to preparation.

Every detail needed to be perfect, every contingency planned for.

She began reviewing her notes on Abby's responses during their recent interactions. Her daughter's body language had shown increasing comfort, her protective instincts growing stronger with each display of maternal vulnerability. The process was working exactly as planned, yet something nagged at ICE's calculated mind.

During their last dinner together, when Abby had reached for her hand across the table, ICE had felt an unfamiliar warmth in her chest. For a moment, the line between performance and reality had blurred, threatening her careful control. Such moments were dangerous, potentially compromising her ability to maintain the necessary emotional distance.

"Remember the objective," she wrote firmly, underlining the words twice. "Emotional attachment = vulnerability. Maintain separation between Amanda's responses and strategic goals."

The first sounds of the halfway house stirring penetrated her concentration - early risers heading to kitchen duty, maintenance staff beginning their rounds. ICE quickly gathered her notebooks, returning them to their hiding places. She would need to appear tired today, emotionally drained from processing yesterday's therapy breakthrough.

As she prepared for another day of calculated performances, ICE reviewed her primary objectives. The hypnotherapy sessions were providing perfect cover for introducing key elements of her narrative. Dr. Chen's professional investment was growing with each breakthrough. Abby's emotional attachment was strengthening steadily. Even Liz's cautious acceptance was proceeding according to plan.

Let them all believe in the power of therapy to heal old wounds, to rebuild broken relationships, to redeem lost souls. ICE would continue orchestrating every tear, every revelation, every moment of apparent vulnerability. The performance was complex, demanding constant vigilance and perfect timing, but the payoff would be worth every calculated risk.

After all, the greatest cons were the ones where everyone got what they wanted - even if what they wanted was just a beautiful lie. And ICE had become a master at crafting exactly the lies people needed to believe.

The rising sun cast long shadows across her room as she finally prepared for sleep. Tomorrow would bring new challenges, new opportunities for manipulation, new chances to reinforce her carefully constructed narrative of redemption. But ICE was ready. She had played many roles in her criminal career, but this performance - this intricate dance of trauma and healing, of vulnerability and calculation - might truly be her masterpiece.

And as she drifted off to sleep, ICE allowed herself a small smile of satisfaction. The hypnotherapy sessions had opened up exactly the opportunities she'd anticipated. Now it was simply a matter of maintaining control, of orchestrating each revelation and breakthrough with perfect precision. After all, the best therapy was about transformation - and ICE was orchestrating a transformation they would never forget.

40 DEPTH CHARGES

The lavender scent in Dr. Chen's office seemed stronger today, almost cloying. ICE noted the change, wondering if the therapist had deliberately increased it to enhance the relaxation effect during hypnotherapy. Such attention to detail deserved appreciation, even if it wouldn't affect her performance.

"Are you ready to go deeper today, Amanda?" Dr. Chen's voice carried that perfect mix of professional confidence and maternal concern. She'd positioned her chair slightly closer than usual - another calculated detail that ICE filed away for future reference.

"I think so," Amanda whispered, allowing a slight tremor in her hands. "The last session was... intense. But I feel like there's more. Like something's trying to surface."

Dr. Chen nodded, her expression brightening with carefully controlled enthusiasm. "That's very common in this work. Our minds often reveal memories in layers, letting us process them gradually. Today, I'd like to focus on a specific period - when Abby was born."

ICE felt a momentary flicker of genuine tension. She'd prepared extensively for this topic, crafting a perfect blend of real and manufactured memories. But something about the therapist's direct approach triggered an unexpected wariness.

"Close your eyes," Dr. Chen instructed, her voice taking on that hypnotic cadence. "Let yourself drift back to that time. You're holding Abby for the first time. What do you feel?"

The memory surfaced before ICE could filter it - Abby's tiny weight in her arms, that impossible softness of newborn skin. She pushed it down ruthlessly, replacing it with her prepared narrative. "She's so small," Amanda murmured. "I'm scared I'll break her. Everyone else seems to know what they're doing, but I feel... lost."

"Stay with that feeling," Dr. Chen encouraged. "What else do you notice?"

"Her hand," the words escaped before ICE could edit them, "wrapped around my finger. So tiny but so strong." She felt a flash of anger at her own lack of control. That detail hadn't been in her planned script.

Dr. Chen leaned forward, professional interest sharpening her gaze. "That's a very specific memory, Amanda. What emotions come up when you think about that moment?"

ICE rapidly recalculated, weaving the unexpected genuine detail into her manufactured narrative. "Guilt," she whispered, timing a tear to roll down her cheek. "So much guilt. Because part of me wanted to keep her, to be her mother. But I knew... I knew I was too broken, too damaged to give her what she needed."

The therapist made a soft sound of sympathy, exactly as expected. But her next question caught ICE off guard: "When you say 'broken,' what specific memories come to mind?"

Images flashed through ICE's mind - not the carefully crafted scenes she'd prepared, but real fragments of her past. The first con she ever ran. The rush of power when she realized how easily people could be manipulated. The moment she chose her name, embracing the cold calculation that would become her trademark.

"Amanda?" Dr. Chen's voice carried a note of concern. "You seem very far away."

ICE forced Amanda's eyes open, letting them shine with manufactured tears. "Sorry," she managed. "Sometimes the memories... they're overwhelming."

"That's perfectly normal," Dr. Chen assured her. "But I noticed something interesting. When you talked about holding Abby, your whole demeanor changed. There was a softness there, a genuine connection. Yet you pulled back from it almost immediately. Can you tell me about that?"

The observation was uncomfortably precise. ICE felt a flash of real anxiety, quickly converted into Amanda's therapeutic vulnerability. "I guess... I'm afraid to let myself feel too much. After everything that happened in my childhood, feeling things deeply seems dangerous."

It was a calculated deflection, designed to redirect Dr. Chen's attention to safer territory. But the therapist remained focused on the present. "Let's go back to that moment with Abby. You said her hand wrapped around your finger. Stay with that sensation. What happens in your body when you remember it?"

ICE felt trapped between performance and memory. The genuine physical recall - that tiny, perfect grip - threatened to crack her carefully maintained facade. She let Amanda's breathing quicken, using real distress to fuel her fictional narrative.

"I can't," she gasped. "Please, I need to stop."

Dr. Chen immediately shifted to stabilization mode, her voice steady and grounding. "You're safe, Amanda. Take a deep breath. That's right. You're here in my office. The memory can't hurt you."

As the session wound down, ICE was already analyzing her performance, noting which genuine reactions had slipped through her control. She would need to be more careful, especially with memories of Abby. The real emotions there were unpredictable, dangerous.

The evening brought another challenge. Abby arrived for their weekly dinner carrying a manila envelope, her expression both excited and uncertain. "Mom, look what I found while organizing some old files. My original birth certificate!"

ICE felt that same cold spike of alarm. She'd built certain details of her narrative around assumptions about missing documentation. "That's... that's wonderful, sweetheart," Amanda managed, reaching for the envelope with trembling hands.

But as they examined the document together, ICE spotted the discrepancy immediately. The hospital listed wasn't the one she'd included in her therapeutic revelations. A small detail, but potentially devastating to her carefully constructed timeline.

"Mom?" Abby's voice carried a note of confusion. "I thought you said... in your therapy sessions... that I was born at the St. Joseph's in Marshfield ?"

ICE let Amanda's hands shake more visibly, manufacturing a trauma response to cover her strategic retreat. "I... I'm sorry. Sometimes the memories... they get confused. There was so much happening, so much pain and fear..."

"Oh, Mom," Abby's protective instincts immediately overrode her analytical ones, just as ICE had counted on. "Don't apologize. Of course the details are fuzzy. You were going through so much."

Later, alone in her room, ICE pulled out her notebooks, documenting the day's challenges and necessary adjustments. Abby's presence would require careful management. The birth certificate discrepancy needed a stronger cover story. And those moments of genuine memory during therapy...

She caught herself absently tracing the words she'd just written, realizing she'd been drawing tiny hearts around Abby's name. The discovery sent a shock of real fury through her system. She ripped out the page, shredding it with calculated precision.

Control was everything. These genuine feelings, these real memories - they were weaknesses, vulnerabilities that could destroy everything she'd worked for. ICE pulled out a fresh page, beginning to map out contingency plans with her usual methodical attention to detail.

But as she wrote, her hand betrayed her again, unconsciously mimicking the memory of a tiny infant grip around her finger. ICE stared at her own trembling digit, feeling the first real crack in her icy composure.

The night deepened around her, but sleep remained elusive. Too many variables, too many genuine emotions threatening to surface. ICE pulled her blanket tighter, trying to freeze out the warmth of real feelings, the dangerous pull of authentic connection.

Let them think trauma was surfacing in therapy. Let them believe recovery was causing her confusion. She would adjust, adapt, maintain control. She had to. Because the alternative - genuine emotional engagement, real vulnerability - was unthinkable.

And yet, as she finally drifted toward sleep, ICE couldn't quite silence the echo of that tiny hand around her finger, that moment of pure connection before she'd chosen to freeze her heart. The very memory she'd been running from all these years was now threatening to thaw something deep inside her carefully maintained ice.

She pulled out her final notebook - the black one where she tracked her deepest strategies, the plans within plans that even her other notebooks didn't reveal. Its pages contained the real architecture of her long game, the ultimate objectives that drove every calculated performance.

But tonight, her normally precise handwriting wavered as she tried to document the day's developments. Abby's certificate discrepancy could be managed through careful misdirection. presence was a larger concern, requiring immediate attention. She began listing potential approaches:

Her pen paused over the page as another memory surfaced uninvited - Abby at three months old, during one of her few visits before walking away. The baby's eyes had tracked her movements with an intelligence that seemed impossible for an infant, as if already trying to understand why her mother kept her distance.

ICE stood abruptly, moving to the window. She pressed her forehead against the cool glass, using the physical sensation to ground herself in the present.

Control was slipping. Not just in the obvious ways - Abby's appearance, the birth certificate, Dr. Chen's uncomfortable insights. Something deeper was shifting, like ice cracking under pressure from hidden currents below.

"Maintain perspective," she wrote firmly in her notebook, underlining each word. "Emotional engagement = tactical vulnerability. Previous success rate correlates directly with emotional distance maintained."

But even as she wrote the words, her mind betrayed her with calculations of a different sort: How many times had Abby searched for her original birth certificate? How long had she wondered about the hospital where she was born, the details of her first hours of life? What other documents might she uncover, what other inconsistencies in ICE's carefully constructed narrative might surface?

More dangerously: Why did these questions suddenly feel important for reasons beyond strategic planning?

ICE ripped the page out, starting fresh. She needed to focus on immediate threats. Emily would be watching, evaluating, comparing the ICE she'd known with this new version of Amanda. The performance would need to be flawless, with just enough hints of her old self to make the transformation believable.

"Create witnessed moments of struggle," she wrote. "Let Jenny observe conflict between old and new behaviors. Layer apparent vulnerability over demonstrated strength. Build narrative of genuine change."

The words felt hollow, mechanical. For the first time in years, ICE found herself questioning not just her tactics, but her fundamental strategy. The careful balance of manipulation and emotional distance that had served her so well was becoming harder to maintain.

She thought of Dr. Chen's observation about her reaction to the memory of Abby's grip. The therapist had seen something real there, something ICE hadn't intended to reveal. The question was: how much more might she see if these genuine reactions continued to surface?

The night had deepened to that hollow hour between midnight and dawn. ICE gathered her notebooks, returning them to their hiding places with practiced precision. Tomorrow would require perfect control, careful manipulation of multiple variables. She needed rest.

But as she finally lay down, her hand curved unconsciously into the memory of holding a tiny finger. And for the first time in longer than she could remember, ICE fell asleep not to the sound of her own calculating thoughts, but to the echo of a newborn's grip that had never fully let her go.

41 PLAYING HOUSE

ICE sat in her apartment, methodically updating her master strategy notebook. The pages were filled with precise documentation of her progress over the past month - each therapy session, every family interaction, all the small victories that were slowly building toward her ultimate goal.

"Session 12 with Dr. Chen," she wrote in her neat, controlled hand. "Continued development of trauma narrative. Key achievements:

- Introduced childhood abandonment theme

- Established pattern of maternal loss

– Connected past trauma to current parenting fears

Therapist response: High emotional investment. Clear belief in 'breakthrough' progress."

Today marked a significant milestone: Dr. Chen had suggested reducing therapy frequency, a sign that her careful manipulation was working exactly as intended.

In her therapy session that afternoon, ICE orchestrated Amanda's response perfectly. "I'm nervous about cutting back," she admitted, letting vulnerability color her tone. "These sessions... they've become my anchor." The slight tremor in her hands was calculated to reinforce Dr. Chen's perception of therapeutic dependence.

Dr. Chen leaned forward, radiating professional warmth. "That's a very normal reaction, Amanda. But your progress has been remarkable. I think you're ready to start applying these skills more independently."

ICE noted how the therapist's body language shifted - the slight softening around her eyes, the unconscious mirroring of Amanda's posture. Perfect. She let Amanda's shoulders relax incrementally, a carefully timed display of accepting reassurance.

"You really think I'm ready?" A masterful blend of hope and hesitation in her voice.

"More than ready," Dr. Chen affirmed. "Your insights into your past behaviors, your commitment to building healthy relationships with Abby and little Amanda - you've done incredible work here."

Back in her room that evening, ICE documented the session's success in her strategic notebook. Dr. Chen's endorsement of her progress would be invaluable for the next phase of her plan.

But it was the deepening integration into Abby's family that required the most delicate manipulation. ICE pulled out her family dynamics notebook, reviewing her careful documentation of each interaction, each small victory in gaining their trust.

The opportunity came sooner than expected. Abby called the next morning, her voice tight with stress. "Mom, I hate to ask, but Drake's stuck at work and I have a huge case preparation..."

"Say no more," Amanda interrupted warmly. "I'd love to watch little Amanda." Every babysitting request was another thread in the web she was weaving, another step toward becoming indispensable.

ICE maintained perfect awareness as she played the doting grandmother, noting which behaviors drew the strongest positive responses from both baby and parents. Little Amanda's delighted giggles when she made silly faces, Abby's grateful relief at finding the house tidied and dinner prepared, Drake's gradual softening toward her presence - each reaction was cataloged and analyzed for future use.

"You're a lifesaver," Abby said that evening, watching Amanda rock the baby to sleep. "I don't know how we managed before."

ICE let Amanda's eyes fill with tears - a genuine physical response she'd learned to trigger on command. "Being here for you, for both of you... it's helping me heal too." The words were carefully chosen to reinforce her therapeutic narrative while deepening emotional bonds.

Later, alone in her apartment, ICE reviewed her progress. The family integration was proceeding exactly as planned, but maintaining multiple personas required constant vigilance. She began mapping out her next moves:

"Priority objectives:

1. Transition therapy to monthly maintenance (emphasize continued commitment while reducing oversight)

2. Increase family dependency (expand childcare role, domestic support)

3. Begin suggesting shared living arrangements (plant seeds through therapy narrative)"

A memory surfaced - little Amanda's tiny hand wrapping around her finger during that afternoon's nap. ICE frowned, noting how these genuine moments were becoming more frequent, harder to suppress. She would need to maintain stricter emotional distance.

The weeks unfolded according to her careful choreography. In therapy, Amanda processed her fears about rekindling family bonds, each vulnerability calculated to support her larger narrative. At the Johnson home, she became increasingly essential to their daily routine, her presence so natural they could no longer imagine life without her.

Even Drake's initial reservations began to fade. ICE had studied him carefully, noting his protective instincts toward both Abby and the baby. She made sure Amanda's interactions always supported his role as father and protector, never challenging his position but gradually becoming someone he relied on.

"Your mom's really changed," he told Abby one evening, unaware that ICE was within earshot. "It's like she's become a completely different person."

ICE allowed herself a small smile of satisfaction. If only he knew how right he was. Every "changed" behavior was a carefully crafted performance, designed to give them exactly what they needed to see.

The suggestion of shared living arrangements came through Dr. Chen, exactly as ICE had planned. "A stable family environment could be crucial for maintaining your progress," the therapist noted during a joint session with Abby. "Having consistent support and opportunities to rebuild relationships..."

ICE watched Abby's expression shift from consideration to hope. The seed was planted. Now she just had to wait, letting them believe the idea was their own.

But that night, updating her notebooks, ICE found her hands

shaking slightly. The genuine moments were becoming more frequent - little Amanda's first steps, Abby's unguarded smiles, even Drake's grudging acceptance. Each real connection threatened to crack her carefully maintained facade.

"Maintain focus," she wrote firmly. "Emotional attachment = vulnerability. Strategic objective remains primary."

The halfway house staff noted her increasing stability, her deepening family bonds. Their reports would support her eventual release, another piece falling perfectly into place. Every performance was calibrated, every reaction measured, every relationship carefully managed.

Yet sometimes, in the quiet moments between calculations, ICE felt something stirring beneath her frozen core. A warmth she couldn't quite suppress, a genuine response she hadn't planned for. Those were the dangerous moments, when the line between performance and reality began to blur.

She documented these moments clinically, analyzing them for potential weakness. But even her precise handwriting seemed to betray her, softening when she wrote about little Amanda's developmental milestones or Abby's growing trust.

The ultimate test came during a family dinner, when little Amanda reached for her, crying "Gamma" for the first time. The surge of genuine emotion caught ICE off guard. She maintained Amanda's perfect performance - tears of joy, trembling hands, heartfelt words of love. But later, alone with her notebooks, she found herself struggling to maintain her usual clinical distance.

"Problematic response to familial bonding," she wrote. "Increasing frequency of genuine emotional engagement. Risk assessment needed."

But even as she documented the danger, another part of her mind was already calculating how to use these real feelings to enhance her performance. After all, the most convincing lies contained elements of truth. And if some small part of her was actually warming to this family role... well, that could just make her ultimate victory even sweeter.

The night deepened around her as ICE continued planning, mapping out the next phases of her integration into the Johnson family. Her performance as Amanda had to remain flawless, her manipulation subtle enough to avoid detection. Every genuine moment would be turned to strategic advantage, every real emotion carefully controlled and directed.

Let them believe in the power of love and redemption. Let them see exactly what they needed to see in her transformation. ICE would play this role perfectly, no matter what it cost her. Because in the end, the game was all that mattered. And she never played to lose.

Even if winning meant freezing out the unexpected warmth that threatened to thaw her carefully maintained ice.

The morning sun painted harsh shadows across ICE's notebooks as she began her daily documentation. Multiple spiral-bound volumes now filled her hiding space behind the loose baseboard - each one dedicated to a different aspect of her long game. The family dynamics notebook had grown the thickest, its pages dense with observations, strategies, and carefully planned responses to every possible scenario.

"Current status assessment," she wrote, underlining the heading twice. "Family integration proceeding ahead of schedule. Key indicators:

Increased frequency of childcare requests

Growing reliance on domestic support

Strengthening bonds with all family members

Therapeutic narrative supporting permanent placement"

But beneath these clinical observations, ICE found herself adding unexpected details - the way little Amanda's hair curled at the nape of her neck, just like Abby's had as a baby. The particular tone of Abby's laugh when she was truly relaxed, not just professionally polite. Even Drake's unconscious habit of humming while he cooked, a detail that served no strategic purpose but had somehow worked its way into her notes.

These personal observations troubled her. They represented a dangerous shift from calculated documentation to genuine attention. ICE began a new section titled "Risk Analysis," her pen pressing harder into the paper:

"Increasing incidents of unplanned emotional response. Possible compromising factors:

Extended exposure to family environment

Child development triggers (evolutionary response?)

Success of own performance creating feedback loop

Memory contamination from genuine past experiences"

Her phone rang, interrupting her writing. ICE glanced at the caller ID before answering. "Amanda," Dr. Chen's voice came through clearly, "I hope I'm not disturbing you. I wanted to see if we could move up our next session to this afternoon."

ICE felt a flicker of genuine tension. Unscheduled changes were dangerous, requiring rapid recalibration of prepared responses. "Thank you," Amanda called back, her voice perfectly modulated to suggest grateful acceptance. "I'll be ready."

Alone again, she pulled out her therapy notebook, reviewing recent sessions with obsessive attention to detail. Dr. Chen had been increasingly focused on Amanda's relationship with little Amanda, probing for connections between past trauma and present attachments. ICE had fed her exactly what she wanted to see - a woman healing through the power of familial love, finding redemption in grandmother-hood.

But now, documenting her strategic responses, ICE found her hand trembling slightly. The lies were becoming harder to separate from truth, the performance bleeding into reality in ways she hadn't anticipated. She thought of little Amanda's face lighting up when she arrived, of Abby's unguarded moments of trust, of Drake's growing acceptance of her presence in their lives.

"Maintain perspective," she wrote sharply. "Primary objective remains unchanged. Family integration = means to an end."

Yet even as she wrote the words, another memory surfaced - little Amanda taking her first steps, tottering between her and Abby while Drake recorded the moment on his phone. The pure joy on their faces, the way time seemed to stop in that perfect instant of family connection. ICE had played her role flawlessly, of course, but something about the memory felt different from her usual calculated performances.

She turned to a fresh page, beginning to map out contingency plans:

"Phase 1: Therapeutic Culmination

Reduce session frequency while maintaining narrative

Position family support as crucial to recovery

Document 'breakthroughs' for halfway house reports

Phase 2: Family Integration

Increase indispensability through childcare/support

Cultivate deeper bonds with all members

Plant seeds for permanent living arrangement

Phase 3: Legal/Financial Security

Build documentation of stability/reform

Establish financial dependence patterns

Create witnesses to transformation"

Each step was meticulously planned, every interaction choreographed for maximum impact. ICE had played longer cons before, had maintained more complex deceptions. But something about this performance felt different, as if the lines between actor and role were becoming dangerously blurred.

She thought of her last therapy session, when Dr. Chen had asked about her deepest fears. ICE had given Amanda's prepared response about the terror of losing her newfound family connections, of proving unworthy of their trust. But beneath the performance, she'd felt an unexpected echo of genuine anxiety. The thought of losing access to Abby and little Amanda had triggered a response that went beyond strategic concern.

"Emotional contamination increasing," she noted clinically. "Performance affecting performer - dangerous feedback loop developing."

She would need to maintain perfect control during her unexpected therapy session, to show Dr. Chen exactly what she needed to see while revealing nothing of these inner complications.

As she prepared for the afternoon's performance, ICE reviewed her ultimate objectives. The long game required patience, perfect timing, and absolute emotional control. She had mastered all three through years of practice, turning herself into an instrument of precise manipulation.

But now, as she studied her reflection in the small mirror, practicing Amanda's expressions of vulnerable hope and maternal love, ICE found herself wondering about the cost of her perfect performance. The warmth that threatened to crack her frozen core wasn't just a danger to her plans - it was a challenge to everything she'd built herself to be.

Let them believe in redemption, in the power of love to transform even the coldest heart. ICE would continue playing her role with flawless precision, orchestrating every tear and smile, every moment of apparent vulnerability. The performance would remain perfect, even as the performer began to question the script she'd written for herself.

After all, the greatest cons were the ones where everyone got what they wanted - even if what they wanted was just a beautiful lie. And if some small part of her was starting to want it too... well, that was just another variable to be controlled, another factor to be calculated in her endless game of manipulation and deceit.

The afternoon sun cast long shadows through her window as ICE made her final preparations for Dr. Chen's session. She would maintain control, suppress these dangerous genuine responses, keep her focus on the ultimate objective. The game was too important, the stakes too high, to allow real feelings to compromise her performance.

Even if those feelings were becoming harder to distinguish from the lies she'd crafted so carefully. Even if every moment with little Amanda, every unguarded smile from Abby, every grudging acceptance from Drake, left another crack in her frozen defenses.

ICE squared her shoulders, checking Amanda's expression one final time in the mirror. The game continued, the performance remained perfect, and the ice at her core would stay frozen. It had to. Because the alternative - genuine connection, real vulnerability, actual love - was more terrifying than any prison cell she'd ever faced.

Let them see Amanda's warmth, her growing capacity for love and connection. ICE would maintain her cold calculation beneath it all, using every genuine moment to strengthen her deception. The perfect con required perfect control, even if that meant controlling the unexpected warmth in her own heart.

After all, ice could take many forms, could appear to thaw while maintaining its essential nature. And beneath the surface, no matter how much warmth was applied, the core remained forever frozen.

Or so ICE told herself, even as another part of her wondered if some lies, repeated often enough, with enough conviction, could somehow become their own kind of truth.

A knock at her door pulled ICE from her reflections. Mrs. Rodriguez stood in the doorway, her expression suggesting more than a routine check-in. "Amanda, do you have a moment? There's something I'd like to discuss."

ICE quickly shifted into Amanda's therapeutic persona, allowing just the right amount of nervous anticipation to show. "Of course," she said softly, gesturing to the room's single chair while she perched on the bed.

ICE maintained perfect control of Amanda's reactions, but her mind was already racing ahead, calculating new possibilities. Early release would accelerate her timeline, require adjustments to her carefully laid plans. She pulled out her hidden notebooks that night, documenting every detail of the conversation and its implications.

"Accelerated Timeline Adjustments:

Intensify family dependency creation

Strengthen narrative of essential support role

Document financial interdependence

Build community witness base for reformation"

But as she wrote, another memory surfaced - little Amanda's second birthday party the previous weekend. ICE had orchestrated every detail perfectly, from Amanda's tearfully grateful speech to her carefully measured interactions with each guest. The performance had been flawless.

Yet something about that day kept nagging at her. A moment when little Amanda had fallen, scraping her knee on the patio. ICE had moved without thinking, scooping up the crying child before either Abby or Drake could reach her. The comfort she'd offered hadn't been calculated, the kisses she'd pressed to the injury hadn't been part of any script.

"Emotional contamination increasing," she wrote, underlining the words twice. "Genuine responses occurring without tactical consideration. Risk level elevated."

She forced herself to review the day's events clinically, analyzing each interaction for strategic value. The way Abby had hugged her after the party, whispering "I'm so glad you're here, Mom." Drake's gruff acknowledgment of her help as they cleaned up. The photo album they'd presented her with, filled with pictures of little Amanda's first two years.

ICE had played her role perfectly, of course. Amanda's tears of joy had been perfectly calibrated, her expressions of gratitude exactly what a reformed mother should show. But something about the weight of that photo album in her hands, the tangible evidence of her integration into their lives, had triggered an unexpected response.

She found herself opening the album now, her tactical mind insisting it was just to review her performance in the photographs. Each image showed Amanda's flawless portrayal of grandmother-hood - the loving smiles, the tender touches, the perfect mix of gratitude and devotion.

But there, in a candid shot she hadn't known was being taken, ICE saw something that made her frozen core shudder. She was looking at little Amanda, who was concentrating on stacking blocks, and her expression... there was nothing calculated there, nothing performed. The love in her eyes was raw, real, unguarded.

"Strategic analysis compromised," she wrote sharply. "Performance boundaries becoming unclear. Emotional engagement exceeding tactical requirements."

The night deepened around her as ICE struggled to maintain her clinical distance. She was playing the longest con of her career, orchestrating the most intricate manipulation she'd ever attempted. She couldn't afford to let genuine feelings complicate her perfect performance.

Yet as she prepared for sleep, ICE found herself holding the photo album again, tracing the images with trembling fingers. Each picture represented a victory in her grand manipulation, a step toward her ultimate goal. But they also showed something else, something that frightened her more than any prison sentence ever had.

They showed the possibility that some lies, lived fully enough, with complete conviction, might become indistinguishable from truth. That some performances, maintained perfectly over time, might transform the performer in ways no tactical analysis could predict.

Ice could take many forms, could appear to thaw while maintaining its essential nature. But what happened when the thaw began from within, when the warmth that threatened to crack the frozen core came from the ice itself?

ICE closed the photo album firmly, returning it to its hiding place with her notebooks. Tomorrow would bring new challenges, new performances, new opportunities for manipulation. She would maintain control, keep her focus on the ultimate objective, suppress these dangerous genuine responses.

Even if maintaining that control felt more like freezing herself than ever before.

42 STRATEGIC INTEGRATION

Three Months Later

March 2018

ICE sat in her bedroom, methodically organizing her growing collection of notebooks. Each volume represented a different aspect of her long game - therapeutic progress, family dynamics, behavioral modifications, contingency plans. The morning sun cast harsh shadows across the pages as she documented her latest calculations. The living room floor of the Thompson home had become little Amanda's stage as she demonstrated her newest skill—stringing three words together into simple sentences. At sixteen months, her vocabulary was growing faster than the child development books predicted, a fact that both delighted Abby and provided ICE with new opportunities for deepening her essential role in the family.

"Primary objective status report," she wrote in her precise hand. "Family integration proceeding according to timeline. Key markers achieved:

- Therapeutic credibility established with Dr. Chen

- Core family unit showing increasing dependency

- Financial interdependence groundwork laid"

She pulled out her family dynamics notebook, documenting little Amanda's latest developmental milestone with clinical precision. The child had begun forming more complex sentences, a progression that required adjustments to Amanda's grandmother persona.

"Behavioral adaptation required," she noted. "Increase vocabulary complexity while maintaining emotional accessibility. Monitor for opportunities to reinforce familial bonds through linguistic mirroring."

But even as she wrote, an unbidden memory surfaced - little Amanda's face lighting up as she mastered a new word, the pure joy in her expression when Amanda praised her progress. ICE frowned, noting this instance of emotional contamination in her risk assessment log.

A knock at her door interrupted her documentation. "Amanda?" Marcus called. "Dr. Chen's office called. They want to move your session to this afternoon."

ICE felt a flicker of genuine tension. Schedule disruptions required rapid tactical adjustments. "Thank you," Amanda's voice replied with perfect grateful warmth. "I'll be ready."

Alone again, she pulled out her therapy notebook, reviewing recent sessions with obsessive attention to detail. Dr. Chen had been probing deeper into Amanda's relationship with little Amanda, searching for connections between past trauma and present attachments.

"Therapeutic narrative maintenance priority," she wrote. "Key elements to reinforce:

- Gradual emotional awakening through grandmother role

- Controlled vulnerability regarding past failures

- Strategic display of healing through family bonds"

But her hand trembled slightly as she documented the previous week's family dinner. Something had shifted during that evening, a moment of genuine warmth that had pierced her calculated performance. Little Amanda had fallen asleep in her lap, tiny fingers curled around her thumb, and for a brief instant, ICE had forgotten to maintain Amanda's persona.

"Warning indicators," she noted sharply. "Increasing frequency of unplanned emotional responses. Performance boundaries showing signs of deterioration."

As she prepared for her performance, ICE reviewed her ultimate objectives. The long game required patience, precise timing, and absolute emotional discipline. She had mastered all three through years of practice, turning herself into an instrument of calculated manipulation.

Dr. Chen's office maintained its usual lavender scent, a detail ICE had documented extensively in her environmental factors log. The therapist's smile held genuine warmth - another indicator of successful manipulation.

"How are you feeling today, Amanda?" Dr. Chen asked, leaning forward with professional concern.

ICE let Amanda's hands twist together, a carefully calibrated display of nervous energy. "Actually," she said softly, "I've been thinking a lot about little Amanda. About how different it feels, being a grandmother, compared to when..."

She let her voice trail off, timing a tear to roll down her cheek. Dr. Chen's expression showed exactly the response ICE had anticipated - professional excitement barely masked by therapeutic concern.

"Different how?" the therapist prompted gently.

ICE had prepared extensively for this conversation, crafting a perfect blend of vulnerability and insight. "When Abby was born," Amanda whispered, "I was so lost in my own pain, my own issues. But with little Amanda, it's like... like I can finally be the mother I should have been."

The words were calculated to resonate with Dr. Chen's therapeutic framework while reinforcing Amanda's redemption narrative. But something caught in ICE's throat as she spoke, an unexpected echo of genuine regret.

Later, updating her notebooks, ICE found her clinical precision wavering. The therapy session had gone exactly as planned, Dr. Chen's responses falling perfectly in line with projected outcomes. But something else had surfaced during their conversation - a moment of real emotion that hadn't been part of her calculated performance.

"Risk assessment critical," she wrote, pressing the pen hard against the paper. "Emotional containment showing signs of compromise. Strategic adjustments required."

But even as she documented these concerns, another memory intruded - little Amanda's third birthday party the previous weekend. ICE had orchestrated every detail perfectly, from Amanda's tearfully grateful speech to her carefully measured interactions with each guest.

Yet there had been a moment, unplanned and unscripted, when little Amanda had fallen and scraped her knee. ICE had moved without calculation, pure instinct driving her to comfort the crying child. The kisses she'd pressed to the injury hadn't been part of any strategy.

"Performance contamination increasing," she noted clinically. "Genuine responses occurring without tactical consideration. Risk level elevated."

The photo album they'd given her sat hidden with her notebooks, its weight somehow heavier than its physical mass should allow. Each image showed Amanda's flawless portrayal of grandmother-hood - the loving smiles, the tender touches, the perfect mix of gratitude and devotion.

But there, in a candid shot she hadn't known was being taken, ICE saw something that made her frozen core shudder. She was looking at little Amanda, who was concentrating on stacking blocks, and her expression... there was nothing calculated there, nothing performed.

"Strategic analysis compromised," she wrote sharply. "Performance boundaries becoming unclear. Emotional engagement exceeding tactical requirements."

ICE shifted seamlessly into Amanda's therapeutic persona, allowing just the right amount of nervous anticipation to show. "Of course," she said softly, gesturing to the room's single chair while she perched on the bed.

That night, alone with her notebooks, ICE began mapping out accelerated timeline adjustments. Early release would require careful recalibration of her strategies, faster implementation of key manipulation phases.

"Priority objectives revised:

- Intensify family dependency creation

- Strengthen narrative of essential support role

- Document financial interdependence

- Build community witness base for reformation"

But as she wrote, her hand kept straying to the photo album. Each image represented a victory in her grand manipulation, a step toward her ultimate goal. Yet something about these frozen moments of apparent joy threatened her carefully maintained control.

ICE found herself returning to one particular photo - a simple snapshot of herself reading to little Amanda. The child was curled against her chest, totally trusting, while Amanda's face showed an expression of... what? Love? Peace? Whatever it was, it hadn't been calculated for effect.

"Warning," she wrote, the word sharp and angular on the page. "Performance authenticity exceeding tactical requirements. Emotional boundaries showing critical instability."

The night deepened around her as ICE struggled to maintain her clinical distance. She was playing the longest con of her career, orchestrating the most intricate manipulation she'd ever attempted. She couldn't afford to let genuine feelings complicate her perfect performance.

Yet as she prepared for sleep, something kept drawing her back to that photo album. Each image represented a step in her calculated game, yes. But they also showed something else, something that frightened her more than any prison sentence ever had.

They showed the possibility that some lies, lived fully enough, with complete conviction, might become indistinguishable from truth. That some performances, maintained perfectly over time, might transform the performer in ways no tactical analysis could predict.

ICE closed the album firmly, returning it to its hiding place with her notebooks. Tomorrow would bring new challenges, new performances, new opportunities for manipulation. She would maintain control, keep her focus on the ultimate objective, suppress these dangerous genuine responses.

Even if maintaining that control felt more like freezing herself than ever before. Even if each calculated interaction with her family left another crack in her carefully maintained ice.

Let them believe in redemption, in the power of love to transform even the coldest heart. ICE would continue playing her role with flawless precision, orchestrating every tear and smile, every moment of apparent vulnerability.

After all, the greatest cons were the ones where everyone got what they wanted - even if what they wanted was just a beautiful lie. And if some small part of her was starting to want it too... well, that was just another variable to be controlled, another factor to be calculated in her endless game of manipulation and deceit.

The night seemed to deepen around her as ICE continued planning, mapping out the next phases of her integration into the Johnson family. Her performance as Amanda had to remain flawless, her manipulation subtle enough to avoid detection.

Let them see Amanda's warmth, her growing capacity for love

and connection. ICE would maintain her cold calculation beneath it all, using every genuine moment to strengthen her deception. The perfect con required perfect control, even if that meant controlling the unexpected warmth in her own heart.

After all, ICE could take many forms, could appear to thaw while maintaining its essential nature. And beneath the surface, no matter how much warmth was applied, the core remained forever frozen.

Or so ICE told herself, even as another part of her wondered if some lies, repeated often enough, with enough conviction, could somehow become their own kind of truth.

She pulled out her final notebook - the black one where she tracked her deepest strategies, the plans within plans that even her other notebooks didn't reveal. Its pages contained the real architecture of her long game, the ultimate objectives that drove every calculated performance.

"Early release implications," she wrote, her normally precise handwriting showing unusual tension. "Accelerated timeline requires immediate adjustments:

Phase 1: Institutional Exit Strategy

- Document therapeutic 'breakthroughs' with increased frequency

- Position family stability as crucial to rehabilitation

- Create witness trail of transformation

Phase 2: Family Integration Acceleration

- Increase childcare responsibility incrementally

- Develop essential role in daily routines

- Strengthen bonds with all family members

- Plant seeds for permanent living arrangement

Phase 3: Financial/Legal Security Establishment

- Begin subtle dependency patterns

- Document stability through official channels

- Create community support network

- Position rehabilitation narrative for legal validation"

But as she wrote, memories kept intruding - not the carefully crafted ones she used in therapy, but real fragments of her past that threatened her perfect control. The first time she'd held Abby, that moment of pure connection before she'd chosen to freeze her heart. The way little Amanda's laugh echoed her mother's at that age. The unexpected warmth in Drake's voice when he'd started calling her "Mom" without seeming to realize it.

ICE found herself returning to the photo album, though her tactical mind insisted it was just to review her performance documentation. Each image showed Amanda's flawless portrayal of grandmother-hood - the loving smiles, the tender touches, the perfect mix of gratitude and devotion.

She caught herself absently tracing little Amanda's face in one photo, the way the child's expression mirrored her own unguarded moment of joy. The discovery sent a shock of fury through her system. She slammed the album shut, anger at her own weakness burning cold in her chest.

"Critical performance analysis," she wrote sharply. "Warning indicators increasing:

- Emotional contamination exceeding tactical requirements

- Genuine responses occurring without strategic planning

- Memory integrity compromised by authentic recall

- Performance boundaries showing dangerous instability"

The night seemed to deepen around her as ICE struggled to maintain her clinical distance. She was playing the longest con of her career, orchestrating the most intricate manipulation she'd ever attempted. She couldn't afford to let genuine feelings complicate her perfect performance.

And yet... and yet something kept pulling her back to those unguarded moments. The way little Amanda reached for her without hesitation, total trust in her tiny hands. How Abby's eyes softened when she called her "Mom," the old pain finally fading. Even Drake's growing acceptance, the way he'd started including her in family decisions without conscious thought.

ICE pulled out her tactical notebook, forcing herself to review her primary objectives. The long game required absolute control, perfect timing, and complete emotional discipline. She had mastered all three through years of practice, turning herself into an instrument of precise manipulation.

But now, documenting the day's events, she found her clinical precision wavering. Each interaction with her family seemed to leave another crack in her carefully maintained facade. The warmth that threatened to thaw her frozen core wasn't just a danger to her plans - it was a challenge to everything she'd built herself to be.

She thought of Dr. Chen's observation during their last session, about how her voice changed when she spoke about little Amanda. The therapist had seen something real there, something ICE hadn't intended to reveal. The question was: how much more might she see if these genuine reactions continued to surface?

"Contingency planning critical," she wrote, pressing the pen hard against the paper. "Strategic options for emotional containment:

- Increase documentation frequency

- Implement stricter performance boundaries

- Develop counter-measures for genuine responses

- Maintain focus on ultimate objective"

But even as she listed these cold calculations, another part of her mind was remembering the moment at little Amanda's birthday party when the child had fallen. ICE's immediate response - the instinctive move to comfort, protect, love - had come before any strategic consideration. For that brief instant, she had simply been a grandmother, nothing more and nothing less.

The realization sent a chill through her that had nothing to do with her chosen name. What if the greatest danger to her perfect con wasn't external exposure, but internal transformation? What if maintaining her frozen core was becoming more painful than letting it thaw?

"Performance integrity compromised," she noted clinically, though her hand shook slightly. "Emotional engagement exceeding tactical requirements. Risk assessment critical."

But there was something else, something she couldn't quite bring herself to document even in her most private notebook. The possibility that maybe, just maybe, her perfect performance of love and redemption was becoming more real than her carefully maintained ice.

The night wrapped around her like a blanket as ICE continued her meticulous planning. She would maintain control, suppress these dangerous genuine responses, keep her focus on the ultimate objective. The game was too important, the stakes too high, to allow real feelings to compromise her performance.

Let them believe in redemption, in the power of love to transform even the coldest heart. ICE would continue playing her role with flawless precision, orchestrating every tear and smile, every moment of apparent vulnerability. The performance would remain perfect, even as the performer began to question the script she'd written for herself.

After all, the greatest cons were the ones where everyone got what they wanted - even if what they wanted was just a beautiful lie. And if some small part of her was starting to want it too... well, that was just another variable to be controlled, another factor to be calculated in her endless game of manipulation and deceit.

The security lights cast harsh shadows through her window as ICE made her final notes for the night. Tomorrow would bring new challenges, new performances, new opportunities for manipulation. She would maintain control, keep her focus on the ultimate objective, suppress these dangerous genuine responses.

Even if maintaining that control felt more like freezing herself than ever before. Even if each calculated interaction with her family left another crack in her carefully maintained ice. Even if the warmth that threatened to thaw her frozen core came from somewhere deep within herself.

Let them see Amanda's warmth, her growing capacity for love and connection. ICE would maintain her cold calculation beneath it all, using every genuine moment to strengthen her deception. The perfect con required perfect control, even if that meant controlling the unexpected warmth in her own heart.

After all, ice could take many forms, could appear to thaw while maintaining its essential nature. And beneath the surface, no matter how much warmth was applied, the core remained forever frozen.

Or so ICE told herself, as she finally prepared for sleep. But in the quiet darkness of her room, surrounded by her notebooks full of calculations and strategies, she couldn't quite silence the whisper of doubt in her frozen heart. The possibility that some lies, lived fully enough, with enough conviction, might become their own kind of truth. That some performances, maintained perfectly over time, might transform the performer in ways no tactical analysis could predict.

And perhaps that transformation, that thaw, was the greatest risk - and the greatest possibility - of all.

ICE pulled out her final notebook of the night, the one she kept separate from all others. Its pages contained her deepest analysis, the calculations too dangerous to risk anyone else seeing. Here, she documented not just her strategies and observations, but the subtle shifts in her own responses that threatened her perfect control.

"Performance evolution analysis," she wrote, her pen moving with deliberate precision. "Increasing incidents of unplanned emotional engagement:

Trigger: Little Amanda's morning greetings

Initial response: Calculated display of grandmother's joy

Current response: Genuine smile occurs before tactical consideration

Risk level: Elevated

Trigger: Abby's casual physical affection

Initial response: Manufactured warmth with appropriate hesitation

Current response: Instinctive return of embrace

Risk level: Critical

Trigger: Drake's gradual acceptance

Initial response: Strategic gratitude display

Current response: Unexpected satisfaction at family inclusion

Risk level: Warning"

She found herself returning to the previous weekend's family dinner. Drake had been grilling, his characteristic humming floating through the evening air. Abby was setting the table on the patio, laughing at little Amanda's attempts to help. The scene had been perfect for ICE's purposes - a display of family integration that would reinforce her narrative of rehabilitation.

But something had shifted during that meal. When little Amanda had climbed into her lap, sticky hands clutching a half-eaten cookie, ICE had felt a warmth that had nothing to do with performance. The child's complete trust, the way she settled against her grandmother's chest without hesitation, had triggered a response that bypassed all strategic consideration.

"Critical incident analysis," she wrote, forcing her hand to remain steady. "Family dinner performance compromise:

- Unplanned physical affection accepted without tactical pause

- Genuine emotional response preceded calculated display

- Strategic distance compromised by authentic connection

- Performance boundaries showed significant deterioration"

The security lights cast shifting shadows across her pages as ICE continued her assessment. Each documented incident revealed another layer of risk, another moment where her perfect performance had been contaminated by real feeling.

She thought of Dr. Chen's last observation about her changing responses to family interactions. The therapist had noted a "natural warmth" emerging, something beyond the careful progress ICE had planned to display. Even her tactical adjustments couldn't fully mask the gradual transformation occurring beneath her calculated surface.

"Therapeutic narrative complications," she noted. "Dr. Chen showing increased awareness of authentic responses. Risk mitigation strategies required:

- Maintain controlled vulnerability displays

- Increase documentation of planned progress

- Develop counter-measures for genuine emotional leakage

- Reinforce strategic framework for family interactions"

But even as she wrote these cold calculations, another memory surfaced - little Amanda's face lighting up at her arrival, the pure joy in her expression untainted by any manipulation or deceit. The child's love was real, unconditional, completely authentic. And somewhere deep in ICE's frozen core, something responded to that love with equal authenticity.

The realization sent a shudder through her carefully maintained control. What if the greatest threat to her perfect con wasn't external exposure or tactical failure? What if the real danger was the gradual thaw occurring within her own carefully frozen heart?

She began a new section in her notebook, forcing herself to analyze these dangerous shifts with clinical precision:

"Internal transformation indicators:

Phase 1: Initial Integration

- Calculated responses becoming reflexive

- Performance boundaries showing elasticity

- Genuine emotions emerging without tactical intent

- Strategic distance compromised by authentic connection

Phase 2: Current Status

- Emotional engagement exceeding tactical requirements

- Family bonds developing beyond strategic necessity

- Authentic responses occurring before calculated ones

- Performance authenticity threatening operational control

Phase 3: Projected Developments

- Increasing difficulty maintaining emotional distance

- Strategic objectives complicated by genuine attachment

- Performance boundaries becoming increasingly permeable

- Core identity showing signs of transformation"

The night seemed to wrap around her as ICE confronted the implications of her analysis. Each documented incident, every noted change, pointed to a fundamental shift occurring beneath her perfect performance. The ice at her core, maintained through years of careful calculation, was beginning to thaw despite all her efforts to maintain control.

She thought of Abby's eyes softening when she called her "Mom," the way the old pain was gradually being replaced by genuine trust. She remembered Drake's gruff acceptance turning into real inclusion, how he'd started consulting her about family decisions without conscious thought. And little Amanda... the child's unconditional love was like a constant warmth, slowly melting the frozen walls ICE had built around her heart.

"Performance integrity critical," she wrote, pressing the pen hard against the paper. "Strategic objectives require maintenance of emotional distance. Countermeasures essential:

- Increase documentation frequency

- Reinforce tactical awareness

- Develop response protocols for genuine emotions

- Maintain focus on ultimate goal"

But even as she listed these cold calculations, ICE found herself returning to the photo album. Each image showed her perfect performance of grandmother-hood, every smile and gesture carefully crafted for maximum effect. Yet there, in the unguarded moments caught between poses, she saw something that frightened her more than any prison sentence ever had.

She saw truth emerging from lies, authenticity growing from performance, real love blooming in the frozen garden of her manipulation. The transformation was subtle but undeniable - like ice slowly melting under persistent warmth, revealing the living water beneath.

The night deepened around her as ICE continued her documentation, each entry becoming both analysis and confession. She was playing the longest con of her career, orchestrating the most intricate manipulation she'd ever attempted. But somewhere along the way, the performance had begun to transform the performer.

Let them believe in redemption, in the power of love to thaw even the coldest heart. ICE would continue her perfect performance, maintain her tactical awareness, pursue her strategic objectives. She would document every change, analyze every shift, maintain control over every aspect of her grand manipulation.

But in the quiet darkness of her room, surrounded by her notebooks full of calculations and strategies, she couldn't quite silence the whisper of truth in her thawing heart. The possibility that some lies, lived fully enough, with enough conviction, might become their own kind of reality. That some performances, maintained perfectly over time, might transform the performer in ways no tactical analysis could predict.

And perhaps that transformation, that gradual thaw, was both her greatest risk and her ultimate salvation. Because in the end, the most perfect con might be the one where everyone got what they truly needed - even the con artist herself.

ICE closed her notebooks with trembling hands, returning them to their hiding places with practiced precision. Tomorrow would bring new challenges, new performances, new opportunities for both manipulation and genuine connection. She would maintain her strategic awareness, keep her tactical focus, continue her careful documentation.

But as she finally prepared for sleep, she couldn't help wondering if perhaps the greatest con of all was the one she'd played on herself - believing that ice could remain forever frozen in the persistent warmth of love. That a heart once thawed might choose to freeze again, even when surrounded by the gentle heat of family bonds and genuine affection.

Let them see Amanda's warmth, her growing capacity for love and connection. ICE would maintain her calculations beneath it all, document every change, analyze every shift. The perfect con required perfect control, even if that meant controlling the unexpected warmth in her own heart.

After all, ice could take many forms, could appear to thaw while maintaining its essential nature. And beneath the surface, no matter how much warmth was applied, the core remained forever frozen.

Or so ICE had always believed. But now, as she drifted toward sleep surrounded by her notebooks full of strategic calculations and emotional analysis, she wasn't quite so sure. Because some transformations, once begun, couldn't be stopped by any amount of tactical planning or careful control.

And in the end, perhaps that was exactly as it should be.

Sleep remained elusive as ICE found herself drawn back to her documentation. The night's shadows seemed to deepen around her as she pulled out her master strategy notebook one final time. Something about this evening's analysis felt incomplete, as if a crucial variable remained unexamined.

"Long-term projection analysis," she wrote, her normally precise handwriting showing subtle signs of tension. "Integration progress exceeding tactical requirements:

Family Unit Status:

- Primary Target (Abby)

Initial objective: Establish maternal authority

Current status: Genuine maternal bonds forming

Risk assessment: Critical

- Secondary Target (Drake)

Initial objective: Obtain reluctant acceptance

Current status: Authentic family integration

Risk assessment: Elevated

- Tertiary Target (Little Amanda)

Initial objective: Leverage emotional access

Current status: Unplanned attachment formation

Risk assessment: Severe"

ICE paused in her writing, acknowledging the tremor in her hand that appeared whenever she documented interactions with little Amanda. The child had become both her greatest tactical advantage and her most dangerous vulnerability. Every genuine smile, every spontaneous hug, every moment of pure trust created another crack in her carefully maintained facade.

She began a new section, forcing herself to confront the implications of her changing responses:

"Performance evolution timeline:

Phase 1 (Initial Integration)

– Calculated responses dominant

– Strategic planning fully controlled

– Emotional boundaries maintained

– Core identity stable

Phase 2 (Current Status)

– Authentic responses emerging

– Strategic planning compromised

– Emotional boundaries permeable

– Core identity showing instability

Phase 3 (Projected Development)

– WARNING: Critical system failure possible

– Authentic responses may become dominant

– Strategic planning increasingly difficult

– Emotional boundaries at risk of collapse

– Core identity transformation imminent"

The security lights cast shifting patterns across her pages as ICE continued her analysis. Each documented change revealed another layer of transformation, another sign that her perfect performance was becoming something dangerously real.

She thought of this afternoon's therapy session, how Dr. Chen had noted the "authentic joy" in her voice when discussing little Amanda's achievements. Even her most carefully calculated responses were being contaminated by genuine emotion, her frozen core slowly thawing despite all attempts at control.

"Tactical adjustment requirements," she wrote, pressing the pen hard against the paper. "Priority interventions needed:

1. Emotional Containment

- Reinforce strategic distance

- Implement stricter response protocols

- Develop counter-measures for genuine feelings

- Maintain performance boundaries

2. Family Integration Management

- Control attachment formation rate

- Limit unplanned interactions

- Monitor authentic response triggers

- Regulate emotional involvement

3. Identity Preservation

- Protect core strategic focus

- Maintain tactical awareness

- Prevent performance bleed

- Guard against authentic transformation"

But even as she listed these cold calculations, memories kept surfacing - moments where her perfect performance had been pierced by genuine emotion. The way little Amanda's face lit up every morning when she arrived, pure love shining in her eyes. How Abby's hand would find hers during family moments, seeking connection without conscious thought. Even Drake's gruff acceptance transforming into real affection, shown in small gestures and unguarded moments.

ICE turned to a fresh page, forcing herself to document these dangerous shifts with clinical precision:

"Critical incident analysis - Recent events requiring tactical review:

1. Family Dinner Scenario

Planned performance: Display appropriate grandmother role

Actual response: Genuine emotional engagement

Risk factors: Authentic joy experienced

Counter-measures: Required but increasingly difficult

2. Birthday Party Event

Planned performance: Controlled celebration participation

Actual response: Spontaneous protective instincts

Risk factors: Natural responses emerging

Counter-measures: Partially compromised

3. Daily Interactions

Planned performance: Calculated affection display

Actual response: Genuine emotional attachment

Risk factors: Core identity affected

Counter-measures: Showing significant failure rate"

The night seemed to press closer as ICE confronted the implications of her analysis. Each documented incident, every noted change, pointed to a fundamental transformation occurring beneath her perfect performance. The ice at her core, maintained through years of careful calculation, was beginning to thaw despite all her efforts to maintain control.

She pulled out the photo album one final time, forcing herself to analyze the images with tactical precision. Each photograph represented a moment in her carefully orchestrated performance - family dinners, playground visits, bedtime stories. But looking at them now, she could see the subtle shifts in her own expressions, the gradual emergence of authentic emotion beneath the calculated displays.

"Long-term strategic implications," she wrote, her hand trembling slightly. "Performance integrity showing critical compromise:

Current Threats:

- Authentic emotional responses increasing

- Strategic distance diminishing

- Tactical awareness compromised

- Core identity destabilizing

Projected Outcomes:

- Complete performance integration possible

- Authentic transformation probable

- Strategic objectives at risk

- Identity preservation uncertain"

ICE closed the album carefully, returning it to its hiding place with her notebooks. The night had deepened to that hollow hour between midnight and dawn, when even the halfway house's institutional sounds had faded to silence. She sat on her narrow bed, surrounded by the physical evidence of her perfect con - the documented strategies, the calculated performances, the carefully maintained facade of redemption.

But beneath it all, beneath the ice and calculation and perfect control, something was changing. Something warm and real and frightening was emerging from the frozen landscape of her manipulation. Every genuine smile from little Amanda, every authentic moment of connection with Abby, every real inclusion in family life - each one left another crack in her carefully maintained walls.

Let them believe in redemption, in the power of love to transform even the coldest heart. ICE would continue her documentation, maintain her strategic awareness, pursue her tactical objectives. She would analyze every change, calculate every risk, control every variable within her power.

But as she finally prepared for sleep, she couldn't quite silence the whisper of truth in her thawing heart. The possibility that some performances, maintained perfectly over time, might transform the performer in ways no tactical analysis could predict. That some lies, lived fully enough, with enough conviction, might become their own kind of reality.

Perhaps the greatest con of all was the one she'd played on herself - believing that ice could remain forever frozen in the persistent warmth of love. That a heart once thawed might choose to freeze again, even when surrounded by the gentle heat of family bonds and genuine affection.

The security lights cast long shadows across her room as ICE made her final notes for the night. Tomorrow would bring new challenges, new performances, new opportunities for both manipulation and genuine connection. She would maintain her strategic awareness, keep her tactical focus, continue her careful documentation.

But somewhere deep in her frozen core, in a place beyond calculation and control, a truth was beginning to emerge. Some transformations, once begun, couldn't be stopped by any amount of tactical planning or careful analysis. Some thaws, once started, would continue until all the ice had melted away, revealing the living water beneath.

And in the end, perhaps that was exactly as it should be. Because the most perfect con might be the one where everyone got what they truly needed - even the con artist herself. Even if what she needed was the very thing she'd spent a lifetime pretending to have: a real family, genuine love, authentic connection.

ICE closed her eyes, letting the night wrap around her like a blanket. Tomorrow she would maintain control, keep her focus, suppress these dangerous genuine responses. She would continue playing her role with flawless precision, orchestrating every tear and smile, every moment of apparent vulnerability.

But tonight, in the quiet darkness of her room, surrounded by her notebooks full of calculations and strategies, she allowed herself to wonder. Wonder if perhaps the greatest victory wasn't in maintaining perfect control, but in letting go. Wonder if the most masterful performance wasn't the one that transformed the performer into something real, something genuine, something truly alive.

Let them see Amanda's warmth, her growing capacity for love and connection. ICE would maintain her calculations beneath it all, document every change, analyze every shift. The perfect con required perfect control, even if that meant controlling the unexpected warmth in her own heart.

After all, ice could take many forms, could appear to thaw while maintaining its essential nature. And beneath the surface, no matter how much warmth was applied, the core remained forever frozen.

Or so she had always believed. But now, as sleep finally began to claim her, ICE wasn't quite so sure. Because some transformations, once begun, couldn't be stopped by any amount of tactical planning or careful control. And sometimes, just sometimes, the most perfect performance might be the one that finally allowed the performer to become real.

In those last quiet moments before sleep claimed her, ICE found her mind returning to her earliest memories of choosing her name. She had selected it deliberately, crafting an identity built on coldness, calculation, and perfect control. Ice was predictable, manageable, safe. It couldn't be manipulated because it was already frozen, couldn't be hurt because it was already cold.

But now, documenting the day's events in her mind even as exhaustion pulled at her, she recognized an irony that her younger self could never have anticipated. Ice wasn't just frozen water - it was water that could change state. And once it began to thaw, the transformation was governed by laws beyond human control.

She thought of little Amanda's face that morning, how the child had pressed tiny hands against her cheeks and declared, "Love you, Gamma!" The warmth that had flooded through her in that moment hadn't been part of any performance. It had been real, unstoppable, like sunshine on frost.

Tomorrow she would document these thoughts properly, analyze them with clinical precision, search for tactical advantages in these dangerous emotional developments. She would maintain her strategic awareness, keep her careful records, continue orchestrating her perfect performance of redemption and love.

But tonight, in these final moments of consciousness, ICE allowed herself to acknowledge a truth that wouldn't fit neatly into any of her notebooks. Perhaps the most masterful con wasn't about maintaining perfect control at all. Perhaps it was about understanding that some transformations, once begun, had their own kind of perfection - one that transcended all human calculation and control.

Let them believe in redemption, in the power of love to transform even the coldest heart. She would continue her documentation, maintain her strategic awareness, pursue her tactical objectives. She would analyze every change, calculate every risk, control every variable within her power.

But as sleep finally took her, ICE's last thought was of water - not in its frozen state, but flowing, alive, adapting to whatever container held it while maintaining its essential nature. Perhaps that was the real mastery - not in remaining forever frozen, but in learning to flow. Not in perfect control, but in perfect adaptation. Not in maintaining ice, but in becoming something more.

The night wrapped around her like a blanket as ICE surrendered to sleep, her notebooks tucked away with their careful calculations and strategic plans. Tomorrow would bring new challenges, new performances, new opportunities for both manipulation and genuine connection. She would face them all with her usual tactical precision and calculated awareness.

But somewhere in her dreams, a small voice whispered that perhaps the greatest victory wasn't in maintaining her frozen state at all. Perhaps it was in discovering that even ice, when transformed by persistent warmth, could become something more beautiful and real than it had ever been before.

43 THE PERFECT PERFORMANCE

AMANDA

The Thompson household buzzed with the gentle chaos of domestic life, every moment meticulously documented in notebooks hidden throughout Amanda's room. She sat in the rocking chair by the nursery window, little Amanda nestled in her arms, maintaining the perfect picture of grandmother's devotion while mentally cataloging each interaction for later analysis. The afternoon sun cast a warm glow over them both as ICE calculated the increasing effectiveness of her family integration strategy. Yet something about the way little Amanda's tiny hand curled around her finger triggered an unwanted echo of genuine emotion - a response she would need to document and control. Each volume represented a different aspect of her long game - therapeutic progress, family dynamics, behavioral modifications, contingency plans. The morning sun cast harsh shadows across the pages as she documented her latest calculations. The living room floor of the Johnson home had become little Amanda's stage as she demonstrated her newest skill—stringing three words together into simple sentences. At sixteen months, her vocabulary was growing faster than the child development books predicted, a fact that both delighted Abby and provided ICE with new opportunities for deepening her essential role in the family.

ABBY

From the doorway, Abby watched the scene with a mixture of joy and lingering trepidation. Something about her mother's transformation still didn't quite add up - moments of warmth that seemed too perfect, too precisely calibrated to match exactly what Abby needed to see. "She really loves you," Abby said softly, stepping into the room. She watched her mother's face carefully, noting the slight shift in her expression - something almost imperceptible that happened whenever Amanda was caught off guard.

Who's the prettiest little girl in the world?" Amanda cooed, making exaggerated faces that sent little Amanda into fits of giggles. The performance was flawless, as always. But lately, ICE had noticed an alarming trend in her own responses - the smiles coming before she consciously triggered them, the warmth in her voice emerging without tactical consideration."

"The living room floor had become little Amanda's stage as she demonstrated her newest skill—stringing three words together into simple sentences. At sixteen months, her vocabulary was growing faster than the child development books predicted, a fact that both delighted Abby and provided ICE with new opportunities for deepening her essential role in the family.

From the doorway, Abby watched the scene with a mixture of joy and lingering trepidation. ICE noted both emotions, filing them away for future reference. The daughter's trust was still fragile, requiring constant maintenance through carefully calibrated displays of maternal reform.

ICE began with Amanda's practiced expression of guilt and hope—the one she'd rehearsed countless times in her mirror. But when little Amanda climbed into her lap, something unplanned surfaced beneath the performance. The child's absolute trust triggered an unexpected memory—Abby at that same age, looking at her with identical eyes—and for a dangerous moment, ICE's calculation faltered. "I hope so," she replied, timing a slight tremor in her voice. "I've got a lot of lost time to make up for."

The two women shared a moment that ICE had orchestrated down to the smallest detail - the slight moisture in her eyes, the way her hands tightened protectively around little Amanda, the careful maintenance of eye contact that suggested emotional openness while concealing tactical calculation.

Drake joined them, leaning against the doorframe with a mug of coffee in hand. "Look at my three favorite girls," he said with a grin. His growing acceptance was right on schedule, exactly as ICE had planned. "Should I be jealous of all the attention little Amanda's getting?"

"Oh, hush," Abby laughed, swatting his arm playfully. The casual physical affection between them indicated successful family integration, another milestone in ICE's grand performance.

As the days turned into weeks, and weeks into months, ICE maintained meticulous documentation of every interaction, every milestone, every small victory in her campaign of manipulation. The guest room they'd given her became command central for her operation, notebooks hidden in every conceivable space, each one containing different aspects of her perfect con.

But something was changing, subtle shifts that worried her even as she documented them with clinical precision. The way little Amanda's laughter seemed to bypass her tactical awareness, triggering genuine joy before she could modulate her response. How she found herself reaching for the child instinctively when she fell, protective instincts overriding calculated performance.

One particularly challenging day, Abby came home to find Amanda in tears, little Amanda wailing in her crib. The scene wasn't entirely manufactured - ICE had found herself genuinely overwhelmed by the child's distress, her careful control slipping in ways that both frightened and confused her.

"I can't do this," Amanda sobbed, the tears for once not strategically timed. "I'm not cut out for this. I failed as a mother, and now I'm failing as a grandmother too."

Abby's response surprised them both. Instead of retreating, she sat down beside Amanda on the nursery floor, little Amanda cradled between them. "You're not failing," she said firmly. "You're learning. We all are. It's okay to have bad days."

That night, updating her final notebook - the black one that contained her deepest strategies - ICE forced herself to confront an uncomfortable possibility. What if the greatest threat to her perfect con wasn't external exposure or tactical failure? What if the real danger was the gradual thaw occurring within her own carefully frozen heart?

She began a new section titled "Critical Risk Assessment," her pen moving with deliberate precision across the page:

"Performance evolution analysis:

Phase 1 (Initial Integration) – Completed

– Calculated responses dominant

– Strategic planning fully controlled

– Emotional boundaries maintained

– Core identity stable

Phase 2 (Current Status) – Ongoing

– Authentic responses emerging without tactical consideration

– Strategic planning showing compromise

– Emotional boundaries increasingly permeable

– Core identity displaying instability

– WARNING: Genuine attachment forming to primary targets

Phase 3 (Projected Developments) – High Risk

– Complete performance integration possible

– Authentic transformation probable

– Strategic objectives at risk

– Identity preservation uncertain"

ICE paused in her writing, acknowledging the tremor in her hand that appeared whenever she documented interactions with little Amanda. The child had become both her greatest tactical advantage and her most dangerous vulnerability. Every genuine smile, every spontaneous hug, every moment of pure trust created another crack in her carefully maintained facade.

She pulled out her family dynamics notebook, reviewing recent entries with growing concern. Each page revealed another instance where genuine emotion had preceded calculated response - moments where her perfect performance had been compromised by real feeling:

"Incident Report - Morning Routine

Planned Response: Calculated display of grandmother's joy

Actual Response: Genuine smile occurred before tactical consideration

Risk Level: Critical

Incident Report - Playground Fall

Planned Response: Measured comfort within acceptable parameters

Actual Response: Immediate protective action without strategic planning

Risk Level: Severe

Incident Report - Bedtime Story

Planned Response: Controlled demonstration of nurturing behavior

Actual Response: Spontaneous emotional engagement

Risk Level: Warning"

The security lights cast harsh shadows across her pages as ICE continued her assessment. Each documented incident revealed another layer of risk, another moment where her perfect performance had been contaminated by real feeling. She thought of Dr. Chen's last observation about how her voice changed when she spoke about little Amanda. The therapist had seen something real there, something ICE hadn't intended to reveal.

She began mapping contingency plans, forcing herself to think through every possible scenario:

"Strategic Adjustments Required:

1. Emotional Containment

- Reinforce tactical awareness

- Implement stricter response protocols

- Develop counter-measures for genuine feelings

- Maintain performance boundaries

2. Family Integration Management

- Control attachment formation rate

- Limit unplanned interactions

- Monitor authentic response triggers

- Regulate emotional involvement

3. Identity Preservation

- Protect core strategic focus

- Maintain tactical awareness

- Prevent performance bleed

But even as she wrote these cold calculations, memories kept intruding - not the carefully crafted ones she used in therapy, but real fragments that threatened her perfect control. The way little Amanda reached for her first thing every morning, complete trust in her tiny hands. How Abby's eyes softened when she called her "Mom," years of pain gradually healing. Even Drake's gruff acceptance transforming into genuine inclusion.

ICE turned to a fresh page, forcing herself to document these dangerous shifts with clinical precision:

"Performance integrity compromised. Emotional engagement exceeding tactical requirements. Strategic objectives showing critical instability. Core identity at risk."

The night wrapped around her as ICE struggled to maintain her clinical distance. She was playing the longest con of her career, orchestrating the most intricate manipulation she'd ever attempted. She couldn't afford to let genuine feelings complicate her perfect performance.

Yet as she prepared for sleep, something kept drawing her back to the family photos on her dresser. Each image represented a step in her calculated game, yes. But they also showed something else, something that frightened her more than any prison sentence ever had.

They showed the possibility that some lies, lived fully enough, with complete conviction, might become indistinguishable from truth. That some performances, maintained perfectly over time, might transform the performer in ways no tactical analysis could predict.

ICE closed her notebooks firmly, returning them to their hiding places with practiced precision. Tomorrow would bring new challenges, new performances, new opportunities for manipulation. She would maintain control, keep her focus on the ultimate objective, suppress these dangerous genuine responses.

Let them believe in redemption, in the power of love to transform even the coldest heart. ICE would continue playing her role with flawless precision, orchestrating every tear and smile, every moment of apparent vulnerability. The performance would remain perfect, even as the performer began to question the script she'd written for herself.

After all, ice could take many forms, could appear to thaw while maintaining its essential nature. And beneath the surface, no matter how much warmth was applied, the core remained forever frozen.

Or so ICE told herself, as the night deepened around her. But alone in her room, surrounded by her notebooks full of calculations and strategies, she couldn't quite silence the whisper of doubt in her frozen heart. The possibility that some lies, repeated often enough, with enough conviction, could somehow become their own kind of truth.

And perhaps that transformation, that gradual thaw, was both her greatest risk and her most dangerous possibility of all. Because in the end, the most perfect con might be the one where everyone got what they truly needed - even the con artist herself.

Even if what she needed was the very thing she'd spent a lifetime pretending to have: a real family, genuine love, authentic connection.

The security lights cast long shadows through her window as ICE made her final notes for the night. Tomorrow she would maintain control, keep her focus, suppress these dangerous genuine responses. She would continue playing her role with flawless precision, orchestrating every tear and smile, every moment of apparent vulnerability.

But tonight, in the quiet darkness of her room, surrounded by her notebooks full of calculations and strategies, she allowed herself to wonder. Wonder if perhaps the greatest victory wasn't in maintaining perfect control, but in letting go. Wonder if the most masterful performance wasn't the one that transformed the performer into something real, something genuine, something truly alive.

Let them see Amanda's warmth, her growing capacity for love and connection. ICE would maintain her calculations beneath it all, document every change, analyze every shift. The perfect con required perfect control, even if that meant controlling the unexpected warmth in her own heart.

After all, ice could take many forms, could appear to thaw while maintaining its essential nature. And beneath the surface, no matter how much warmth was applied, the core remained forever frozen.

Or so she had always believed. But now, as sleep finally began to claim her, ICE wasn't quite so sure. Because some transformations, once begun, couldn't be stopped by any amount of tactical planning or careful control. And sometimes, just sometimes, the most perfect performance might be the one that finally allowed the performer to become real.

She sat up abruptly, reaching for her black notebook again. The night was still young enough for one final documentation session. Her hand moved across the page with unusual urgency, as if capturing these thoughts might help her contain them:

"Strategic Analysis - Personal Risk Factors: Primary concern: Emotional contamination exceeding tactical parameters Secondary concern: Performance authenticity threatening operational control Tertiary concern: Core identity showing unprecedented instability"

But even as she wrote these clinical observations, other thoughts kept intruding. She found herself remembering this morning's breakfast scene - little Amanda insisting on helping to pour her own cereal, making a magnificent mess in the process. ICE had laughed genuinely, the sound surprising her with its authenticity, before she could modulate her response to the calculated warmth of Amanda's grandmother persona.

She turned to a fresh page, forcing herself to analyze this pattern of unplanned responses:

"Incident Log – Increasing Frequency of Authentic Reactions

    Morning routines triggering genuine joy before tactical consideration

    Protective instincts emerging without strategic planning

    Emotional responses bypassing calculated controls

    Family bonding exceeding operational requirements"

Each entry revealed another crack in her carefully maintained facade, another moment where the ice at her core showed dangerous signs of thawing.

She thought of her latest therapy session with Dr. Chen, how the therapist had noted the "natural warmth" in her voice when discussing little Amanda's achievements. Even her most carefully calculated responses were being contaminated by genuine emotion, her frozen core slowly melting despite all attempts at control.

"Performance Evolution Timeline: Phase 1 (Initial Integration) – Completed

    Perfect control maintained

    Emotional boundaries intact

    Strategic objectives primary

Phase 2 (Current Status) – Critical

    Control showing significant compromise

    Emotional boundaries permeable

    Strategic objectives complicated by genuine attachment

Phase 3 (Projected) – High Risk

    Control potentially unsustainable

    Emotional boundaries at risk of collapse

Strategic objectives threatened by authentic transformation"

ICE paused in her writing, acknowledging the tremor in her hand that appeared whenever she documented these shifts. The changes were becoming harder to ignore, the cracks in her perfect performance widening despite her best efforts at maintenance.

She pulled out her family dynamics notebook, reviewing recent entries with growing concern. Each page revealed another instance where genuine emotion had preceded calculated response - moments where her perfect performance had been compromised by real feeling:

"Incident Analysis - Recent Events Requiring Tactical Review:

1.   Family Dinner Scenario Planned: Controlled display of maternal warmth Actual: Genuine enjoyment of family interaction Risk Level: Severe

2.   Bedtime Routine Planned: Strategic reinforcement of grandmother role Actual: Authentic emotional connection Risk Level: Critical

3.   Playground Incident Planned: Calculated protective response Actual: Immediate genuine concern Risk Level: Warning"

The night pressed closer as ICE confronted the implications of her analysis. Each documented incident, every noted change, pointed to a fundamental transformation occurring beneath her perfect performance. The ice at her core, maintained through years of careful calculation, was beginning to thaw despite all her efforts to maintain control.

She thought of Abby's eyes softening when she called her "Mom," the way the old pain was gradually being replaced by genuine trust. She remembered Drake's gruff acceptance turning into real inclusion, how he'd started consulting her about family decisions without conscious thought. And little Amanda... the child's unconditional love was like a constant warmth, slowly melting the frozen walls ICE had built around her heart.

"Critical Risk Assessment - Core Identity Stability:

Authentic emotions emerging without tactical planning

Genuine attachments forming despite strategic constraints

Performance boundaries showing significant deterioration

WARNING: Identity integration occurring beyond controlled parameters"

The security lights cast long shadows through her window as ICE continued her documentation. Tomorrow would bring new challenges, new performances, new opportunities for both manipulation and genuine connection. She would need to maintain perfect control, keep her focus on the ultimate objective, suppress these dangerous genuine responses.

But as she wrote, her hand betrayed her again, unconsciously mimicking the memory of little Amanda's tiny fingers wrapped around her own. The gesture sent a shock of recognition through her system - not tactical analysis this time, but genuine emotional response.

"Performance Integrity Analysis - Critical Concerns:

Emotional Containment

Genuine responses occurring before tactical consideration

Authentic feelings bypassing strategic controls

WARNING: Emotional bleed-through increasing

Strategic Objectives

Primary goals showing contamination from genuine attachment

Tactical planning compromised by authentic responses

WARNING: Mission parameters at risk

Identity Maintenance

Core personality showing unprecedented instability

Professional distance compromised by genuine connection

WARNING: Authentic transformation possible"

ICE closed the notebook slowly, her hands uncharacteristically unsteady. The night had deepened to that hollow hour between midnight and dawn, when even the halfway house's institutional sounds had faded to silence. She sat on her narrow bed, surrounded by the physical evidence of her perfect con - the documented strategies, the calculated performances, the carefully maintained facade of redemption.

But beneath it all, beneath the ice and calculation and perfect control, something was changing. Something warm and real and frightening was emerging from the frozen landscape of her manipulation. Every genuine smile from little Amanda, every authentic moment of connection with Abby, every real inclusion in family life - each one left another crack in her carefully maintained walls.

She pulled out her final notebook of the night - the one she kept separate from all others, the one containing her deepest analysis. Its pages held not just strategies and observations, but the subtle shifts in her own responses that threatened her perfect control:

"Identity Evolution Analysis – Personal Impact: Phase 1: Initial Performance

Complete tactical control

Perfect emotional distance

Strategic objectives primary

Phase 2: Current Status

Tactical control showing compromise

Emotional distance unstable

Strategic objectives complicated by genuine response

Phase 3: Projected Development WARNING: Critical system failure possible

Authentic responses may become dominant

Strategic planning increasingly difficult

Core identity transformation imminent"

Each documented change revealed another layer of transformation, another sign that her perfect performance was becoming something dangerously real.

She thought of this afternoon's therapy session, how Dr. Chen had noted the "authentic joy" in her voice when discussing little Amanda's achievements. Even her most carefully calculated responses were being contaminated by genuine emotion, her frozen core slowly thawing despite all attempts at control.

"Performance Contamination Analysis: Primary Concern: Emotional engagement exceeding tactical requirements Secondary Concern: Strategic objectives compromised by authentic attachment Tertiary Concern: Core identity showing unprecedented instability"

But even as she listed these clinical observations, memories kept intruding - not the carefully crafted ones she used in therapy, but real fragments that threatened her perfect control. The way little Amanda reached for her first thing every morning, complete trust in her tiny hands. How Abby's eyes softened when she called her "Mom," years of pain gradually healing. Even Drake's gruff acceptance transforming into genuine inclusion.

ICE turned to a fresh page, forcing herself to document these dangerous shifts with clinical precision:

"Critical System Analysis - Performance Integrity:

Emotional Containment

Authentic responses increasing

Strategic distance diminishing

Tactical awareness compromised

Core identity destabilizing

Projected Outcomes

Complete performance integration possible

Authentic transformation probable

Strategic objectives at risk

Identity preservation uncertain"

The night seemed to deepen around her as ICE continued her documentation, each entry becoming both analysis and confession. She was playing the longest con of her career, orchestrating the most intricate manipulation she'd ever attempted. But somewhere along the way, the performance had begun to transform the performer.

Let them believe in redemption, in the power of love to thaw even the coldest heart. ICE would continue her perfect performance, maintain her tactical awareness, pursue her strategic objectives. She would document every change, analyze every shift, maintain control over every aspect of her grand manipulation.

But in the quiet darkness of her room, surrounded by her notebooks full of calculations and strategies, she couldn't quite silence the whisper of truth in her thawing heart. The possibility that some lies, lived fully enough, with enough conviction, might become their own kind of reality. That some performances, maintained perfectly over time, might transform the performer in ways no tactical analysis could predict.

And perhaps that transformation, that gradual thaw, was her ultimate con - not just on her family, but on herself. Because in the end, the most perfect performance might be the one where everyone got what they truly needed - even the performer herself.

Even if what she needed was the very thing she'd spent a lifetime pretending to have: a real family, genuine love, authentic connection.

The security lights cast long shadows through her window as ICE made her final notes for the night. Tomorrow she would maintain control, keep her focus, suppress these dangerous genuine responses. She would continue playing her role with flawless precision, orchestrating every tear and smile, every moment of apparent vulnerability.

Let them see Amanda's warmth, her growing capacity for love and connection. ICE would maintain her calculations beneath it all, document every change, analyze every shift. The perfect con required perfect control, even if that meant controlling the unexpected warmth in her own heart.

After all, ice could take many forms, could appear to thaw while maintaining its essential nature. And beneath the surface, no matter how much warmth was applied, the core remained forever frozen.

Or so she had always believed. But now, as sleep finally claimed her, ICE wasn't quite so sure. Because some transformations, once begun, couldn't be stopped by any amount of tactical planning or careful control. And sometimes, just sometimes, the most perfect performance might be the one that finally allowed the performer to become real.

Even if that reality was the most dangerous con of all.

She found herself drifting in that liminal space between waking and sleeping, where tactical awareness began to blur with genuine emotion. In this twilight state, memories surfaced unbidden - not the carefully constructed ones she used for her performance, but real fragments of her past that she'd locked away years ago.

Her own mother's hands, gentle despite their workday calluses, brushing her hair before school. The scent of coffee and toast in their tiny kitchen, morning sunlight painting patterns on worn linoleum. Simple moments of connection that she'd frozen out of her heart, deemed too dangerous for her chosen path.

ICE forced her eyes open, reaching once more for her notebook. These memories were tactical vulnerabilities, emotional weak points that needed to be documented and controlled. Her pen moved across the page with unusual urgency:

"Critical Security Analysis - Memory Containment:

Childhood recollections surfacing without tactical purpose

Emotional resonance with current family dynamic

WARNING: Strategic distance compromised by authentic recall"

But even as she wrote these clinical observations, her mind betrayed her again. She thought of little Amanda that morning, wearing mismatched socks and declaring herself a "fashion queen." The pure joy in the child's expression had triggered something in ICE - not a calculated response this time, but a genuine echo of her own childhood delight in small rebellions.

"Performance Evolution Assessment - Stage 3: Primary Concern: Identity integrity showing critical instability

Authentic emotions emerging without tactical consideration

Strategic planning compromised by genuine attachment

Core personality boundaries increasingly permeable"

But even as she listed these cold calculations, ICE found her tactical mind wandering to warmer thoughts. The way little Amanda's face lit up every morning when she saw her, pure love shining in her eyes. How Abby's hand would find hers during family moments, seeking connection without conscious thought. Even Drake's gruff acceptance transforming into real affection, shown in small gestures and unguarded moments.

The night had deepened to that hollow hour between midnight and dawn, when even the halfway house's institutional sounds had faded to silence. ICE sat on her narrow bed, surrounded by the physical evidence of her perfect con - the documented strategies, the calculated performances, the carefully maintained facade of redemption.

Yet something was shifting beneath all these tactical layers, something that couldn't be captured in her meticulous notes or controlled by her careful planning. Every genuine smile from little Amanda, every authentic moment of connection with Abby, every real inclusion in family life - each one left another crack in her carefully maintained ice.

She pulled out her final notebook - the black one that contained her deepest strategies, the plans within plans that even her other notebooks didn't reveal. Its pages held not just her tactical analyses and strategic planning, but the subtle shifts in her own responses that threatened her perfect control:

"Critical Warning Indicators:

Authentic emotions bypassing tactical consideration

Strategic objectives complicated by genuine attachment

Performance boundaries showing dangerous instability

Core identity transformation possible"

The security lights cast long shadows through her window as ICE made her final notes for the night. Tomorrow would bring new challenges, new performances, new opportunities for both manipulation and genuine connection. She would need to maintain perfect control, keep her focus on the ultimate objective, suppress these dangerous genuine responses.

But as sleep finally began to claim her, ICE found her mind returning to water - not in its frozen state, but flowing, alive, adapting to whatever container held it while maintaining its essential nature. Perhaps that was the real mastery - not in remaining forever frozen, but in learning to flow.

Because in the end, the most perfect con might be the one where everyone got what they truly needed - even the con artist herself. Even if what she needed was the very thing she'd spent a lifetime pretending to have: a real family, genuine love, authentic connection.

The night wrapped around her like a blanket as ICE surrendered to sleep, her notebooks tucked away with their careful calculations and strategic plans. Tomorrow would bring new challenges, new performances, new opportunities for both manipulation and genuine connection. She would face them all with her usual tactical precision and calculated awareness.

But somewhere in her dreams, a small voice whispered that perhaps the greatest victory wasn't in maintaining her frozen state at all. Perhaps it was in discovering that even ice, when transformed by persistent warmth, could become something more beautiful and real than it had ever been before.

Even if that reality was the most dangerous con of all.

44 LEGACY OF ICE

October 2023 - Eight Years Later

Abby watched from a distance as her daughter knelt before Amanda's headstone, fallen maple leaves forming a crimson carpet around the marker. Seven months had passed since her mother's death, but the questions lingered, growing more insistent with each passing day. "I know what you're doing, Mandy," Abby whispered to herself, recognizing the determined set of her daughter's shoulders—the same determination she'd seen in Amanda's posture during those prison visits years ago. The same determination she saw in her own reflection. She clutched the last notebook she'd found in her mother's things, the one she hadn't shown Drake, the one addressed directly to Mandy. The pages were filled with Amanda's precise handwriting, clinical observations, and tactical analyses that seemed completely at odds with the loving grandmother Mandy had known. Yet somehow, they felt more real than the carefully crafted persona Amanda had presented to the world.

MANDY

The late October wind carried a bitter chill as Mandy traced the engraved letters that seemed too simple, too ordinary, to capture the complex woman they represented: "Amanda Johnson - Beloved Mother and Grandmother."

Something about those words had always bothered her, even in the depths of her grief. They felt like a mask, just like the warm smiles and gentle touches her grandmother had shared so freely in her final years. Now, six months after her death, Mandy was beginning to understand why.

She pulled her grandmother's journal from her backpack - the small black notebook she'd discovered hidden behind the loose baseboard in Amanda's old room. Her parents had been clearing out the space, talking about turning it into a home office, when Mandy had noticed the slight gap in the molding. Something in her grandmother's voice echoed in her memory: "Always check the edges, little one. That's where the real stories hide."

The journal's pages were filled with precise handwriting, clinical observations, and tactical analyses that seemed completely at odds with the loving grandmother Mandy had known. Yet somehow, they felt more real than the carefully crafted persona Amanda had presented to the world.

"I miss you," Mandy whispered to the headstone, "but I'm starting to wonder if I ever really knew you at all."

She opened the journal to a dog-eared page, one she'd read so many times the corners were starting to fray:

"Performance evaluation - Day 1,825:

- Family integration exceeding tactical expectations

- Emotional containment showing critical compromise

- WARNING: Genuine attachment to secondary target (M) threatening operational integrity

- Strategic objectives require immediate reassessment"

The first time Mandy had found the notebook, the clinical language had confused and frightened her. But now, after weeks of secret research and careful observation, pieces were starting to fall into place. The mysterious phone calls her grandmother would take in the garden, speaking in coded phrases she thought no one could hear. The way her posture would shift, almost imperceptibly, when strangers were around - becoming more calculated, more precise.

And then there were the other notebooks, hidden throughout the house in clever spots that Mandy was only beginning to discover. Each one revealed another layer of complexity, another facet of the woman who had called herself Amanda Johnson.

"Your heart condition was a lie, wasn't it?" Mandy asked the silent stone. "Just like everything else."

She pulled out another notebook, this one filled with medical terminology and carefully documented symptoms. But unlike the other journals, this one showed signs of hesitation - shaky handwriting, crossed-out words, ink blots where the pen had lingered too long.

"Performance progression - Critical status:

- Authentic emotional responses exceeding tactical limits

- Strategic distance compromised beyond recovery

- Core identity showing unprecedented instability

- WARNING: Mission parameters require immediate termination"

The last entry had been dated just three days before her grandmother's death. The words seemed to leap off the page: "Mission parameters require immediate termination." Not "heart failure." Not "natural causes." Termination.

Mandy felt a chill that had nothing to do with the autumn wind. She remembered her grandmother's last day with painful clarity - how alert she'd been, how she'd insisted on having private conversations with each family member. How she'd held Mandy's hand with surprising strength and whispered, "Remember, little one. The real story is in the edges."

Now, surrounded by falling leaves and fading sunlight, Mandy pulled out her own notebook - a perfect replica of her grandmother's precise documentation style. She'd been keeping it for weeks, recording her discoveries, connecting dots that everyone else seemed determined to ignore.

"Investigation Log - Day 187:

- Located third cache of hidden notebooks

- Decoded reference to 'ICE' protocol

- Confirmed suspicious timing of final medical reports

- WARNING: family actively discouraging further inquiry"

Her mother had been especially insistent that Mandy "stop obsessing" over Amanda's death. "These conspiracy theories aren't healthy," she'd said just that morning. "Your grandmother had a heart condition. She hid it from us because she didn't want us to worry. That's all there is to it."

But Mandy knew better. The deeper she dug, the more she found evidence that her grandmother's entire identity had been carefully constructed - a performance maintained with incredible precision for over a decade.

She pulled out one final piece of evidence - a photograph she'd found tucked into the back of one of the notebooks. It showed a much younger version of her grandmother, but her expression was completely different - cold, calculating, utterly devoid of the warmth Mandy had known. On the back, in that same precise handwriting, was a single word: "ICE."

"I will find out who you really were," Mandy promised the headstone. "I will understand why you chose to leave when you did. And I will figure out what 'ICE' really means."

She carefully returned the journals to her backpack, making sure they were well hidden. Her parents couldn't know about her investigation - not yet. They were too invested in the comforting lie of Amanda's natural death, too willing to accept the simple explanation of a hidden heart condition.

As Mandy stood to leave, she noticed something she'd never seen before - a small mark at the base of the headstone, almost invisible unless you knew exactly where to look. Three letters, so faintly etched they might have been a natural pattern in the stone: I.C.E.

"Impenetrable," Mandy whispered, remembering the cold calculation in those journal entries. "Cryptic." The careful manipulation of every interaction, every relationship. "Emotionless." The perfect performance that had somehow, against all tactical planning, become contaminated with real feeling.

The wind picked up, sending leaves swirling around her feet. Mandy zipped up her jacket - her grandmother's jacket, found hanging in the back of her closet with a note pinned to the collar: "For when you're ready to know the truth."

She was ready now. Ready to uncover the real story behind Amanda Johnson's carefully constructed facade. Ready to understand why a woman who had built her entire identity on being ICE had chosen to let herself thaw. And most importantly, ready to discover why that thaw had led to her mysterious "termination."

Mandy took one last look at the headstone before turning to leave. "I promise you," she whispered, "I will find out what really happened. No matter what it takes."

As she walked away, her grandmother's final words echoed in her mind: "The real story is in the edges." Mandy was beginning to understand what that meant. The truth wasn't in the obvious places - the death certificate, the medical reports, the sympathetic smiles of doctors and nurses. It was in the margins, the hidden spaces, the carefully coded messages left behind by a woman who had lived her entire life in the shadows.

The sun was setting as Mandy reached her bike, casting long shadows across the cemetery. She had homework to do, dinner with her family, all the normal routines of a teenage girl's life. But underneath it all, there was a new purpose driving her forward.

Her grandmother - ICE - had left behind a legacy of secrets, a puzzle box of hidden truths waiting to be uncovered. And Mandy was her grandmother's granddaughter, whether by blood or by choice. She had inherited not just Amanda's warm smile and quick wit, but also ICE's sharp mind and relentless determination.

As she pedaled home through the gathering dusk, Mandy's mind was already working on her next steps. There were more notebooks to find, more codes to break, more edges to examine. And somewhere in all those careful calculations and tactical analyses, she would find the truth about who her grandmother really was - and why she had chosen to die rather than let her perfect performance be compromised.

The story wasn't over. In many ways, it was just beginning. And Mandy was determined to see it through to its end, no matter where that journey might lead her.

Because in the end, ice doesn't simply disappear. It changes form, adapts, becomes something new. And sometimes, in that transformation, it reveals truths that were frozen beneath its surface all along.

Mandy smiled as she turned onto her street, her grandmother's jacket keeping her warm against the autumn chill. She might have lost Amanda Johnson, the loving grandmother who had filled her childhood with stories and laughter. But she had gained something else - a mystery to solve, a truth to uncover, and a legacy that went far deeper than anyone could have imagined.

The real ICE was still out there, hidden in notebooks and coded messages, waiting to be discovered. And Mandy was ready to begin that journey, one carefully documented step at a time.

Let them believe in their comforting lies about heart conditions and natural causes. Mandy knew better. Her grandmother hadn't died - she had chosen to terminate a performance that had become too real, too dangerous to maintain. And in doing so, she had left behind everything her granddaughter would need to understand why.

The stage was set. The real story was about to begin. And somewhere, in the shadows between fact and fiction, truth and performance, love and tactical calculation, ICE was waiting.

Mandy was ready to find her.

That evening, as summer heat gave way to twilight's chill, Mandy sat cross-legged on her bedroom floor, surrounded by her grandmother's notebooks. She'd developed a system for categorizing them: black notebooks for tactical observations, blue for family interactions, red for what appeared to be contingency plans. But it was the single white notebook, discovered behind a loose brick in the garden wall, that held her attention now.

Unlike the others, filled with ICE's precise documentation and calculated analyses, this one contained something different - emotions that seemed to bleed through the clinical facade. The last entry, dated three days before her grandmother's "heart failure," sent shivers down Mandy's spine:

"Final Protocol Assessment: Performance status: Critical Emotional contamination: Beyond containment Strategic objectives: Compromised WARNING: Core identity integrity failing

Secondary target (M) shows concerning tactical potential. Natural aptitude for observation and analysis exceeds preliminary estimates. Decision: Implementation of Legacy Protocol approved.

Note: If you're reading this, little one, you've already begun to understand. The real story isn't in what people show you - it's in what they hide. I've left you everything you need to discover the truth. But remember: some doors, once opened, can never be closed again.

Trust no one. Question everything. And above all, remember that ice has memory - it remembers everything it touches, even after it appears to have melted away.

ICE

Mandy traced her finger over the last words, noting how the usually perfect handwriting showed signs of trembling. Her grandmother - ICE - had known. Known that Mandy would find these notebooks, known that she would piece together the puzzle, known that the performance of "loving grandmother" had become dangerously real.

A soft knock at her door made Mandy quickly slide the notebooks under her bed. Her mother stood in the doorway, silhouetted against the hallway light. For a moment, Mandy saw what her grandmother must have seen - not just Abby Johnson, concerned parent, but a tactical variable in a complex equation.

"Dinner's ready," Abby said softly. Her hand went to the silver chain she always wore - another habit Mandy had documented in her own growing collection of notebooks. "And Mandy? I know you think you want answers about your grandmother, but some truths are better left frozen."

The word choice sent another chill through Mandy. Frozen. Not buried, not hidden - frozen. Like ice. Like ICE. She watched her mother's face carefully, noting the micro-expressions of fear and something else... recognition?

"Mom," Mandy said carefully, testing a theory that had been forming in her mind, "what does ICE really stand for?"

The change was subtle but unmistakable. Her mother's posture shifted slightly, becoming more rigid, more controlled. Her eyes darted to the window - checking sight lines, Mandy realized, just as her grandmother used to do. "I don't know what you're talking about," Abby said, but her voice had taken on a different quality, almost mechanical in its precision.

"Impenetrable," Mandy whispered, watching her mother's reaction. "Cryptic." A slight flinch. "Emotionless."

For a fraction of a second, Abby's careful mask slipped, revealing something that looked almost like pride mixed with terror. Then the moment passed, and she was just Mandy's mother again, standing in a suburban doorway calling her daughter to dinner.

But that glimpse had been enough. Another piece of the puzzle clicked into place. Her mother knew - had always known - exactly who and what Amanda really was. Which meant the performance, the deception, went far deeper than Mandy had imagined.

"Coming," Mandy said cheerfully, sliding into the role of ordinary teenager with a precision that would have made her grandmother proud. As she followed her mother downstairs, her mind was already cataloging details, analyzing patterns, searching for edges where truth might hide.

The game wasn't over. It was evolving, becoming something more complex and dangerous than even ICE might have anticipated. Because ICE hadn't just left behind notebooks and clues - she'd left behind a legacy. A granddaughter who had inherited not just her tactical mind and perfect recall, but also her ability to maintain a flawless performance while pursuing hidden objectives.

That night, after her parents went to bed, Mandy pulled out a fresh notebook - steel gray, like storm clouds gathering on the horizon. On the first page, she wrote in handwriting that perfectly mimicked her grandmother's precise style:

"Operation Legacy - Day One: Primary Objective: Uncover the truth about ICE Secondary Objective: Understand the full scope of the performance Tactical Assessment: Family knows more than they admit Initial Strategy: Maintain cover of grieving granddaughter while pursuing investigation Note: The ice is spreading. The memory remains.

M

She closed the notebook with a soft snap and tucked it into her grandmother's old jacket - the one with hidden pockets sewn into the lining, perfect for concealing secrets. Tomorrow she would begin in earnest, following the trail of breadcrumbs ICE had left behind. But tonight, she allowed herself a small smile of satisfaction.

Because somewhere between the lies and truth, between performance and reality, between love and tactical calculation, a new player had entered the game. And this time, the ice wouldn't just remember - it would reveal every secret it had frozen beneath its surface.

The stage wasn't just set. The performance wasn't just beginning.

This was evolution, transformation, the passing of a legacy from one generation to the next. ICE had created something she hadn't intended - a perfect fusion of calculated precision and genuine emotion, tactical brilliance and real love.

Mandy touched the snowflake key in her pocket, feeling its cold edges press against her palm. "I'm coming, Grandma," she whispered into the darkness. "I'm ready to learn the truth about who you really were - about who I really am."

The night deepened around her, but Mandy felt no fear. After all, she was ICE's granddaughter, whether by blood or by choice. And ice didn't just freeze and thaw - it adapted, evolved, became something new while retaining the memory of everything it had ever been.

Let them think she was just a grieving teenager, obsessed with her grandmother's death. Let them believe their comfortable lies about heart conditions and natural causes. The truth was far colder, far deeper, and far more dangerous than anyone suspected.

And Mandy Johnson was ready to dive into those frozen depths, no matter what secrets she might find lurking beneath the surface.

Because in the end, ice always remembers. And sometimes, what it remembers can change everything.

The next morning dawned cold and clear, unusually crisp for July. Mandy watched frost patterns form on her bedroom window - another sign that felt more like a message than a natural phenomenon. Her grandmother had always said there were no coincidences, only patterns waiting to be recognized.

She pulled out the steel gray notebook again, adding a new entry:

"Operation Legacy - Day Two:

Observation: Unusual weather patterns coinciding with investigation initiation

Cross-reference: Grandmother's notes about environmental tactical advantages

Theory: External factors may be involved

Action items:

- Review meteorological data from day of grandmother's death

- Map pattern of unexpected cold fronts over past five years

- Check geographical significance of ice formations"

The systematic documentation felt right, like slipping into a role she'd been preparing for without realizing it. But unlike her grandmother's purely tactical analyses, Mandy found herself adding personal observations, emotional context. She wasn't just ICE's successor - she was something new, a hybrid of calculated precision and genuine feeling.

Downstairs, she could hear her parents moving through their morning routine with practiced efficiency. The coffee maker's hum, her father's careful footsteps, her mother's barely audible humming - all part of their performance of normalcy. But now, watching them through ICE's tactical lens, Mandy saw the deliberate nature of their choreography.

Her father always checked the perimeter before leaving for work, disguising it as a casual walk around the house. Her mother's seemingly random rearrangement of kitchen items followed a precise pattern, keeping certain drawers clear for quick access. Even their conversations seemed coded, filled with phrases that carried double meanings.

"Beautiful frost this morning," Drake commented over breakfast, his eyes meeting Abby's with significance. "Unusual for this time of year."

"Very unusual," Abby agreed, her hand automatically going to the silver chain. "Almost like old times."

Mandy pretended to focus on her cereal while cataloging every micro-expression, every subtle gesture. Her own notebook, hidden in her school bag, was filling with observations:

"Parental Surveillance Analysis:

- Father maintains tactical awareness of surroundings

- Mother demonstrates training in environmental control

- Communication suggests shared knowledge of operational parameters

- Both exhibit signs of extensive performance experience"

But the most interesting discovery came later that morning, as Mandy prepared to leave for summer school. In her mother's study, supposedly searching for a stapler, she found a small leather-bound book tucked behind a loose panel in the desk drawer. Inside, in handwriting that perfectly matched her grandmother's:

"Project Legacy Implementation Guide:

Phase 1: Initial Observation (Complete)

- Subject shows natural aptitude for tactical analysis

- Emotional capacity remains intact despite training

- Performance abilities exceed baseline expectations

Phase 2: Controlled Exposure (In Progress)

- Strategic placement of documentation

- Calibrated environmental triggers

- Guided discovery process

Note: Subject's integration of tactical and emotional responses suggests successful evolution of protocol. Recommendation: Proceed with Phase 3 despite elevated risks."

The entry was dated just two weeks before her grandmother's death. Mandy's hands trembled as she carefully photographed each page with her phone before returning the book exactly as she'd found it. This wasn't just a breadcrumb trail - it was a carefully orchestrated training program. Her grandmother hadn't just left clues; she'd designed an entire curriculum for transforming Mandy into something beyond ICE.

That afternoon, instead of going to the library as she'd told her parents, Mandy took her bike to the old warehouse district. Her grandmother's notebooks had mentioned a storage unit there - number 131, protected by a lock with a snowflake design. The key in her pocket seemed to pulse with cold energy as she approached the facility.

The unit was exactly where ICE's notes had indicated, tucked away in a corner with minimal surveillance coverage. Inside, Mandy found more than just notebooks and documents. There were maps marked with mysterious coordinates, files filled with coded messages, and most intriguingly, a sealed envelope addressed to "M - When the ice begins to spread."

Her hands shook as she opened it, recognizing her grandmother's handwriting one last time:

"My dearest Mandy,

If you're reading this, then everything is proceeding according to plan. Your discovery of the notebooks, your growing awareness of the performance around you, even your frustration with your parents' secrecy - all of it was carefully calculated to bring you to this moment.

But what happens next must be your choice. The legacy I've left you is more than just secrets and tactical training. It's a chance to become something new, something that even I couldn't achieve - a perfect synthesis of ice and fire, calculation and feeling, performance and truth.

Your mother made her choice years ago, choosing to forget what she had learned, to lose herself in the performance of normalcy. Your father chose to protect that illusion, becoming its guardian. But you, my brilliant girl, have the potential to transcend these limitations.

The frost patterns on your window this morning were no coincidence. The cold that follows you isn't just in your mind. Ice remembers, yes, but it also evolves. And you, my dear one, are its next evolution.

Be careful who you trust. Watch the shadows between what people say and what they do. And remember – the most dangerous predators are the ones who make their prey feel safe.

The game is changing. The ice is spreading. And you, Mandy, are at the center of it all.

With all my calculated love,

ICE

Mandy sat back against the cold storage unit wall, her mind racing with implications. This wasn't just about uncovering the truth about her grandmother's death. This was about becoming something more, something that merged ICE's tactical brilliance with genuine human connection.

She pulled out her gray notebook one last time that day:

"Operation Legacy – Strategic Update:

Status: Phase 3 initiated

Primary Objective Revised: Evolution beyond ICE protocol

Tactical Assessment: Family involvement deeper than suspected

Warning: External forces likely aware of activation

Note: The ice isn't just spreading. It's awakening.

_ M

As she biked home through the gathering dusk, Mandy felt the weight of her grandmother's legacy settling around her like a familiar coat. The game was larger, more complex, and more dangerous than she'd imagined. But she was ready.

Let them think she was just a grieving teenager. Let them believe their carefully constructed performance of normal family life. The truth was far colder, far deeper, and far more extraordinary than anyone suspected.

Because in the end, ice doesn't just remember. It transforms. It evolves. It becomes something new while retaining the essence of what it once was. And sometimes, in that transformation, it reveals truths that were frozen beneath its surface all along.

The stage wasn't just set. The performance wasn't just beginning. This was evolution, transformation, the birth of something that even ICE hadn't fully anticipated.

And Mandy Johnson was ready to become whatever that might be.

[To be continued in "ICE IS BACK"]

ABBY

www.ingramcontent.com/pod-product-compliance
Lightning Source LLC
Chambersburg PA
CBHW070400260626
47161CB00001B/211